Z E N I T H

Andrew Matarazzo

ZENITH

"You may live to see man-made horrors
beyond your comprehension."

—Nikola Tesla, 1898

TABLE OF CONTENTS

1 3 2 2 14
2 6
10 19
5 3 4
7 2 4
17
6 8 13 3
10 7 10 7 11 10
2 12
1
10
19
7 10 4 3 7 14 10
10 7 11
10
14
19 2 3 5 10 5
17
6 8 3 7
10 7 11 10 2 12
1 14

6 MONTHS LATER

1. TYE

An automated voice sounded throughout the hall. *PLEASE REPORT TO COMMISSARY. PLEASE REPORT TO COMMISSARY. PLEASE REPORT TO COMMISSARY.*

As expected, I'd hardly been able to get any sleep during my first night here, but the wake-up call still sent a jolt through my body.

I sat up on the narrow bed, my arms sore and bruised from all the blood drawn in the last few months. Since being brought to Ylem, my worst nightmare had come true—I was a lab rat now.

I could see the other captives through the glass dividers that were now sliding aside to let us out into the common areas. They stirred in their tiny rooms as the bright lights kicked on. Our pods were the only personal space we had here at the Ylem camps. Though, 'space' was a generous way to put it. Inside each pod was merely a small bed, a sink, and a toilet behind a curtain.

All of us lined up outside our pod doors as an armed guard waited down the hall to escort us. In single file, we followed him out of the bare white hall and into a larger, more open space, equally as sterile, but with guards in every corner.

Five long tables graced the middle of the vast room. A large line had formed in front of a single tablet mounted on the wall.

"Sign in and wait for your assignment!" yelled another guard, as part of the line was lagging while a few boys roughhoused.

When I arrived here the day before, I noticed right away that we were all boys, and figured the girls were being kept in a separate wing. No one looked older than late twenties, but most were around my age.

I'd been isolated for so long, I felt overwhelmed by so many bodies being around me now. I kept my head down in line and tried my best to blend in. At least we were all wearing the same light blue jumpsuit, eerily reminiscent of the border camps.

All I was told was that every one of us here was an 'Angel'—a name given to anyone who had special properties in their blood that made them immune to the virus. I'd gathered that whatever that unique trait was varied from person to person, but my blood was somehow one of a kind, a blessing and a curse. It was the reason I'd been hunted down and brought to Ylem for further study.

I could still hear Secretary Croft's words in my nightmares. "*God's Blood*," she called it, that day she captured me. Listening carefully during all my medical visits, I'd tried to piece together what exactly made my blood so rare, but I still wasn't entirely sure.

It was my turn to select my name for check-in on the screen. I clicked it and it flashed green in confirmation. When I stepped out of line, I noticed a second line had formed in front of a pickup window on the other side of the room. An unpleasant-looking lady handed out breakfast trays.

"Tye, right?" asked a voice from behind me.

I turned to see a guy a bit taller than me, well-built with a bright smile. I shook the hand he held out in greeting.

"How'd you know my name?" I asked.

"It's on our pod doors," he said with a laugh. "I'm Vale."

More than half the Angels here looked sickly and exhausted, but somehow, he had a glow about him.

"Hah, got it. Nice to meet you. Sorry, I'm a bit lost. It's my first day."

He put a vascular arm around me and led me to the breakfast line. "Don't sweat it. It doesn't take long to get the hang of things. Every day's exactly the same."

My throat got tight at the thought. "How long have you been here?"

"About six months."

“Jesus Christ,” I said under my breath. I’d expected him to say only a few weeks by the looks of him.

“It’s whatever. No family or friends left in the real world. At least here I have some. Grab some food and come sit with us,” he said, stepping out of line to join a group at one of the tables.

“You don’t want any breakfa—”

“Take one and step away, please,” said the saggy-faced lady as she slid me a tray.

I eyed the food with distaste. It was just another detail that made this camp feel like a prison. I couldn’t tell if my stomach was rumbling from hunger or protest.

Vale was flagging me down as I walked towards the tables. I sat across from him.

“This is Tye,” he said to the group of boys.

Some nodded, and others greeted me, but I got the sense that they weren’t in the mood to be overly social.

Vale didn’t have a tray. The guy next to him, freckled and dark-haired, was trying to get him to take a bite of his soggy powdered eggs.

“You have to eat something, dude,” he said, holding the fork up to Vale’s mouth.

“I’m *goood.* I’ll eat at lunch. I don’t have an appetite in the AM,” Vale said, taking the boy’s hand and redirecting the fork back to his own mouth.

“You gotta keep up your strength when they’re taking this much blood,” the boy said through a mouthful.

We watched as two Angels were escorted out for their assignments.

“You have an appointment today?” Vale asked me.

I shrugged. “How am I meant to tell?”

“Did your name light up red or green?”

“Green …”

The boys all let out a synced “oof.”

"Yeah, you do," said Vale. "*Ongoing research.*"

"How many more tests can they possibly do?" I asked. "I just got here after *months* of testing."

"It's what they do," said the guy beside Vale. "Once you get assigned a family, it'll get better."

"A family?" I asked while pushing my food around my tray.

"Once they're done with all the diagnostics and studies, you become a family's personal blood source to drain as needed."

My face must have paled, because Vale seemed to notice my shock. "There's no pleasant way to put it," he said somberly. "That's the point of these camps: to farm us like a product to be used by the rich families who live in Ylem. They want to be immune like us. I think a lot of these tests are because they're still perfecting the process."

"How is that better ... ?"

"Well, you'll get out of here for a bit, see the city," said another of Vale's friends. "Some families are nice enough. Might even feed you real food, or let you hang for a bit after the transfusion. Vale landed a pretty decent fam."

I swallowed a bite of food with difficulty. None of that sounded better at all. All my fears were manifesting before my eyes. Surviving alone in the desert, even in total isolation, was easier to cope with than the thought of being a science experiment for life.

I'd escaped once, almost twice, but escaping again was absolutely impossible. I managed to catch a glimpse of Ylem the day I was transported there. It was a mecca: a blatant display of wealth and power, with towering buildings and complex structures, and a bordering wall so high it reached the tip of the tallest high-rise. And it seemed there were guards every few feet.

I was awestruck. How something this vast could go undetected by the world for so long was mind-boggling. I didn't even know what part of the country we were in, or if we were in the U.S. at all.

PLEASE REPORT TO RECREATION. PLEASE REPORT TO RECREATION. PLEASE REPORT TO RECREATION.

It was clear in the way that everyone finished off their small portions and stood up that they were conditioned to cooperate and behave. As a unit, we moved through an opening that had formed on one end of the Commissary and found ourselves in a massive dome-shaped area.

We were technically outdoors, but the dome above was screened in. There were plastic chairs set up all along the perimeter of the curved walls, probably for us to sit in and wait for our appointments. Gym equipment and a large shelf of books and magazines were all that was left to take in.

The Angels spread out, some aimlessly walking around, while others rushed to snag their favored activity, all under the watchful eye of several armed guards. I saw Vale and his crew make their way to the gym equipment.

I didn't want to seem like a shadow, so I sat on one of the waiting chairs and tried to calm my anxiety by taking in a deep breath of fresh air. It was the first time in ages I'd felt natural oxygen.

From the day I left my childhood home and life as I knew it was gone, it felt like a never-ending battle to catch my breath. Surviving, running, hiding, and suffering. My friends had become my only sense of safety and comfort, and even they were separated from me—some didn't even make it.

There wasn't a single day I didn't try to imagine what their lives were like. I knew Riley was with her dad, and had a new baby by now. Ava had Otto and her mom. Dustin and Willa were together, and even though Willa lost her brother, she was going to find her parents.

Sometimes when I was sad, I would imagine myself with them again: conversations we'd have, fun things we'd do... I didn't really know what life was like in the safe zones, but I tried to imagine it being as normal and calm as the before-world felt compared to now.

At least, now that I was captured for good, I could stop running and try to live out my own existence the best way I could.

A few guards walked past me, escorting some Angels out. One of them was Vale's freckled friend, who waved to me. I was dreading my turn. I remembered the last trial, when they had to draw blood from a vein in my calf because the ones in my arm had been poked so many times.

"Ey, tinkerbell, let me out-bench you," a beefy guy shouted at Vale from across the way.

He approached Vale with a few guys flanking him. I couldn't imagine how Vale earned that insult, considering he was pretty fit, and though younger than the other guy, he was slightly taller.

"You're on, but let's make it a bet," said Vale, approaching the weights.

A bunch of guys were gathering around the gym equipment now, so I decided to join them.

"Two hundred on the plates. Whoever gets in more reps," the beefy guy challenged.

"And loser has to do what?" Vale asked, clearly familiar with this guy's game.

"See that guard by the bathrooms, short one?"

"Yeah..."

"Loser walks up to him and gives him the finger. You'll have to spend the night in the tank."

Vale laughed. "You're about to spend the night in the tank, then. Hope you like it there."

The bigger guy started to stretch while his friends loaded up the bar. He lay back on the bench and heaved the bar up with ease. He huffed loudly as he powered through three or four, the bar bending from the bulky weights, while his friend stood on standby to spot him.

The onlookers all counted together. *Seven! Eight!* He was shaking dramatically, but he got two more in with difficulty before slamming down the bar, beet-red in the face.

"Let's fucking go!" he said, pounding his chest. "Easy ten!"

I hoped this was not the daily culture here, because I felt very out of place. If I tried that weight, I'd probably snap at the elbows.

"Tye, come spot me," Vale said, planting himself on the bench.

My face burned, likely turning even redder than his competitor's. "Ah, I don't know, man..."

"I won't need it, it's just for good measure," he assured me.

Reluctantly, I stood behind him, letting my hands hover under the bar as he lay back. He gripped it firmly, then pushed into a powerful first rep. The first five seemed like a cakewalk, but when he hit six, he was visibly slower.

"You got this, Vale!" shouted someone from the crowd.

He got two more in.

"Beast mode, V!" encouraged another.

I could tell Vale was well respected and liked around here, simply by the differences in the way people watched him versus the first guy. He was on his ninth rep when he started shaking uncontrollably. I grew nervous that I'd need to step in, imagining the weights falling onto Vale's neck because I couldn't hold the bar up. I'd bulked up a little bit with age, but under such survival conditions, it was hard to keep muscle on.

Vale hit the tenth rep, but was blue in the face.

"Don't touch the bar!" his challenger yelled at me as I inched closer.

"One more," I said to Vale as he trembled, and not only did he hit an eleventh rep, but he got an extra one in before dropping the weights violently onto the rack, jumping up and letting out a huge breath of relief as his friends rallied around him.

The other guy spat on the ground. "You're lucky I did a transfusion yesterday. I would've cleared you at full strength—"

"Right, right. Enjoy the tank," Vale said, wiping the sweat from his forehead. His friends laughed.

Clearly pissed, the losing guy trudged over to the guard as everyone watched in anticipation, barely holding back their snickering. He went up to the stoic man, who tightened his grip around his holstered gun.

"What do you want?" he asked threateningly.

The beefy guy hesitated for a moment, looking back at all of us watching, then finally turned back around and held up his middle finger in the guard's face.

With lightning speed, the guard drew his weapon, which I now realized was a taser, and fired into the offender. The guy instantly dropped to the floor, convulsing as other guards came to assist.

The dome filled with laughter, but I couldn't help but wince as they dragged him away.

"Cut it out or you'll spend the rest of the day in the pods!" threatened another guard.

Finally, the crowd dispersed. Vale hung back and came over to me. He planted himself on a nearby chair, still catching his breath.

"Such a tool bag. Steer clear of him," he said.

I sat next to him. "Don't think he'll be challenging me anytime soon," I said, jokingly flexing my arm. "I'm a string bean."

Vale burst out laughing. "We'll bulk you up. We got nothing but time."

A nurse holding a tray came over and handed us two cups each, one containing a handful of pills and another some blue liquid. I only accepted because Vale didn't hesitate.

"It's just vitamins to help replenish our blood," he assured me, knocking them back.

I stared at the pills for a beat, then mirrored Vale. It was then I spotted his friends waving at us, waiting by the gym equipment.

"I'll be there in a minute!" he called to them. "Let me catch my breath."

"Go, I feel like your friends didn't think much of me at breakfast," I said, grinning to mask my insecurity.

"I promise, it's not that. It's just hard for them to invest in newcomers. A lot of people don't come back from the clinical trials. We've lost a handful already."

I dropped my forced smile and eyed the prick marks under his biceps. "How'd you end up here?" I asked.

He gave a sarcastic-sounding chuckle, as if to say, *Where do I start?* "Well... my dad was a big-time engineer. He was recruited to project manage construction on one of the border walls after the big outbreak. Me and my mom were put in housing near the site, but there were Needle-Mouths all over the place, and the military was spread thin trying to contain the safe zones. One got in our place in the middle of the night and my mom didn't make it, and I got bit trying to get her out of there."

He showed me the scar on his calf. Unlike mine, it was very prominent.

"Since my dad was working for the government, I got treated pretty quickly. But at that point they didn't really have a protocol, so they kind of put me in a holding cell to monitor the infection. My dad even came to visit me to say goodbye... but I never changed. Weeks passed, they ran all sorts of tests, and then they realized my blood wasn't compatible with the virus."

"I take it they didn't let you go back with your dad?" I asked, recalling my own traumatic separation from the ones I loved.

"For a few days. But then, suddenly a whole new team took over, and I was put through a bunch more tests. At first, I was down because they said it could potentially help with vaccines and cures, but then I realized I was very much a prisoner for science. I asked to go back with my dad, and they told me he'd taken a bad fall and didn't make it."

"That's bullshit."

"I know. Trust me, I know... Conveniently, it was once the wall was finished, too. Months went by and I sort of became numb, let them do what they needed to do, hoping it'd be over soon, but the world just kept changing so fast and there was no real life to go back to anymore. I was handed off to Ylem and have been here ever since." He started to re-tie his shoelaces, which seemed like an escape from the subject. "How about you?"

I didn't even know where to start. I felt like I'd lived a hundred lifetimes. I knew I definitely shouldn't share how I'd escaped the border and that my blood was somehow different than even his. I couldn't handle the thought of more eyes on me.

Three guards interrupted us before I could respond. Two of them took me by the arms. "Time for your appointment," one said.

Vale saluted me as the third guard pushed him in another direction.

My heart started to race as they escorted me down a series of halls and into an elevator. We traveled several floors up. I couldn't imagine what sort of testing I'd be subjected to today—it seemed they'd done every test imaginable before I'd even made it to the camps.

The doors slid open to reveal a cavernous laboratory with different stations set up all around the room. Scientists and researchers worked diligently, not even looking up from whatever tests they were monitoring.

A nurse approached me holding a tablet. She turned the screen towards me and asked, "Is all of this information correct?"

It showed my photo, full name, and stats. "Yes ..."

I couldn't help but notice the long list of notes directly under my image, but she turned it back towards her too quickly for me to read it.

"This way," she said, setting off at a brisk walk. The guards pushed me to follow her. While we made our way to the other end of the lab, the researchers I passed began to stare and whisper, clearly recognizing me in some way.

We finally reached a large silver door where my escort placed her palm over a scanner, prompting the door to hiss and slide open. Behind it was a large doctor's office, with mechanisms and monitors surrounding an examination table.

Though the nurse left me, the two guards stayed, ushering me forward to sit on the table. A few moments later, in walked a third person, who I assumed was the doctor who would be torturing me today. He walked over to the sink and washed his hands before greeting me.

"Tye. How are you feeling today?"

I met his gaze and somehow, he seemed familiar. He must've seen my expression change because he said, "I'm Dr. Chiron. I treated you when you arrived at the state border."

My face turned hot. Part of me was angry, associating him with the start of all of this, but the kindness in his eyes disarmed me somewhat. I remembered he was one of the nicer parts of my experience at the border.

"You look different without the hazmat suit," I noted.

In fact, his face was much more worn out than I remembered. He'd clearly been overworked.

He ignored the comment. "We've concluded that if you have Angel's blood, you can't transmit the virus. At least, not if it's airborne." He started to prepare a needle.

"What's the torture gonna be today?" I asked.

He looked at me regretfully. "Hopefully it won't be too bad. They assigned me to head your trials since we're familiar. If it's any consolation, they're hoping it will ease your mind."

He tied a rubber band around my bicep, and I flinched from the bruising. "Ease my mind? Nothing will ease my mind while I'm being held prisoner."

Gently, he placed the needle in a healed part of my vein. I turned so as not to see the blood drain. "We believe that Ichor is compatible with all blood types, but this is just a precaution to confirm the theory. Then, we can place you with a household."

"Ichor... ?"

"God's Blood. *Your* blood. Just one of the various unique properties it holds."

I looked at him steadily. "Why am I different? Why are they so set on keeping me captive?"

He glanced at the two guards by the door before removing the needle from my arm and bandaging me up. "You're set for today, Tye. I'll be seeing you soon."

Back in my pod, as the lights dimmed for curfew, I felt dizzy with my racing thoughts. Though Chiron seemed willing to tell me more than he was allowed to, it didn't escape me that the last I saw him, he was a government employee, and that now he was serving Ylem.

It was apparent that the government and the powers behind Ylem were linked, if not the same entity altogether. Of course, for an enormous metropolis like Ylem to remain a secret for so long, it had to have been interlaced with all sorts of high-powered officials.

"Hey, Tye," came a voice, accompanied by a knock on the glass door of my pod.

I looked up to see Vale's freckled friend, his arm bandaged from his appointment earlier. "Hey."

"Since you just got here, do you mind if I leave this book I finished and grab one from you? They haven't added any new ones to the shelves for a while and I'm burning through them."

For the first time, I noticed the three books stacked on my bedside table.

"Oh, yeah, of course," I said, laying them out on my bed. "Take whichever."

"Thanks. I'm B, by the way. Sorry we didn't chat much earlier, I was anxious about my transfusion today."

"Don't sweat it. I'm just floating around trying to get my bearings... Did you get through it okay?"

He shrugged. “I can’t stand the family I’ve been placed with.”

That made me feel uneasy. Dr. Chiron had said they were trying to match me with my own family to donate to. I hoped they would be at least tolerable.

PLEASE REPORT TO PODS. LIGHTS OUT IN FIVE. PLEASE REPORT TO PODS. LIGHTS OUT IN FIVE. PLEASE REPORT TO PODS. LIGHTS OUT IN FIVE.

B took the middle book off the bed. “You’re a lifesaver. Get some rest, Tye. Tomorrow we do it *allll* over again.”

2. WILLA

I'd gotten used to the constant drone of overhead choppers and distant protests, but the one sound I had yet to adjust to was a baby's cry.

Amid the sound of Riley comforting her daughter in the other room, I rolled over, untangling myself from my sheets. Across the room, Ava's bed was vacant. Thanks to her resourcefulness, we had secured better housing, but we were still sharing rooms. Something I didn't mind. Having my friends around had been a huge factor in my healing. Despite the chaotic environment of the safe zone, I felt at peace around them.

Although I was dealing with it better than my parents, there were days when Malik's death still hit me with full force. Having space from them had done me good, though. Little by little, I'd carved out a routine.

All of us had taken on minor jobs around the city. Ava helped with refugee files, I had a few shifts at the local food hall handing out rations, and Otto was a mechanic for the military forces in the area. Our government-issued bank cards were loaded with our meager earnings every other week, just enough to get us by.

With people now returning to their once-abandoned homes and others scrambling to find a place amid the housing shortage, it was common for multiple families to share a living space. Eventually, we'd all moved into this bigger house with Riley, her father, and her newborn daughter, Rio.

With hospitals over capacity, she'd gone through a painful home-birth. Though she made it through, the aftermath was also challenging. Baby supplies were hard to come by, and expensive, but with all of our support, they were both doing well.

I slipped on my sweats and headed to Riley's room. "Need anything?" I asked, watching her gently bounce her fussing daughter.

Riley looked up. "Sorry, did she wake you again?"

"I don't mind, really. Can I help?"

Rio's cries softened as she looked up at me with big blue eyes.

"You already are," Riley said, putting the now burbling girl back in her makeshift crib—something Otto had surprised her with when we moved in.

I leaned over and gently caressed the baby's cheek. Her gummy smile was contagious; I couldn't help but smile back. "I'm more worried about your sleep than mine," I told Riley. Though just as beautiful as ever, her face definitely showed signs of new motherhood.

"Is it weird that I love when she cries for me?" she cooed. "Yeah, sleep's great, but she's so attached. Nothing beats that feeling."

A knock on the door made us look up. It was Ava's mother.

"How's she doing?" she asked, lighting up when she spotted Rio, now dozing off again. "I don't mind staying here if you guys are going to the protest."

"Are you coming?" I asked Riley.

Word had spread that another massive rally was happening in the city center. With the military presence so intense, these gatherings were becoming less frequent, but it was a great place for us citizens to regroup and exchange information.

"Yep, Ava and Otto are gonna meet us there after work."

Ava's mom sat on the chair next to the crib. "I know I always say it, but be safe. There's a lot of these rebel groups causing havoc out there. I know they say they're on our side, but the 'safe zone' isn't feeling so safe anymore."

"We'll be in and out," said Riley, kissing Rio softly on the forehead.

Protests had been going on since the early rumors of the planes spreading chemicals, but now that Thirteen's exposé had been circulating in the media, tensions were higher than ever. We'd all been on the edges of our seats for months, waiting for a major shift now that Zenith was outed for intentionally causing the plane crash and silencing their past employees, but no real change had come.

The media used the shocking headlines for clickbait, talked about it while it was a hot topic, then slowly allowed it to fade as if it were all hearsay. Even backed by concrete evidence, the chilling details barely caught fire. I suspected, somewhere under the radar, the story was being buried and dismissed. Not only had Zenith done this before, but it was becoming more and more obvious that our own government was somehow intertwined with the events that unfolded. They continued to be vague and point blame at other possible causes.

Luckily, the people would not allow that to go unnoticed. What was left of the internet had become a hellstorm of information wars, massive uprisings sprang up at every major government building, and rebel groups had become our only allies in fighting back. The suppressive military force that had once been for protection now seemed to be looming solely to keep us in line.

"Show me what democracy looks like!" a woman shouted through a megaphone among the sea of angry civilians.

They called back, "THIS IS WHAT DEMOCRACY LOOKS LIKE!"

Hundreds of people lined the streets, holding their angry signs high. The energy was explosive. Rallies like this were nothing new, but the sheer numbers that showed up today were astounding. It seemed like the whole state had unified in uproar. Otto, Ava, and Riley stood beside me, joining in on the chorus of angry shouts.

"Who spread the virus?!"

"MIDAS SPREAD THE VIRUS!"

That name still boiled my blood. I first learned it through my brother, and it became an obsessive focal point in my day-to-day thoughts.

Midas Rothfield was a tech trillionaire who had acquired Zenith just prior to the plane crash at Ground Misery. He was the very man responsible for the mass layoffs and company reform—a shift that would ultimately lead to the spread of the virus.

With all the evidence against him, his name was prominent among the people, but he still hadn't been spotlighted in mainstream media. It almost seemed like they were purposely avoiding his name, even when speaking on the plane crash and Zenith. Every day, the divide between the media, the government, and its citizens became clearer.

"MIDAS IS THE VIRUS! MIDAS IS THE VIRUS!"

Through the dense crowd, I saw my friend Cleo pushing her way over to us. Her bright red hair stood out among the dusty palette of protestors.

"Hoped I'd see you guys! How's Rio?" she asked with endearing concern.

"She's good for now," Riley assured her. "Any luck getting baby stuff in the last raid?"

"Nothing useful, but we're hitting a distribution center next week," she said, lowering her voice. "I'm on it."

"You're the best," I said.

Cleo moved in closer. "Did you guys hear about the second plane crash?" she asked grimly.

My knees nearly buckled. "*What?*"

"There's rumors some second plane was found on its way to Canada. They're investigating the crash site ... or so they say."

I had no words; Otto spoke before I could. "What makes them think it's related to the Zenith plane?"

"Not sure yet. I just heard from one of my sources this morning. I'm sure it'll be all over the news by this afternoon. You know they love blasting out trauma porn."

My friends and I traded grave looks. Though I'd shared valuable insight with Cleo before, she had no idea how linked I was to everything that had happened. The prospect of a second plane crash flooded me with worry.

Someone bumped into me hard. The crowd had started to congeal, squeezing my friends and me against each other.

Six large military trucks pulled up to the scene and a battalion of armored soldiers poured out. Hardly any of them were over the age of thirty, which was partly the reason the crowds rarely took them seriously.

"That's enough! Disassemble immediately!" came a voice over a loudspeaker.

A symphony of booing ensued, but we'd learned the hard way that if the military wasn't met with compliance, things would get messy.

"Let's get back," said Ava as the crowd became agitated. Though passionate about the injustice we faced, Ava always remained the level-headed one in our group.

In contrast, Cleo flashed a middle finger to the soldiers as we walked away. "I'll tell you more if I hear anything!" she called to us as the current of bodies pushed us apart.

Back at the house, the four of us walked in on Ava's mom and Riley's dad sitting in front of a small television in the living room. It was clear right away that something was off. Normally, they'd greet us with great relief that we'd come back safe, but today, they were fixated on the newscaster on screen.

"-still looking into whether there are ties to Zenith. Reports say that there were no obvious biochemicals aboard the aircraft, but that it appeared to have been shot down. U.S. and Canadian air forces claim they had no involvement, which could mean the crash was either intentional or staged."

An image of the plane flashed up on the screen: a dark gray cargo plane with a large red X spray-painted on the exterior.

It was like a punch to the gut. I'd seen that plane before. It had haunted my dreams often, the sight of Tye boarding it and the knowledge that I might never see him again.

"Guys," I said, so hoarsely my voice didn't even sound like my own. The whole room turned to me. "That's... That's the cargo plane that rescued Tye."

Everyone seemed to process the words with difficulty. The use of his name had become less and less frequent under our roof, as time passed and his absence became harder to face.

Ava looked between me and the screen a few times before asking, "How do you know that's the one?"

I frowned, recalling what I knew. "The red X. And it was heading to Canada. I'm one hundred percent sure it's the same plane."

The energy in the air changed. Riley froze, Ava audibly swallowed, the parents looked at me in total shock, and Otto fell back onto the couch.

Riley turned to her dad. "Did they say if anyone was found on board?"

"Just the pilot, shot dead..."

The room was spinning. "They must've taken him," I said, struggling to breathe through my words.

"To those camps?" asked Otto, his anxiety clearly rising to join mine.

Although we didn't know where it was, I'd informed them all of what Maverick had shared about Ylem, the secret city. Tye was meant to be taken there and used for his blood. Something I knew to be his deepest nightmare.

"They must've. Whoever took down that plane knew about Tye's blood and took him."

Riley began to pace. "So, what now? We can't tell the authorities that you tried to smuggle him out of the country, and we already know our government's probably in on this!"

I felt that familiar urge bubble within. The unyielding drive to protect and save the ones I loved. And my love for Tye was unlike any other, but this truly felt like an impossible dilemma. We had no idea where Ylem was, nor the means to march in there and save him. "Maybe Thirteen has some advice… He has the best grasp on all of this," I thought out loud.

"When's the last time you heard from him?" asked Otto.

"Months. Before I got here. I have his contact, but I've been afraid to reach out in case it compromised him."

"Well, his exposé's already out there now. It's as good a time as ever," Ava pointed out.

While the others stayed glued to the TV, trying to make sense of the crash, I dug through my single drawer of belongings.

At one point in time, Thirteen had given me a Post-it note with Tye's last known coordinates written on it. I only noticed months later that his own number was written discreetly on the other side.

I held it in my shaking hand. I'd memorized it long before now—hardly needed the paper at all. For so long I wanted to reach out, but once the data went public, I wasn't sure who Thirteen's enemies were. Luckily, my contributions to his cause remained anonymous.

I picked up the house phone and dialed, my lungs tightening with each number. It rang. I held my breath…

"Hello?"

His voice sounded different from what I remembered. I wet my dry lips. "Thirteen?"

"Willa? Hi-Hello! This is his son, Rowen."

He sounded much older than I'd always imagined him. I took a deep breath, caught off guard. "Rowen? Hi. I've heard a lot about you… Is he around?" There was a long pause on the phone. "If this isn't a secure line, you can call me back—"

"It's secure, but... my father's no longer with us. He died in a car crash a few months back."

Deflated, I sank down on the edge of my bed. "A car crash... ?"

"Yes... I'm so sorry you're finding out like this."

That sounded all too suspicious.

"I know... It's suspect," he added in response to my silence.

"I'm so sorry, Rowen. He was a great man. Are you doing okay?"

"Getting by... but I've taken over where he left off. I'm filled in and working tirelessly with the network he's created. The work's far from over."

"I want to talk with you about some stuff, but I still think it should be in person," I told him. "Just in case."

"I know where you are. I'll come by tomorrow afternoon for a chat."

"Okay. Just be careful. See you then."

We sat around the repurposed picnic table in the dining room, waiting anxiously for a knock on the door. My finger traced circles around the rim of my mug.

Despite Riley's dad having made us a substantial lunch, my stomach was in knots. It was difficult to enjoy the hard-earned meal. He'd taken one of the tougher jobs available, assisting at the border camps in different roles, as they were more understaffed and overwhelmed than ever. Though he was worked to the bone, his earnings were significantly better than any of ours. He loved treating us when he could.

Ava's eyes were wide, her fork suspended in mid-air. "We need to start spreading the word about Ylem. Not enough people are talking about it."

"We hardly know anything about it," Otto reminded her. "Except for what Mav told Willa."

"Rowen will fill us in," I said, pushing the unseasoned potatoes around on my plate.

"Look, I know I never met Maverick," said Riley's dad, "but it's pretty obvious he told them Tye was on that plane. With everything you've told us about him, I just don't see how there's any other answer."

Even with months having gone by, I still struggled to forgive Mav. It was easier not being in contact with him, but parts of me missed him and other parts resented him.

When I didn't respond, Riley chimed in. "Do we know why Maverick knew about Ylem when no one else did? That alone is fishy..." She wiped Rio's mouth, and the baby let out a coo. "See, even Rio thinks so."

"He said they have something on him. I guess he landed in some sort of blackmail situation and was forced to work with them. I don't know what to believe, really," I said doubtfully.

A knock on the door pulled our focus. I shot up from my seat almost instantly. Peeking through the blinds, I saw someone waiting at the door, a hoodie and baseball cap hiding their face.

I opened the door slowly, waiting for the person to speak first.

"It's Rowen," he said quickly, looking around to make sure no one was watching us.

"Come in," I said, and locked the door behind him.

Rowen looked so much like his dad, there was no doubt he was who he claimed to be. He even wore the same style of rounded glasses I remembered Thirteen wearing when we met, possibly even the very same ones—a sad detail that made me feel sorry that Rowen had to bear the burden of his father's legacy without him.

He closed the blinds one by one before joining us at the table. I could see a number of creased stress lines on his face, though he couldn't have been too much older than me.

"I can't stay long," he said, putting a friendly hand on my shoulder. "Can we speak in private?"

"Everyone in this room's like family," I told him. "Everything I know, they know. We can speak freely."

He nodded, but still looked hesitant.

I spoke to the room. "Rowen's picking up where his dad left off. He's running the network now."

"Glad to finally meet you all. Sorry it's not under better circumstances," he said timidly.

"Did you see the latest plane crash?" I asked him.

"We're looking into it, but it doesn't seem to be one of the spreader planes."

"I know ... " I swallowed to relax my tightening throat before saying it out loud. "Tye was aboard that plane. I know he was wanted at Ylem for whatever's in his blood. Do you think they're behind that crash?"

His eyebrows arched when I said Ylem, clearly surprised that I even knew about it. That was a detail yet to be mentioned in his father's exposé.

"It's likely. What have you heard about Ylem?"

"Only that it's a stronghold where the rich are hiding. Probably hoarding the cure for themselves," I said with distaste.

"My father left Ylem out of his reports so we wouldn't compromise getting our assets inside. We have a few people there now," Rowen revealed. "It's very hard getting messages in and out, but from what we've learned, it's a vast city. When we got a hold of some early blueprints, it was clear they began construction decades ago. Zenith's owner, Midas Rothfield, headed the project."

The room was heavy with silence, until my voice broke it. " ... *What?!*"

"Midas used Zenith to end the world while building a safe city in secret."

"So he had a full plan all along," Otto said, looking defeated.

It felt like the temperature in the dining room had dropped several degrees.

"And the blood harvesting? What are you hearing about that?" Riley dared to ask.

Rowen visibly swallowed. "The research camps are headed up by leading scientists. They're working on new ways to keep the Ylem residents immune to any future exposures. Essentially, they're waiting for the world to rot and self-implode while they adapt and thrive in their bubble…" There was pain in his timbre. "The border camps were filters to catch anyone with some form of immunity. It was the first sign we had that the government was working in tandem with Ylem's research."

My hands were starting to shake from anger. If there was any doubt that Tye had been taken there, it faded with every word Rowen spoke. I couldn't imagine what all those kids were going through.

"Why would the government help a terrorist like Midas?" Ava blurted out.

"Because the heads of our government want what we all want—to be safe and secure. They've struck deals with him to live in Ylem, with their families, in exchange for their cooperation," Rowen confirmed regretfully.

"So Midas is behind *everything*?" I asked, venom on my tongue.

"He's definitely the core of it, but to execute something of this magnitude, there's no doubt his web of corruption is wide. We've had confirmation there are many world leaders living there…including our own president."

Ava's mom spilled her water, quickly standing to dry it with a nearby dish towel. Even though it was painfully obvious our government was failing us, hearing this directly made my stomach churn.

"Where is it?" asked Otto.

"It's very remote. Hard to find precisely on any existing map, but we're working on more accurate coordinates."

"Is that why no one's tried to take them down?" Riley asked, her temper visibly rising to the point where she handed Rio to her father so she could pace. "There's plenty of big rebel groups out there fighting back. And other countries? It should be their first stop!"

"There have been attempts, but all failed miserably. No one comes back. It's difficult to reach as it is, but they even have jamming satellites so aircraft can't fly near it. With every billionaire from around the world under one roof, their resources are incalculable. They have a strong defense force, but their most significant protection is their barrier wall. It dwarfs any border wall of ours."

My friends and I traded horrified looks.

"So what you're saying is, there's nothing we can do?" Ava asked.

"Not for the time being, no. But trust that we *are* working on it. Ylem needs to be taken down from the inside," he said simply. "A head-on attack would need immeasurable logistics, and information we simply don't have. They are few, but our network is trickling into their veins. We're working on figuring out an alternative infiltration route. For now, it'd be good to start spreading the word that Ylem exists and is very much the enemy. The more citizens understand, the more support for our cause will rise."

These weren't the answers I was hoping for when I'd asked Rowen to visit. If anything, I had ten times the number of questions I had before. But I couldn't bring myself to ask any more with the way my mind was spinning. If Tye was there, he wasn't safe.

Rowen was visibly anxious to get going, so I walked him to the door.

"Rowen, please keep an ear out for any word on my friend. And if there's anything I can do to help take down Midas, or Ylem, I'm here. Nothing would make me happier."

He smiled.

"What?" I asked.

"You're exactly how my father described. You have a big fire in you. The best thing you can do right now is keep yourself safe. I imagine you'll be an invaluable asset when the time comes. So much of what's already in motion is because of you."

I smiled back. “I’m ready,” I said as he stepped outside. “And Rowen… I’m here for you too. If you need anything.”

Even with his hood back up and his head lowered, I caught sight of his sweet dimples before he took off down the sidewalk.

3. TYE

I was only four days in and already feeling incredibly claustrophobic, between the pods and the constricted common areas we were confined to.

I even caught myself joining in on workouts with Vale and his friends, purely out of extreme boredom. His friends were slowly warming up to me, but Vale was the real light in the dark during my first week here.

He reminded me a lot of Hunter in the way that he made it a point to make me feel included while I was still green. Unlike what Hunter eventually became, Vale was very even-keeled and positive. For the twenty four hours that he was away for his transfusion and enjoying the leisure time his assigned family granted him, I felt thoroughly lost trying to fit in with the more seasoned Angels.

In my attempt to get to know more of them, I realized that many had lapses in their memory from their early symptoms. Some didn't know what their names used to be and had adopted new ones. When I overheard a few different accents, it dawned on me that there were Angels imported here from other countries. A couple didn't even speak English at all.

I sat in the rec area library, trying my best to get through a chapter of some mediocre fantasy book, but my mind was so all over the place, it was hard to retain any of what I was reading.

My name had flashed red on the tablet for the last few days, so I was not needed for any appointments. Though I was happy I wouldn't be going through more tests, I was eager to prod Dr. Chiron for more answers.

In between thinking of Willa and my friends, I'd combed through a Rolodex of theories in my mind about what could be so exceptional about my blood that would justify its given name, *God's Blood.*

I didn't know enough about cells or blood types to make any plausible guesses. In high school, my biology class landed in the middle of the school day after lunch, so it was usually where I dozed off in a food coma while my teacher yapped on.

A shadow passed over the pages of my book and I looked up to see a nurse standing over me, holding a stack of faded white towels.

"Shower day," she said flatly, handing me one.

It was scratchy to the touch. I'd been so consumed with getting through each day, I'd hardly remembered that it'd been days since I was able to bathe. We were lucky that things around here were kept so sterile, or it'd be unbearable to stand next to anyone.

The nurse continued to hand out towels, while a line formed near the restrooms on the other side of the dome. I'd been through enough to know there would be limited hot water, so I joined the line in a hurry.

I spotted Vale right away, since he was taller than the few guys ahead of me. He was sweatier than usual, having probably pushed his workout harder knowing it was shower day.

As the group funneled into the restrooms, a sliding glass door opened to our right and I could see a locker room just beyond it.

Vale saw me following the crowd. "Tye Guy's first shower day. Thank god. You were starting to smell like a hamster." He whipped me lightly with one end of the towel.

"Shut up," I laughed. "Do we get shampoo and stuff, or is that another privilege we have to earn?"

"Nah, they have some," he said, shucking his jumpsuit off.

All around me, everyone started to undress.

"Is it stalls, or—"

"Communal. So get comfy, my friend," Vale laughed, tossing his boxers into a locker like a basketball.

I should've never expected an ounce of luxury like privacy, so my shock was hardly warranted. Nervously, I put my clothes in a locker, trying my best to cover myself with my small towel.

I wasn't so much embarrassed about my body or assets; it was more the humiliation of feeling like an inmate with no sense of autonomy. The way we were treated here was infuriating.

Stepping into the large open room, I found a free showerhead and tried my best to hang my towel nearby, then quickly got going. As predicted, the water was barely lukewarm.

Next to the towel hook were a few dispensers with body wash and shampoo. I tried to block out everything around me, keeping my back to the others, and washed myself quickly.

I could hear everyone comfortably talking among themselves. Clearly, this was nothing they hadn't seen before. Most of them had been here much longer than me. I turned around to face them, trying to fake my own comfort level.

I noticed we all shared matching bruises from needles and probes.

Vale was across the way, mid-conversation with his best friend B. "So to do this, she dips him in the river, which is the boundary between earth and the underworld, and the waters have magical properties," B was explaining passionately. He saw me looking over. "Vale doesn't like reading, so I just give him the synopsis of every book I finish."

Vale was rinsing the soap from his hair. "He's like my own little podcast."

B rolled his eyes.

Another friend of his called over from the other side of the room. "I actually heard about another cool legend."

"Which one?" Vale asked, shutting the water off and reaching for his towel.

"Godzilla!" his friend shouted mockingly, pointing at Vale's private parts.

Everyone cracked up.

"You spend a lot of time looking at it, huh?" Vale shot back, taking his time covering it with his towel.

I couldn't help but laugh myself. I was just glad all the attention was off me.

Simultaneously, all the showerheads shut off, yet no one was left with suds in their hair, clearly aware they were on a limited timer. I hadn't gotten to wash my hair at all, but at least my body felt clean. A guard came in to start ushering us back to the lockers to get dressed.

That afternoon in the Commissary, I sat at the usual table with Vale and his posse, a few missing having gone to their assignments for the day. I noticed Vale had given his tray to one of his friends and wasn't eating, and this time, B wasn't around to force-feed him.

"This is definitely the same sausage we had for breakfast that they just cut up and mixed with rice," he said, staring at my plate.

"I know it's junk, but don't you get hungry?" I asked.

"I eat good on transfusion days. My family's chill."

I was happy to hear Vale was comfortable, but I couldn't bring myself to imagine feeling anything positive about a family I was enslaved to.

LINE UP IMMEDIATELY. LINE UP IMMEDIATELY. LINE UP IMMEDIATELY.

That was an announcement I hadn't heard before. Vale caught my hesitation and tapped my shoulder, urging me forward as everyone abandoned their seats to line the Commissary walls.

"What's going on?" I whispered worriedly.

He was scanning the room. "Not sure. They've only done this once before, when someone stole a guard's taser..."

The guards seemed too subdued to make me think there was a threat at hand. They stationed themselves in an orderly fashion around the room while the rest of us held our breath waiting for their next move, but to my surprise, the main door slid aside and a new group appeared.

A unit of soldiers clad in metallic gold uniforms marched in behind a woman whose presence alone held the room in check. I recognized her right away: Secretary Croft. The one who tore me from the cargo plane to bring me here.

The room seemed to hum with nervous energy. The camp guards didn't even make eye contact with her, just stood at attention with their heads down. During my early weeks in Ylem, I'd learned through observation that she was some sort of very high-ranking military officer.

What few interactions I'd had with her were cold. Her appearance here today could only mean bad news, so when she walked right up to me, my mood took a sharp downturn.

"A word?" she asked curtly.

Two of her soldiers grabbed me on either side and directed me to follow. I saw Vale tense with confusion before I was pushed out into the dome.

The door closed behind us and I stood alone with Secretary Croft and her men.

"What now?" I asked, barely holding back my resentment towards her.

"You've been assigned."

I felt a jolt in my stomach. The time had finally come. "All the theatrics just to tell me that?"

"I had to evaluate your condition and cooperation myself. Those stunts you tried to pull in your first weeks here will not be tolerated where you're going. Are there going to be any issues moving forward?"

I was hardly compliant when I arrived in Ylem, even tried to make a run for it a few times, but I learned the hard way that resisting did no good.

Since I didn't answer, she continued. "We're taking you for your first transfusion—"

"Please don't do this—"

"—and if you refuse, it'll be done by force. If I were you, I'd do my best to make a good impression. Your life can be a lot easier here if you use your gifts wisely."

I stared at her, tears of frustration welling in my eyes.

She ignored them. "Understood?"

I could only hope that whoever I was assigned to would be more like Vale's family than B's. Deep down, I wanted to relent and try to have a decent quality of life, but the thought of being used in this way made me sick. With immense difficulty, I nodded.

"Good. Come," she said.

Her ensemble ushered me back through the Commissary towards the halls. I caught one last look of shock from Vale and his friends before a blindfold was slipped over my eyes.

They'd done this before. My eyes had remained covered for the entirety of my travels to Ylem. It was obvious they couldn't risk any prisoners knowing the layout of the facility.

It was only once we boarded some sort of moving vehicle that my blindfold was removed. I could see now that we were in the compartment of a sleek metro train. Once my eyes adjusted to the sunlight, I had an intense, visceral reaction to what I saw outside the window.

The train was weaving in and out of complex high lines throughout an unbelievable metropolis. Even the quick glimpse I'd caught on my first day couldn't have prepared me for the scale of the cityscape.

It must've taken thousands, if not tens of thousands of workers to construct a city like this. Where were all those people? How on earth had word not spread of a place like Ylem? It was haunting to think of how money and power could make anything happen ... or not happen.

The architecture throughout was interesting and unique, clearly having been designed by top craftsmen. One building stood out among the rest. Planted in the heart of the city was a giant spherical black construct, nestled among a prominent patch of lush greenery, like a modern-day garden of Babylon. I couldn't peel my eyes away. When comparing it to the new world I'd come to know, decayed and desolate, my brain was having a hard time processing everything I was seeing. I hated the fact that I could not deny this city was breathtakingly beautiful.

"The Basilica," said Croft, following my gaze to the giant sphere.

I gaped at it. "What is it?"

"It's where we're headed."

In less than fifteen minutes, the metro pulled into an underground station where we were greeted by more golden soldiers. A very obvious security checkpoint.

Led by Croft, our entourage funneled out of the train cabin. The soldiers saluted her respectfully, then a few broke off to pat me down. When I was cleared, the whole unit moved towards a massive elevator.

It seemed a little overboard to need this much supervision when I was unarmed, but over ten soldiers, including Croft, stepped into the elevator with me. It climbed several floors before opening into a grand circular foyer.

A single, sharply dressed man stood there to greet us. "I'll take him from here," he said.

Croft nudged me forward. "Let me know if there's any issues," she said to him, her hand gripping my shoulder a bit too tightly for comfort.

While the houseman ushered me through the halls, I was mesmerized by the ornate details. I hadn't been anywhere so polished in ages. Everything in the new world was crumbling or unkept.

"Please wait here," he said, showing me to a large sitting room.

Reluctantly, I sat on the emerald-green velvet couch. On the coffee table, a crystal water pitcher and glass were left for me on a silver tray. After a beat, I poured myself a glass, noticing that my hand was shaking.

I looked around at all the art filling every possible inch of the room. Whoever lived here had a boundless collection. There was a noticeable abundance of Roman and Greek statues everywhere. Some paintings even looked familiar to me. It wasn't beyond the realm of possibility that when the world crashed, the rich scrambled to snatch these forsaken treasures off the black market.

It was hard to imagine the level of wealth and power that lived under Ylem. This building alone was more like a palace, and it was just one of many the train had sped past.

The houseman returned, clearing his throat to announce himself. I peeled my eyes away from a large painting of two men immersed in a game of cards.

He beckoned. "This way."

Because of the spherical construction of the mansion, it felt like we were walking in circles as I followed him through more hallways. Finally, we entered an extravagant lounge where two people waited: one familiar, the other a stranger, with medical equipment set between them

Dr. Chiron stood next to an imposing man. The man stood up, his movements slow and controlled. The lustrous sheen of his silky robes matched the richness in his glowing skin.

"Wow… There. He. Is. I've been looking forward to meeting you." He spoke in a deep but soft voice. His eyes were pale blue, cold as they regarded me, his black hair making them even more piercing. There was something vampiric about him, which was fitting considering it was my blood that brought me here.

"…Hi," I said, hesitantly.

"Midas," he said, shaking my hand with a firm grip. It was soft, as if it had never seen a day of manual labor. "Thank you for being here."

Like I had a choice. I nodded an acknowledgement to Dr. Chiron as Midas sat in one of the plush lounge chairs, lifting his sleeve to bare his vein.

"Tye, you can sit when you're ready," said Chiron timidly.

They knew I'd never be ready, nor willing, but it was all just aggravating formalities. I sat on the opposite lounge chair, eyeing the IV stands and tubing. Chiron hooked Midas to some electrical monitors, then did the same to me.

"This will be painless," said Midas, looking at me like I was one of the art pieces in his collection. "I'm excited to see how the Ichor translates."

I scoffed. "That makes one of us."

He chose not to acknowledge my tone. Chiron prepped his arm with the needle, then moved onto mine, wiping it first with alcohol. I turned away as the needle entered my vein, but through my peripheral vision, I could see the tubing turn red.

"It won't require much," said the doctor. "Let me know if you experience any chills or concerning sensations."

I just then noticed several armed guards in gold, standing like suits of armor in the corners of the room. I swallowed hard.

"Tell me, Tye: how has your stay at the camps been?" Midas asked.

I couldn't help but feel the seemingly pleasant delivery had some taunting behind it. "What do you think?"

"Well, you'll be spending a lot more time here if all goes well with today's transfusion."

"No thanks."

This time, his gaze held mine for just a few seconds too long, shrinking me. He had an effortless dominance to him. "We have big plans for you, Tye. It would be in your best interest to go along with them."

I didn't like this man one bit. The way he spoke, his words were definitely coated with threats. His stare made me so uncomfortable, I couldn't help but look at the blood funneling from my IV pack to his. I did feel a bit lightheaded, but I wanted to get out of here as quickly as possible. Stopping it now would only delay that.

"You're mythical, you know that?" Midas asked, as if fascinated by my story. "We were almost sure your readings were unique because you weren't actually bitten, but after some deep analysis of the infection, it was clear your DNA really is one of a kind."

It was also clear he knew much more about my blood than I did.

"Are you ever going to tell me what exactly makes me so special? Besides my blood being compatible with everyone?" I asked.

Midas smiled. I caught myself checking for fangs, just in case. "In due time. There are still more tests to be done."

His condescending tone was maddening. My fist clenched, making the needle twitch.

Although I was eager to get out of Midas's lair, I wasn't so keen on being trapped at the camps again. It felt even more suffocating now that I had tasted the outside. Vale and B were both out for their own transfusions, so I waited anxiously in my pod, picking at my arm bandage.

I was fantasizing about all the ways to break out of here, but unlike at the border, there was no plan that seemed even a tiny bit achievable. The camera in the top-left corner of my pod was a reminder of that.

I heard him before I saw him, greeting a few neighboring pods before appearing in the doorway of mine.

"You good?" Vale asked. "What was that all about?"

"I got assigned."

"So? How was it? Are they chill? Sick house?" My face must have told him everything he needed to know. "Shit ..." He sat on the corner of my bed. "Was the house cool, at least?"

"Define cool." I shook my head. "It was weird as fuck. Looked like an evil snow globe."

The warmth in his expression dimmed. "Wait, you went to the big sphere?"

I frowned at him, confused. "Yeah, the one in the middle of everything."

"Dude ..."

"What?!"

He stood up. "That's the Basilica. That's where the head honcho lives."

"What? Midas?"

"Yeah, that's the guy who started all of this. He used to own Zenith, and he built Ylem."

Now I stood up. "*Midas* is the guy who started it all?!"

"No wonder they came to get you like that. I thought you were in trouble."

It felt like my skull was going to shatter. Anger boiled under my skin. My teeth clenched with the realization that I had just been in a room with the man responsible for all the agony life had become.

"Are you okay?" Vale asked as I fell back down onto my bed.

"Not really, no. I'm gonna be helping the guy who's directly responsible for the loss of everyone I love? He gets to be immune, while everyone out there gets infected?!"

My breathing became heavy. Willa had mentioned Zenith and its part in the outbreak. Although at the time we couldn't be sure what the intentions were, it was clear now that Midas had orchestrated a devastating collapse while knowing he could watch safely from Ylem, his stronghold.

Vale put a calming hand on my head. "None of us want to be helping them ..." Then, unexpectedly, he sat next to me and hugged me. Tucking his head into my shoulder, he whispered, "There's stuff happening in the shadows that could get us out of here. Just try to get through these next few months."

I slowly pulled him off of me to look him in the eye. I had to be sure that I'd heard correctly, that he wasn't joking around.

He motioned to the camera with an almost undetectable head nod, and I knew I couldn't make him repeat it, so I just nodded back.

These next few months would be grueling.

4. WILLA

There was definitely a new energy under our roof. Although we continued on with our week, the charged information Rowen had shared with us sparked a shift in our reality.

Underneath the small talk and daily routines, we felt a pressure building. Tye had likely been captured, Midas was at large, and a whole secret society of corruption loomed.

It'd been a while since I'd felt this helpless. If Tye were somewhere in the contamination zones, I would be back out there in a heartbeat, but Ylem was a whole different ballgame. If groups of rebels and foreign military were trying and failing to infiltrate, it was unrealistic to think I could manage an attempt. And unlike the contamination zones that I was at least familiar with, Ylem was a total blind spot.

I was due at the cantina for my shift. After tying up my bed-tangled locs, I went downstairs to find Ava and Otto packing up for their own work days, while Riley was washing something outside with the hose.

"What's she up to?" I asked, grabbing a piece of cold toast from a tray on the counter.

Ava zipped up her backpack. "Rio's diaper. She's been reusing a cloth while we're out of them."

Before I could react to the heartbreaking news, Riley came inside. She picked up on my concern right away. "It's working, for now," she sighed.

I tried to offer some comfort. "Cleo said she's on it. I'm sure we'll get some supplies soon."

She gave me a tight-lipped smile.

Riley and I had bonded a lot in the last six months. Her own sister's abrupt passing made her the ideal sounding board for everything I was experiencing, and she helped me process so much of my mourning for Malik.

Before I came back, I was terrified to face her. She had once been—and in my opinion, still was—in love with Tye. And my feelings for him? They weren't exactly subtle. Anyone could see it in the way I talked about him, acted around him.

But Riley never faulted me for it. She assured me her love for Tye wasn't romantic anymore, and even said she admired me for everything I'd done for him. After that conversation, something shifted. We only got closer from there.

Otto put his hefty toolbox by the door. "How've you been sleeping?" he asked me, clearly seeing on my face that it'd been a rough week.

"Well, it was hard before Rowen's visit, so you can imagine what it's like now. I'm really worried about Tye."

I hadn't dreamt of Tye the way I used to. It worried me that maybe our connection wasn't as strong as it once was. I was relieved not to be having as many nightmares as before, but my sleep was still restless. Maybe he truly was safe, and all my dark intuitions stemmed only from anxiety.

Otto gave me a warm hug. "Tye's strong," he said. "We're gonna figure this out."

With Dustin still deployed, Otto had really stepped up to take care of us girls during all the transitions. Even though it frustrated him having to service the controlling military forces, his earnings were decent and he was great about helping to support us.

Ava joined in the hug and we laughed. Otto added an extra kiss for his girlfriend.

"I'll probably be back early evening," he told us. "I think the parents want to have dinner all together tonight if it syncs up."

"We should be back before you," said Ava. "I got a lot done last night, so I just have a few housing intakes to register."

They kissed again before Riley helped prop the door open so Otto could carry his toolbox out to the military escort vehicle waiting outside.

Ava was probably the only reason we'd found some normalcy among the chaos of reentry. Her talent for researching and organizing had been essential in getting us all situated. Our earning cards, our jobs, and even the house we lived in were all thanks to her. It was likely she was busying herself to avoid the pain of losing Tye and her father, but we made sure to always make her feel valued.

"Since you mention Cleo," she said, going through one of the kitchen drawers, "she gave me this from the last raid." She placed an old flip phone on the laminate counter. "It's a burner phone."

"For what? Bro, are you a spy?" Riley asked, checking it out.

"I was thinking about calling in an anonymous tip about Ylem, and Midas potentially hiding there. I still have that ad from the newspaper about reporting valuable info, and I feel like it's worth a try. I mean, Rowen said getting the word out there could push the cause."

My distaste for the media and how useless they'd proven to be made me hesitant to support the idea. There were very few outlets with any integrity left.

"What're you thinking?" Riley asked, like she could see the opinion forming on my face.

I shrugged. "I just have a hard time believing the media will make a difference, but there haven't been any stories on Ylem, so maybe it'll work out."

"It's a reputable reporter," Ava said. "She's done some of the better think pieces I've read. And besides, it'll be totally anonymous if we use the burner. I don't think there's anything to lose."

"Okay, then," Riley agreed. "Do your thing, girly."

Ava picked up the phone. "Yeah?"

"Go for it," I said.

She unfolded a piece of newspaper she'd taken from the same drawer and dialed the number. As she waited, Riley's dad came downstairs holding a naked Rio.

"Is her diaper thingy ready?" he asked his daughter, holding the baby as if she were radioactive. "Last time, she peed all over me."

Riley laughed, taking Rio and planting a big kiss on her cheek. We lowered our voices as Ava broke away, taking the phone into another room.

"Who's she talking to?" Riley's dad asked.

"She's calling in a tip about Ylem and Midas," I replied.

He looked concerned. "Is that safe?"

"It's not her personal number," Riley said, patting Rio gently on the back.

I caught a few words from the other room, 'Midas' and 'fugitive' among them.

"You have work today, Pops?" Riley asked him.

"Yeah, leaving in a bit with mama bear. Things have been non-stop at the border."

Ava finally came back into the kitchen. "Yes ... I can't disclose that ... You can check records for reference ... "

"Put it on speaker," Riley whispered.

Ava switched it over.

"Great! Can we follow up with you at this number?" asked the friendly-sounding reporter.

"Prefer not. The info's good, I promise you," Ava replied.

"We hope so. Thanks so much. Just be careful, Ava."

The call ended. She looked up at me with dread in her eyes.

"What?" I asked. The conversation had sounded straightforward enough.

She took the battery out of the phone and snapped the flip cover from the dial pad.

" ... I never told her my name."

The uneasy feeling I was left with carried over, even after we parted ways. On my way to work, I couldn't help but feel I was being watched. It was a feeling I'd always had since helping Thirteen, but today I felt like I was under a microscope.

I took the longer route, opting to walk down the busier streets towards the cantina, all the while thinking about the possibility that all of us were spotlighted as potential problems for Zenith and the government powers at play.

The food hall I worked at was a big hub for everyone in the district to receive their weekly rations. Grocery stores still existed but were few and far between, not to mention very understocked. Most people relied on the food banks to get by.

I used to love going to the grocery store. Some of the best memories I had growing up involved making big shopping runs with my aunt during the holidays. She'd always credit me as her sous-chef when her big feast was ready.

This place had none of the charm grocery stores had. Soldiers were parked at different points of the entrance and inside. It had an unfortunate ambience, but with supplies being scarce, the food hall had become a target for looters.

Among the young adults, two children broke off and approached my station. They looked like twins, a boy and girl, not much older than Archer would've been. I'd seen them before.

"Two packs, please," said the boy.

"You guys doing good?" I asked, handing them the prepackaged rations from the big crate behind me.

"The family that used to live in our house came back, so we have to move," said the girl, worry on her face.

"I had to move too," I said, leaning over the counter, "but now we got a better place, so don't worry too much."

They smiled and ran off with their food packs. It was still common that survivors were under thirty, which meant there were many left without parents or caretakers. I was happy they were still coming around.

A guy, slightly older than me, was next in line. I handed him a bag, but he dropped it, the contents spilling out onto the floor.

"So sorry!" I said, scrambling to help him, but he didn't move. I picked up a few items and stared up at him. He was shaking. "Are you okay?"

He looked down at me with dark, crazed eyes. Instinctively, I reached for my guns, but there was nothing there. I wasn't allowed to be armed in the safe zone. I stepped away only seconds before blood from the man's nose leaked onto the floor.

BANG!

Everyone screamed as a soldier took him down.

"Clear out! Everybody, clear out!" he yelled as more soldiers positioned themselves around the hall.

I followed the crowd back outside. Shaken, I watched as they secured the building. Word of infections happening in the safe zone was becoming more common. The vaccines that helped with airborne immunity simply weren't enough anymore. It tore at my soul, knowing that one day, safe zones might not exist. Not without a cure. Not with Midas keeping it locked away in Ylem.

The hours seemed to tick by as I waited for everyone to get home from work. Riley was surprised when I showed up at the house early, but I filled her in. She too was growing increasingly worried by the reports, keeping Rio in sight at all times.

I helped her get started on a basic meal of potatoes and thawed-out chicken, deciding it'd be a nice gesture to have dinner ready when everyone returned.

When we were all seated at the dinner table, I told the others about what had happened during my shift.

"That's the closest it's been to our house," Ava's mom pointed out. "It's happening more and more, but I haven't heard of one around here."

"And just outside the border wall, there's more Morts than ever. They're thinking about installing landmines along the perimeters if the numbers keep going up," Riley's dad added.

I used my knife to cut a piece of chicken with a little too much force. It made an unpleasant scraping sound against the plate. "Has there ever been a breach in any of the other safe states?" I dared to ask.

The parents traded a look, clearly deciding if they should share. Ava's mom took a bite to bail out, so Riley's father spoke. "One. They got it under control, but a few months later, there were so many infections popping up that that safe zone was a complete loss. They evacuated those they could and it was abandoned."

An unpleasant static hung in the air.

"How about I share some good news?" suggested Otto, easing the tension. "I got a call today while at work. Guess who?"

"Dustin?" Riley guessed hopefully.

"Good guess, but no."

"Who?" Ava pressed.

"My birth mom."

Everyone stopped eating.

"Really?" I asked. "That's a huge deal. How'd you feel about it?"

Otto had shared with me that he had a lot of unresolved trauma around his birth mother, who had abandoned him when he was very young. Reconnecting with her now, after all the mayhem, was a true miracle.

His eyes were glossy. "I guess I'm not sure yet. I mean, I'm obviously happy to hear from her. It just feels hard with my parents being gone."

Ava put her hand on his back. "Well, you don't have to make any decisions. You know she's there when you're ready."

"Where did she say she was?" Riley asked.

"Neighboring state, if you can believe it. Would be an easy visit. She marked me as family. Apologized for not calling sooner, but apparently she's been making moves in her safe zone. Said I'd be proud of her, but didn't want to say more on the phone."

Seeing Otto's hopeful face made me think of my own parents. I'd been optimistic that once we reunited, our past issues would feel smaller. Something we could finally put in perspective and move past. But when I came back, I found out pretty quickly that wasn't the case.

The food hall was closed for contamination protocols, so I decided to take the day to visit my parents. We'd been doing better since having time and space apart, but there was still work to be done. Losing Malik was a big blow to all of us.

I hadn't been home in weeks, and seeing how much it meant to Otto just to hear from his mom made me feel like maybe it was time I biked over to see mine and try to make things right.

Biking was one of the only things I still genuinely enjoyed. Unlike Seabird's quaint charm, our city felt more like a military base these days, but riding still gave me a sense of freedom. I was grateful to even have a bike. Ava's mom had managed to get one for our household through her job.

The weight of Ava's call and Rowen's warning still lingered, so I stayed on high alert. I avoided eye contact with every soldier I passed. It was better that way. The last time I rode alone, a few had catcalled me from their posts.

Eventually, the city blocks gave way to quiet suburbs, and I reached the checkpoint for the housing district where my aunt lived. Finding her place was still tricky since every house looked the same, but she had started making it feel more like her own. A small cluster of potted plants and flowers on the porch helped me spot it.

I parked my bike out front and knocked gently, almost hoping they weren't home. It only took a few seconds before I heard "Willa baby!" and my aunt Solana greeted me with a hug.

I instantly felt myself lighting up. It was hard not to when I saw her. She had voluminous decorated hair and dressed brightly, which stood out even more against the dusty backdrop of the world.

As always, the house smelled like food, somehow still appetizing despite the limited ingredients available.

"I didn't know you were coming! I would've made something more special!" she said, immediately leading me to the kitchen to stir some yellow rice.

"It's okay, I just wanted to stop by. Are Mom and Dad here?"

She looked surprised that I asked to see them. Normally, I avoided them unless we happened to end up in the same room.

"Of course, baby. Is everything okay?"

"Yeah. I just want to talk."

I met my parents at the dining nook while Aunt Solana served us a plate. I was hyper-invested in the food, biding my time to figure out just what I wanted to say.

They both seemed to be in a good mood. Their hugs lingered longer than usual, and my dad even complimented my new septum ring—something he used to constantly get on my case about.

"How're your friends doing?" he asked. "Did you hear from Dusty yet?"

"Dustin. No, not yet, but the others are all doing good."

"Are you guys earning enough?" my mom asked. A very typical concern of hers.

"Yeah, we all chip in."

There was an awkward lull while silverware clinked against plates.

"We're glad you came by," my dad said, as if trying to fill the silence.

I took a deep breath. "Yeah. I was just thinking...I wanted to apologize—"

"Willa," my mom interrupted, but her tone was soft. She put her silverware down and looked at me, her face flooding with emotion. "You don't have to apologize. *I* do."

"We both do," my dad added.

My aunt stood up and pretended to busy herself with something in the sink. I wasn't expecting this, but it was a welcome surprise.

"Losing a child," my mom started with difficulty, "your firstborn... It does something to you. I wasn't thinking about anything else. How you also lost someone."

My dad put a comforting hand on my mother's back. "Now we've had some time to process, we're both very sorry for how we took the news. It'd been so long trying to get updates on him, to find him. It was a shock. And somehow, through it all, we knew *you* would make it through."

My mother dabbed at her face with her napkin. "Malik had an incredible mind, but he wasn't the same kind of smart you are. You always adapted and thrived... It was something I admired. Deep down, I knew we'd find you, but Malik... I'm sorry for everything I said. We love you very much."

"Thank you for trying to rescue him. It was more than we could have ever done," added my dad, clearly trying his best not to crack.

I caught myself using the back of my hand to stop my own tears from streaming down my face. All I'd ever wanted was for them to acknowledge that I'd tried everything I could to save him. That they'd lost a son, and I'd lost a brother, but they *still* had a daughter.

"I love you too."

5. TYE

As I sat in the Commissary, poking at the powdered eggs on my breakfast tray, I started to understand why Vale couldn't stomach the food. With a few weeks under my belt, it was getting harder and harder to accept that this would be the new normal.

I'd managed to get by a few days without my name flashing green on the check-in tablet, but today I wasn't so lucky. I let out a huff of disappointment as green appeared. Whether it indicated a transfusion or another testing appointment was yet to be seen.

When I talked to some of the other Angels to ask how often transfusions were done, I was told it seemed to vary by family and blood type.

I hadn't seen Midas since our first encounter. I kept fantasizing about ways to take him out the next time I saw him, but I knew they were just delusions of grandeur. He was heavily guarded, and I was at the complete mercy of Ylem and how they decided to treat me. My valuable blood would only protect me so much if he was murdered at my hand.

There was a point in time when I wouldn't have been able to even let the thought of killing someone fully form in my head, but my time alone in the desert had changed me. The trials of survival had made my emotions secondary.

When I escaped the border facility and realized I was on the wrong side of the wall, whatever hope I had left vanished. After months of surviving, then weeks of being tortured and studied, I was ready for it all to end. Being thrown back into the contamination zone wasn't just a setback—it was psychologically crushing.

Standing under that wall, I felt so close to my friends, but so far from them. Reuniting seemed impossible, but something in me refused to believe our stories were over. That quiet belief gave me just enough energy to keep going.

I waited until nightfall before inching across the open landscape, using clusters of rock for cover from the search helicopters overhead. I had no idea where I was going, only that I wasn't going back to their prison.

When I reached the canyons, I ran into a Mort—one who had clearly once been military. I used the gun I'd stolen at the border to take it down, then stripped it of its jacket and spare magazine.

The next few days were hell. I hid in small grottos, too scared to start a fire and risk being spotted. If the cold or hunger didn't kill me, dehydration would. One morning, I noticed the lining of my jacket had collected droplets of dew overnight. I managed a small sip, but I knew that wouldn't last me long.

I was surprised I survived that first week at all. The search parties were relentless. The only upside to the military presence was the abandoned campsites they sometimes left behind. I found ration bars and a blanket—small wins that kept me alive. But the real thing that kept me moving was the thought of getting back to my friends. Back to Willa.

It was hard to put my feelings for her into words. I'd only had one real relationship before, and that was with Riley. We'd had a strong connection, and I cared about her deeply, but I never felt that thing people in movies talked about. Sometimes I worried we were just playing the part, both too stubborn to admit something was missing.

With Willa, it wasn't like that. The connection wasn't surface-level. Yes, she was breathtaking, but it went way beyond that. Being with her felt otherworldly, like we'd known each other for years instead of months. The kind of closeness you'd expect to grow into much later in life. And when she came looking for me, it confirmed what I already suspected—that what I felt wasn't one-sided.

Every day without her weighed heavier than the last.

"You're gonna miss the movie. Finish up," said B, walking past my table and towards the pods.

"Movie?"

"They're projecting a movie onto the rec room wall."

"Where're you headed, then? Rec room's that way."

He rolled his eyes. "They already screened this movie last month … and the month before. It's just another form of torture. Anyway, I'm gonna go start a new book. I'm done with the one I borrowed. I'll toss it in your room."

I put my tray in the cleansing bin. "I'll come snag it. Too anxious to sit through a movie."

"Assignment today?" he asked with empathy as we headed for the pod hall.

"Yeah … "

I followed him around the corner to his quarters. Half of his tiny room was covered in books, like a mini library.

"Here," he said, handing me the one I lent him. I could see it was worn from being carried around wherever he went.

"Not that I'm gonna read it, but thanks."

"You say that now, but you're still green. Just wait 'til those few months hit."

The thought of the time ahead gave me an instant headache. "Alright, I'll hang onto it. Thanks, B—"

I nearly dropped the book. My eyes had landed on the name tag outside of his pod door.

BECKETT T.

He seemed to clock my disbelief and instantly looked concerned. "You okay?"

"B? *Beckett Taylor?*"

Now his face shifted to confusion. "That's my name ... How'd you—"

"Wait, wait, wait," I said, pacing. My head was spinning. "Sorry- I- I met your brother! And Xander ... Xander, do you remember him?!"

He fell back onto the edge of his bed, his freckled cheeks reddened like wine. "How on earth—"

"Your brother was at the border camp with me! We were being held together, for our blood. I heard you were taken out of there and he stayed behind—do you remember that at all?!"

His eyes weren't focusing, but he nodded faintly. "Barely ... Was he okay?"

I swallowed. "I think so ... Parker. He lost his memory."

Tears were forming in Beckett's eyes. "When I first got here, I couldn't even remember my name ... I just knew it started with a B." With obvious difficulty, he asked, "And Xander?"

I sat next to him on the bed. "He was with my group after the outbreak ... He didn't make it." Before Beckett could take the hit, I quickly went on. "But he told me about you! He loved you so much. It was the last thing he asked for. Told me if I ever found you, to tell you you were the only one he ever loved, and he was *so* sorry ... I can't believe I actually get to tell you."

Despite the tears streaming down Beckett's face, he wore a huge smile. "I loved that kid more than he realized. I remember him more than my own family, even. I knew everything he said to me when we broke things off was out of fear, but I really never thought I'd feel like that about anyone ever again. Thank you for telling me."

"Of course. I hope it brings you some peace. For him to think of that in his final hour means it was really important to him."

He nodded, his eyes distant as if he were recalling memories. "... Meeting Vale healed a big part of me, but this really is a chapter closer. I'm glad he had you there with him."

"Are you and Vale a thing?" I asked.

"It's not obvious?" he asked with a laugh. "We get shit for it daily. Only reason they won't say it to our faces is because Vale could kick their ass."

We laughed together.

"Well, I hope you feel loved," I said. "By both of them."

A guard suddenly appeared in the doorway. "Tye, you're due," he said sternly.

The moment of levity was instantly snuffed out. I stood up to leave.

"Really, Tye. Thank you," Beckett said, just as I was pulled away.

I was somewhat relieved to find out that I'd be seeing Dr. Chiron for further studies rather than a transfusion. I was brought to the lab where I was seated on his examination table, relenting to his probes and needles.

With the guards standing by, I knew I couldn't ask him what was really on my mind: *What is going on with my blood?*

"We've prepared a test subject for a phase one experiment," said the doctor, placing a glass tank on a nearby countertop. Inside was a sleeping lab rat, hooked to electrical wiring and monitors. I felt like I was looking at a miniature model of myself.

After sticking me with a needle, Chiron took the vial of blood and used it to fill a syringe.

I still felt uneasy about Dr. Chiron's allegiance. Last I'd seen him at the border, he claimed to be an innocent bystander, drafted into service during the global emergency.

"So how'd you end up here?" I asked boldly. "When we first met, it seemed like you were brought to the border to help. Now you're mixed up in the corruption of it all..."

He stayed busy with his task, not making eye contact. "I have a family, Tye. We were offered safety here, and I did what was necessary."

My respect for him was teetering.

He flipped on one of the monitors connected to the lab rat, and I realized it showed a heart rate graph. The straight line and low hum revealed the rat was not asleep; it was dead.

"What kind of experiment is this?" I asked, grimacing as he injected the lab rat with my blood.

"This subject is infected. We're testing a hypothesis."

As always, the vagueness spiked my cortisol. I watched for nearly ten minutes in silence, fidgeting anxiously with my arm bandage.

"If you can't elaborate on why I'm different, can you at least explain what makes me like the other Angels?" I asked eventually. "How's our blood immune?"

This question clearly wasn't off limits, because Chiron turned to me and calmly began to explain. "Some people have a genetic makeup that contains a unique mutation that allows the body to resist and repair the effects of the virus."

I believed he was making an effort to dumb it down for me, but it was still tough to follow the details. "And those mutations transfer over in a blood transfusion?"

"It's more complex than that, but with our technology, yes. The special stem cells enter the recipient's bloodstream and merge with their cells, reprogramming their immune system to behave like the Angel's. Upon entering, they actively spread the mutation throughout the recipient's body, effectively upgrading their DNA for a period of time. The changes aren't permanent, but they can last long enough to resist infection or even reverse early transformation."

"So our blood's the answer for a cure, then? Or at least immunity... immunity the rest of the world will never have."

Chiron turned away from me again, but I caught a glimpse of his shame-stricken face. "As it currently stands, the proprietary technology belongs to Ylem."

Beep... Beep... Beep...

My own heart monitor went off suddenly. It was only Dr. Chiron's sharp reaction that made me aware something out of the ordinary was happening. He was jotting down notes in a hurry, while calling for the nurses to assist. The commotion seemed unnecessary. Other than my simmering frustration, I felt fine. Then I realized: it wasn't *my* heartbeat reacting—it was the lab rat in the tank!

The rodent's furry belly rose and fell in quick huffs. Its beady dark eyes opened, before it suddenly turned over and scurried around the tank, fully back in motion.

How is that possible? My skin tingled with the haunting realization. Through the frenzy of nurses now in the room, Chiron held my gaze, as if to say without words that what I was seeing was the answer to my burning question: my blood was different from the other Angels because it wasn't just immune. It could apparently heal—and bring an infected body back to life!

I did not sleep a single wink overnight. My pounding heart continued to race after seeing the rodent spring up again. The weight of the universe crushed me against my mattress. So many possibilities for what this could mean for the world poured into me like a biblical flood. Suddenly, the given title of *God's Blood* didn't feel so dramatic. This was why they'd put so much effort into capturing me. This was why they needed me more than any other Angel.

I hardly understood the effects or limitations, but my mind automatically jumped to the evil that could be done. Certain people weren't meant to be brought back from the dead...

A lump formed in my throat as tears gathered in my eyes. *Why me?* As if I wasn't already resentful for how my teen years had turned out, now I was some sort of deity freak? At a minimum, I wished I could use my abilities to bring my parents back. I missed talking to my mom about everything. And spending time with my dad.

When I first saw them as Morts, my understanding of the world was instantly turned upside down. Those kinds of things just didn't happen in real life. Nothing was off the table now. It was clear that I possessed an ability straight out of fiction—like Midas called it, *mythical.* It made everything feel like I was looking through a haze as my mind reasoned with yet another new version of reality.

The next morning, salt hit the wound when my name lit up green again. Like my soul wasn't already heavy—two days in a row felt brutal. I figured whatever theory they'd confirmed must've earned me double the tests from now on. Or worse...maybe they expected me to start resurrecting people left and right.

All morning, I felt like I was choking on something. I wanted to vent to the others, but I was still in denial that it was even possible.

Right away, I was peeled away from my friends at breakfast and taken to the metro in a blindfold. I wasn't surprised to be going to Midas. He must be so eager to gorge himself on my blood now that the experiment had succeeded. Like a human leech.

I didn't say a single word on the ride to the Basilica. When I walked into the lounge room, I knew Midas could instantly tell I was drastically more guarded than the first time we met. Chiron could hardly make eye contact, looking extra busy as he set up our transfusion mechanisms.

When ten minutes of uneasy silence had passed, Midas's cold eyes finally landed on mine. "Tye. You really should embrace your gift. Most of the world is so common. You are lucky to have greatness in you."

I scoffed. "You want me to walk around like some god now? I don't even know what you guys are gonna do with me."

"I see you have a lot of anger built up," he said, with a countering attitude that softened me. "What would ease your mind? What would set us on a good path to becoming allies?"

I locked eyes with him for as long as I could, thinking about my answer. 'Allies' would be a stretch, but taking advantage of his flattery was in my interest. "Tell me everything... about Ylem, about Zenith."

It was the first time I saw even a glimpse of his façade flickering, but not for long. He gave me an icy smile. I guess he hadn't expected this topic to be at the top of my mind. "I'm an open book," he began. "Simply put, the world needed a reset. Society had become completely clouded by mediocrity. Darwinism was once the great equalizer, but it was failing us. The average, common people clung to the coattails of those of us at the top, burning through the earth's resources without contributing an ounce of value themselves. We, the pioneers, the visionaries—it was simply time for us to cut the fat."

My jaw was clenched so tight, my ears were ringing—the way the words flowed out of him so easily, like he'd pitched this all before.

"I started building Ylem over a decade ago. I reached out to every figurehead of every country, the billionaires and trillionaires at the forefront of innovation—our resources were unmatched, and the circle grew surprisingly quickly. Now, not all of them knew what the true end goal was, but the promise of eternal luxury and protection wasn't a hard sell.

"So, while Ylem was growing into a powerful mecca, I acquired Zenith. It had the perfect infrastructure to execute the vision. All that needed to be done was a few tweaks to the treatments it was already spreading through the atmosphere, and the whole thing unfolded as planned."

The way he told the story like it was simply a childhood memory was stomach-turning.

"So you *meant* for all this to happen?"

"Nearly all. The chemical mutagens reacted differently with some DNA. We didn't anticipate the violent mutations. It was meant to be a total wipeout, clean and simple, but instead we got those abominations. Anyhow, it was a small redirection. That was when we built our walls."

I glared at him, wishing it would cut his throat. "Do you know how many friends I've lost because of you?"

"The mutagens we used were purposely designed to target older and weaker bodies, not those in your age group. We wanted the youth to have a chance—"

"I'm not talking about what you intended. I'm talking about what you've done! My parents are gone. Everything's gone!"

Dr. Chiron started to gently remove the needles from our arms, looking like he was trying his best to shrink himself and not get involved.

Midas had no visible reaction to my raised voice, although his guards did step forward from the walls. "The ones who still matter are all here. The greatest minds and the most powerful people in the world. You'd be shocked by how many you'll recognize."

A chill crawled up my back. "So clearly you're not going to use our blood to help anyone outside of this city. Who *are* you bringing back to life with mine, then?"

The question got a strange reaction out of him. At first I thought he was surprised I'd finally figured it out, but when his taunting smile faded, it seemed more like it had eased him. "Why don't you stay for lunch?" he asked evasively. "I have things to attend to elsewhere in the city, but the staff will take care of you."

"I'm good."

His glare bore into me. "I insist."

Dr. Chiron had just finished wrapping my arm with gauze when the golden soldiers lifted me from the chaise. I only resisted for a moment, but relented when they pushed me out into the hall.

After traversing a few spiral staircases and corridors, we arrived on what seemed like the main floor. It was a cavernous, open living room with tall, curved glass windows bordering the circular space. A long, sleek stone island divided the sitting room from the gray, tonally monochromatic kitchen. The antique statues and art displayed all around contrasted with the futuristic appliances and soft LED lighting. A chef wearing a gray uniform was busy preparing something that smelled divine.

I hardly noticed that the guards had left me until I realized the houseman I met on the first day had replaced them. "Make yourself comfortable. Lunch will be ready shortly," he said, carrying some plates into the next room.

I'd just started to pace around the room when Midas entered in a hurry, now in a perfectly tailored pinstripe suit. He grabbed a glass of water and a handful of pills from a small silver tray on the onyx countertop, downed them in a rush, then turned back to me.

"I'm late. Enjoy lunch. I'm leaving you with my personal security agent. Only the best for the most valuable asset in the world." The generous words did not match his demeaning tone. He glided out of the room, leaving behind a faint smell of expensive cologne.

I watched the chef finishing up the final touches of garnish on the elegant china plates. He was serving some sort of fish with purple mashed potatoes and thinly sliced artichoke. I hadn't seen food like this since my fifteenth birthday, when my mom had saved up to take me to a Michelin-star restaurant as a surprise.

The houseman ushered me into the hallway, where a guard in gold waited to escort me. "He'll take you to the dining room."

I almost choked on the sudden gulp of air I took in. I recognized the guard! His white-blond hair, his tattooed neck… I tried with great effort to mask the fact that I knew him. *Maverick*. He looked so much healthier than when I'd last seen him. The youth had come back to his skin.

He barely made eye contact with me as we started down the hallway. I wasn't sure if his calm reaction was a front or if he'd known I was in Ylem all along.

"Actually, I need to use the restroom," I said to him, just loud enough for the houseman to overhear.

Maverick stopped in his tracks, opening a door to his right that led into another corridor. "I'll show you to it," he said stoically.

As soon as the door closed behind us, I turned to him, immediately dropping the pretense. *"What are you doing here?!"*

He looked around before shoving me into the bathroom and following me in. It was an ornate washroom with multiple stalls. Mav opened each one to make sure we were alone before he replied.

"I'm still indebted to the government, and they're tied to Ylem, so I offered my services. They think I never found you. To them, this is the first time we're meeting, so we can't be caught talking like this."

I was happy to see someone I knew, but I still didn't trust Maverick. Although in the end he'd saved me from Dame, his gold uniform was a reminder that he was working with the enemy.

"So you didn't tell them I was on that plane?"

"No. They caught wind of it through the radio channels Dame was using."

"Where's Willa? Is she okay?" I got my words out fast, aware that we had limited time.

Her name instantly pulled his features downward. "I think so. We made it back to the border after you left. I have an old squadmate in Safe Zone 32 who spotted her not too long ago. She's with your other friends."

Safe Zone 32. In contrast to his mood, mine lit up. Nothing made me happier than to know they were all together and that she was safe.

"And Dustin?"

"He went to fight on the frontlines."

Maverick reached for the door, letting me know our time was up. I quickly grabbed him by the arm and we locked eyes.

"Are you with Ylem or against?"

"You can trust me," he hissed. "I don't have anyone left. I'm just staying out of trouble."

I stared at him through narrowed eyes before returning to the hall.

6. WILLA

With my pistols concealed at my back, I rushed outside the house to see what all the commotion was about. People ran frantically in every direction along the neighborhood streets. I stood on the doorstep, my heart pounding as I tried to make sense of the scene.

I was expecting another Mort, but my confusion turned to dread when I spotted a military brigade cruising down the street after the crowd.

"Halt and comply!" a soldier yelled from the open window of a Humvee, his gun aimed at the crowd.

Other soldiers on foot managed to tackle and restrain a few fleeing citizens. As I scanned the crowd, my eyes locked onto a young man darting between the houses, his face etched with fear. As he ran by, I reached out and pulled him inside.

The guy stumbled to the floor behind me as I locked the door and shut the blinds. "What's going on out there?!" I demanded.

Riley, Ava, and Otto met me in the foyer. "What's happening?" asked Otto, eyeing the stranger at my feet.

The guy took a moment to catch his breath before responding, his words coming out in a rush. "There's been a serious attack by a rebel group on the nearby military base."

My mind reeled with the implications of such an attack. Of course there was plenty of civil unrest in our area, but I'd never imagined it would escalate to anything this bold.

Suddenly, I realized maybe it wasn't such a good idea to have brought him in. "Were you part of it?"

The young man sank onto the nearest chair. "No, not directly. But we were standing by to help them."

"How the hell did they pull that off? Those bases are airtight," Riley said.

"Guess not. We had help from the inside," he replied, lowering his voice. "Even some of the soldiers are getting fed up with the way things are. They've started fighting back against orders from the government too."

Ava picked nervously at her fingernail. "I can't even keep track of who's on whose side anymore. How many of these groups are there?"

"There's definitely a few factions," said the guy, still catching his breath. "There's thugs causing chaos for their own gain, rebel groups against the government, and insurgent forces trying to stage attacks on Ylem."

My friends and I exchanged silent glances of surprise. It was the first time we'd heard another citizen mention the secret city.

The sound of a faraway gunshot broke the silence. Ava parted a slit in the blinds to peer out of the window. "The street's clear now. I think maybe you should get going before more military come looking," she said, masking her obvious unease with a soft tone.

The young man joined her, peeking out through the gap before thanking us and leaving, disappearing down the block.

The others looked as visibly shaken as I felt. I put a comforting hand on Riley and Ava's shoulders. "I'm meant to see Cleo tomorrow to get Rio some stuff. I'll ask her about all this."

The volatility carried into the next day. Military presence had thickened. I was stopped several times on my bike ride through town and questioned about where I was headed. I stayed calm and told them I was meeting a friend at the coffeehouse. It was the only one in the area, which meant it was always crowded. Ideal for blending in.

I locked my bike to the fence out front and headed in, spotting Cleo's fiery hair at her usual table in the back corner. I pushed past the line of eager patrons and sat across from her. Her leg bounced with nerves.

"I know it's pretty bland, but I got you a cup of coffee. They're out of milk again," she said, sliding over a second mug.

"Thanks. I take it you're caught up on what happened last night?" I asked, lowering my voice the best I could over the café chatter.

A small smirk broke through her stressed expression. "Caught up? I was in on it."

I was hardly surprised. Cleo was one of the few friends I'd made in the safe zone. I first met her in FORESIGHT training and her tenacity stood out immediately, one of the many reasons she was among the rare few who'd made it back to the border alive.

With her foot, she nudged at a bag under the table, pushing it over to me. "I got the diapers, by the way. Some other supplies for her too."

I grabbed her hand in place of a hug. "Cleo, you're a queen."

"Right?" she said jokingly, before her demeanor grew serious. "These raids are getting harder each time. Things are reaching a boiling point and the military's cracking down hard. Check this."

She pulled a wrinkled newspaper out of the tote bag hanging over the back of her chair. It was the latest issue of the *Pinnacle Post,* one of the last remaining independent publications that still managed to exist in the current climate. On the cover was a huge photo of Midas with the headline:

The Most Wanted Man in the World Hides in Ylem

I felt a sudden surge of intense anger. Midas's smug expression behind his cold eyes made me want to tear the paper to shreds. I'd seen him grace the cover of publications in the past, but that had been because of his technological accolades. Now, it was an article on his crimes. He'd finally been called out by a major outlet.

Cleo went on. "The military's been swiping these off doorsteps and newsstands. The numbers fighting back are growing and they're getting scared. I mean, some of them are even turning on each other now. They're realizing all the higher-ups are in hiding and have left the shithole states for them to manage. They're all pawns."

I folded the newspaper discreetly, handing it back to her. "So are there plans being made to take Ylem out? 'Cause if there are, I want in."

Cleo looked at me as if calculating her answer. "I'm not involved in all that. I'm just trying to make this place livable for me and the ones I care about, and maybe knock some corrupt heads off on the way. There's been groups who've tried attacks on Ylem and failed miserably."

Rowen had said the same, but it seemed there was some restrategizing happening in secrecy.

Cleo clearly saw the disappointment on my face. "Willa," she said, lifting my chin to make me meet her eyes, "you don't have to take on the whole world. Do what you can *here*."

I nodded to appease her, but I wasn't convinced.

My daydreams of taking out Midas stayed with me until sunset. Despite my conflicting emotions regarding the morality of killing *people* as opposed to Morts, when it came to protecting the ones I loved, mercy was out of the question. Midas was responsible for the loss of so many I loved: Imani, Archer, my brother, and now Tye.

I wanted to get to Ylem so badly, but it wasn't just about Midas or getting Tye back. There were people there who could cure the world of this awful plague, and they were being selfishly hoarded. If it wasn't evil enough to have created such a destructive experiment, they were adding insult to injury by making sure the cure would never reach the masses. Those other kids with miracle blood had to be saved somehow. Even if Ylem was taken down, who was thinking about the prisoners there?

After a rationed dinner, Riley and I sat on the floor of the living room on Rio's blanket. She was in a fresh diaper and chugging a bottle of formula, visibly in bliss over the rare treat. Riley had thanked me about a hundred times throughout the day, no matter how much I reminded her it was all Cleo's doing.

We'd spoken at length about the latest Ylem article. It confirmed the existence of the stronghold and where Midas was hiding, but it never mentioned the blood operations going on there. She could see my spirit was dim.

"I just remember you telling me that when your brother died, you felt lost, like your purpose was taken away…I don't want you to create a whole story about Tye being there because you want that spark again," said Riley.

Her tone was kind, but I felt vulnerable at her words. She always went straight to the point. "You don't think Tye's at Ylem?" I asked, trying not to sound defensive.

"I'm saying, there's no way to really know. Even if he *was* on that plane, he could've escaped after the crash. He could've been found by people who helped him. I just don't want you to get caught up in going up against a power like Ylem when we simply don't know if Tye's actually there. He could be somewhere else."

I felt like she was trying to convince herself more than me. "Do you really believe that?"

She busied herself with a button on Rio's onesie. "I'm trying to… because thinking of him having to suffer more, alone, is way harder. Wherever he is." Rio cooed softly, finishing the last sip of her bottle. Riley laid her over her shoulder to burp her. "Look, I wish I could be on the frontlines with you, helping to find him. I just… have to think of Rio now."

"Of course, and Tye would want the same."

"That's the thing, he would. That boy is so special."

"It'd be so nice having him here, living with us again. Having him around just makes everything better," I said.

After a beat, Riley started laughing.

"What?" I asked, catching her contagious smile.

"I just remembered something hilarious Tye told me once. He has terrible FOMO. When he was a kid, he used to hold his pee for hours so he wouldn't miss a single moment with his friends. He'd hold it so long his legs would tremble, just so he wouldn't have to stop playing with them. It makes so much sense knowing him now."

I laughed, but there were tears in my eyes, because I wished more than anything he'd made it through the border like the rest of us. He deserved to be here, without missing a moment.

Ava came down the steps and sat on the couch, laying out some paperwork in front of her. "Did you guys see the *Post* article? Word's out about Ylem."

"Yeah. We were just talking about Tye. What d'you think? You think Ylem really got him?" Riley asked, her voice cracking with emotion.

His name was a topic we usually avoided around Ava. With her being the most sensitive among the group, we were careful when to bring him up.

"One thing I learned about Willa is that her intuition's borderline supernatural. So if you think they have him, then I do too," she said to me, her lips going tight to hold back tears.

Riley stood up to go, breaking off from the touchy subject. "I'm gonna go put her to bed."

"Okay. Night-night, baby Rio," said Ava as we watched them head upstairs. She turned to me and lowered her voice. "It's crazy how I can still see Gage's eyes in hers."

I'd witnessed the complicated dynamic between Ava and Riley following Riley's pregnancy, and I was always impressed by how they'd managed to grow so close after a rocky start. "You okay?" I asked gently.

"Yeah. It feels like a lifetime ago, to be honest. I love Rio, and Riley ... I just spent so many nights in that warehouse imagining what the other side of it all would look like. Crazy to see how it played out for us."

"In an alternate reality, we'd all be going to college parties right now."

We both laughed. Then, she said earnestly, "Sometimes I wonder what we're gonna be like as adults. I mean, we're basically skipping our teen years."

"Well, if anything, there'll be nothing we can't handle," I said, and meant it.

"Helps having Otto and my mom around... and you, of course. I know you're still mourning too, but I really admire how strong you've been."

"Letting me stay here with you guys really got me back on track," I told her. "I really wouldn't have gotten through it if you weren't so welcoming."

"Good. I'm glad you're doing better. My mom's been doing better, too. I think Riley's dad's been good for her. Losing my dad has been hard on me, of course, but when it finally hit her... I've never seen her like that. I'm just glad she has someone to lean on now, who understands what it's like. We've all lost so many people."

I reached out and grabbed Ava's hand. As if my thoughts had transferred through touch, she squeezed my hand tighter. "We're gonna find Tye," I said. "We never thought we'd see him again when we were separated at the border, and then we did. We'll see him again."

I was pulled out of my shallow sleep by a knock on the door. Otto cracked it open and peeked in. He was still in the tank and boxers he always slept in, telling me it was still very early in the morning.

He was holding a phone, which he quickly handed to me. "Rowen," he said seriously.

Like I'd been hit with a shot of caffeine, I was up and awake in an instant. "Hello?"

"Meet me on Ruin Road in twenty."

I biked through the military-infested streets to the more secluded part of town. Ruin Road was a nickname for a street of abandoned stores that were never repurposed. It was such a low-traffic area, even soldiers found it unworthy of their time.

Rowen ushered me into an old, gutted deli.

"Everything alright?" I asked, leaning my bike against the grimy wall.

"There's been confirmation that Tye's in Ylem. As suspected, he's at the camps there."

I took in a jagged breath. Deep down, I'd known it all along, but hearing it out loud hit like a gunshot. "Is he okay?"

"Seems so, but they're doing extensive testing on his blood. Though, that's not the reason I asked you here in person," said Rowen, shifting from one foot to another. "An opportunity's presented itself. One of our contacts inside Ylem was ordered to recruit more servants to assist some of the wealthy families there. It's an incredibly rare occurrence for Ylem to allow outsiders in. Most of the families came with their own trusted entourage."

Suddenly, I understood what he was implying. "You want *me* to go?"

"There'd be an intense vetting process and background check, but we'll sort that for you. I realize it's a demoralizing position to apply for, but—"

"I'll go. I'm in."

His eyelids fluttered. It looked like he was bracing himself to deliver more news. "You won't have contact with any of us... and there's no telling how long you'd be there before we're able to dismantle Ylem. You'll have an entirely new identity. You won't be able to interact with Tye, but you'll be able to help when the time's right."

My head was suddenly crowded with all the things that could go wrong. "Won't they recognize my face? I was in FORESIGHT, and spotlighted for being close with Tye."

"It's your name that's recognized in data profiles, but we'll replace your digital and DNA trail entirely. Do what you can to change your appearance. The hair, your nose ring, anything to minimize in-person recognition. If you survive the initial vetting process, they won't look into you once you're there if you stay out of trouble. You'll be approved, I guarantee it."

I felt familiar rage simmering in my chest. "And Midas? If he's taken out, the whole thing crumbles, doesn't it?"

He looked worried. "In theory. But if you were to get inside Ylem, it would be solely as a resource. You can't risk compromising our operations. Lie low, blend in, and adapt until you're needed. Even if you see Tye, you'll have to protect your new identity."

I'd fantasized about getting close to Midas and saving Tye, but now the opportunity to make it all happen had come so suddenly, and not without sacrifice. I recognized that I tended to do first and think later, but I'd be trading in all my friends here for an uncertain chance to save another. It was a hard pill to swallow.

Rowen seemed to pick up on my initial eagerness melting away. "You told me to let you know how you could help, so I'm telling you, but you don't *have* to do this. You're already a hero. Everything you did for my father, for the cause ... "

"How would I get there?" I asked, still thinking it through.

"There's transport arranged. Three days from now."

"And what's your plan for Ylem, with the network?"

"Our biggest priority is getting a hold of the captives with immune blood. There's been little progress on a cure here, but Ylem is light-years ahead. We won't be able to get to them without dismantling their defenses." As if by subconscious instinct, Rowen lowered his voice. "The forces against Ylem are slowly growing. The next time we attack will have to count. Each time there's a failed attempt, they strategize and reinforce their fortifications. While you're there, it may seem like there's no hope, no visible progress, but everything has to be in place for a strike from within."

My hesitation was logical, but my heart was pushing me to go. I loved my friends and family here in the safe zone, but Tye needed me more. Rowen needed me. And despite Cleo telling me not to take on the world, I believed the world needed me too.

Every grueling step I'd taken to get here, I'd had someone backing me up. Imani when I left home, Tye and his friends when she was gone, Archer and Dustin when I reentered. This time, I'd not only be going in blind, but also alone.

"I'll be ready in three days. Keep me posted."

He looked at me with a worried smile, then hugged me. The gentle embrace was like a hug from the universe itself, reminding me that even if I felt alone when I left, I'd have people on my side.

The energy around the dinner table was heavy. No one was sure about my decision to go to Ylem. I could tell everyone was holding back a flood of doubts so I wouldn't feel scared, but I knew they wanted to get Tye back just as much as I did, and if I played any part in taking down Ylem, they had to support the plan.

"Three days ... Feels like this is happening so fast," said Ava.

"And they're *sure* Tye's there?" her mom asked.

"They're sure," I said. "Rowen said they'll need me when the time's right. I'll have a new identity." I took a long sip of water. "There'll be no contact with you guys for a while, but Rowen said they're working on a takedown from the inside. I'll get us out of there when they strike."

"Can we go with you somehow?" asked Otto eagerly.

Ava looked at me like she was wondering the same thing.

"I think if we're seen together anywhere, it'll raise the alarm. It'd be more noticeable. I have to go alone."

My friends looked pale with worry. They'd seen the lengths I'd go to for Tye and knew my mind was made up.

7. TYE

On the train ride back to the camps, I thought of more ways to end Midas, though I wasn't sure it was even possible now with my blood running through his veins. Would he spring back to life? I still had no understanding of how it all worked. I had a million questions and no one to answer them.

Then I wondered, would whatever pulsed through my veins keep *me* alive forever? When I was first infected, the symptoms were hardly threatening. I wondered about more severe scenarios. What if I were shot, or hit by a car? What were the boundaries of my newfound 'gift?' The next time I saw Chiron, I would press him again. He seemed willing to talk to me, but it was clear he was ordered not to share more than necessary. If only there was a way to speak to him in private, without the guards breathing down our necks, the same way I'd managed those few minutes with Maverick.

Meanwhile, Maverick's presence in Ylem and his connection to Willa made me feel less alone in this strange place. Despite the comfort it offered, I stayed cautious, and aware that him being here might not be mere coincidence. The fact that Midas's personal security guard was someone from my past meant Mav either had situated himself perfectly, or was meant to keep an eye on me.

Somehow, the only person I trusted in Ylem was Vale. He'd proven he truly cared about my well-being, taking me under his wing when he had no obligations to. I felt good about Beckett, too, although I wasn't ready to share the news about my genetics with either of them just yet.

Vale's assurances that efforts were underway to free us fueled my motivation to get through each day. While I wasn't sure of his exact role in these plans, his words kept my spirits up.

Walking into the dome, I was relieved to find Vale right away at his usual hangout spot—the weight racks.

"Can I talk to you?" I asked as he finished a set.

"Absolutely," he said eagerly, stepping away from his pack.

We pulled up two chairs to the reading area, each of us grabbing a novel and pretending to be immersed in the pages.

"How'd the transfusion go?" he asked, as if he'd been waiting all day to know.

"That guy's seriously evil. Everything that's happened is because of him," I said, keeping my eyes on the page in front of me. "You said there's a plan underway to get out of here, right? I want *in*."

Vale couldn't help but look up from his book, eyes darting around to make sure no one was listening. "If you really want to play a part, get as close to Midas as you can. None of us have even been near the Basilica, and you're getting in the same room as him."

"I can't take him out, though, there's guards everywhere—"

"Of course, I'm not saying that. Don't try anything. We might need you later on, but for now, just listen and learn as much from him as possible. The more we know, the better we can plan against—"

"You two!" a guard cut in. "Date night's over." He approached us with an intimidating stride. "I know you don't read, Vale. Whatever you're up to, cut it out."

Vale tried to hold back an uncomfortable laugh. "Don't tell B about my new boyfriend, okay?" he said sarcastically to the guard, taking my hand in a dramatically romantic way.

We both laughed.

Throughout the next week, I focused on being more cordial with Midas during my few transfusion visits. It required Oscar-worthy commitment. His arrogance was enough to make me break, but it was his formidable presence that made it hard not to be guarded around him. My efforts seemed to be working, though. He felt lighter around me, allowing me to have proper meals every visit and often leaving me to enjoy the comforts of his home for hours at a time, whether he was there or not.

I started to understand why Vale was significantly healthier than the rest of us. There was no denying the transfusions were awful, but the perks of time away from the camps were an undeniable benefit.

Life went on as usual, until things within the camps took a morbid turn by the weekend.

LINE UP IMMEDIATELY. LINE UP IMMEDIATELY. LINE UP IMMEDIATELY.

Muscle memory made me tense up like stone, as if I'd looked into Medusa's eyes. The last time I'd heard those robotic words, Secretary Croft had come to make my life even worse.

This was an early wake-up call. The Angels lined up in an orderly fashion along the walls of the Commissary, half of them with crusted eyes and disheveled hair.

Vale looked even more tense than I felt.

"Do you know what's going on?" I asked in a whisper.

His eyes were shifting chaotically. "Have you seen B? He wasn't in his pod."

I joined him in scanning the room, realizing Beckett wasn't in the lineup.

Before I could answer, Beckett was brought into the room by a couple of guards, but they didn't seem to be manhandling him like he was in trouble. In fact, they sat him in a corner rather professionally and looked to be questioning him.

Beckett's face was tear-streaked; he looked distraught. Vale took a step forward, but I put my hand out to stop him when I saw a third guard already reaching for his taser. He relented.

As we buzzed with worry, more guards entered the Commissary, wheeling in a medical cot with a body bag on top.

There was a collective wave of whispers around the hall. I knew this scene well. It was how I'd escaped the border holdings, but it was also how they unceremoniously removed fallen bodies.

Once the procession of guards passed through the hall with the cot and the others returned to their stations, the whistle was blown to let us know we were free to move about again.

Vale instantly ran to Beckett, still sitting deflated in the corner. "Are you okay?! What was that about?"

B hugged him and Vale gave him a tender kiss.

"I found one of the foreign kids in the bathroom ... Just last week he was telling me he couldn't take it in here anymore," Beckett explained, panicked breaths escaping between each word.

Vale hugged him tighter. "Let's get some fresh air."

The death of one of our own hung heavy in the air for days, but the appointments for testing and transfusions didn't stop. With no regard for the mental effects our suffering had on us, they continued the blood harvesting like nothing had happened.

My urgency to fight back skyrocketed. I couldn't accept that this place would be where I spent the rest of my life. I wasn't going to be driven to madness. I had to get Midas comfortable around me, and quickly. The more I knew about him, the more I'd understand Ylem. Maybe somewhere there was a fault in their system, and an escape plan could reveal itself.

To my disappointment, my name lit up green on the check-in tablet. As I waited for my escorts over breakfast, I had Hunter on my mind. He, too, had once taken his own life. Even though it was heroic, he'd been battling demons way deeper than my understanding.

The guilt still found me, now and then. I regretted how things ended between us. And even more, I carried the weight of knowing he gave his life to save us at a time when we were barely speaking.

I tried to hold on to the version of him from before the fallout. Some of my best memories were with Hunter. Accepting who he became—and who he revealed himself to be in the end—wasn't easy. But that final moment? That was the Hunter I'd always known was in there. The one I loved like a brother.

A portly guard grabbed me by the shoulder and led me along the familiar path to Chiron's quarters. I was relieved that today involved testing rather than a visit to Midas. After everything that had happened this week, I wasn't sure I could hide my resentment from him.

I was surprised when the guards got off the elevator on a different floor than usual. What I saw when we stepped out and turned the corner was more surprising still.

The entire floor was one big room. Chiron stood before a group of well-dressed individuals, all of them seated in a semicircle. Considering their tablets and reading glasses, I figured they were here to observe and take notes. I hardly paid them any attention anyway, since I was distracted by a large mechanism with snaking tubes coming out of all sides and leading into four chambers along the back wall.

As I joined Chiron at the center of the room, I started to tremble when I realized what exactly I was looking at. Each chamber contained a body, in some form.

The first tank held a woman, screaming for help as she clutched the meat of her bloodied arm. She slammed her palm against the wall, and I saw the wound was a familiar-looking bite mark.

In the neighboring tank, a seemingly dead body lay still. From its distorted features, I could see it was a Mort. Probably one that had lost its revival spurt without a recent bite of another.

In the next chamber over was an active Mort, violently clawing at the glass, eager to feed on its limp neighbor.

And in the final cell, a lifeless young man with no visible wounds. Goosebumps rose on my forearms. He seemed to be a cadaver, here for whatever experiment this was.

All of the bodies were connected to a tangle of tubing and wires.

"What is all this . . . ?" I choked out.

Chiron busied himself with contraptions connected to various monitors. "Take a seat," he said, pointing me to the blood-drawing station.

"What the fuck is this?!" I asked again to the room.

My escort guards stepped closer with their weapons out.

Chiron lowered his voice to me. "If you cooperate, you might very well learn answers to many of your questions." He then addressed the room. "The following experimental treatments will use Ichor blood on subjects at varying stages of the viral infection. The primary focus is to evaluate the Ichor blood's capabilities across different infection stages and its potential to reverse fatalities."

Now, I understood: this was not a test for me. It was a test of how my blood affected different bodies. My heart was screaming at me to run from this room—no part of me wanted to relent to the experiment—but my mind needed to understand it all.

I moved slowly toward the center seat within the mechanism. Settling into it reluctantly, I extended my arm to Chiron. The soft murmurs of the onlookers filled the room, their tones hushed and barely audible over the wounded woman's cries for help.

Once Chiron inserted the IV, a light illuminated the struggling woman behind the glass. The thin tube leading from my arm to hers began to fill with red, and right away her agitation died down. The monitors and screens started to buzz with information. Chiron and the others all seemed to be annotating on their tablets.

I locked on the woman, who slowly let go of her arm wound. It seemed to look less severe than it had only moments before. Though she continued to groan, she was settling.

My heart pounded on as the next cell was lit up. The motionless creature lay there in a contorted position. I watched as my blood now flowed into its veins. I waited anxiously with my jaw clenched, expecting it to stand up, but other than a slight color change in its skin, it seemed not to react right away.

I started to feel lightheaded when the blood drained into the next cell. The frenzied Mort inside it instantly stopped scratching the glass and stood in place for a moment, as if processing what was now pulsing through its body.

My vision was blurring, but I tried to keep my eyes on the Mort and see how it would respond.

"Drink this," said Chiron, handing me a cup of neon blue liquid.

In my disorientation, I took it without question. From the first sip, I felt instantly replenished.

Finally, my blood seeped into the cadaver in the last chamber. I could feel my body protesting the amount of blood they were draining from me today. Through my fading vision, I could just make out Chiron changing my IV, then everything went black.

When I came to, I was still seated, but clearly a significant amount of time had passed. The tubing linked to my arm was now filled with the same blue liquid I drank earlier.

"Are you feeling okay?" Chiron asked.

I was too in shock to answer, processing the changes in each of the test subjects.

The woman's arm was no longer bleeding, though a wound was present. She looked exhausted from her struggles, slumped in the corner of her cell.

"Subject 1," Chiron began, addressing the room. "Post-administration, the bleeding from the arm wound ceased, and the injury exhibits signs of accelerated healing, akin to a weeks-old wound. However, the subject appears significantly fatigued."

The observers frantically typed away on their devices.

The formerly lifeless Mort was still lying down, but now, its once shriveled skin was evened out and its dark eyes were human again. The half-man stared up at the ceiling of its tank, breathing in quick huffs. Just like with the lab rat, my blood had been able to reverse and revive the infected body.

"Subject 2. Notable physical rejuvenation. The skin texture normalized, and eye color returned to a human-like appearance. The subject regained consciousness after being deceased for several weeks."

His counterpart next door was also looking human again. Though still pale and sickly looking, he was much more human than Mort now. A chill ran up my spine, imagining what he might have experienced while dying and coming back again.

"Subject 3. There was a noticeable reversion from the infection's physical manifestations. Although the subject still appears pale and weak, its condition is markedly improved over its initial infected state."

My eyes finally landed on the dead body at the end of the room. It was the only subject that showed no change. The body still lay lifeless in its tank.

"Subject 4. No change was observed. The subject remains deceased with no visible reaction to the Ichor blood treatment. Which we anticipated, as this cadaver had no infection in its blood to start with."

The babble of excited conversation from the observers pulled me back from my whirling realizations.

"We will continue to observe the subjects in the coming weeks, but thus far, all of our research and hypotheses have been confirmed," Chiron concluded.

The researchers were devouring the data, their fingers flying over the keys as they eagerly typed up every detail.

Despite being horrified by what I had just witnessed, a sense of overwhelming clarity washed over me. Everything had been laid out before my eyes: my blood had the power to reverse death, as long as the body was infected. The scientific details eluded me, but I was buzzing with this epiphany.

For a moment, I envisioned the profound impact this could have on the world. Millions of lives could be reclaimed, families mended, and friends reunited; so much that was lost could be restored.

But my hope quickly dwindled. Ylem didn't intend to save the world. It planned to keep me for itself. And I was just one person. I couldn't give my blood to everyone. Today had made that painfully clear.

As I wandered through life in the camps, each step felt mechanical. Life continued, yet I drifted through it all, detached and distant, as though I were viewing everything from behind fogged glass.

With each passing day, though I couldn't be certain how many there'd been, I wrestled with the ever-growing turmoil inside of me. Even Vale and Beckett remained at arm's length, clearly noticing I needed some space. They offered a listening ear, but I was hesitant to share my ordeal with them, thanks to a gnawing fear that saying it all out loud would confirm my reality, branding me an outcast forever. Maybe if I never voiced it, I could somehow make it all disappear.

Then today happened. My name flashed green on the sign-in screen, and an hour later, one of the guards called out, "Tye!"

It was time to face Midas, the architect of all the twisted experiments. This would be the first time I'd seen him since learning everything he had avoided telling me.

On the train ride, I maintained a calm and collected attitude; these trips had become routine. However, inside, I was struggling to calm the storm raging in my head.

Chiron had made it clear—Ichor's reviving power only worked on bodies touched by the virus. I'd seen it myself. One of the test subjects stayed dead. Which meant even with my blood in him, Midas was just immune. If someone assassinated him, he wouldn't be coming back.

I tried my best to force those dark fantasies from my thoughts. When I saw Midas, I would need to stay composed and begin subtly laying the groundwork of trust between us.

When we arrived at the Basilica, it wasn't Midas's usual houseman who greeted me but Maverick, standing in the foyer with a blank expression, trying a little too hard to hide our familiarity. When my escorts left me with him, he pushed me towards an ornate elevator just off the lobby.

It was tubular, carved from what looked like black marble. When it started to rise, Maverick said, "Don't speak." I was taken aback by the abrupt command, until I noticed the camera in one corner of the ceiling.

I took a deep breath to steady my strong heartbeat, then noticed that we'd already passed the floor where Midas usually took my blood.

When the doors opened, they revealed a lush rooftop garden, overflowing with healthy-looking plants and trees. I could hear the sound of trickling water as Maverick walked me down the stone path. The chorus of birds coming from the canopies felt so foreign compared to the silence of the contamination zones.

As if the garden itself wasn't already a sight to behold, I caught glimpses of the city view off the curved edge of the giant sphere. I hadn't seen it from a vantage point like this before. I felt like I was looking at a computer-generated cityscape—so many interesting structures, and a striking newness that other cities with history didn't have. Everything I was looking at had been built so quickly, it was of the now.

The path ended at a circular platform in the center of the rooftop, covered by a linen canopy. Seated in a circle of carved wooden chairs were a group of impeccably dressed people. Among them was Midas, wearing a matching set of cobalt silks.

He was deep in discussion, but when he saw me, he visibly brightened and there was a noticeable shift in the others. They sat up straighter and looked at me like I was a notable celebrity or something.

Maverick stepped to the side, leaving me standing on display before them.

"Tye," said Midas, getting to his feet. The others rose to mirror him. "We were just talking about you."

I smiled through a clenched jaw. I was sure word of the recent experiment had reached them all by now. I could feel them eyeing me, probably dreaming of who in their own lives they could bring back. Or if they could have my blood in their veins, too.

The way they seemed to show respect for Midas made me feel this was some sort of council meeting he was leading, but as I looked around at each of them, they too appeared to be figureheads in their own right.

I did a double-take when I spotted a very familiar face: our very own president of the United States. Her eyes flickered away from mine when I met her gaze, a tinge of embarrassment flashing across her face.

Anger boiled inside me. The last I'd heard, she was on national broadcasts, feeding people hope that things could still be contained, all the while knowing she had her own escape plan.

"We'll continue this meeting another time," Midas said to his colleagues.

They said their goodbyes and soon, only Midas and Maverick remained with me in the garden. Midas took his seat again, and gestured for me to sit nearby.

I tried to mask my discomfort by sitting right away. "How's your day been?" I asked pleasantly.

"Lots of movement on important matters."

His vague answer sparked some anxiety in me, but I stayed composed. "About me?"

He smiled. "Some. After the last experiment, there's a lot to get done. I won't bore you with the intricacies, but I do have a question for you."

I swallowed. "Sure. What is it?"

"How would you like to live here at the Basilica?"

In my shock, I almost looked at Maverick by mistake, but played it off like I was looking out at the city.

Midas went on. "I appreciate how cooperative you've been, and it's in everyone's interest to keep you happy and healthy."

That part nearly made me lose it, but still, I kept my composure. "Are there more tests to be done?"

"The worst is behind you, but you'll have to go back to the camps for testing once in a while. Otherwise, you'll be very comfortable here. Much better than you could ever hope for at the camps."

I couldn't help but feel there were ulterior motives here, but I had some of my own. Vale would go nuts knowing this opportunity had fallen into my lap. I would not only be in the same rooms as Midas, but living under the same roof too.

"Can I think about it?"

Midas looked taken aback. "It shouldn't require much thought, but if you insist." He rose, and I instinctively did the same. "Maverick, take Tye to the transfusion lounge. I'll be there shortly."

This time, my forced smile didn't hold.

8. WILLA

No matter how hard I tried, I couldn't picture what Ylem would look like. The thought of an untouched city, filled with all the luxuries of the old world, seemed so unfathomable. All I'd seen since leaving home was decay and destruction.

There was a time when Morts were the most terrifying thing I'd ever known, but now, they hardly made my hands tremble. I'd come to know much worse: loss, loneliness, heartbreak, and evils I'd never imagined could exist in humanity.

As I pedaled my bike faster, I took in the brisk air washing over my face and through my hair. With one hand still on the handlebars, I lifted the other to touch my locs. My hair had been a huge part of my identity my whole life. So much so, it was the first thing that would have to go in order to throw off anyone who would recognize me. My aunt was excited to help me, though I still hadn't decided if I should tell her or my parents the reason behind the dramatic change. The fewer people I involved, the better.

Last I'd heard from Rowen, my new identity was secured. Tomorrow, I'd be picked up at the crack of dawn and become Ylem cargo. I'd had a burning tension in the pit of my stomach since the moment I'd agreed to go.

The metropolis was Mort-free, but the threat of being exposed hung over me. I'd be brushing shoulders with some of the most evil, corrupt people—and the worst part was, I'd be serving them. Morts or not, I'd have to watch my back all the same.

While my parents were out working their bi-weekly stocking jobs, my aunt had transformed our living room into a makeshift salon. She'd set a chair in the center and laid out a tray of brushes and oils, and a clean towel—fully prepared for the makeover.

I couldn't help but smile, even though changing my hairstyle wasn't something I was exactly excited about.

Aunt Solana had told me it'd be a long process, so I sat patiently while she draped the towel over my shoulders. She gently let down the two messy buns I'd thrown up earlier.

"I've always wanted to pamper you like this," she said, starting to brush out the first loc. "You were never really a girly girl."

"Well, today's your lucky day," I said, gritting my teeth as the comb tugged at my long hair.

"Why the sudden change? Is there a lucky someone?" she asked good-naturedly.

She had known about my preferences before anyone else, but it was only recently that she'd begun to understand that sexual attraction and romantic interest were not the same thing. What she didn't know, and would likely never guess, was the real reason I'd asked for a makeover.

"There is," I said.

She stopped combing. "Really?!"

"His name's Tye ... but I just wanted a change, really."

In the wall-mounted mirror, I could see her smiling from ear to ear, resuming untangling the dread. "I won't pry. I know you hate that, but I'm very happy to hear it. You've always been so fiercely independent. I sometimes thought you'd want to be on your own your whole life."

"Well, I'm learning that doing everything alone isn't always best."

We spent nearly three hours brushing through my hair. It'd been years since I'd seen it unwoven, and though it was a big change, I still looked too recognizable. After some debate, we decided to cut my hair shoulder-length.

As the bundles of hair dropped to the floor, a surprising wave of emotion came over me. It was really happening. Tomorrow, my life would change yet again.

"Willa, you look unbelievable. I love it!" my aunt said after running some oil through the new cut.

I walked up close to the mirror. I was shocked by how big a change it was, but amazingly, I felt it really suited me. I removed my septum ring and took in the new version of myself.

"Thank you, Auntie. I love it too."

Back at our shared place, the praise for my new look was short-lived. When the parents arrived home from work, they looked visibly shaken, and the mood completely changed.

"What happened?" Ava asked her pallid mom with concern, leading her to sit on the couch.

Riley's dad sat beside her, putting a comforting arm over her shoulder. "There was a major breach at the border camp. They've contained it, but it was a madhouse."

A palpable sense of fear settled over the room. "Morts got through the wall? Or did someone inside the camps turn?" Otto asked gravely.

Ava's mom spoke with a shaky voice. "One of the refugees in temp housing somehow went undetected. Turned overnight, and no one caught it until he'd already bitten four or five people."

"The Morts were taken out quickly, but the aftermath of figuring out how it all happened caused a lot of chaos," said Riley's dad.

"This is getting out of hand," said Riley, holding Rio closer to her chest. "Just the other day, they removed an infected from the town center. This is exactly how it happened at the start of everything. We had that weird flu that spread, then it seemed to be under control, and the next time it popped up we got this mutated version that ruined the world. Is it evolving again, or are there just so many infected that we can't contain it anymore?"

The thought of the virus further evolving, and this time without Zenith's tampering, was straight out of nightmares. The pressure to retrieve any chance of a cure from Ylem was mounting. Who knew how long these supposed safe zones would hold?

"No matter the cause," Riley's dad said, "the military's stretched thin, and volunteers at the border keep dropping the worse things get outside the wall. If our lives are at risk, like they were today, we'll have to reconsider our jobs. We can't let anything happen to us. We're not leaving you all alone again."

Ava's mom squeezed his hand. "Let's try to make the rest of the day a good one. Willa leaves tomorrow. I did a food run yesterday, so how about we all get in our PJs and cook something nice?"

While the others prepared and cooked in the kitchen, I sat with Otto in the living room. They refused to let me help, and while Otto could build a car from nuts and bolts, he somehow couldn't find his way around an oven.

"The short hair makes you look like a badass! How you liking it?" he asked.

I laughed feebly. "I'm not supposed to look badass. I'm meant to be a servant."

"Then you're a badass servant with a badass bob!"

"Thanks, dummy. And how're you holding up? You talk to your mom again?"

He looked like he was trying to keep the smile on his face, but it receded slightly. "I did, yeah. I was planning to take some time off work to see her next week. Ava's worried, though. She thinks I might not be able to make it back if anything happens while I'm gone. And with the way things are going, I'm nervous about it too."

"Would you ever tell your mom to come here?"

"I'm not sure I want to open my life up to her like that... Not yet, at least. For so long, I've imagined what I'd say when I confronted her about leaving me as a kid. I froze last time I saw her. No telling how I'll react this time, no matter how much I prepare."

"Otto, you've handled some crazy shit since then. You can handle this. And it's going to be so good for you."

His smile came back. "Thanks, Willa."

Riley came in from the kitchen, rocking a crying Rio. "Sorry, she got scared of the oven timer going off."

Riley's dad followed her in and took Rio in his arms. "Awww, come here, little princess. She needs Pop Pop."

He started walking around, gently bouncing the girl to calm her. Riley watched as they went into the other room.

"He's been so great with her," she said, half to herself and half to us.

"Were you nervous he wouldn't be?" Otto asked.

She sat on the floor in front of us. "I don't know, he just changed a lot after my sister's accident. In some ways, I think he feels like he's getting a second chance at raising a kid. Especially since Rio's named after my sister," she said with a wistful smile. "The other day, he said he thinks I'm an incredible mom."

I didn't need to see her face light up to know how much that meant to her. Things had been rocky between Riley and her dad after her sister passed, and for a while, she was terrified of becoming a parent herself.

"You are," I said. "Seriously. I hate that I won't be here to help you with Rio, but she has the best family. You and your dad are gonna make her an amazing person."

Her smile looked bittersweet. I could tell she was grateful for my words, but sad at the realization I was leaving.

Emotions were still running high after dinner; our impending separation was creeping closer. There was no way I'd be able to get any sleep tonight. I kept catching myself grinding my teeth as I organized the few belongings in my room. Nothing would be able to come with me to Ylem.

My two pistols were the only things I owned that would be hard to leave behind. Yes, weapons were an extremely valuable commodity these days, but to me, they were more than that. My father's gun I'd left home with, and Malik's I'd taken up in his name, were the two tokens of my past that had seen everything I'd seen. It was strange to think two worldly objects held so much credit for the fact that I was still here, alive.

I wrapped them in one of my band tees and put them under my mattress.

Though they tried their best to pull an all-nighter like the rest of us, the parents had fallen asleep next to Rio on the couch while the rest of us talked into the morning. I insisted that my friends all go to bed, but I was grateful they didn't. Though they probably couldn't tell from what I let on, I was uneasy about leaving. I had no idea what to expect or who was coming to pick me up.

We moved to the backyard and sat around a firepit Otto had built a month earlier. In the glow of the flames, I could see a nostalgic smile on his face.

"This reminds me of night watch at the warehouse," he said.

"We've come a long way, haven't we?" Ava said, holding his hand.

"I hate that we're gonna be separated again," Riley lamented, "but if anyone can survive Ylem and make it back, it's you and Tye."

I nodded, feigning confidence.

"Will Rowen be able to make him a new identity too, so he can get back here?" asked Ava.

I hadn't even thought ahead that far. "We'll see. Rowen's biggest priority now is to get those prisoners out of there so we can work on a cure. I don't expect Tye will come live with us right away with all the work that has to be done to invent one," I said, only coming to the realization as I said it.

"I heard they're called 'Angels' at Ylem, the ones with the special blood. I overheard a couple of soldiers talking about it while I was doing repairs," Otto shared.

"Oh god, is Ylem some Christianity bullshit?" scoffed Riley.

Otto chuckled. "Who knows, but that's what Tye is to them. Or maybe not. We still don't know what sets him apart from the others."

"Once I get to Ylem, I'll find out more," I said.

Otto threw another log into the pit. "What d'you think the people are like there?"

"Rich snobs," Riley replied immediately.

We laughed.

"Everyone's probably trying to outdo each other," Ava said, with a tone that only seemed half-humorous.

"Bro, I literally don't even think about brushing my hair anymore," said Riley.

We stifled more laughter so as not to wake the baby.

A jolt of nerves hit me suddenly when I noticed the glow of a morning sun just barely brightening the night sky. My friends seemed to notice the change in my mood.

"Willa," Ava said, "thank you for doing this."

She hugged me, and the others joined in. I squeezed them tight, determined to never forget this feeling, because it could be the last time we were together this way.

As a unit, we stepped out onto the front porch. The soft morning sun bled onto the street. A large black shuttle bus with tinted windows was parked on the corner. A single armed guard waited by the car door. He looked military, but his uniform was different—a monochrome gray.

I turned to my friends. "I love you guys, you hear me? Take care of each other."

Their eyes were glossy.

"Take care of *yourself,*" Otto said, his voice cracking with emotion.

"If you find out that Tye's not there, do whatever you can to make it back," said Riley.

"'Til then, we'll keep tabs on anything we can do from here to help against Ylem," Ava added.

Otto put a loving hand on my shoulder. "We'll be waiting for you."

I started towards the van, purposely not looking back at my friends before my emotions could make me change my mind. It felt like I'd known them my whole life.

The guard scanned my face with a tablet. My stomach was churning with nerves. "Aria Sterling?" he asked.

With forced confidence, I said, "Yes."

He patted me down, then slipped a blindfold over my eyes and assisted me inside the bus. It was an obvious precaution—not just to keep us from knowing the route to Ylem, but also to make sure none of the new recruits could recognize one another. When I heard the door shut, I felt my pulse quicken. I took the nearest seat and inhaled a deep breath as the shuttle began to move.

Throughout the long ride, I braced myself for a surge of emotions as the reality of it all sank in. Leaving behind my family and friends to embark on another new chapter should have been overwhelming, yet the expected flood of feelings never came.

It was as if I was watching the situation from a distance, detached from the expected breakdown. While I could acknowledge the devastation of parting ways, it felt like the logic was separated from any sentiment. I had no concept of permanence anymore. People were temporary.

I finally heard the shuttle doors slide open and footsteps all around me. I was being led somewhere new. The chilly air told me I was outside, and by the strong wind, I could tell it was somewhere in the open.

A man's voice could be heard at my side. "Aria, please hold out your fingertip."

Reluctantly, I presented it. A sharp pain made me flinch. They were testing my blood.

"Cleared," I heard him call out to someone.

My boots clanked on a metal staircase as I was led up some steps. The familiar hum of a plane's engine filled my ears. So, this was how we'd be getting to Ylem. I imagined this plane belonged to them, unaffected by their own jamming satellites.

I was escorted to my seat. I could hear murmurs of other voices, but nothing I could fully make out.

Before long, the plane took off with a turbulent start that mirrored the state of my nerves. With no idea of how long the flight would be, and the blindfold over my eyes, it felt like I was in purgatory. Aimlessly floating in darkness, waiting to find out my fate.

The hum of the plane's cabin brought me to thoughts of Tye and the last time I'd seen him, boarding the cargo plane. Just before that, he'd asked me to make sure I took care of the others. I'd promised him, yet here I was, leaving them again.

At that point, Tye was optimistic about making it to Canada safely. We didn't know what was to come. Riley's dad suspected Mav was the one who'd revealed the escape plan to Ylem, and although it was definitely not beyond the realm of possibility, something in me still couldn't discard Maverick, despite his past betrayals.

I'd seen the good in him countless times. He'd protected me and Archer. Sailed us to safety, got us out of being captured multiple times, helped me at Ground Misery. Maybe it was because of his connection to my brother, who saw Mav's kind heart despite his life choices, but I still missed him.

Yet, missing and trusting were very different feelings. I hoped that wherever he ended up, he'd get clean and free himself from whatever debt he'd trapped himself in. I knew he wanted that too.

I'd been so sure that everything we'd gathered at Ground Misery and all of Thirteen's work would dismantle Zenith and the powers around it. I had hoped that it would help so many people with a cure and finally change the way things were going...but I was wrong. And so was Thirteen. He'd once said my friend's deaths wouldn't be in vain. It was hard for me to believe that.

The only undeniable victory was that Midas couldn't hide anymore. Even though he seemed untouchable, the spark had lit the fuse, and a firestorm was coming. I felt my heart rate go up the instant he crossed my mind. Soon, I'd be the closest I'd ever been to the source of all this evil. I wondered if I even had it in me to remain calm if I came across him. Which of the hundred horrible ways I'd thought of for killing him would I choose?

"Drink up," came a man's voice to my right. I felt a cold plastic cup nudge my hand.

I tried to smell it before it touched my lips. It was scentless. When I took too long to take a sip, he said, "It's water. We have a long flight. *Drink.*"

Still, I hesitated.

"A long flight" was an understatement. It felt endless, especially with my eyes still covered. I drifted in and out of shallow sleep. I was allowed a bathroom break at one point, but I never heard the door close. I was sure I was being watched.

At last, I felt the wheels hit the runway. My stomach was hollow with nerves. When we came to a stop, I could hear the commotion of the other passengers and protocol jargon as I waited for the next move.

The familiar voice of who I imagined to be the handler urged me to get up. He pushed me towards the exit, guiding me down another set of metal steps. The fresh air should've felt euphoric, but my blocked vision still stifled me.

As I stood in place, I could hear the group of voices dwindle, as if they were all being taken in different directions one by one.

A hand guided me somewhere for a few minutes until, finally, I was seated in a chair and my blindfold was removed.

I squinted, my eyes trying to refocus. I was in an office of some sort. An older woman sat before me behind an elegant-looking desk. Endless paperwork was stacked all over it, nearly burying the desktop computer to her right.

Despite her deep smile lines, she did not smile at me. Her face was serious and borderline unimpressed as she looked me up and down. "Welcome to Ylem, Aria. I'm Mother June. I oversee the aides," she began, in a flat-toned English accent. "Look here." She snapped a shot of my face with her tablet. "We're cross-referencing your blood test with your identity records. This may take a second."

My insides went cold. Surely Rowen would've anticipated a deeper dive than just a simple scan of my face? I could feel the sweat forming under my palms as I gripped the arms of my chair.

She read whatever info was scrolling over her screen. Her eyes lifted to meet mine, seemingly gauging my reaction to her digging. I kept my face neutral, but I was holding my breath. Finally, a positive-toned chime sounded from her device.

"Good," she said, emotionless. I let myself breathe again. Rowen had pulled through.

She threw a canvas bag onto her desk, unzipping it and displaying the contents to me like a well-rehearsed bit. "This is your care kit with everything you'll need. You're required to maintain impeccable personal hygiene at all times. The three uniforms provided must be kept clean and worn according to the standards set forth by the family you serve."

I eyed the gray sets of clothes on the desk. They looked similar to medical scrubs.

"Aides must comply with all orders without hesitation or question. Failure to obey promptly will result in immediate disciplinary action. You must maintain the utmost professionalism and discretion.

"Conversations with or about the family you serve must remain confidential. Disclosing any information about their personal lives, business dealings, or the internal operations of their household is strictly forbidden and will be severely punished... Are you following?"

After hours of silence and darkness, the bombardment of information was overwhelming. I nodded as earnestly as I could.

Her pursed lips made me think she wasn't convinced. "You're very lucky to be here. It's extremely rare that we recruit outside resources into Ylem. Don't mess it up for yourself."

My hands were still tightly gripping the armrests of my chair, but I tried to smile pleasantly.

She repacked the bag and handed it to me. When I took it, she stood to walk me to the door.

"The guards will escort you to your assigned home. Remember everything I told you and try to learn quickly on the job."

My hand was on the doorknob to leave, but she suddenly turned me around to face her, her expression very different from before. It was soft, almost concerned.

"And Willa... rest assured, you are not alone," she whispered, just before the door opened and the guards took me away again.

9. TYE

The clatter of lunch trays filled the cafeteria as I shuffled in line, the familiar, bland aroma of today's lunch—a mushy stew that seemed to have given up on flavor long before it reached our spoons—wafting through the air.

Most days, the noise was an overwhelming mix of loud teens and shouting guards, but today was oddly calm. A lot of the guys were out at appointments, which left the room feeling hollow.

I grabbed my tray and scanned the room, spotting Vale and Beckett already seated at our usual spot at one end of the long table. It was strategic: far enough from the others that our hushed conversations wouldn't carry, but not so isolated as to catch the guards' watchful eyes.

As I approached, Vale gave a quick nod, his eyes flicking to the empty seat across from him, while Beckett pretended to be engrossed in his food.

"The last supper with Tye Guy," he said, miming tears. "How you feeling?"

Sliding into my seat, I kept my voice low. "The food won't be missed, that's for sure."

It had only taken a few days for me to commit to the decision that the Basilica would be my new home. Both Vale and Beckett had been encouraging of such a prime opportunity to get closer to Midas and his inner workings.

"You gonna miss *us,* at least?" asked Beckett sincerely.

"Of course. But they said I'll be back here sometimes for more tests, so it's not the end of the three amigos."

Vale gave me a fist bump, his eyes soft and thoughtful, reminding me that he saw me as a close friend. The realization struck me—I hadn't been fully open with him lately, especially about the turmoil stirred in me by everything I'd learned about my blood.

I took a deep breath. "Can I tell you guys something big?" I asked, lowering my voice even more.

"Always," said Vale and Beckett together.

I checked to see if anyone was listening, but everyone else was caught up in their own chats. "All these crazy tests they've been doing on me… Turns out my blood isn't the same as the other Angels. It's immune, yeah, but it can somehow bring someone back—"

"Tye," Vale cut in, "we know already."

I winced. "How—"

"I've known about you since day one."

"…But, how? *I* didn't even know—"

"Like I said, there's things happening in the shadows. Just trust that."

A guard strolled by, close enough for Beckett to prompt a subject change. "It's one of my favorite books, actually," he said enthusiastically, before taking a bite of the mush.

I didn't push too hard on the subject, but it was clear that Vale was part of some network I wasn't knowingly involved in. It gave me a small boost of confidence as I parted ways with them and left for the Basilica that evening. I felt part of something bigger, like I was more than just an eavesdropper.

The golden guards left me in the foyer, and once again, Maverick was there to greet me. The houseman was by his side this time, but it was Mav who approached me first.

"Welcome home," he said without emotion. "I'll show you to your quarters."

I hadn't yet seen the place at night. The maze of hallways was dimly lit, and every few turns would reveal a gorgeous display of large candles burning on elegant console tables. There was a gothic ambiance that made me feel I was somehow being led to a dungeon.

When we got to the bottom floor, it was far from that. A wide, maroon-carpeted hallway ended in a sleek wooden door. Maverick swung it open to reveal a massive circular bedroom with a four-poster bed at the center. I could see the bathroom off to one side, its marble countertops glinting in the low light of the grand chandelier above. If it weren't for the fact that there were no windows in the room, I may have let myself believe I was no longer a prisoner.

"I have first shift outside your door. Another guard will take over in a few hours," said Maverick as I looked over the room.

I opened a drawer and found multiple sets of socks and underwear. Another revealed shirts. It was a fully stocked room. "What are you guarding me from? Isn't this place the most heavily guarded spot in Ylem?"

"Well, turns out you're the most valuable asset in the world, so you can never be too careful."

I scoffed. I hated how that sounded. "Maverick... how could you be working for this guy?"

He stepped inside and shut the door behind him as I sat on the corner of the bed. "I told you why."

"You're indebted to them somehow, but *why*? *How*?" I could see his jaw clenching in discomfort. "Maverick, if I'm gonna trust you, you have to trust me."

He opened the door and looked outside before closing it again. It took him a full beat to speak. "I made some reckless choices, back when I was the worst version of myself. I was high out of my mind, driving fast... and I caused a wreck. The young driver didn't make it. I panicked and ran.

"For years, I thought I got away with it... but eventually they caught up with me. The kid I killed was the attorney general's son. I'll spare you the details, but I had no choice but to work for them as a crony or spend my life in prison. It was the only option left."

He shifted uncomfortably, his voice hardening. "I thought I could manage it, that it wouldn't get this far. I never knew the full picture. And now, I have no one left. Not even her. So here I am."

I felt a surge of anger, yet he sounded so earnest and vulnerable that I couldn't help but empathize. I had also made some out-of-character choices to avoid life as a prisoner. It was difficult to fault his reasoning.

I wanted to offer some comfort, but I had to guard my emotions. Despite his reasons, he was still working for Midas. I couldn't fully consider him an ally just yet.

I was saved from a response by a knock on the door. Maverick opened it quickly.

It was the houseman. "Is everything with the new room to your satisfaction? I hope it meets your expectations," he said to me. His unfriendly tone did not match the inquiry.

"It's wonderful," I said, mirroring his energy.

The houseman came back in the morning to bring me a small breakfast tray of delicious pastries and set aside my clothing for the day. He let me know I was expected in the transfusion lounge in a few hours. Although my new home was a far cry from the camps, it was business as usual.

There was no denying it—my new living quarters were the best setup I'd had since being forced to leave home. Better than the Don Lux Hotel, even. Despite my building anxiety, the luxurious silk sheets, fluffy pillows, and clean scent of my new room had put me into a sleep that lasted the entire night without interruption.

The hot morning shower under the waterfall cascading from the ceiling almost made me feel guilty for how much I enjoyed it. I felt bad for the other boys, like I was a sellout, even though I knew my intentions were for the greater good.

Once dressed, I made my way out into the hall. A guard in gold, one I didn't recognize, stood waiting at the other end. I noticed these elite guards of Ylem carried actual guns, unlike the lowlier camp guards. I followed with no resistance.

He brought me up to the lounge where Chiron and a smiling Midas awaited. He was sipping orange juice from a crystal glass.

"Good morning, Tye," he said. "Hopefully you're feeling good about your decision to stay?"

I pushed aside my murderous thoughts, instead saying, "I am. Thanks for having me."

I sat promptly in the chaise beside him, offering my arm to Chiron, who looked taken aback by my eagerness.

Midas seemed to appreciate my friendly energy. With his free hand, he poured me my own glass of fresh juice and set it on the glossy stone table between us.

I took the glass and smiled, masking my discomfort as blood began to drain from my arm vein.

"Are you feeling better now that some of your long-standing questions have been answered?" he asked, watching the blood flow.

The subject was an immediate trigger for me. Was he testing my composure?

I kept my tone even. "Much better. Just wondering what comes next. Who are you planning to revive?"

My boldness appeared to catch him off guard. I realized I might have accidentally matched his intensity. My question clearly affected him. He shifted ever so slightly in his seat.

Like me, he kept his voice calm. "There's still a lot more work to be done before it's attempted on anyone important."

I couldn't help but feel his words were calculated to imply that no one outside his circle was considered 'important.' His cold smile made me reach for my glass, taking a sip for reassurance.

Chiron started to remove the IVs and patch us up.

"How would you like to see more of the paradise I've built?" asked Midas, standing and adjusting his silk nightwear. "Get some fresh air?"

After being confined for so long and only catching brief glimpses of Ylem from the train, my curiosity was undeniably piqued. However, it was the strategic advantage of understanding Ylem's layout that ultimately pushed me to agree.

"I'd like that."

"Great," he said, heading into the hallway, Maverick appearing at his side. "I'll have the houseman put aside the appropriate clothes for you. There's an equestrian event that will be fun for you to see."

Chiron and I exchanged a look. I couldn't imagine anyone enjoying a horse race while thousands of people were dying outside of these walls.

"Can't wait," I said, wondering if my forced sincerity was believable.

As the train buzzed gently along the tracks, I found myself in a compartment unlike the usual ones I'd sat in between the camps and the Basilica: plush, velvet seats, gold-trimmed curtains, and the faint scent of warm wood filling the air.

This was clearly Midas's personal carriage, and it screamed luxury in every corner. The golden guards stood at attention at either end of the car, their eyes ever-watchful. Maverick was seated two seats behind Midas.

Across from me, Midas reclined his seat. His mood seemed unusually light today, a sharp contrast to the usual air of intimidation he carried. I turned to the window, watching the city landscape blur past me. It was still hard to believe that a place the size of Ylem had been constructed in secret. The scale, the resources, the sheer audacity—it was mindboggling.

I realized this train ride could be an invaluable opportunity. Knowledge was power, and in my position, I needed all the power I could get.

I fidgeted with my armrest. "It's beautiful," I began, keeping my tone casual but curious. "How did you build something like this? I can't imagine how much money and manpower it took."

Midas turned his gaze towards me, a slight smile playing on his lips. "Money was never the issue. Everyone I brought into the fold had to make significant contributions to the project as a trade for the safety and luxuries that Ylem provides. As for the labor, everyone involved in the development was compensated in some way."

I was listening, but my eyes stayed fixed on the immaculate structures, each one more interesting than the last. "How did you manage to keep it hidden for so long?"

"I suppose a bit of history wouldn't hurt." He leaned back, contemplating for a moment. "Every aspect was planned down to the smallest detail. And every individual to whom Ylem was ever mentioned was meticulously logged into our database. We knew everything about them, even their darkest secrets, ensuring that if the name Ylem was merely whispered, there would be consequences. Naturally, we had our own methods for handling any loose ends."

I nodded to show I was interested. I had to tread carefully, and push for more information without raising suspicion. "And what about all the people who work here at Ylem and make it run? Your staff, the scientists, the soldiers. How did they become part of it?" I was hoping to hear about potential vulnerabilities in the Ylem machine.

Maverick, seated behind Midas, was listening intently. His expression remained unreadable, but I could sense he was weighing every word.

"Most of the powerful families here already had extensive infrastructures in place," Midas replied. "Their combined staff and workers alone outnumber the families here. As we expand, we occasionally recruit from outside. It's extremely rare, but it's a once-in-a-lifetime opportunity to live here behind the wall—serving, but safe nonetheless."

I could only imagine what sort of vetting process would be in place for an outsider to end up here.

As the train continued its journey, a stadium came into view, its modern architecture standing out against the backdrop of the city. It was an impressive sight, but it also made me realize just how empty and pristine the city had felt until now. Crowds of citizens had gathered outside the entrance of the stadium. The atmosphere was electric.

The train slowed as it approached a bustling station hub. It was a hive of activity, with multiple trains coming and going in all directions. The sheer scale of the operation was overwhelming.

The golden guards deboarded first, clearing a path for Maverick to lead Midas and me out onto the platform. As a unit, our entourage headed for the entrance to the stadium.

We moved through the crowd towards a private elevator off the entrance hall. All eyes were on us. Although Midas seemed familiar and friendly with the onlookers, the guards allowed no one to approach.

When the elevator doors opened at the top, we were inside a luxurious suite, situated high above the main seating areas and offering a panoramic view of the entire stadium. It had large windows and plush seating, creating an atmosphere of elegance and exclusivity. This suite was clearly reserved for VIPs.

I recognized some of their faces from the Basilica's rooftop garden. The others I didn't know, but they definitely knew me. They whispered and stared at me in awe.

The guards stationed themselves, and Midas made himself comfortable. As for me, I was all but pressed against the window, overwhelmed by the spectacle of the stadium below.

Hundreds of well-dressed individuals chatted among themselves as they waited for the event to begin. I had assumed it would be a horse race, but the lack of track marks on the field made me reconsider. The horses were trotting around aimlessly; all of them looked spooked and agitated, nothing like disciplined racehorses.

Before I could figure out what was happening, a new procession of guards entered the room, escorting a newcomer whom Midas and the others stood up to greet. Almost instantly, I was captivated by her presence, feeling a surprising sense of admiration that left me momentarily speechless.

She was a silver-haired beauty, but I guessed her hair must've been dyed because she couldn't have been far from my age. It was cut in a modern, shoulder-length style. She wore an emerald jumpsuit, structured in a fashion-forward way. Fitting, because her lean body type and striking bone structure looked to be right out of a fashion magazine.

She placed a kiss on both of Midas's cheeks before nodding politely to some of the others in the room. When her blue eyes landed on me, her expression took me by surprise. She clearly recognized who I was, but she seemed to let out a sigh, like she was sorry to see me here. She gave me a small, sympathetic nod before sitting beside Midas.

"Tye." His deep voice cut through the chatter around us. "Come meet my daughter."

I stared at them. For some reason, I'd never considered that Midas had any family at all. "Hello," I said feebly, reaching out to shake her hand. "Tye."

"Harlow," she said, shaking my hand with the kind of formality that felt more political than personal.

A blaring horn sounded, turning our attention to the field below. The stadium erupted in cheers as a rabid, ferocious creature was unleashed among the horses.

My jaw dropped. It was clearly a Mort, but it looked bigger and more deformed than any I'd ever seen before. The horses ran and kicked wildly, panic in their every movement. The Mort pounced on its first victim, a brown-spotted horse, bringing it down with brutal force.

Cheers erupted from some of the people in the suite, while others let out sounds of disappointment. A cold realization washed over me. This wasn't a horse race; they were betting on which horse would be the last one standing. The shock of it all hit me hard, and I glanced at Harlow.

She wasn't watching, occupying herself with some hors d'oeuvres on the back table. I decided to join her. I couldn't stomach watching how something that to me was a nightmare was being used as mere entertainment for the people of Ylem.

"Isn't this *so* fun?" she asked me sarcastically.

"Sure," I said, throwing a small tart into my mouth. I noticed that Maverick was watching us closely.

Another cheer mixed with boos rang out.

"It's awful. They use horses since they can't turn. Somehow they're very strict about how many Dark-Eyes are allowed within the walls, even though we're all allegedly immune ..."

Her energy was so different from Midas's. She was sarcastic but charming, and seemed to be uncomfortable with Ylem culture despite being an inherent part of it.

The Mort was now mounted on a black horse, biting into its neck like it hadn't tasted flesh in ages.

"Do these ... events happen often?"

She closed her eyes as if it pained her to reply. "Every day it's some weird fucking show, like everyone has to prove just how out of touch they are."

A violent sound made us both wince. I dared to peek down onto the field and saw a gray horse still bucking, while the rest of the herd lay on the ground in a bloodbath. The crowd erupted in another mix of cheers and groans.

Judging by the way people began collecting their winnings and mingling again, it seemed the first round was over.

"Harlow," called Midas.

She didn't move. Instead, he came over to us, with him, a tall red-headed man in an expensive-looking leather outfit. I swore I caught Harlow rolling her eyes before she turned and nodded politely to him.

"This is Angus Astor," Midas told her. "You know of his family and their contributions."

She held out her hand and he kissed it gently.

"Pleasure," he said in a German accent.

He seemed pleased to meet her, but she immediately turned back to the food table and grabbed a finger sandwich.

“If you’ll excuse me, I have to scoff this down.” She then put the whole thing in her mouth and started chewing rather loudly, to the point that Midas reddened with embarrassment and Angus backed away.

“I will reintroduce you when my daughter is not trying to play class clown for her new friend,” Midas said through gritted teeth.

Angus bowed his head politely and rejoined some of the others who were mid-celebration.

Midas reached for Harlow’s arm. He maintained an even expression, but his tone was threatening. “If you continue to embarrass me when I’m trying to introduce you to people you will *need* one day, I will make sure you have less freedom to do so.”

Harlow didn’t look intimidated at all. “Stop trying to pawn me off. No matter how many men you bring me, it won’t change the fact that I’m not interested in them.”

I watched in surprise as Midas’s powerful presence diminished in the shadow of his daughter’s.

10. WILLA

I pressed my forehead against the cool glass of the train window, my breath fogging up the pane. The city of Ylem unraveled before me like a painted masterpiece, every detail looking too perfect to be real. I wondered which of these grand buildings were the camps holding Tye, and where else in the city I might find members of Rowen's network.

I'd never seen anything like this. Glittering skyscrapers reached for the sky, their mirrored surfaces reflecting the soft light of dusk. It was breathtaking, yet the perfection of it all felt haunting.

In the distance, I could see the massive walls, an intimidating barrier separating this oasis from the rotted and destroyed world beyond. The difference was staggering. Beyond those walls was desolation, a sad reminder of what humanity had become: a world where only the rich and powerful could find refuge in a place like Ylem.

The sheer injustice gnawed at me. Survival was a necessity, but the fact that money and power dictated who got to live in safety while others suffered was deeply disturbing.

The train glided smoothly on until it stopped at a platform in front of a magnificent high-rise. I marveled at how such tall structures could be built in secret.

With my pack in hand, I was escorted off the train by two guards dressed in golden uniforms, a clear distinction from the dusty gray uniform I now wore.

Inside the high-rise, I was immediately struck by the opulence of the lobby. Polished marble floors gleamed under the dim lighting. A tranquil water feature dominated the center of the space, its gentle trickle the only sound breaking the silence. The air was scented with a faint hint of eucalyptus, adding to the surreal atmosphere of luxury and calm.

I was guided through the lobby toward a private elevator tucked away to one side. More golden guards stood by it, their expressions unreadable.

In the elevator, one of the guards pressed a single button labeled *Penthouse*. Unlike buildings I'd been in before, this one had no other floors. Its multi-story base seemed to exist solely to support the grand penthouse at the top. Whoever lived here obviously possessed an ungodly amount of wealth and resources. The sheer audacity of it all made my blood boil.

At last the doors parted, and with the small parade of guards, I stepped into a stylish foyer. The space was surprisingly cool and hip, far from the stuffy luxury I'd expected.

The first thing that caught my eye was the pop art all over the walls, vibrant and colorful. The furniture was an eclectic mix of vintage pieces. It all had a lived-in, welcoming feel. It reminded me of the cool lounges my artist friends and I used to frequent in the city.

The guards left without a word. I stepped farther into the open-concept space, only to find I wasn't alone. Two men in gray were tidying the living room, while in the sleek kitchen just off the main room, a chef laid out pots and pans. None of them looked up at me.

I felt awkward, not knowing my next move, until I heard a voice coming from down the hall. "Manny, will you make that yummy pasta again this eve?"

Coming around the corner into the lavish kitchen was a lean young woman with glossy silver hair. She was wearing an elegant mint-green silk set, a far cry from the gray uniforms the rest of us were wearing. Clearly, this was the owner of the impressive home.

The chef, Manny, smiled at her. "Of course, ma'am. My pleasure."

"Thank god. You really outdid yourself—oh, hey," she said when she saw me.

I bowed to her clumsily.

She started laughing. "Don't ever do that again. I know they tried brainwashing you, but I'm chill." I felt my cheeks flush. "*Finally* they sent some estrogen. I had to beg Mother June myself, 'cause my dad insists on an all-male staff."

She had an effortlessly cool presence, and her dyed silver hair gave off the kind of vibe that reminded me of the crowd I used to run with. But looking around at the lavish home of a millionaire's kid, I dismissed the thought. It was probably just a carefully curated act.

"I'm Harlow," she said, reaching out to shake my hand.

I respectfully shook it back, noticing her soft pale skin next to my worn brown hand. No matter how 'chill' she was, I was still in service to her. It was wildly uncomfortable. "Aria," I said simply.

"You're gorgeous, too. Let me show you to your room?"

One of the guys in gray stepped into the kitchen. "I can do it, Harlow, don't worry—"

"No, it's okay. I'll take her. Come, Aria."

On a secondary floor, the doors opened to reveal a rather plain room, devoid of the hip style I'd seen so far. But what it lacked in ambiance, it more than made up for with its stunning views. Floor-to-ceiling windows showcased the entire city of Ylem, twinkling in the night in all its crafted glory, the massive walls looming in the distance.

"You'll take this room," Harlow said, switching on the soft lighting.

Despite it being intended for a maid, this room was far better than any setup I'd had since leaving home. The bed looked inviting, with crisp white linens neatly tucked in. A small but comfortable-looking armchair sat by the window. There was even my own bathroom.

"It's nice. Thank you."

"As long as you keep up with what they told you to do, you're free to use the house. Just play the part when guards and any visitors are here."

Her apparent kindness was a far cry from what I'd expected from my new employer.

A doorbell chimed upstairs. "Speaking of visitors ... " she said.

I was still uneasy in my new surroundings, so I put my bag down and followed her back up the stairs.

Waiting by the elevator doors were two golden guards escorting a young man in a jumpsuit and an older woman in medical scrubs into the foyer. He was washed out, with dark circles under his eyes. Couldn't have been much older than Archer was. He did not look happy to be here.

Harlow waved the guards off and knelt down to the boy's level. "I'm so sorry," she said empathetically. "I already told them to stop bringing you, so this'll be your last session, okay?"

The boy nodded weakly.

The nurse moved into a sitting room across the way. Harlow and the boy sat across from each other in a pair of lounge chairs. The nurse started arranging the tubes and wiring attached to some weird medical device in the center of the room. I watched in confusion until I saw her inserting IVs into their arms. It suddenly became clear—I was witnessing firsthand how Ylem used the Angels to gain immunity.

I stared in horror as the blood transferred from the young boy's arm into Harlow's veins. She refused to watch the ordeal, her face covered in shame. I couldn't imagine why. She likely had the choice not to partake, yet here she was.

I saw the boy pale even more, his skin turning almost ghostly. Was this what Tye was being put through? My stomach churned violently, and a wave of nausea hit me suddenly. I turned and rushed down the hall, desperate to find a bathroom. Thankfully, I spotted one nearby and stumbled inside, barely making it to the marble toilet before vomiting.

My face was hot with embarrassment. I shouldn't be drawing any attention. I gathered myself, throwing some cold water on my face from the gleaming sink. A few beats later, there was a knock on the door.

"Aria?" Harlow called.

I opened the door. My expression must have been judgmental; she looked equally concerned and embarrassed.

"Sorry, I should've warned you about the transfusions. They're morbid, I know. Ylem takes some adjusting to."

I'd been here for just a few hours, and I'd already seen enough to confirm how twisted Ylem truly was. If this was the daily reality for the Angels, it only fueled my determination to bring it all down.

I schooled my face, remembering that I had to maintain my alias and fulfill my purpose here. Rowen had told me to lie low until I was needed. "I just get queasy when I see blood. Don't worry about it."

"Why don't you lie down? I'm sure you've had a long day," she said, walking me back down to my room.

I sat on the edge of the bed, my eyes darting to her arm bandage, still processing what I'd seen.

"It's horrible," she admitted. "I wouldn't do it if my dad wasn't forcing me to. He has eyes everywhere ... and I'll admit, when you spend enough time here, you get numb to things."

"So your dad lives here too?" I asked, trying to redirect the conversation to a place where it would be easier for me to mask my judgment.

"God no, he's overbearing enough. I insisted on having my own place. He lives there." She pointed out of the window at a spherical black building not too far in the distance.

"That's a *house?*" I asked in disbelief. Its architecture and size looked more like that of a museum. It seemed like the entire city was built around it.

"Hideous, I know, but it's *the heart of Ylem*. Just like my father."

My throat tightened, barely allowing any words to escape. "... Like him, how?"

"All of this," she said, making a sweeping motion out at the metropolis with her hand, "is my father's life's work. I'm just stuck in it."

My ears rang. My mind raced with a hundred thoughts at once. I had walked straight into the viper's nest. *She's Midas's daughter.* With Mother

June being part of Rowen's network, it was surely no coincidence that I'd been placed here. He must have orchestrated everything. Harlow was a direct link to Midas and held the key to everything we needed to know about this place.

"I'll admit, though, I don't ever want to be infected," she went on. "The transfusions make us immune. I've seen what the virus does. I'd rather deal with the discomfort of these weird medical experiments than turn into one of those Dark-Eyes."

Despite her being related to the most hated man on earth, I still found Harlow's energy docile, warm even.

A golden guard appeared at the threshold, his hand resting on his weapon. "Ma'am? Is everything okay?"

"Why wouldn't it be?" she snapped back at him.

"You ended your transfusion early—"

"That boy isn't doing well. I already told them to stop sending him."

"I will relay again, ma'am."

"Leave us."

Hesitantly, he did.

"Are you hungry? Do you need anything?" Harlow asked me kindly.

"I'm okay. If I'm not needed, I think I want to get some rest."

"Of course. I'll see you in the morning."

I woke up the next morning to the sound of the curtains being yanked open and the flood of harsh sunlight. I squinted and spotted one of the aides by the window, his movements urgent.

"Get dressed quickly," he instructed, his tone leaving no room for questions.

I stumbled out of bed, throwing on my uniform as fast as I could. My mind still foggy with sleep, I followed him upstairs.

The other staff members were gathered in the foyer, their posture respectful and attentive. They were greeting a formidable-looking woman dressed in gold military gear who was flanked by two other soldiers and a nurse.

Also beside her stood a boy of around my age, with dark hair and freckles. He was wearing the same jumpsuit that the sickly-looking Angel had on the night before. It didn't take long to put two and two together. This boy was another Angel—sent to replace the last. His eyes held a mixture of fear and defiance.

It crossed my mind that when I did find Tye again, he may be very different from how I remembered. Who knew what other tests and tortures they were putting him through?

Whether my energetic connection with him was fading, or the trauma I'd endured was blocking my swevens altogether, the idea of his suffering still echoed through my body. And that alone was proof that my feelings for him hadn't gone anywhere.

Even after all the anguish that attachment had brought me, I had fully surrendered to my feelings for Tye.

Harlow entered the scene and seemed immediately confused. "What now?"

The commanding woman stepped forward. "Your transfusion was cut short yesterday. You requested another Angel, so I brought you one. This one matches your blood type and didn't get along with his last assigned family. We're hoping he'll have better luck here." She turned her piercing gaze onto the boy, as if the last part was a threat.

Harlow rolled her eyes. She didn't seem to be affected by the woman's imposing presence at all. "Thanks, Secretary Croft."

"Of course. Why don't you show the nurse and Beckett here where you're most comfortable having them carry out the transfusion?"

Harlow walked off, the other two in tow.

Croft's attention landed on me. "Aria?" I flinched. "A word?" She walked past me into the next hall, waiting for me to follow.

It took a great deal of effort to unfreeze myself from where I stood. I could've sworn, by the way she said my name, that she wasn't convinced at all. This would probably be the end of my journey, before it had even begun. *She knows who I really am.*

I met her in the hallway. Her sharp features showed no signs of levity. "You were appointed to be Harlow's personal aide. I'm here to make sure you understand what that means."

I let out a small breath of relief. My cover was still safe. "Mother June explained it all."

"Harlow has a tendency to blur the lines when it comes to her position and her staff. It will be up to you to maintain your duties and stay in line."

My fists clenched by my sides. "Understood."

"She's the next successor to Ylem. She has many responsibilities, none of which include befriending the help."

Her insult would've otherwise bothered me, but 'successor' was the part that stuck out to me the most. If Harlow were to take over from Midas one day, did that mean she was an only child? Did she have no mother who would take the leadership position? I hadn't even considered what would happen with Ylem *after* Midas was taken out. I'd assumed it would all fall apart.

"I'm here to serve," I muttered tightly. It seemed like the right thing to say.

"I hope so. Carry on."

I walked aimlessly around the spacious penthouse until I found the living room, where the nurse was clearing away the remaining equipment following the transfusion.

Harlow, looking flushed and self-conscious, made her way to the breakfast table and pulled out a chair. "Beckett, come eat something." He looked at her like she was pulling his leg. "You like salmon Benedict?"

Beckett's face lit up, but he approached the table so slowly, it seemed he was waiting for the guards to tackle him. Finally, he took a seat near Harlow.

The guards nearby watched disapprovingly, but judging by the way they remained at their stations, this must've been a common occurrence.

"Aria? Come sit," she called.

Before I could, one of the other aides piped up. "We have her breakfast in the back kitchen, ma'am."

"That's okay, I'm sure this food here will do just fine," she replied, with a friendly but pointed tone.

I joined them in the seat opposite Harlow. There was an overwhelming amount of food on the table, clearly beyond anything three people, let alone one person, would be able to finish on their own.

Beckett dove straight in, collecting a large amount of food on his plate and scoffing it down in a hurry. He'd probably not had a meal like this in ages.

I waited for Harlow to take her modest portion before putting a few things on my own plate.

"This looks amazing. Thank you," I said.

She smiled, pulling up the sleeves of her elegant bathrobe. "Everything's grown or sourced here in Ylem."

I imagined that among all the wealthy families living here, some must own massive supply chains. When the outside world collapsed, their resources would have most likely been redirected to their new home.

"Where's the food from the camps sourced?" Beckett asked with a grin. "The sewers?"

Harlow let out an uneasy laugh.

"The camps?" I asked, my interest piqued.

"Where they keep the Angels," she said, busying herself with her food. "My dad refuses to let me visit, but I know they're awful. I'm sorry, Beckett. I hope you can find some comfort when you visit here."

He smiled with difficulty, his cheeks bulging with a mouthful of biscuits.

I tried to look overly invested in my poached egg so I didn't seem too eager to pry. "Is that where they keep all of them?"

"When they're not with their assigned families for transfusions, yes."

"Look, I hate the transfusions," Beckett began through a full mouth. He swallowed. "But you're already way better than the last family I had. They were—"

"Watch yourself," Secretary Croft cut in as she sauntered into the room. Beckett turned red. Croft addressed the other guards nearby. "Take him back to the camps. He can finish his food on the way. Harlow, I have important things to cover with you."

While the guards escorted Beckett away, Croft tapped me on the shoulder to dismiss me. She took my seat across from Harlow as I stood to the side.

"I apologize for these matters being discussed within your home, but given that you didn't find it important enough to attend the last few council meetings, it's my duty to keep our future leader in the know," she said. "There are some things that are mandatory to bring to your attention so that you may be aware of what's going on outside your preferred bubble."

Harlow pushed her food aside dramatically. "Of course. I'm all ears."

"Another insurgent group was destroyed outside our borders. There's cause for concern because this time, it wasn't just a ragtag team of rebels—there were actual soldiers among them. Deserters who've abandoned their units from the different states. It seems some are turning against their government, and in turn, against us."

I tilted my head subtly, pretending to admire a painting on the far wall while focusing intently on Croft's words.

"Their numbers are nowhere near those of our forces, of course, but it's the first time since our conception that we've seen this type of counterforce. Word's spreading that your father's responsible for what the world became and that he's here. Our location's becoming more and more compromised.

"We're still confident that nothing they have will match our defenses, especially with all the relevant world leaders under our roof. But it's important that you understand the beginnings so that we may better prepare for what's to come."

Harlow seemed to be processing the information, but at the same time, she was rolling a grape between her pointer finger and thumb disinterestedly.

"I know you and your father don't always see eye to eye," Croft pressed, "but it might benefit you to start showing some interest—playing the political game and attending some of these social gatherings so that you can build alliances and be more involved in the workings of this metropolis. You *will* have to lead one day."

Finally, Harlow looked up. "It's concerning, yes, but my dad's in his fifties. I think with all the science relating to health and longevity, he's far from leaving me on my own. I have time to learn. Unless you specifically think that he's in danger for some reason…"

Croft paused thoughtfully, as if crafting her response. "We've built a great city of the future, and things had to be destroyed for it to exist. Naturally, people will want it to fail. We can never be too careful, nor too prepared."

I could've sworn Croft's eyes met mine for a second, but I quickly busied myself, picking up some leaves from the floor around the base of a potted plant by the table.

The gravity of Croft's words hung heavy in the air, and I realized that beneath the surface of Ylem's perfect façade, an undercurrent of tension was steadily growing.

Harlow's nonconformity was my opportunity. It was a crack in the armor I would take advantage of.

11. TYE

I woke up with that familiar knot in my stomach, the one that comes when you know something awful is about to happen. Today was the first time in weeks I had to go back to the camps for another test. Just thinking about it made me feel anxious, but underneath it all was the faintest hint of excitement that maybe, just maybe, I'd see Vale and Beckett. They were my lifelines in all this mess; the weekly transfusions had already stretched my nerves thin. But even the thought of my friends couldn't fully shake off my dread.

I was starting to get used to the strange pace at the Basilica. The staff coming and going, the soldiers always around—it had a certain rhythm to it. Not exactly comforting, but predictable.

Or maybe I was just numb to everything. Numb to all the trauma that had dulled the sharp edges of my new reality. Sometimes it was hard to tell.

It was getting harder and harder to remember the faces of my friend group. The details, once so clear, were now fading, like old photos left out in the sun. I couldn't help but feel a pang of sadness whenever I realized that. So much had happened since I'd seen them, and the more time passed, the more those memories seemed to slip away.

As I got dressed, I tried to recall Riley's voice and the way she would always sing while getting ready or driving us somewhere after school. Ava's hilarious expression whenever I'd jump out and scare her in the school halls. Otto's proud smile after finishing one of his incredible contraptions. Dustin, always there when I needed him, a steady presence in a world that often felt like it was crumbling around me.

And then there was Willa. She was *always* on my mind, a beacon of light through the chaos. I was so relieved she'd never boarded that cargo plane with me. She was worthless to Ylem, and probably would've been killed. The thought of losing her was unbearable.

Willa was extraordinary. She had so many qualities I didn't. She was scarily intuitive, able to sense things and act on them. She was someone who made things happen, no matter how difficult or dangerous. And when she set her mind to something, there was no stopping her.

While I'd gotten stronger, bolder, and less sensitive over time, I still felt delicate compared to her. Her strength was something I admired, something I wished I had more of. Even though I'd grown, I could always predict that she'd be one step ahead.

But despite everything, just thinking about her brought me a small sense of peace. It reminded me that there was still good out there, things worth fighting for. It gave me the strength to face whatever came next.

Willa must have been on Maverick's mind, too. It was the first topic he brought up in the train carriage on our way to the camps. This rare moment of solitude was an unexpected opportunity. Today, Mav was assigned to escort me, as Midas was occupied with preparations for an upcoming event, accompanied by Secretary Croft.

Only two golden guards were present, stationed outside the doors at either end of the carriage. Maverick spoke under the cover of the train's constant hum.

"The way she used to talk about you... Do you feel the same way about her?"

I was caught off guard by his sudden, personal question. Yet, each time Maverick revealed his vulnerabilities, it became easier to believe that he was genuine and that his past mistakes were behind him.

"I love her very much."

His shoulders slumped, but a trace of relief was visible behind the hurt in his eyes. "Good. It makes me happy knowing she has people who'll take care of her. I promised her brother I would, and I failed."

"Well, I can't take care of her while I'm trapped here," I slung back. He had no readable reaction to that. "You were close with her brother, right?" I asked, deciding to steer the conversation in a different direction.

I could tell the thought stung him.

"Malik had a way of making you feel like he really saw the deepest part of you," he said, staring out of the window.

"Just like Willa."

"Just like Willa," he agreed. "I wish I could undo so much of my past. It feels like half my life I was a prisoner to my addictions, and now in the other half, I'm a prisoner of Ylem."

I gave him a light nudge on his knee so he'd turn back to face me. "Well, you don't have to be, Maverick. We can find a way—"

"Stop."

I only did because the train had pulled into the camps and the guard was already approaching with the blindfold.

The usual faces greeted me as I walked through the doors. Some nodded in recognition, others barely glanced up. It was as if I had never left. The routine, the monotony, it all felt like stepping back in time.

In the rec area, the Angels were scattered about, each finding their own way to stave off the boredom. Some were engaged in half-hearted games, their movements sluggish and uninspired. Others sat in small groups, murmuring quietly or staring off into the distance. It was a depressing sight, as expected.

I caught sight of Vale leaning against a wall near the squat rack, catching his breath. He spotted me and flashed a bright smile. I returned it, walking over to him and giving him a big hug.

"Finally! How long you back?" he asked enthusiastically.

"Not long. They told me to wait until I'm called for more testing. What'd I miss?"

His smile twisted into a grimace of disgust. "You don't wanna know."

"Tell me."

"Dude … They're starting a breeding program for the Angels. Trying to replicate our bloodlines."

"What?! What do you mean?"

"We had to provide … *samples.*"

A clammy sweat prickled the back of my neck. "If that's why I'm here today—"

"Yo, fairies!" a voice broke in.

We turned to see the burly guy who had challenged Vale on my first day here. He approached with his usual puffed-out chest.

"Not now, Brock, we were about to kiss," Vale said sarcastically.

Brock scoffed. "You kicked lil' Beckett to the curb, huh?"

"He got assigned a new family today. What d'you want?"

An impish grin stretched across Brock's dim-witted face. "I heard Tye here's serving the evil overlord. Word is you're his little pet and getting special treatment."

"What's your point?" I asked mockingly.

Brock stepped a little too close to me. Vale put his arm out, but Brock ignored it. "You tell that piece of shit to let us *all* out of this shithole or if I ever see him, I'll personally curb stomp that motherfucker—GAAAH!!"

Brock suddenly dropped limply to the floor. A security guard had tased him in the back. Both Vale and I watched in joyful shock as he was dragged away by a group of them.

"Get back to your activities or you'll be sent back to the pods for the day!" one yelled before slamming the rec room door.

Realizing the guards were occupied by the disruption, I took full advantage of our unsupervised moment and dragged Vale to a corner of the room.

"V, I really want to be in the loop of what you're planning. Midas is getting more comfortable around me, and if I know the plan, I'll be better at helping you guys."

He shifted uncomfortably. "There are so many moving parts that took months of careful planning. I know you mean well, but I don't want you to do anything thinking you're helping, only to accidentally mess things up. It's best you stay out of it until we need you. Even a tiny mistake can ruin everything."

My frustration simmered. "At least tell me this: how long do I have to tough it out? When's it happening?"

He hesitated, his eyes skipping around to see if anyone was listening, before finally leaning in and speaking quietly. *"New Year's Day."*

And that was all he was able to say before the guards funneled back into the dome.

Soon enough, I found myself in Chiron's office, bracing myself for whatever today's misery was. Vale's words were still fresh in my mind.

Chiron was preparing a suspicious-looking needle, much larger than any I'd been stuck with before.

"Is this a joke? I'm already bruised head to toe, and now you're sticking me with *that*?"

Chiron tied my bicep with a rubber strap. "We're inserting our new nanotechnology into your bloodstream. It will monitor you and teach us how we can further develop a permanent cure. There may come a day when transfusions are no longer needed."

So one day I'd be disposable, great. I had no fight left in me to protest. I was just happy he wasn't forcing me to take part in the breeding program.

"I know you can't tell me, I get it, but I still don't understand who you're bringing back from the dead if it's not the people outside of Ylem. Isn't everyone here immune and thriving?"

"Sometimes, it's not about using the technology and research. The real value is in the knowledge and possibilities we gain, which lay the groundwork for future advancements."

As always, he was skirting around the point. The way he kept his eyes on the guards proved it.

As the needle was inserted into my forearm, I changed course. "Why'd you get into medicine in the first place?"

The question seemed to have pulled a heartstring. His eyes became distant and glazed. "Aside from virology being fascinating... to make a safer world for my family."

I couldn't help the small laugh that escaped me. "But you'll settle for a safe bubble city instead?"

He busied himself with wrapping a bandage around my sore skin. "I've tried to be as helpful to you as I can. What more do you want from me, Tye? I'm limited by a hundred factors."

It was the first time I saw his professional attitude slip. The guards even perked up.

I had to be strategic. Any report back to Midas could kick the hornet's nest. "Nothing, I guess."

I decided to stop there. I hoped my point was made and he'd remember why he was doing all of this—the bigger picture. To help the *world.*

On my way back to the Basilica, my unease from the latest test lingered, but it was the looming mystery of the New Year's event that truly filled me with anxiety. While five months seemed like an eternity to wait, it still felt far too soon to execute such an elaborate plan.

The city was fortified with mammoth walls and teeming with soldiers on every corner. Whatever Vale and the insurgents were planning had to be monumental, because once they set off the plan, if it failed, Ylem would crack down and root out everyone involved. There would be no second chances.

Halfway through the ride back to the Basilica, a wave of commotion forced the train to slow down. A trio of attack helicopters was circling the city, weaving in and out of tall buildings, their spotlights scanning the streets below.

"What's going on?" I asked Maverick, who was pacing the carriage and listening in on his earpiece.

He planted himself in the seat across from me. "An Angel escaped. She managed to break free during her transfusion and somehow made it far enough to run and hide."

I looked out at the cityscape, hoping I'd spot the bold hero. I felt a jolt of worry, seeing how aggressively the choppers maneuvered. There was no way she'd make it outside the walls, even if there was a way out. This was just a small taste of Ylem's forceful response to any deviation from their strict regime.

The frenzy carried throughout the Basilica when we arrived. Soldiers were coming in and out of Midas's quarters, delivering and relaying messages.

Secretary Croft was on her way out when Mav and I stepped into Midas's grand office space. Rich mahogany bookshelves lined the walls, filled with leather-bound volumes as well as modern-looking books, all beautifully organized.

At the center stood a carved oak desk where Midas sat in a high-backed leather chair. Elegant touches like bronze statues, antique globes, and gold-framed artwork decorated the sophisticated room.

Through the panoramic glass window, he was watching one of the choppers that had landed on a bridge a few miles off. When I got closer, it was clear to see by the brigade of soldiers surrounding the area that they had found and captured the runaway Angel. I felt a stab of disappointment in my chest.

"Tye," Midas greeted, turning his attention to me. "I hope your appointment today was manageable."

His calm energy didn't match the chaos outside; he didn't seem bothered by the disruption at all. As if he had no doubts that the systems he had in place would correct the situation within minutes and there would be no trace of any disturbance.

"It was easy enough," I replied.

"Would you like to join me for dinner?"

The offer surprised me, but it was validation that he was feeling less guarded around me. "Sure. Can I shower first, then meet you in the dining room?"

"I was thinking I'd pay a visit to one of our most decadent bistros, run by a renowned chef who happens to be a friend of mine. Does that sound of interest?"

I'd never even considered Ylem's commercial establishments. The concept seemed so out of place somehow. "Sounds nice."

"Great. Maverick, when he's ready, bring him down to the car."

"Yes, sir."

Soon after, I found myself inside a luxurious armored vehicle. Up front, a driver sat behind a glass divider, his eyes focused on the road ahead. Through the tinted windows, I could see a military vehicle leading our convoy, with another one bringing up the rear. We were a fortress on wheels, cutting through the streets of Ylem.

I adjusted my suit, feeling out of place in such fancy attire. The fabric was smooth and expensive, but my outfit was nothing compared to what Midas was wearing. Sitting across from me, he was a vision of opulence, his burgundy suit dripping with lavishness. It was as if he was trying to embody the wealth and power of Ylem itself.

Maverick sat in the rearmost seat, silent but ever-watchful. I glanced out of the window again, the city passing by in a blur.

Our car was the only one on the road. As we drove through, I couldn't help but marvel at how different the city looked from this angle. It felt even bigger. I caught glimpses of people going about their evenings—families gathered, friends laughing on street corners, couples strolling hand in hand. It all seemed like the old world, yet so far removed from reality.

The golden uniforms of soldiers stood out against the peaceful scenes, their presence unmistakable on every block, saluting as we passed.

Finally, we pulled up to a unique-looking building. Its teardrop shape and all-chrome exterior made it stand out among the surrounding architecture.

The driver stepped out and opened the door, and both Midas and I followed Maverick towards the entrance where other guards were standing by. A greeter appeared and led us inside.

The interior was dimly lit, the soft lighting casting a warm glow that made the place feel both chic and sophisticated. It was minimalistic, yet every detail screamed high-end. A few tables were occupied by other patrons, all dressed in expensive-looking attire.

As we walked past, they stood to respectfully acknowledge Midas. I could've sworn I recognized one of them as an A-list actress from some films I'd seen. Midas gave them all a courteous wave, and they returned to their conversations.

We were then shown to a back table in a private room, the isolation making it clear that we would be dining alone. Maverick stood alone just outside the door. I hadn't expected this; the sudden intimacy made my heart race with nerves. What could this elaborate occasion be?

Intricately crafted ceramics lined the shelves, adding a touch of artistry to the room. A single candle flickered on the table, casting shadows that danced along the walls.

Midas took a seat and I followed suit.

"What do you think of the place?" he asked, breaking the silence.

"It's ... impressive," I replied, struggling to find the right words. "I've never seen anything like it."

Midas smiled, a hint of amusement in his eyes. "I thought you might appreciate it. It's one of my favorite spots in the city."

I nodded, still trying to piece together the reason for the theatrics. "Is anyone else joining?"

He leaned back in his chair, his expression derisive. "Just us."

A knot formed in my gut as his words sank in. This was more than just a dinner. It was a prelude to something significant. I took a deep breath, trying to calm my nerves.

"... Okay," I said, watching the waiter serve the first course of what was clearly a preset menu.

The black china plate was adorned with a tiny spoon of caviar and sprinkled with gold leaf. Even with the artistic presentation, I hardly had an appetite thanks to my stomach churning with anticipation.

"A pre-meal taste," Midas said as he took a spoonful. "My daughter loves this place too."

I chewed mine with reluctance, but the decadent taste was undeniable. "I'm glad I got to meet her. I didn't know you had family here."

The waiter poured us some rich red wine.

"Only her. I had to cut out the rest of my family years ago. As soon as I had major success in my field, they only saw me as an opportunity, what they could gain from me. It was a necessary severance."

I tried to keep my curiosity in check, but these small glimpses beneath his persona were important. "What about Harlow's mom? Is she not here in Ylem?"

He stopped with his wineglass halfway to his lips, a flicker of discomfort crossing his face before he resumed taking a sip. "She is."

It was clear this was a subject he wasn't comfortable diving into. Maybe they were separated or taking some time apart. I decided not to press my luck.

The waiter cleared our plates and presented ornate bowls of pink broth with some sort of foam floating on top. My first sip revealed the distinct taste of lobster.

"What does your daughter think about all of this?" I asked, hoping to shift the focus.

"We have opposing views on many things. She has a lot to learn. She's still too soft for it, but one day she'll inherit Ylem and take my place."

And that day would surely come once Midas was out of the picture.

"My daughter doesn't grasp the broader context of how the world was spiraling toward its end, regardless of my actions. The way people were mistreating the earth, political systems crumbling, resources depleting more and more, and the sickness that was already spreading even before I tampered with it."

I concealed my clenched fist under the table. "I've been wondering, why the need for Angels if there's no virus within the walls? Why's immunity so important?"

He took a sip of his soup before replying. "The risk is always present. Especially as new strains emerge, or the airborne contamination strengthens. If Ylem's going to be around for thousands of years to come, surely it will come in contact with some form of it. And our latest research suggests that over time, as our blood mixes with the Angels', our people may evolve to be naturally immune. Especially as the breeding program develops."

My spoon clanked a little too hard against the rim of my bowl. I tried to cover by setting it gently to one side as if I was finished.

For the next course, the waiter brought out a large smoking stone with a marbled cut of meat cooking on top. He placed it at the center of the table, then expertly sliced it to serve us each a delicate portion. At any other time, my mouth would've been watering, but Midas was in the middle of giving me a critical look into Ylem's agenda.

"I heard... What's this breeding program? Am I next?"

Another smile stretched across his face, hinting at unspoken thoughts. "In your case, the circumstances are more unique. Your blood type needs to be matched with one that offers the highest probability of passing on your rare abilities to the next generation. It would be a shame if this gift ended with you, but it turns out we did find someone who's highly likely to produce a child with the same blood makeup as you. Not only would it be a miracle, but it would also ensure your bloodline stays connected to Ylem for generations to come. A strategic chess move on the board for both of us."

I sat frozen, my mouth slightly open, unable to process what I'd just heard. "…Who is it?"

He took a slow, deliberate sip of wine, as if to toy with me. "My daughter, Harlow."

And there it was. The reason he had planned this extravagant show. What he was asking of me was utterly insane. Internally, I was screaming, doing everything I could to resist the urge to reach over and strangle him right then and there.

I was barely eighteen. My birthday had come and gone while I was surviving alone in an airplane hangar in the middle of the desert. His mind was so twisted.

"I'm a bit young to be a dad, don't you think?" I ground out through a tight jaw. "And Harlow can't be much older."

"The child will be cared for sufficiently. And naturally, you won't be engaging in any intimate activities with my daughter. My daughter has…specific tastes when it comes to romantic interests. Either way, she'll carry the baby, but the process would be done through a lab, carefully monitored and assisted."

I was on the brink of being sick. I abandoned my food completely, pushing the plate away.

"Tye, you're going to be here for many years to come. Do try to enjoy Ylem and understand the vision—"

In a sudden burst of rage, I stood up and swiped my plate from the table. It hit the floor with a crash, shattering into dozens of pieces and prompting Maverick to enter quickly with his weapon drawn.

It was obviously not the reaction Midas was expecting from me. His face turned hauntingly dark. "I've been generous with you, yet you're clearly not showing me the same respect!" he scolded. "Perhaps some more time in the camps will remind you of the path you should be on. Whether you consent or not, it *will* be done, but I assure you, your cooperation will make things much easier for you." He rose in his chair. "Maverick, take him back to the camps. He'll stay there until he learns his place."

And with that, I was forcefully marched out of the restaurant, while the patrons watched in shock.

12. WILLA

I stood in the upstairs of my Seabird home, where sunlight streaked through the dusty hallway. Laughter sounded from my brother's room, a reminder of our hours spent talking there. I stepped closer, hearing two voices—was it us?

My hand reached for the doorknob, and as I slowly opened the door, I saw Malik with someone... but it wasn't me—it was Imani!

I woke with a start, the vivid dream lingering in my mind. It was the first time Malik had appeared to me in a dream since he passed—and one of the rare ones I hadn't had in a long time. I was happy to see him and Imani, but now, as I lay in the soft sheets, a heaviness settled over my heart.

I'd been at Harlow's penthouse for a full week now, enough time to learn the routine. As the early morning light filtered through the heavy curtains, I quickly rose and pulled out my gray uniform, ready to start the daily chores with the rest of the staff.

Despite my initial determination to find a reason to hate Harlow—the daughter of a man I wanted to see burn—I found myself struggling. I wanted to despise her, to hold onto the anger and use it to fuel me. But Harlow made it difficult. She was kind to everyone, her demeanor gentle and genuine. She seemed to move to the beat of her own drum, avoiding the flashy events that the other wealthy families indulged in every night.

Each day, as I worked alongside the other staff members, I searched for flaws, for some indication that she was like her father. Yet, I found none. Harlow was different. She moved through life with a grace and independence that was both intriguing and frustrating.

As I buttoned up my shirt and tied my hair back, I couldn't shake the image of Malik's face from my dream. His eyes had been so clear, filled with a warmth I hadn't felt in so long. It was a brief moment of comfort, a fleeting connection to a happier time. If only Malik knew what the theories in his letters had unraveled. Now, as reality set in, the weight of my mission pressed down on me once again. I wondered when I might run into Midas, but until then, I needed to stay focused.

With a sigh, I stepped out of my room and joined the others, ready to face another day in Ylem.

My early hours were filled with routine tasks. I cleaned the large windows, dusted the rooms, emptied the trash, and wiped down the counters and art displays.

As I finished gathering a few fashionable pieces of laundry from Harlow's expansive walk-in closet, I was startled when she rounded the corner.

"Hey," she said, sitting at her ornate vanity at the other end of the closet.

"Sorry, I was just picking up."

"Oh, don't apologize. I'm just touching up my makeup really quick." She patted some shimmering powder onto the apples of her cheeks. "Do you wanna go for a walk?"

I shouldn't have been surprised by the offer; Harlow always treated me more like a companion than a maid. Having been cooped up for so long, I thought the idea sounded infinitely better than doing more chores.

"Sure, that sounds nice."

We walked the trail of a botanical garden only a few blocks away from her skyscraper. The path ran through a raised platform that provided gorgeous views of the city.

Despite the two guards following us, they were far enough behind that Harlow and I were able to converse without listening ears.

"This is the only place I feel sane in this city," she said.

I couldn't help but notice the birds singing in the treetops, something I hadn't heard since before the outbreak. "It's beautiful."

"You were brought here from the outside, right?"

I quickly went over my prepared backstory in my head, just in case she pried. "I was."

"What's it like?"

I let out a knowing laugh, but I decided not to divulge more than I needed to. "It's a nightmare. Hard to even describe out loud."

Her brow wrinkled with concern. "I can only imagine. We moved to Ylem when I was ten. I hardly remember it."

"It's nothing like this ... Even compared to before the outbreak, I'd say this feels pretty different. To me at least."

"I'll admit, I've only known some version of this life. I'm very lucky. Sometimes I feel guilty, even. I wonder why someone like me can be born into all of this privilege, while there's kids out there born into hardship."

Her words sounded heartfelt.

"Well, you can only control what you do with that privilege. That's what matters," I said cautiously, not wanting to overstep.

"I've begged my father to undo his wrongs, but he's adamant about his mission for a *new world*. There's no going back for him now."

The familiar fury bubbled in my chest. I took a deep breath of the fragrant floral air. "So I take it you two aren't close?"

She settled on a garden bench near a trickling waterfall. "We never have been. I was close to my mom before she passed. I blame him for what happened."

I blinked quickly, trying not to give away any shock. "I'm sorry to hear that." I knew better than to reveal too much, like how I could relate to losing loved ones, but I couldn't pass up the opportunity to find out more. "I lost my older brother. We were very, very close."

She took my hand, inviting me to sit beside her. "Aria, I'm so sorry. Was he infected?"

"No, thankfully. It was a bad wound. Is that what happened to your mom, infection?"

"Yes. It helps me, knowing she's kept here in Ylem, but I miss her so much, it aches." A tear rolled down her glittered cheek, leaving behind a streak of sorrow. "I can still see her face at the exact moment she turned..."

Now I knew why the burden of inheriting Ylem fell to Harlow alone. "She may not be with you in person, but I can see all the amazing things she shaped in you," I said, gently squeezing her hand.

Her expression warmed, and I could tell my words resonated deeply with her. "Thank you, Aria. You have a good soul."

As touching as our walk was, I was thrown right back into chores when I got back to the house. The usual family concierge was out for routine viral testing, so I had to do a grocery run for the chef, Manny. Even though it was a mundane task, I was eager to see more of the city for myself.

My conversation with Harlow stuck with me. Even she understood that her father's actions were destructive and the cause of so much loss. I hadn't dared ask too much about how her mom got infected, but I couldn't help but wonder how Midas could live with himself, knowing his power-hungry ways hurt his own daughter. He could turn a blind eye to the rest of the world, but he couldn't escape her.

A driver eventually picked me up at the front of the building. I sat in the backseat of the luxury SUV and watched the world outside the tinted windows speed past. The road was eerily empty; there was no sign of the bustling metropolis I'd imagined. With all the trains constantly zipping by, I figured that having a car must be a perk reserved only for the top tier.

We drove past a giant spherical building, a black-glassed structure I'd seen every day from the window of my bedroom, but this was the closest I'd ever been to it. The sheer size of it was overwhelming, and the notable increase in security around the property, visible even from this distance, was telling. This was where Midas lived. I couldn't help but fantasize about storming in there and ending his reign of terror now, but I knew the reality—I'd be shot and killed before I could even make it within a few blocks of the place.

Soon, we arrived at the marketplace. Carrying my shopping bag, I stepped into the grocery store, which felt like stepping into the future. The sliding doors opened with a soft hiss, revealing a minimalist, beautifully organized space. Sunlight streamed in through large skylights, illuminating the wide aisles. I'd fantasized about places like this during various moments of starvation on my journey.

It was clear that only personal shoppers were permitted here. Everyone browsing wore gray uniforms and a significant number of guards stood by, monitoring them.

Everything was perfectly arranged, with floating shelves displaying products in neat, visually pleasing setups. Digital labels provided all the information needed, from nutritional details to the family name of who had provided what. In the produce section, fruits and vegetables were organized in geometric patterns. Every section was efficient and easy on the eye.

I grabbed a cart and unfolded the list the chef gave me, starting down an aisle and avoiding eye contact with any of the other soldiers. As captivated as I was by the surreal experience of being back in a fully-stocked grocery store, I tried to be quick yet thorough in collecting the ingredients for the required dish, some sort of herb-crusted lamb, and thought back on some tips my aunt gave me when we used to cook together.

It was while I was debating the ripeness of the tomatoes that I overheard two of the guards nearby.

"I mean, they never stood a chance on the frontlines. The number of Teeth out there nowadays is wild."

"Well, yeah, that's why most of them are retreating back to the bordered cities. Finally realizing they lost the fight."

The mention of the frontlines grabbed my attention. That's where Dustin was stationed last. The news was unsettling. I couldn't go on living if I lost Dustin too.

"That's why these young gun soldiers are joining rebel groups now. They're waking up to the fact that they were always collateral and never stood a chance out there. Now they need another purpose and they wanna get back at their governments—it's fuckin' pathetic. No sense of honor."

"Well, they'll cut it out soon. They're in way over their heads with these petty attacks on us. Failing every time. It's like a paper boat in the ocean—" The soldier stopped mid-sentence. "Hey, you!"

I quickly threw a few tomatoes into my bag and moved towards the herbs, but he palmed my shoulder and spun me around.

"Why do you look familiar to me?" he asked, eyeing me with suspicion.

My heart pounded in my chest like a drum, each beat echoing the fear now coursing through my veins. "I've never seen you before," I said meekly.

"Yes, you have ... You don't recognize me?"

I swallowed to buy time. "No, I—"

"I work for Harlow. I had a few night shifts at her place last week. Saw you there."

My shoulders, which had been tightly hunched, finally relaxed and dropped. "Oh, right—"

"You two! Back to your stations," came another voice.

One of the other soldiers, clearly higher ranked, ordered the gossiping men back to their corners. I quickly broke away and strode down the nearest aisle, my heart still racing with residual anxiety.

That was close.

As organized as the market was, I was overstimulated by the newness of it all. It took me a long time to complete the extensive shopping list, especially with Dustin on my mind. I got back to the penthouse much later than I'd anticipated.

"You're lucky this is for tomorrow's meal and not tonight's," Manny chided as I entered the kitchen.

I left the groceries on the counter and the other aides began to unpack them. I then went and found Harlow in the living room. She was surrounded by a full glam team, getting some final touches done.

"Aria! I was starting to think you got lost or something," she said with a carefree laugh. "I have to go to this awful gala tonight. I missed too many and now my dad says he's starting to look bad, so I have no choice."

"You look amazing at least," I offered.

"Leave us," she told her entourage, and they left the two of us alone. "Thanks. I like to dress up, but there's no one there I care to impress... That's why I enjoy having you around. You're not snooty and fake like the other girls who try to befriend me."

I laughed lightly.

"Wait, Aria—would you come with me?" she asked suddenly.

"Me? I-I don't know if that would be a good—"

"I'll let you borrow something! Oh, please. It'll be so much more fun if you're there with me. No one'll think twice about it. People bring their assistants all the time."

I felt my smile drop.

"I didn't mean it like that," she said quickly. "Please? It'd make me so happy to have some girl time."

"If you want, of course—"

"Hell yes! Okay, come with me!"

Harlow whisked me away to her closet, a wonderland of insanely high-end outfits that left me both amazed and overwhelmed. She was like a whirlwind, pulling dress after dress off the racks, each one more extravagant than the last. We tried on countless looks, her excitement infectious, making the experience surprisingly fun despite the opulence.

Eventually, we landed on a look that couldn't have been further from my usual tomboyish style: a blood-red silk dress with off-the-shoulder sleeves. The dress clung to my frame, the rich fabric of the skirt flowing elegantly as I moved. Harlow's enthusiasm was contagious, and despite my initial hesitation, I found myself smiling and twirling in front of the mirror, both of us laughing.

The glam team swooped back in to finish the look, adding the final touches to my hair and makeup.

Before long, we were dropped off at the gates of a massive estate, where people dressed to the nines were funneling in, their laughter and chatter filling the city air.

I couldn't help but get lost in the fantasy for a moment. The estate was a vision of luxury, every detail crafted to impress. But as we approached the entrance, reality crashed back in. Midas may very well be here.

My heart began to race, adrenaline pumping through my veins. I took a deep breath, bracing myself for whatever was to come.

Inside the grand hall, I watched Harlow make her obligatory greetings. She was very good at playing the part, but I'd known her long enough to notice her forced smile slipping in between conversations. Eventually, she'd made her rounds, and we were able to enjoy some snacks and drinks in a quiet corner of the ballroom.

"What's this event for?" I asked Harlow in a whisper, having noticed the number of uniforms mixed in with the elegant outfits among the crowd.

"Most of the families here contributed forces to our military. Different world leaders and such. But I couldn't tell you any more. All these events blur together."

I took a large swig of champagne.

We were interrupted by a trio of teens, two girls and a boy dressed in extravagant clothes.

"Oh, Harlow, you made it out of the house! Glad we got to see you, finally," one of the girls said, her tone dripping with sharp friendliness.

They completely ignored me, almost closing me out of the circle entirely.

Harlow kept her composure, her smile never faltering. "Well, my good friend here convinced me," she said, nodding towards me. "Aria."

My face grew hot as the trio looked me up and down, judging me with their eyes.

The boy smirked. "We are 'osting a rooftop party at my pent'ouse tomorrow afternoon," he said in a French accent. "You should come, but you will 'ave to come alone as we are at full capacity."

Harlow didn't miss a beat. "I'm busy," she replied coolly.

Realizing they weren't going to get the approval they wanted, the three of them walked off, whispering among themselves.

As soon as they were out of earshot, Harlow and I exchanged a glance that nearly made me burst into laughter.

Just as our smiles subsided, a chime silenced the room, drawing everyone's attention.

On the raised platform at the far end of the ballroom, Secretary Croft approached a mic. She was in her usual golden uniform, but a cape now draped off one shoulder. Even when she was in uniform, her features made her stand out with an air of regalness.

"Honored families of Ylem, I hope you are all enjoying the night. I will try to make this brief so we can continue our beautiful evening. I would like to take a moment to address a military matter while I have your attention."

I could tell by the way the energy in the room shifted that the guests took her words seriously.

“As many of you are aware, there was a recent attempt on our walls. The rebel group responsible was indeed larger than what we usually encounter. However, I wanted to personally assure you that they stood no chance against our formidable defenses. Our security measures are stronger than ever thanks to your joint contributions.

“In response to the increasing threats, we have reinforced our jamming signals for aircraft and enhanced our anti-missile systems. Nothing will ever come close to breaching our walls. Our defenses remain impenetrable, ensuring the safety and security of Ylem.”

There was a wave of applause, a stark contrast to how her words made me feel. How in the world would Rowen pull off a successful attack on a place so heavily protected? Even from the inside, it sounded unlikely.

“Additionally, our top scientists continue working tirelessly, and new possibilities are coming to light. The attacks will most likely continue when the outside learns of our innovations, but we will not falter. With Ylem holding the cure and paths to immunity, we *will* become not only the last nation standing, but the most powerful one.”

This time the applause was twice as loud, with cheers of approval and pride.

“And now, it is my honor to introduce the visionary leader who has made the coming together of the most powerful people in the world possible. Please welcome, Midas Rothfield.”

I felt rooted in place, unable to move. Goosebumps erupted all over my skin. I whispered his name under my breath, almost as if trying to make sense of it.

As Midas took the stage, the room’s atmosphere changed, like the oxygen had been taken away. His presence was suffocating, his rigid posture and sly smile dripping with arrogance.

Still, the respect he commanded was undeniable. The crowd erupted in more cheers. I felt a chill as his cold blue eyes seemed to sweep over me as he scanned the crowd. Finally seeing him in person was surreal and terrifying. The man responsible for everything that had broken me.

"Thank you, thank you… I stand before you today with news that marks a significant milestone in our journey. Our research has achieved a remarkable breakthrough. The Angel Program is developing in ways we only dared to hope for. While I can't divulge all the details just yet, I promise that an upcoming event will showcase the full extent of our scientific advancements."

His confident voice reinforced his dominance, and the room hung on his every word. My hands were starting to shake with rage. Tye was surely collateral damage in all their cruel explorations.

"Are you okay?" Harlow whispered to me, placing a kind hand on my back.

I gave her a weak smile, hoping it was convincing enough for her to buy it for the moment. She turned back to watch her father.

"I want to extend my deepest gratitude for your unwavering contributions to our vision. It is your support and dedication that have made these advancements possible. Together, we are stronger than ever before, and the future of Ylem is brighter than we could have imagined."

The room exploded into another round of applause, and this time, my chest tightened so much, it was hard to breathe.

"I'm going to the restroom. I'll be right back," I told Harlow, and rushed out of the ballroom into the adjoining hall.

Even the act of putting distance between Midas and me brought me instant relief. I'd spent so long fantasizing about taking him down that just seeing him in the flesh sent a shockwave through me.

I managed a few minutes alone in the marbled bathroom, calming myself. I took a swig of water from the faucet, trying to steady my breathing. Finally, Harlow came in with concern all over her face.

"Aria, is everything okay? You're worrying me."

"Yes. Sorry. I haven't had alcohol in a while. Think I drank too fast."

She dabbed my damp forehead with a soft handcloth. "Well, I called the driver so we can head home. He's out front."

She gingerly led me out into the hallway, where a sudden procession of soldiers strode past with Secretary Croft and Midas. I flinched, quickly falling behind Harlow, my heartbeat quickening.

It wasn't just his imposing presence that unsettled me. My eyes darted from one stern face to another, and it was one of those faces that made my breath catch in my throat.

Just a few soldiers behind Midas, watching him say goodbye to his daughter, was a striking head of white-blond hair. Recognition hit me like a jolt of electricity. His face, the unmistakable tattoos. *Maverick!*

Time seemed to slow as I struggled to process the sight of him, a flood of memories and emotions overwhelming me. It was all too much.

I shrank back further, trying to make myself as small as possible. If it wasn't for the ridiculous outfit and heavy makeup, he might have spotted me. My mind raced, questions and fears swirling chaotically. *He's still working for them?!*

I could feel my palms growing clammy, but like a gift from the universe, one of Harlow's guards directed us to the exit out back, where the car awaited us.

I sat facing Harlow in a leather seat of the spacious car. "I shouldn't have come. I'm sorry I ruined the night."

"Are you kidding? I just had to show face. I wanted to get out of there the second the speeches started. It's getting harder to listen to my dad talk about all this science shit... It takes me right back to losing my mom."

I wanted to change the subject to anything that would get my mind off Maverick, and to keep her from noticing how strangely I'd acted. "Can I ask how she got infected?"

She looked away for a second, gathering her thoughts before finally locking eyes with me. "...My mom used to be a well-known medical photographer, documenting treatments and outcomes. She put it down for a long time once I was born, but she started it again when all my dad's work began with Zenith.

"Because they were keeping things so secret, she was one of the only people he trusted to document it. She was exposed to the virus. Even all the safety protocols weren't enough, being that close to the source. I blame him, fully. He was messing with things he shouldn't have ever gone anywhere near. She slowly turned into one of those things, right in front of me. Probably one of the first Dark-Eyes to ever exist."

Hearing her firsthand account of Midas's early plotting was chilling. "Harlow, that's horrible. I can't even imagine how hard that was on you."

"He keeps her body here, preserved in a morgue. Even after death, he treats her like some test subject. I don't think I'll ever be able to forgive him..."

My own turmoil with my parents seemed trivial compared to what Harlow had experienced. I took her hand and moved to sit next to her. "I think it's amazing who you've become, despite your parents," I said.

Harlow suddenly leaned over and kissed me. I pulled away, not from feeling threatened, but from utter surprise and being caught off guard.

Her face immediately turned red, a deep blush spreading across her cheeks. "Aria, I'm—I'm sorry. I don't know why I did that. I guess I drank too much as well."

I quickly tried to remedy her embarrassment. "It's okay. I just—I don't feel physical attraction to anyone like that," I stammered. "It's not you."

I offered a smile, hoping to ease the tension. Harlow's eyes searched mine, and I could see the mixture of emotions flickering in them.

"It won't happen again," she said, finally. "Friends last longer than lovers anyway."

We both laughed as the car pulled up to her high-rise.

13. TYE

Being back at the camps for a few days now had been like stepping back into a nightmare I'd briefly escaped. The prison-like culture was hard to readjust to, especially after experiencing the luxury of the Basilica, even if it was just for a short time. The downgrade was almost unbearable, each day a reminder of what I'd lost.

But I still couldn't shake just how insane Midas's proposal was. Bringing a child into this torn-up world seemed cruel, and I knew they wouldn't stop until they replicated whatever gene made my blood so rare. The thought of him using his own daughter this way made my skin crawl.

I remembered how scared Riley was when she found out she was having a baby. It was an added obstacle on top of all her other fears. If only she was here to let me know how it all turned out.

Being forced into parenthood was bad enough, but my feelings for Willa complicated everything even more. Having a kid together had never crossed my mind, but I definitely envisioned a future with her, whatever that looked like. The idea of being with her forever seemed impossible now, but it still made me happy to picture it.

Scarier still was the prospect of being tied to Ylem forever. My kid would be a byproduct of their horrific experiments. It was a future I didn't want, but considering my limited options, it felt like I was trapped. Each day in the camp, I felt heavier with the realization that I was at an impasse, the weight of it pressing down on me.

I'd confided all of this in Vale and Beckett, and they agreed Midas was an outright tyrant, but what they remained steady on was that I needed to play the game. They were of the mindset that if Midas was going to get his way, whether I agreed or not, I may as well make it easier on myself, and use the agreement to get back in his good graces after I'd ruined whatever headway I'd made.

The boys were up to date with everything I'd learned from Midas, but when I pressed Vale about his progress with New Year's Day, he made me promise not to speak another word about the plan. As much as I was itching to learn more, I stopped bringing it up.

We were getting dressed in the locker room after a quick shower, one of the few places where the guards actually gave us privacy. Still, we had to be careful. There were always ears around.

"I didn't realize I'd been placed with his daughter until I overheard one of the guards talking about it on the way back to the camps," Beckett said, fully caught up in recounting his new station.

"She seems nice enough," I said, keeping my voice low, "but I still can't imagine her carrying my kid..."

Vale shook his wet hair out. "As it stands, both of you are in great positions for the cause. Consider yourself lucky and stay sharp."

All three of us quickly made to finish dressing when a guard entered the changing room.

"Vale, you're due," he said sternly.

"The bloodsuckers await," Vale said sarcastically, buttoning up his jumpsuit. "See you two later."

With a quick peck on Beckett's cheek, he left with the guard.

Beckett and I sat together in the Commissary, picking around some glob of what was almost shepherd's pie. Despite the noisy environment, Beckett's mood seemed heavy, like he was lost in his thoughts.

"Are you okay? I thought you were happy to get assigned somewhere else. You said your last assigned family was awful," I said, hoping to spark a bit of his usual enthusiasm.

Beckett glanced up at me. "It's not that. I've just been thinking about Xander a lot lately. It's like the memories have slowly been coming back after we talked about him."

I felt a stab of empathy. I couldn't blame Beckett. Even though I hadn't known Xander that long, his death still affected me. All that Beckett must have been feeling, having his heart broken by Xander and being left with all the unfinished business they had, only to find out he'd died tragically, was a lot for anyone to process.

"I get it. I'm sorry for springing it on you."

"No, I needed to know. It felt like an open wound that would never heal. At least now it can start."

"You know," I began cautiously, "you can always talk to me about it, even if it's painful."

Beckett gave a small nod, his eyes reflecting a mix of pain and gratitude. "Thanks, Tye. I've been keeping it to myself. It's just hard to put that on Vale. I never want him to feel like he's not as important to me as Xander was. I guess, I just really want to know... how did it happen? How did he go?"

I paused, looking down and composing myself before meeting his gaze again. As much as I didn't want to recount the experience, I could tell it was important for him to know.

"We ran into some hostile survivors. It led to a shootout and Xander got hit. He fought hard, but we just didn't have the tools to help him... He had his friends by his side, though, right up until the last second."

I watched as he absorbed the news, his expression shifting through a range of emotions. "Thank you," he choked out, a tear escaping the corner of his eye.

I was back in Chiron's medical examination office, a place that never failed to unsettle me. It wasn't just the imposing guards watching closely; there was something about Chiron that kept me on edge. He didn't quite fit the mold of an enemy, but he wasn't my ally either. One thing was certain, though—seeing Chiron always meant I'd be subjected to some uncomfortable experiment of the week.

As I sat there, my mind raced. Did he already know about Midas's plan for me to conceive with Harlow?

My silent question was quickly answered by Chiron. "Today, I'll need to collect a sample from you so that we may begin the artificial conception process. Is that something you're open to doing willingly?"

His tone was as professional and unemotional as ever, but I could see a flicker of discomfort in his eyes. The words hit me like a punch to the gut.

"Do *you* have any moral issues with this?" I asked, feeling a surge of anger. "Forcing us to have a kid, bringing a baby into this messed-up world? And not to mention, for selfish scientific reasons. I can't imagine Harlow wants any of this, either."

Chiron sighed, his usually calm manner slipping just a bit. "I've seen scientific nightmares I never imagined possible come to life. This isn't going to be the thing that shakes me. I'm sorry you're caught in the crosshairs of our research, but ultimately, you're only responsible for providing a sample. Surely you can do that."

I took a deep breath. I hated that I was even in this position, and Chiron's clinical detachment only made it worse. "I think we both know there's no real choice for me here," I replied, unable to keep the bitterness from my voice.

Chiron didn't answer, but the slight shift in the guards' posture told me everything I needed to know. This was happening whether I liked it or not.

I stared at him, frustration and surrender washing over me. It was clear that Chiron, despite his own morals, had resigned himself to the role he played in this corrupt place.

I took the sample cup he offered me and followed a nurse to a bathroom down the hall.

The following day, I was surprised to learn how quickly my compliance was relayed to Midas. A brigade of golden guards, this time led by Maverick, arrived to return me to the Basilica. Not wanting to risk being seen interacting with Vale and Beckett, I shot them a subtle look of reassurance before I was blindfolded and swept away.

On the train, Maverick removed my blindfold and sat across from me, his expression more charged compared to his usual neutrality.

"Secretary Croft too busy for me again?" I asked to break the silence.

He seemed to catch himself bouncing his leg anxiously and stilled. "She's with Midas. There's a military parade later today."

I arched my eyebrows. "Why on earth's a parade necessary?"

He glanced around to make sure the two guards outside the carriage doors still had their backs to us. "After the last few attacks on the wall, Midas wants to make sure the people of Ylem maintain full confidence that we're untouchable."

I couldn't help but clock his use of 'we.' As well as the fact that his leg started bouncing again. It seemed everyone was off lately. "You good, Maverick? What's going on?"

He took another look at the guards before meeting my eyes. "If I tell you something now, you *can't* react. They may not be able to hear us, but any sign that you and I are exchanging more than common pleasantries, we're both fucked."

My stomach dropped at his warning. The mere anticipation of what he was about to reveal was already jarring. "... Okay."

"Swear it."

"*Promise.* What is it?"

He seemed to struggle with the words, but eventually... *"I saw Willa here in Ylem."*

Nothing could have prepared me for those words. Despite everything that had crossed my mind, it was so unfathomable that even after he said them with such solemnity, it sounded like an elaborate joke. As it sunk in,

I forced myself to remain silent and still, just as I'd promised. I felt a sudden wave of lightheadedness.

"What... What do you mean? How is that—"

"I have no idea how she did it, but we know how Willa is. It was her."

I couldn't think straight. Suddenly, my reality had shifted, like I could feel her somewhere out there. I even found myself looking out at the city, as if I'd spot her in the window of some nearby high-rise.

"Where did you see her?" I asked, trying to keep my face from showing too much shock in case the guards were watching.

It occurred to me that she could be a prisoner here. That the forces behind Ylem had finally caught up to her.

"It looks like she's been recruited to work for Midas's daughter. How she pulled that off is beyond me, but they were together at an event. Clearly, they don't know it's her. She looked different, like she'd changed as much of herself as she could. She may've spotted me, but she made sure not to let on."

The train was starting to slow as we got closer to the Basilica. I spoke faster. "Does she know I'm here?"

I could tell Maverick had already considered this. "I'm assuming that's *why* she's here. Whatever she's up to, she's not acting alone."

I avoided his eyes at those words. Just because Maverick had confided in me, I still couldn't trust him enough to let him in on any knowledge of the secret coalition working against Ylem. Willa must've been in on it. It made perfect sense.

Just as the train came to a stop, a sudden wave of happiness overtook me. I couldn't help but smile to myself, knowing that she was here and that, once again, Willa had gone to impossible lengths to find me.

As I arrived at the globular mansion, the houseman swiftly plucked me from Maverick's side and led me directly to my quarters. He handed me a formal outfit he had picked out and said, "The guards in the hall will escort you to Midas when you are ready."

I felt a little overwhelmed by how quickly I was thrown back into their circle, but I didn't want to question anything. It was better we all forgot my outburst. I dressed quickly, and the guards escorted me to Midas's room, of all places.

When I walked through the grand doors, the room was so large that I didn't spot Midas right away. His room took up the entire top floor, with a dome-like ceiling so high that he had an entire Stegosaurus skeleton in the foyer of his bedroom, towering over a luxurious sitting area.

His triple king bed, the base carved from beautiful dark stone, was against the back wall. Various artifacts and art pieces were placed among the fine furniture around the room. It looked like an elegant bedroom within a museum, but it wasn't eclectic. Everything seemed to have been curated with impeccable taste.

Midas had two aides help him finish dressing before he walked out of what looked like an equally outlandish bathroom. He greeted me with a hint of lingering annoyance, no doubt due to our last encounter, but quickly returned to the cold, even tone that I remembered from when we first met.

"Welcome back," he said. "It's good to see you've come around."

I felt the weight of his icy gaze. It was clear that our last interaction had left a mark, and I feared that Midas's trust in me had backtracked.

I knew I had to do something to set things right. With immense difficulty, almost biting the inside of my cheek, I forced out the words I dreaded to say.

"I'm sorry, Midas." My voice was barely above a whisper. "I appreciate you letting me stay here. I shouldn't have acted out like that."

I was nervous that he could tell I didn't mean it, but I could sense a flicker of appreciation in him. He tilted his chin slightly, acknowledging my apology.

"You took the news better than my daughter at least," he said with a sigh of frustration, before taking a seat in one of the leather armchairs to slip on his polished dress shoes.

"You're young, and I didn't consider that you might not grasp the full context of our work here. I tried to use your blood within me to transfer to an infected. It's apparent no one else can inherit the reviving effects of your abilities through transfusions, so it's crucial to replicate your genes for the future—we can't risk losing this extraordinary gift in a hundred years, or if anything happens to you. We've collected many Angels from around the world, but none possess what you have. Such phenomena haven't been recorded since ancient texts and myths. This is *monumental,* Tye. When I learned that my own daughter had an ideal blood type, it made perfect sense to link you two, even if the baby has to be conceived in a lab. It's a necessary move in this intricate game, and you're a key part of the board."

The tail end of his point reminded me that I was, in fact, not a human being to them.

Just as it seemed we were about to delve into the heart of the issue, the door swung open and Secretary Croft walked in, holding an important looking envelope. "Here's the official announcement speech. Are you ready?" she asked Midas.

A sense of unease settled over me. An announcement? The way the black envelope was sealed with an excessive amount of tape seemed ominous.

"I am," he responded, putting it in the inside pocket of his golden-brown wool blazer.

As Midas and his entourage began to leave the room, Secretary Croft held me back. She fixed me with a stern look and said, "Mind your behavior, Tye. We're all watching you."

I swallowed hard. The gravity of her words lingered as she pushed me down the corridor to follow the others.

When I stepped onto an open floor somewhere in the middle of the sphere, I was immediately struck by the sight of golden soldiers everywhere. Maverick was among them, a rifle at his side.

"Where's my daughter?" Midas demanded, his tone cold and commanding.

"She refused to attend, sir," one soldier replied, clearly nervous to deliver the news.

Midas's expression darkened, but he didn't respond. Instead, Secretary Croft and several guards led him out onto a wide, curved balcony overlooking the city. The whole affair looked like a well-choreographed dance.

When I was brought closer to the tall glass doors, I saw an ocean of people below, and beyond them, legions of soldiers and war vehicles. The sight was mind-blowing. It was my first real glimpse of Ylem's vast population and its formidable defenses. The cheers from the crowd were so loud that they shook the windows.

Maverick stepped out, leading me onto the balcony to join Midas. The noise of the applause grew even louder. My face grew hot as I realized they were all looking up at me now. Like I was some symbol of Ylem's scientific achievements. I wanted to disappear, but I was frozen by the ferocity of Midas's followers.

The parade today was clearly more than just a show of strength; it was a demonstration of power, a reminder of Midas's control over every aspect of our lives.

He reached into his jacket and pulled out the envelope. The crowd fell silent as he opened it. He approached the microphone before him and began to speak.

"My people, many of you were brought into my fold because you had significant influence and power. Talents and gifts that greatly contribute to society. Today, we are a combined force of nature, and only getting stronger. You know me for my extraordinary contributions to both tech and science, but before we enjoy today's parade, I'd like to include you in my next venture."

I scanned the spectators, seeing the awe on their faces.

"I brought you to Ylem to guarantee your safety from the primitivism beyond our walls. To ensure you could continue enjoying the lifestyles you were accustomed to, despite dwindling resources, leeched away by the lesser people of the outer world. And to offer you immunity from a virus that still ravages everything outside these border. I've spoken to the heads of your families, and to my trusted council, and we are all in agreement. As we continue to see resistance to the growth of Ylem, and a rapid increase in infections outside, we are implementing a new battle plan: an extermination."

I slowly turned to look at Midas, dreading what he'd say next.

"We are coordinating strategic aerial bombings around the world, which will not only significantly deter any powers from rising against us, but also reduce the number of infected roaming and spreading the virus. Together, we will secure the future of Ylem and maintain our dominance!"

As the crowd exploded into a deafening roar of support, a cold wave of terror washed over me. I felt a surge of panic for my friends and the rest of the world. My mind raced, picturing the devastation these bombs would leave, the lives lost, and the chaos that would ensue.

Maverick and I exchanged a look of concern; it was clear that even he hadn't been aware of this plan. Fear and helplessness twisted in my gut.

Midas quieted the crowd again with a simple raise of his hand. "And now, turn your attention to the streets behind you, and witness the forces we have—"

BANG!

Screams rang out at the sudden sound of a gunshot. I might've thought it was part of the parade if it wasn't for the spider web of cracked glass that appeared just behind Midas's shoulder. The shot had missed him by inches.

Chaos swirled around me. Golden guards jumped on top of Midas to shield him as a second bullet whizzed by.

BANG!

Midas was quickly whisked inside, while Maverick drew his weapon and pushed me down behind the railing, before Secretary Croft grabbed me by the back of my collar and pulled me inside. I only had a second to witness the crowds dispersing as soldiers flooded in to secure the areas below.

Has the New Year's plan been set off early? Those shots were aimed at Midas's head!

Croft moved swiftly and with purpose, dragging me deeper into the bowels of the grand structure. The cacophony of shouts and gunfire began to fade, muffled by the mansion's thick walls.

The descent was disorienting, the once familiar corridors giving way to darker, more unwelcoming hallways. My heart pounded with adrenaline.

When we reached the lowest level, Midas stood still, visibly shaken—a sight I'd never imagined. His usual mask of composure was cracked, fear filling his eyes.

"What the hell was that out there?!" he yelled.

Secretary Croft's voice cut through the tension as she barked orders at the soldiers. "I want every floor swept and secured! Go!"

Midas hurried to a metallic door embedded in the wall, scanning his hand on a sleek palm reader. The door slid open with a mechanical clank, revealing a large emergency bunker.

"Come, *now*!" Midas's voice snapped me out of my daze, the urgency in his tone undeniable.

I hesitated. I was surprised his concern extended to me, until I remembered I was nothing more than an important asset to Ylem.

Secretary Croft stepped forward, her expression tense. "We don't know where that bullet came from. You stay in the bunker with him 'til I find out," she ordered, her voice resolute.

I stepped inside the cavernous square. The sudden realization that I'd be stuck here, alone with Midas, was unnerving.

Midas called out to her. "Tell Maverick to go retrieve my daughter!" he commanded, his voice echoing in the enclosed space.

The door sealed shut behind us with a final thud. The room shuddered, and I felt a strange sensation of movement, as if the entire bunker was an elevator descending deeper into the earth.

Finally, it came to a stop. Midas and I stood awkwardly in the silence, which felt stark against the hurricane of chaos we'd just escaped outside.

Eventually, he collapsed onto a large couch against the wall, catching his breath. Although the bunker was furnished and clearly well supplied, I hoped we wouldn't be here long enough to need any of it. I could barely look at Midas after the plans he'd revealed.

He somehow always managed to push the limits of his madness. I was trying to keep my composure, but every week it seemed he found a new way to prove that his evil had no bounds.

Whoever let that shot off must've felt the same way. The only mistake they made was that they missed.

Surely with all the soldiers present, they'd never get away with it. I was shocked they even managed to position themselves to take the shot at all. I only hoped that if they were part of the collective Vale worked with, they wouldn't all be exposed when the shooter was caught.

I couldn't help but imagine Willa, somewhere hidden in the crowd, firing that gun at Midas. He was, after all, the source of so much of her pain. But if it was Willa, one thing was for sure: she wouldn't have missed. She wouldn't have compromised the greater plan unless she had a guaranteed opportunity to take him out.

I was itching to get back to the camps and see what Vale knew about all of this, but for now, this personal moment with Midas was a chance to learn more about the bombing plans. Maybe I'd be able to bring details back to Vale and his coalition.

Midas was now pouring himself a glass of wine from a polished concrete bar at the back of the room.

"I bet you're disappointed they missed," he said coolly.

I forced down a lump in my throat, but said nothing.

"I know you think I'm a monster, Tye. But one day you'll see."

I chose my words carefully. I had to make him believe we were starting anew. "If I'm gonna be here for the rest of my life, I want to understand you. I'm trying, Midas. I really am."

He seemed to accept that answer, pouring me a glass of wine and handing it to me. We both took a seat across from one another.

I kept my tone conversational. "Your whole philosophy is that the people outside these walls aren't worthy because they drain resources and don't contribute. But what about the younger ones who won't get a chance? I know a kid my age who's a genius inventor and can make anything out of scraps. I have another friend with a newborn baby. How can you know what they'll become if you bomb them all?"

He smiled, but it was absent of any soul. "Your sentiment's noble, but it's impractical in our current reality. Resources are finite, and the world's overrun with chaos and disease now. The chances of survival for those children and your friends, despite their potential, are slim. If anything, extermination is an act of mercy. We must focus on preserving and advancing those who are already secure within Ylem. By ensuring our survival and progress, we create a future where our children and their potential can be realized. It's a bitter truth, but sacrifices must be made for the greater good."

The harshness of his words boiled my blood. I didn't know why it still shocked me. This new plan was the old plan. He'd always wanted a world reset, and his first attempt didn't pan out the way he'd hoped. He truly believed in this ruthless logic, and based on what I saw at the parade, it was clear the people of Ylem did too.

I had to steer the conversation in a different direction or I risked exploding on him again. "Will they bring Harlow here, or does she have her own bunker?"

The real motive behind my question was to find out if Willa was okay.

He took another sip of his wine. "It's protocol that she be brought to the Basilica's bunker if unobstructed. She should've been here today, but she always lets her emotions get in the way of her duties... She's perpetually angry with me, no matter what I do."

I could tell the assassination attempt had left him feeling mortal and vulnerable.

"When her mother was infected from contamination, Harlow decided then and there that I was to blame for it all. It happened because of my research, under my watch."

I suddenly felt the blood rush to my feet. I put my wineglass on the table to make sure I didn't drop it. "I thought you said her mom was here in Ylem?"

"She is. Cryofrozen. I hoped one day there'd be a way to undo what happened to her. And now there is..."

As honorable as that seemed, the hairs on the back of my neck stood up as I connected the dots. Midas intended to use my blood to resurrect his infected wife. "... Me?"

"You."

The heavy tension in the room was suddenly interrupted by a voice over the intercom. *"This is Secretary Croft. The shooter has been apprehended. It was a disgruntled soldier who seemingly acted alone. We're looking into it, but your daughter's safe and waiting for you upstairs. You're clear to move out."*

Midas gave me a hard look, making it clear his moment of vulnerability had passed. He walked over to the keypad and pressed something that raised the bunker back up to its original position.

I was thankful for the rush of fresh air as the doors slid open, revealing a crew of guards ready to take us back to the main floor.

14. WILLA

Maverick betraying me was one thing, but actually seeing him walking side by side with Midas was gut-wrenching. The moment happened so quickly that I questioned whether I'd truly spotted him at all, or if it was my paranoia playing tricks on me. The last time I'd seen him, he was at his lowest point—his face gaunt from relapse, torn between his feelings for me and Ylem's grip on him.

He looked healthier and stronger now, but his golden uniform left no room for doubt: he was still under their command. Whether it was through blackmail, as he claimed, or by choice, wasn't my current concern. I was worried he'd blow my cover now.

I couldn't even begin to guess what kind of leverage they had on him. After we left him at the border camps, there was no way of knowing if he'd gone crawling back to Ylem and exposed Tye's escape plan.

I still thought about him, and hoped he was okay, but I'd had no choice but to cut all ties. His betrayal had gutted me, and having seen him walking freely among the enemy had been eating at me all week.

Having some leisure time today in Harlow's indoor pool was a welcome distraction from it all. Aside from the guard hovering over us.

"I get you're doing your job, but can you maybe stand guard *outside* the door? It's a bit creepy, watching us in our bikinis."

Harlow was as blunt as ever. I tried to hide my smirk.

The guard turned so red, I could almost see the blush reflected in his metallic uniform. "Of course, ma'am."

He quickly left to take up his new position, and Harlow and I let out the laugh we were holding back. It echoed off the lofty tiled ceiling.

"It's been nice having you around. I'm so happy to finally have someone who gets me," Harlow said genially, sipping her orange spirit.

It'd been easier than expected to get close to Harlow, not only because I actually liked her, but also because it was clear she was lonely and really just needed a friend. A factor I was sure Rowen and June had considered when pulling the strings to plant me here.

"It has its perks," I joked.

She splashed me in retaliation. "Wish we could get some sun on the deck tomorrow, but there's some military parade I'm dreading. Lately, it feels like my father says *every* occasion's mandatory."

The thought of Ylem's forces marching on full display immediately sucked the fun out of the room. Rowen did say they were so formidable that Ylem would have to be strategically taken out from the inside rather than head-on.

I made an effort to keep things light, sensing Harlow was already stressed by her father's summons. "With your silver hair, you look like a real-life mermaid swimming around," I told her.

She brushed a hand through it. "I'd better! This color takes so much maintenance. I only dyed it so I'd look as opposite from my father as possible. The jet-black hair was always a dead giveaway."

Harlow had been vocal about her disapproval of her tyrannical father, but I wondered what that meant for the future.

"When you lead this place one day, what d'you imagine it'll be like?"

I watched her closely to ensure I wasn't crossing a boundary, but she seemed too lost in thought to object.

"I try not to think that far ahead. I don't agree with how Ylem does things, and I know the outside world stands no chance without the Angels. I guess I'd release them, if that's what they wanted."

"D'you think there's any chance your father would go for that before then? I mean, if you guys are developing a cure, there's gotta be a point where they're not needed here anymore, right?"

"I don't think so." She dipped her head back in the water, as if to wash away the shame of her answer. "I love him, but I lost faith in him a long time ago."

I couldn't seem too invested, so I grabbed my drink from the edge of the infinity pool and took a long sip before speaking. "I didn't have the best relationship with my parents, either. I get it."

"... I just want my mom back," Harlow said solemnly. "My only hope now is the Ichor. They're saying this one Angel's blood is different from all the others. That it can actually *revive* someone from the dead and heal their infection for good."

My drink nearly spilled as my head swam with the revelation. Suddenly, it all clicked into place—Ylem's intense focus on Tye now made perfect sense. I floundered, struggling to form a coherent response because I *knew* she was talking about him.

All I could muster up was, "... What do you mean?"

"I don't get all the sciencey parts, but that's what I know," she said. "They've been expediting all the trials so that my father can try it on my mom. To bring her back."

I kept my hands underwater so she wouldn't see them shaking.

"I'm nervous, though," she continued, pushing up to sit on the edge of the pool and wringing out her pearly hair. "I wonder if she'll be the same ..."

Before I could ask her more about it, or learn anything about Tye and his exact whereabouts, one of the aides came into the pool atrium.

"Harlow, the nurse is here and ready for your transfusion," he said.

I couldn't help but notice the brief flash of jealousy in his eyes as he glanced my way. It was common among the other staff these days; they had all noticed Harlow favored me.

Harlow unrolled a crisp towel from a lounge chair nearby. I did the same.

"If I must," she said begrudgingly. "Aria, maybe don't watch this time. Get some fresh air and tend the garden 'til I'm done?"

Even though I wasn't actually queasy at the sight of blood—I'd seen oceans of it on the battlefield—I had no problem obliging her. Fresh air sounded great after what I'd just learned.

"Sounds good."

Leaving Harlow to her transfusion, I changed and made my way to the rooftop garden, a common feature atop the major buildings in Ylem. From this height, I could see the verdant green roofs on all of them, a sharp contrast to their sleek exteriors.

Stepping onto the grass, I felt transported to another world. The space was designed to resemble an ancient Greek garden, complete with marble statues and lush greenery. The sounds of birds filled the air, and I took a moment to absorb the serene view.

As I wandered further in, I noticed other aides tending to the garden. I joined in, picking up a watering can and filling it at a nearby faucet, then began watering the plants along the border of the rooftop.

Now understanding why Tye was so important to Ylem, I considered the implications of his ability to bring a dead person back to life. The potential for both good and evil was immense. What could this mean for the world? The possibilities were endless and overwhelming, and with his blood being the true definition of a miracle, it seemed there was no hope he'd ever get the freedom he wanted so badly.

Naturally, the thought crossed my mind—who would I bring back to life if it were possible? I pictured Malik, still lifeless in my parents' bed. If the Morts hadn't reached him, he'd still be there. Then there was Imani on the shelter floor; Archer, in the depths of Ground Misery...

I forced myself to halt my wandering mind. I had no real understanding of what Tye was capable of, or how any of it worked.

In my daze, I almost didn't notice the two aides pausing their tasks. They rose to their feet to greet none other than Mother June, who had just stepped out into the garden. She was holding a clipboard and pen, looking at me over the rims of her large square spectacles. She dismissed the two boys, and I realized she'd come to speak with me alone.

Her showing up at Harlow's house made me anxious, but remembering her last words comforted me. She'd proven to be the only person in this metropolis I knew to be on Rowen's side for sure.

"Take a seat, Aria," she said, gesturing to a small seating area near the corner of the rooftop. The choice to use my alias made it clear she was still being cautious about playing our parts.

From my seat at the corner table, I could see the entirety of Ylem and the preparations for the parade forming below us.

She positioned the clipboard in front of her as if to begin taking notes. "I'm here to carry out an evaluation on your performance working under Miss Rothfield."

I nodded, accepting the necessary pretense.

"It seems she's taken a special liking to you. That's good."

"It's been ... a better experience than I expected," I admitted.

Mother June looked around the garden like she was confirming we were alone, then placed her glasses on the limestone table between us. "We don't have much time, as this interview's meant to be short, but there's news."

I leaned in as she lowered her voice.

"Messages are becoming near-impossible to get in and out as Ylem tightens its defenses, so this may very well be our last contact. More soldiers on the outside are joining our cause. Even foreign military now know that their leaders have fled here while they've been left to stabilize their countries without them. All the while, more coalitions are forming around the states. There are those who are trying to unite them all in one single attack on Ylem."

I felt a surge of adrenaline, making my entire body alert and tense as I took in what she was saying. "When are they planning that?"

"New Year's Day. The military will be on high alert, so the attack will have to be carefully timed. But traditionally, Ylem is deep in celebration on that day, which is when their defenses are at their weakest, comparatively. Even so, it won't be easy."

"What can I do?"

"Pretend this conversation never happened, and continue to station yourself strategically as you have, until further notice."

I was itching to get more involved, but Rowen had warned me this would be my assignment. "And what about Tye? Do you know about this 'Ichor?'"

"Yes. That was only confirmed recently. It's one of the main reasons people are joining our militia now—everyone wants their loved ones back. It's a cause that's easy to rally behind. The Angels may hold the key to a future cure, but the hope surrounding Tye's abilities is what's really fueling the push to bring Ylem down for good..."

Her words trailed off as another aide came out into the garden and began scattering seeds around for the birds.

Mother June reached for her glasses and put them on again, turning back to her clipboard.

"Sign here, Aria," she said, just loud enough to be overheard, handing me the silver pen.

I could see a list of categories, all pre-rated and filled out already. Trying my best to come up with an impromptu signature, I signed on the dotted line as my alter ego.

Aria Sterling

Mother June stood and left me unceremoniously. I only had a few minutes to stare out at Ylem before I had to get back to work. As I processed what she'd told me, I watched the sun dipping behind the towering walls and the trains meandering through the city. People strolled along the clean sidewalks, with soldiers stationed on every corner. The thought of it all being wiped out soon left me feeling a strange mix of guilt and vindication.

New Year's Day was only a few months away, and I couldn't begin to picture what such an attack would entail. With so many moving parts, I could only assume there were other undercover players like me waiting to make moves.

Back in the main part of the penthouse, another aide informed me that my dinner was ready in the servants' hall. The way he delivered the message had a subtle edge. It was rare that I joined the other staff for meals these days. I could sense the jealousy simmering beneath his words, a clear indication that he'd noticed how often I got to dine with Harlow at her table.

As I made my way to the kitchen, I caught sight of Mother June leaving. She moved with her usual urgency, her gaze fixed straight ahead, never acknowledging my presence. But something in the fleeting glance between her and Chef Manny snagged my attention. It was brief—almost nothing—but enough to make my instincts prick up.

Manny met my eyes for just a moment, a silent acknowledgment, before turning back to the stovetop. There seemed to be a connection there, something unspoken between them. The thought that he might be part of the network brought a small, unexpected comfort. Though I'd never dare ask him outright, the idea that someone in this house might be quietly looking out for me gave me a little relief.

Quiet acts of resistance, like his, mattered just as much as the louder ones. If Manny really was part of the network, it meant I wasn't as alone as I felt.

And now, with word spreading and armies forming to join our cause, it finally felt like the sacrifices my friends and I had made—to expose

Midas, to reveal the horror behind Zenith—were leading somewhere. For the first time, there was momentum behind us.

That didn't mean we were safe. There was still time for everything to fall apart. I couldn't afford to let my guard down, but I let myself have this moment, to believe that maybe we were finally on the right track.

Maverick's loyalty, though, remained a question mark. When the time came, would he stand with us, or would he retreat to the safety of Ylem's shadow? I couldn't be sure. And not knowing where he stood—it bothered me more than I wanted to admit.

One thing was clear: whatever this attack looked like, it had to be merciless and brutal. They had to strike hard and fast, ensuring that this time, Midas and everything he stood for would be brought to its knees. Failure wasn't an option. Not when so much was at stake.

Just as I was finishing up my meal, Harlow walked in, her presence immediately commanding attention from the other aides, who paused eating and stood in respect. She didn't usually venture into these quarters.

I noticed a bandage on her arm. She looked tired, worn down by the weight of her guilt I knew she felt each time she participated in a transfusion.

She nudged me towards the hallway. "I have to go to my father's. He wants to talk to me," she said, her voice laced with a mix of annoyance and resignation. "He says it's something important. I'm only going because I think it's about my mother."

"You gonna be okay?"

"I'm sure he'll say something to set me off, like always, but yeah, I'll be fine. I've been anxious to find out when they're going to do it."

The thought of her mother's corpse flowing with Tye's blood suddenly made my stomach hurt.

"If you need anything when you get back, feel free to wake me up if I'm in bed already."

She hugged me tightly. "Seriously, you're the best. I'm sure I'll be there 'til late, so I'll just see you in the morning."

The day had been exhausting. The sheer amount of information I had to process left my mind in a chaotic state. I tried my best to get some rest, but my dreams were turbulent, filled with unsettling visions of strange experiments performed on Tye, and of Ylem engulfed in flames.

I was startled awake by the sharp sound of glass shattering upstairs, followed by Harlow yelling at someone. My heart raced as I scrambled to get dressed in the dim morning light seeping under the curtains.

I quickly made my way to the main floor, where I found Harlow in a heated argument with a soldier. It looked like she'd thrown a glass against the wall in anger, leaving fragments scattered across the floor.

"I won't be attending anything he's at for the rest of his fucking life!" Harlow shouted, her voice shaking with fury.

The soldier, visibly trying to remain composed, replied, "The military parade isn't until this afternoon, so take some time to calm yourself and—"

"Get out!" Harlow interrupted sharply, her eyes blazing as she pointed to the door.

The soldier looked defeated as he turned and left, closing the door quietly behind him.

Harlow stormed off to her room, slamming the door with enough force to make the walls tremble.

Some aides rushed in to clean up the broken glass, but my focus remained on her. Ignoring the nervous energy around me, I made my way to her room and knocked cautiously on the door.

There was no answer.

Taking a deep breath, I pushed the door open slightly, and the sight that greeted me made me pause. Harlow was curled up in her huge circular bed, the silk pillowcase soaked with tears. Apparently, I wasn't the only one who'd had a rough night.

"Harlow, hey. What's going on?" I asked, sitting at her bedside and extending a comforting hand to rest on her back.

I was nervous to hear her answer. It was the first time I'd seen her not looking impeccably put together. Seeing her like this, broken and sad, was jarring.

She sat up with her back against the headboard, but couldn't bring herself to look at me. "My father's disappointed me so many times, but this one really takes the cake. You're not gonna believe what he's asking of me."

I braced myself.

"The Angel I told you about—Tye, the one with the Ichor—my father wants me to have his child!"

I instantly felt lightheaded. Nothing could have prepared me to hear those words. "What? How does that—"

"Through the labs! It's so disturbing! He's trying to replicate Tye's genetics, and apparently, mine have a high chance of making a baby that will have the Ichor too. My father treats us like fucking science experiments. First my mom, now me!"

When I was too shocked to offer any comfort, she went on. "He doesn't think of *anyone* as a human being! Not the Angels, not his own family... That's how we ended up here. He puts his ambitions above all else. He treated the world like it was his own personal Petri dish that he could experiment with to get what he wanted, no matter the cost."

The news hit me like a punch to the gut, leaving me breathless and reeling. Morally, it felt like an abomination. Bringing a child into the world under these conditions, purely as a tool, was a horrifying thought.

I felt for Harlow, but the thought of Tye being forced into this made my heart ache. I knew he must also be feeling trapped, suffocated by the weight of Midas's demands.

But there was more to it than just the moral horror. I had feelings for Tye—deep, complicated feelings that I hadn't fully sorted through yet.

And now, knowing that he was being pushed into this, forced to father a child with Harlow, even if they weren't expected to be intimate…it twisted something inside me. A mix of jealousy, sorrow, and anger welled up, leaving me feeling raw and exposed. Of course, I'd envisioned what my future with Tye would look like, and although it never included a child, hearing that he might have one with someone else didn't feel right.

I wanted to protect him, to shield him from this nightmare, but as it stood, I was powerless against any of it. All I could do was stand by and watch as he was pulled deeper into a web of cruelty, and hope that somehow, we could all mentally survive all of this long enough to see Ylem fall.

I was stuck between needing to comfort Harlow and deal with my own feelings. All I could manage to say was the truth. "I-I'm in shock right now. I'm so sorry, Harlow."

There was a knock on the door, and another aide came in to open the curtains, trying their best to do their job without invading Harlow's space.

Despite their efforts, Harlow did not appreciate the intrusion. "I don't want to be bothered for the rest of the day. Tell the others," she said, clearly and assertively, yet still polite.

The aide dipped his head and quickly left us.

Through the tall glass windows, I could see crowds already gathering in the city center, getting ready for the military parade as the vehicles started lining up.

"Do you want me to stay?" I asked, feeling a bit out of place.

She shook her head. "I'm sorry I dumped that all on you, it's not your problem to worry about. I think I just need some time to process what I'm gonna do."

I stood up to go, briefly holding the headboard for support as the room seemed to be spinning. "I'll come back to check on you in a bit."

Despite my difficulty focusing, I went about my assigned chores around the penthouse. Life back in the safe zones was brutal, no question—scraping by, barely surviving day to day. But Ylem? Ylem culture was delivering blow after blow, each one hitting harder than the last.

I'd come here to learn what I could, to integrate into this twisted world, but even with everything dark I'd uncovered about Midas and his plans, it felt like the shadows were only deepening. Every day, what I knew grew heavier, and with it, the sense of helplessness chipped away at me.

The New Year's attack couldn't come soon enough. The not knowing, the uncertainty about what exactly was going to happen and what my role would be—it was driving me insane. But for now, I had no choice but to bide my time.

As much as I wanted to strike against Midas, that moment was still out of reach. My more immediate concern was my need to get to Tye—to let him know I was here, that I had his back no matter what he was being put through—but the camps they'd put him in were still a mystery to me.

Later that afternoon, as I was wiping down the panoramic windows in the living room, I saw the massive crowd gathering around Midas's sphere, and that feeling of being helpless only worsened. In the distance, soldiers were all lined up with their war vehicles.

I tried to tune it out and just focus on my task, but the cheers from the crowd were impossible to ignore, penetrating through the glass and echoing around the room.

I figured Harlow could hear it too, so I decided to go check on her again, see if she'd at least eaten something since the morning.

When I stepped into her grand quarters, I was relieved to see a silver tray by the door with the remnants of a half-eaten meal, and Harlow sitting at her vanity, braiding her hair. It looked like she was doing much better than when I'd left her.

"Hey," she said somberly, looking at me in the reflection of the ornate vanity mirror.

I sat on the edge of her bed behind her. "If you're not going to the parade, would you want to get some sun on the deck after all?"

Harlow smiled, then gestured towards the window as the chanting crowd continued to buzz in the background. "Don't think it'll help take my mind off everything, with this going on. I feel a bit better now that I've had a minute. It was more the shock of him asking that of me, but I am *never,* not in a million years, going to consent to that, regardless of his distorted logic for why it's such a good thing."

It was unsettling how quickly my mind accepted that Midas wouldn't bother seeking her consent to achieve his goals, judging by the way he operated. "How can he think that could possibly be a good thing?" I asked.

She dragged the brush through her hair with increasing intensity, each harsh stroke reflecting the clear anger that was bubbling within her. "The way he spoke about it would make you sick. My father's convinced that if I have a child with Tye, it'll secure Ylem's future. The kid would have Tye's rare blood, which he sees as a safety net for Ylem's immunity if anything ever happens to Tye.

"It's all about leverage and keeping control—he wants to make sure Ylem stays untouchable, with no one able to challenge us. It's like he's trying to create this perfect legacy that'll keep Ylem on top for generations, and he'll do whatever it takes to make that happen. He keeps using the fact that I'll inherit this place one day, and saying that these decisions are to set everything up for my success, but I don't want *any* of it!"

"But he can't force you, can he?" I asked, trying to find reason in the insanity.

She tied the end of her braid and turned to me. "I don't even know him anymore. I think I really reached my limit." She flinched as the crowds outside cheered even louder than before, and shook her head in disappointment. "*That's* what I'm inheriting. A bunch of elitists who can live here happily while they ignore—"

BANG!

Both of us jumped, and the cheering outside turned to screams.

We rushed to the window. From this angle, we couldn't see the platform the crowd was focused on, but the soldiers flooding into the throng and the panic that ensued made it clear that the gunshot wasn't part of the show.

The sound of a second gunshot made Harlow go so pale, it seemed her skin and hair had become one color.

"What's happening?!" I asked.

Before we could make any sense of it, three golden guards barged into the room. One immediately pushed me aside as they flanked Harlow.

"What's going on?!" she demanded.

"Some sort of attack, we're looking into it!" one of them said.

"We're awaiting orders on how to proceed while they secure the area!" said another.

Harlow and I looked at each other in disbelief. A disruption like this within the Ylem walls was wildly out of the ordinary.

If Rowen and Mother June hadn't emphasized so strongly that the timing of an attack had to be precise, I would have thought this was all part of the plan. So, whoever was behind it couldn't have been involved in the network.

It wasn't far-fetched to think that Ylem had other enemies, but something like this was bold and reckless, especially with so much military force around today.

I stared out of the window, almost paralyzed, watching the spectators duck while soldiers fired at someone in the crowd. I wasn't able to see who they took down as an overwhelming number of security staff swarmed them.

More golden guards flooded Harlow's room, barking orders into their comlinks as they swept through, checking behind curtains and along the balcony doors. Two of them stepped outside, scanning the street below with their weapons drawn. Through the open window, I could hear others shouting from the halls—"Secure the perimeter! Get eyes on the north entry!"—as boots pounded along the marble floors.

It wasn't until the comms chatter quieted that one of the guards turned toward me. He broke off from the others and grabbed my shoulder. "You shouldn't be in here," he said. "We need this room secured."

As he dragged me away, Harlow tried to stop him. "Leave her!"

"Ma'am—"

Just then, the door swung open and all the guards raised their weapons. To my complete shock, Maverick stood in the doorway. The moment our eyes met, everything inside me tensed.

The silence was so long, I was expecting the guards to shoot him down out of suspicion. Neither of us moved, neither of us spoke—just a long, heavy pause as we sized each other up.

Maverick's next move could change everything. Both of us were behind enemy lines, and I realized that whatever was about to happen, I would have to be ready.

Then, without having said a word to me, Maverick shifted his gaze to Harlow and the guards behind her. "There's been an attempt on your father's life. He's okay, but I've been ordered to take you to the Basilica immediately while they investigate."

His voice was steady, but the tension didn't dissipate. If anything, it only heightened. He hadn't exposed me, but he hadn't given me any reason to trust him, either.

Had he spared me, or was he protecting himself? He knew I had dirt on him just as much as he had on me. We'd both go down together.

15. TYE

The golden guards led us back up to the main floor, where the frantic energy of the incident's aftermath remained. Midas's entourage was in full debrief mode, their voices overlapping as they reported to him.

"The shooter was eliminated."

"An investigation is underway."

"We have an ID on him, and they're tracking his recent activities."

Through the whirlwind of voices and information, I saw Secretary Croft pull Midas aside. Her expression was tight as she quietly delivered the news. "Your daughter's here. They've shown her to her quarters."

Midas didn't hesitate. "Bring her to me," he demanded, his voice sharp with authority.

But the look on Secretary Croft's face told me this was more complicated than he realized. "She's saying she doesn't want to see you, and that she won't be staying long..."

Croft's voice trailed off, but Midas didn't wait for her to elaborate. He stormed off, a horde of security following in his wake, and I was swept along with them.

They flanked Midas as he angrily strode through the curved hallways of the mansion. The walls seemed to close in as we approached the far end of the spherical structure.

When we finally reached the doors to Harlow's room, Midas didn't bother knocking; he pushed them open with a force that made them slam against the walls. I hung back with the guards, standing just outside in the hallway, but even from here, I could hear everything.

Harlow's voice cut through the air, sharp and angry. "I told you, I don't want to see you!"

Midas's voice was raised and filled with the kind of authority that demanded obedience. "You don't get to make that choice, Harlow! Do you realize someone just tried to take my life? *This* is how you act when the family's in danger?"

"*Now* you care about family?" she shot back.

"As much as you'd like to paint me as a heartless tyrant of a father, I do. An attack on me is an attack on the family. You will stay under this roof for the time being. For your safety."

"I don't want to! If you care about me, you'd care about how *I* feel when you ask me to do what *you want.* You don't! You steamroll through everything!"

The surrounding guards kept their heads down, doing their best to appear disinterested, but it was clear they were all tuned in to the argument.

"I am trying to protect you, and to teach you so you can lead this place one day—"

"I never asked for that! If you're bringing Mom back, then give it to her!"

The brief pause that followed revealed just how much the mention of his late wife unsettled Midas. "... Your mother can't be next in line. We don't know the state she'll be in once revived. It will take time to adjust."

The sadness in his voice seemed to catch Harlow off guard, and her tone was softer when she spoke again. "I will stay here while you figure out if there's still a threat, but don't try to control me. Just give me space."

I expected Midas to rebut, but instead, he came back out into the hall and shut the doors behind him.

It was clear he hadn't realized I was close by. The way he looked at me made it obvious he was embarrassed that I'd overheard the exchange, though he quickly masked it by addressing the lead guard.

"Take Tye to get his dinner, then show him back to his room. The rest of you, report to your stations outside and reinforce the security already in place. We'll need extra eyes around the Basilica."

That night, the mansion was eerily quiet. The usual bustle of security stationed in every hallway was absent. Instead, they were all positioned around the perimeter, guarding every possible entry point. The stillness felt suffocating, especially after the chaos of the day.

I lay there in my room, staring at the ceiling, unable to fall asleep. The day's events kept replaying in my mind, especially the fight between Harlow and Midas.

I was probably the only other person who could truly understand what Harlow must be going through. Being used like a variable in an experiment felt incredibly wrong. It was unnatural, especially for the two of us, being so young, having to conceive in such a contrived way, on top of everything else going on in the world. How could Midas expect either of us to accept something like that without resistance?

My thoughts were interrupted by a knock at the door. At this hour, it was usually Maverick on shift to patrol the lower level where my room was.

"Come in," I called out, sitting up.

As expected, Maverick entered the room and closed the door quietly behind him. His expression was focused, and he wasted no time. "Throw on a shirt," he said, his voice low but urgent. "There's someone I want you to see, and we can't take too long. There's less guards inside the house tonight, so it's now or never."

Confused but intrigued, I hurried to get dressed and followed Maverick out of the room.

He was on high alert, peeking around corners as we moved through the dimly-lit hallways. I expected us to head up to the main level, but to my surprise, we stayed on the lower level where most of the staff slept.

Maverick led me to a room down a hall I hadn't been through before. He stopped at the door, his hand on the knob. "Go in. If you hear me tap on the door, it's time to go. If you hear me talking to anyone, hide until I come get you."

"Maverick, what's this abou—"

"Go!" he hissed urgently.

With no other choice, I pushed open the door and stepped inside, my heart racing with anticipation and a hint of fear.

And then, my heart nearly stopped altogether.

"Willa—"

She jumped into my arms and we hugged so tightly, as if we were trying to fuse into one. I spun her around, happiness bursting inside of me.

I looked into her hazel eyes. They were anxious and radiant at the same time.

She looked different—her overall health, her hairstyle. I was happy to see she appeared to be well taken care of, which was no surprise if she'd been in Harlow's care.

"Tye," she said, as if speaking my name out loud would make this moment undeniably real. "What are you doing here?!"

As our eyes locked, the world around us seemed to disappear. We crashed into each other, our lips meeting in a kiss so intense it felt like nothing else had ever mattered.

She was here. She'd pulled it off. The impossible had happened, and despite everything, we were finally in the same room again.

In that instant, it was the most uplifting moment I'd experienced since this whole nightmare began.

"Midas keeps me here. I can't believe *you're* here," I whispered, holding her face in my hands.

"Harlow insisted I come with her. She's been good to me." She scanned my arms and winced at all the needle marks. "How are you? Are you okay?"

"I am now."

We were smiling again. She took my hands in hers and squeezed them tight.

"Were you at the parade? Do you know who took that shot?" she asked, turning serious again.

"I was, but no, I was hoping you knew. I know there's a secret group against Ylem. Some attack's happening on New Year's—"

"I know. I'm part of the network. They placed me with Harlow. I wasn't there, but I don't think it was them."

"Of course you're in the network. I *knew* it," I said, bursting with admiration.

The way we were jumping right back into everything was like we'd never missed a beat.

"I don't know much more, but they told me to stand by and lie low," she said.

"Same here. One of my friends at the camps is part of it too. Did you hear about Midas's parade speech?"

Her face fell. "What now?"

"It's really bad, Willa," I warned, taking a moment to figure out how to even speak the words. "... He's gonna drop bombs around the world. Something about stopping the spread, and getting rid of rising forces against Ylem."

She walked over to the corner of the bed and sat, as if to keep herself from falling. "When?" she asked, her voice laced with fear.

"He didn't say, but if they catch wind of the New Year's attack, or if threats like today keep happening, I'm sure it's not far off."

"It just keeps getting worse... With Ylem on high alert now, I don't know how we're going to warn the others in the safe zone. I was told getting messages back there was hard as it is."

"Maybe Maverick can help?" I suggested.

The way her entire body tensed up at the mention of his name proved she was still harboring anger towards him. Understandably so. She lowered her voice even more. "We can't trust him, Tye. He's a wild card."

"Well, he's the reason I'm here talking to you."

Her eyes darted to the door, as if she was sending him her disapproval right through it.

"I know he made some really bad choices, but I've talked to him," I explained. "I don't think he told them I was on that plane. I think he truly cares about you and wants to help."

"Tye, you have no clue about the things he said to me when we were close, only to go back on them. I know there's good in him, but he still can't be trusted. Be careful what you tell him."

I decided not to push it. We had so much to catch up on and limited time, and I had no idea when I'd see her again. "How are the others?"

"The safe zones are a mess, but they're doing alright. We all live together. Everyone's healthy. Riley's daughter Rio's a happy baby. Otto and Ava are still together, and good. Their parents have been great with us. The only one we haven't heard from is Dustin. He had to report to the frontlines after you left."

I felt a smile spread across my face at the mention of my friends, but it quickly faded into a frown when I thought about Dustin still alone out there in the thick of it. He'd done so much for us.

I could see it was a point of worry for Willa, too. She took a deep breath as if to keep herself from getting emotional.

"How about your parents? Did you find them?" I asked gingerly.

"I did. Things are better with them. Losing my brother was hard on all of us."

I sat on the bed next to her and pulled her close. "I'm not gonna lose you again, Willa. This time we're sticking together for good."

Her face brightened, and we leaned in for another kiss, but before our lips could meet, a voice out in the hall made us quickly pull away.

My blood ran cold as we heard footsteps approaching. I rushed to crawl under the bed, Willa quickly sitting at the vanity across the room to make herself look occupied.

Though it was muffled, I could hear another guard's voice addressing Maverick.

"Midas wants you back at your station on his floor. I'll take over."

After a beat, Maverick's steps faded away, and the silence that followed felt eerie. I wasn't expecting to be stuck here overnight. My mind raced as I prayed Maverick would come back to get me like he said. If he didn't, if something went wrong... we were both finished.

The silence dragged on, nerves twisting in my gut. But then, finally, Willa crouched down by the bed, pulling me gently by the arm. She led me into the cramped adjoining bathroom, where she closed the door behind us and turned on the shower, the sound of water masking our whispers.

To my surprise, she was smiling. The humor in her eyes caught me off guard, but I could see it was her way of coping with the insanity of the situation. It reminded me of those times with Ava—how we'd dissolve into laughter at the worst possible moments.

I perched on the counter, pulling her close, feeling her warmth against me as the tension slowly drained from my body. For a few minutes, we stayed like that, holding onto the quiet connection between us.

Her hands traced down my arm, fingers lightly brushing over the bruises and needle marks etched into my skin. The reminder of everything I'd been through stung, but having her there made the weight of it easier to deal with.

Her smile melted away. "An Angel..." she murmured, as if grappling with how the word had become twisted here. "Harlow told me about the baby."

"... Yeah. Seems she and I both think Midas has reached a new low. I don't know what to do."

"I don't know if there's anything you *can* do. They'll find a way to make it happen no matter what, because they want that power that's in your blood."

Hearing her say it made it feel like I couldn't pretend it wasn't happening anymore. I felt tears well up in my eyes. "I can't believe all of this is happening. Of all the people in the world, why did it have to be me?"

She looked me firmly in the eye, as if to make sure I really felt her next words. "I can't think of anyone else who could get through all of this and still keep it together. And you got friends like me, like Riley and Ava. Otto and Dustin. We're going to fix things, and you're going to get out of this."

I rubbed away the tear before it could slip down my cheek.

Even with the weight of the conversation, I couldn't help but feel grateful for the extra time with Willa.

"Willa, promise me," I whispered, my voice coming out hoarse. "Promise me you'll keep yourself safe. We need to be careful."

"Of course. We'll keep each other safe. We can't trust anyone else except each other. We just need to make it until New Year's."

We talked a bit more about Vale, battle plan theories, and who else was in the network, our voices shielded by the steady rush of the showerhead—until we realized keeping the water running any longer might raise suspicion.

Eventually, exhaustion took over. Willa slipped into bed while I wedged myself under the bedframe, hoping for at least a few minutes of rest until Maverick returned.

Surprisingly, sleep came easier than I expected. Despite the cramped space, Willa's presence brought an undeniable calm that settled over me.

But peace was fleeting. Morning came quickly, and with it, the chaos of the previous day resumed.

I woke to the sound of the housemaid entering to wake Willa. She lingered, watching as Willa dressed and hurrying her to tend to Harlow upstairs.

The moment they left the room, I barely had time to process my relief before Maverick's arm shot under the bed, yanking me out by the arm.

"Come on." His voice was low, urgent.

We darted down the halls and back to my quarters.

I could see the tension in his body language—he was just as rattled by the close call as I was, but I couldn't help feeling a surge of gratitude for how he'd given me that moment with Willa.

"The doctor's here to see you," he said, his tone clipped.

It wasn't long before I realized Maverick wasn't taking me through the usual corridors to the transfusion lounge. He instead left me at the threshold of a large salon room I hadn't seen yet.

At the far end of the room sat a few onlookers in lab coats, holding tablets. I recognized at least two of them from the last experiment.

Dr. Chiron ushered me in and led me to the transfusion chair at the center. As I was trying to figure out why I'd been brought to this unfamiliar room, I spotted a steel-framed gurney just a few feet away.

The motionless shape of a body lay beneath a stark white sheet, the sight sending a cold wave of realization through me. My transfusion wasn't for Midas today.

"Tye. I'm happy to see you're safe," Chiron said earnestly.

I peeled my eyes away from the body, noticing the sparse number of guards in the room. It seemed every available soldier was still being utilized around the premises.

"Thanks."

"We're conducting today's experiment here in the Basilica for security reasons," Chiron said as he connected my IV.

I spotted several cameras set up on tripods at each corner of the room. I imagined there were others watching remotely. Once again, I had no choice but to comply.

Chiron addressed the onlookers. "Let's review Ichor's limitations before we begin today's demonstration."

He pulled a small clicker from his lab coat pocket. The lights dimmed, and a projection of text was cast across the opposite wall. The way his eyes locked onto mine made it clear—he wanted me to pay close attention, as if hoping the presentation would answer some of my pressing questions.

“There’s a window after death in which Ichor can be effective. If the body has decayed too much, Ichor cannot restore the cells because the tissue damage is too extensive,” he began.

“For living recipients, the process of transferring immunity from any Angel is not instantaneous. The blood must be transfused over a period of time, gradually reprogramming the recipient’s immune system and cellular repair mechanisms to mimic the donor’s.”

I was doing my best to take in every detail. As anxious as I felt, these were the answers I desperately needed, the ones that had been fueling my deep sense of unease.

“Ichor can heal wounds and cellular damage caused by the virus, but it can’t regenerate limbs or organs that have been completely destroyed. It can only repair existing tissue, even if badly damaged. The sooner the transfusion is administered, the greater the chance a severe injury can be fully healed,” Dr. Chiron concluded, just as the lights in the room came back on.

My attention was pulled back to the covered body as Chiron slowly removed the sheet to reveal a shriveled-looking Mort. It was long and lanky, like one of the more progressed types.

“The primary focus today is how the Ichor will affect a previously cryofrozen specimen,” he said as he began connecting the IV to the body.

It was starting to click. They needed to know, because the next time they tried this, it would be on Harlow’s mother.

As I watched the red stream of my blood flow through the tube, my heart pounded so hard I could feel it in my throat. The needle stung as it drained me drop by drop, and I couldn’t shake the sick feeling that came with seeing it course into the lifeless body lying across from me.

Its skin was an unnatural shade of gray-blue and covered in dark, jagged veins. Its eyes, bulging and black, were wide open, staring blankly at the ceiling.

I watched the crimson fluid seep into the Mort's veins. Nothing happened at first, like my blood was being swallowed into a black hole, but I knew better.

After a long, tense wait, the first sign was subtle—a faint twitch in one of its fingers, as if its body was trying to remember what it felt like to be alive. The monitors beeped louder. I held my breath.

Slowly, the black veins began to pulse, faint but noticeable; my blood was reactivating something deep inside the Mort. The gray-blue skin color started to change, the frostbite-like hue warming into a sickly white. It was like watching ink dissolve in water.

The Mort's face, twisted in a ghoulish expression of death, began to relax. The hollow cheeks filled out just slightly; the lips lost their blue tint. It was eerie, watching the transformation—a slow crawl from death to something almost living.

Its blackened eyes started to change, and I saw the faintest glimmer of brown irises beneath the dark sheen.

Its hand jerked again, this time more violently, and then its whole body shuddered. My stomach clenched as I watched it start to move. The head twitched to the side, like it was trying to orient itself in a world it no longer recognized.

It was human now... almost. But not quite. Its skin, though no longer gray-blue, was still too pale, too waxy. Its eyes—eyes that had once been dead—now looked terrified, lost.

It sat up slowly, like the effort was costing it everything. The movement was awkward, unstable, a body still figuring out how to use its muscles.

For a moment, I locked eyes with it—or him. I could see the struggle in his face, the faintest flicker of recognition. There was still something off about him, something not quite right. He was human now, yes, but not entirely. There was still that strange, distant hollowness in his expression, like a part of him was lost, left behind in death. He was alive, but not the same.

The room buzzed with excitement, but all I felt was a deep, growing dread. This was what they wanted—what Midas wanted. Proof that my blood could reverse his wife's death. But what kind of life would this be? What was this man, now?

I watched as the other technicians rushed over to examine him, the man I had unwittingly pulled back from the beyond. My eyes stayed locked on the scene until Dr. Chiron swiftly unhooked me from the equipment and wrapped my arm. Before I could process what had happened, the golden guards were already escorting me out.

"Thank you for your participation, Tye," Dr. Chiron called after me, just as the doors closed on the chaotic frenzy of excited researchers.

As the golden guards led me down the hall, my nerves felt shot. The sight of that body coming back to life—it shouldn't have rattled me as much as it did. I'd seen it done before. But this time felt more intimate, more vulnerable, and I couldn't shake the feeling that it had worked too quickly. They had clearly refined the process.

My body was exhausted from the transfusion, and I expected to be brought back to my room, but instead they ushered me into the elevator.

When the doors opened, I was back in familiar territory—Midas's office. He was waiting, as always, standing in front of a large monitor. I could see it in his expression—he'd watched everything. He seemed pleased, almost smug, his eyes glinting with a satisfaction that made my skin crawl.

The last thing I wanted was a repeat of the blowout we'd had before. I couldn't afford that right now. I braced myself for whatever praise or critique he might have following the demonstration, but he threw me for a loop.

"I want to talk to you about my daughter," he said, his voice calm and deliberate.

My mind reeled. After his insane demand the last time we spoke, what could he possibly want now? I couldn't imagine anything worse, but with Midas, there was always something.

"Go ahead," I said dully.

"The fertilization process has begun, and now that I know my wife will be back with us shortly, I need my daughter and me to be in a better place. With yesterday's attack and the ongoing attempts on our city, I need my family to stand firm and be a symbol of strength through all this chaos."

"And how can I help with that?"

"I would like you to spend some time with her. Get to know each other, make her feel more comfortable with the idea that you'll share a child. I don't expect her to be romantically interested, but I do think you may find some commonalities and maybe even the start of a friendship. You're both integral parts of Ylem's future."

My left hand instinctively moved to the bandage on my right arm. "Don't you think I'm doing enough for you already? Living here's great, but where do we draw the line?"

Midas smiled, almost like he appreciated my attempt at negotiation. "What more can I do for you? What would guarantee your best effort?"

I didn't have to think about it. It came to me instantly. "Don't drop the bombs you're planning."

He laughed out loud. "Something realistic. I'm asking you to spend some time with my daughter, and you're asking for the lives of millions—"

"Then Safe Zone 32, specifically. Spare it."

For a moment, he seemed caught off guard, as if he hadn't expected me to drill down to such a precise location. His eyes flickered with thought, and I could almost see the gears turning in his head. He stayed silent, thinking it over, his fingers tapping lightly on the desk.

Then, after a long pause, he nodded. "Safe Zone 32," he said slowly. "Fine."

Relief washed over me, but it was quickly followed by a creeping sense of worry. I'd gotten what I wanted—he'd agreed. But had I been too specific? Highlighting Safe Zone 32 was like putting a spotlight on the place. It was clear now that I cared about it, that there were people there I was trying to protect. My friends.

I'd given Midas something to hold over me. I had no choice but to hope I hadn't just marked a target on the very people I was trying to save.

16. WILLA

The past week at the Basilica had felt like living in the lion's den. I was so close to Midas, yet I hadn't even seen him. After the assassination attempt, he seemed to be lying low, tucked away in his sprawling mansion. The few times I thought I might catch a glimpse of him, it was always from a distance, just a shadow in a far-off hallway. It was frustrating—being here, being this close, and still feeling so far.

As much as being at the Basilica made me feel suffocated, the real frustration came from not being able to be near Tye. After everything we'd been through, seeing him again had filled me with a relief I couldn't quite put into words. I found him. He was alive, and despite the trauma he'd gone through, that familiar spirit I loved so much was still there. But the Basilica was a fortress of its own, massive and carefully monitored, and that meant we were never in the same place at the same time. We couldn't acknowledge each other, couldn't steal a second of privacy. It was driving me crazy. Every time I caught a glimpse of him, my heart jumped, but I had to play it cool, to pretend I didn't even see him.

Harlow had been doing the same, avoiding Tye as much as she could. The awkwardness between them was obvious, considering they were expected to have a kid together—something that made both of them uncomfortable, although she hadn't even agreed to it yet. I could tell it was eating at her too, the whole situation feeling more wrong every day.

The only person I was glad to avoid was Maverick. Even though he was the one who'd brought Tye to see me, I still didn't trust him, not fully. He'd somehow managed to weasel his way into Midas's inner circle, which unsettled me more than I liked to admit. The fact that I was still walking around free suggested he hadn't betrayed me, at least not yet, but that didn't mean the shoe wasn't going to drop at any moment.

For now, there were bigger questions on my mind. I'd been listening for any information I could pick up about the would-be assassin. Rumors were swirling among the staff that the attacker was a rogue soldier in Ylem's army, but none of it was useful. It was just the same recycled gossip about heightened security and how fortunate it was that Midas survived. Nobody seemed to be able to confirm why it had happened, and there was no chance I'd be able to get any info out of Mother June or Chef Manny with the way things were.

At least I had Harlow. She'd been leaning on me more than ever. She was restless, constantly on edge from not being able to return to her home across the way. She knew it was for security reasons, but she hated being stuck here with nowhere to go and nothing to do but wait. The more time passed, the more she seemed to withdraw, relying on me to fill the void. I didn't mind it. She'd been the better part of my time in Ylem, and when big things happened, by her side was exactly where I needed to be.

Now, as I tidied up her room, Harlow sat in front of her vanity, getting her hair touched up with fresh silver dye. She was quieter than usual today, barely acknowledging the stylist.

I carefully hung one of her decorated jackets in the huge wardrobe, turning back around to find her eyes on me. There was no need for words; I knew that look meant she wanted to talk.

My silent recognition must have been all the signal she needed because, with a subtle nod, she waved off the stylist, who quietly left the room.

As soon as the door closed, she let out a long breath, like she'd been holding it until we were finally alone.

I sat down across from her on the bed. "What's going on?"

"They're doing it this week."

A flood of awful possibilities of what she could mean hit me all at once, a reminder of just how bad things were in Ylem.

She took a breath, then continued, her voice quieter now. "They're bringing back my mom."

The hairs on my arms instantly stood up. I tried to pull back my reaction from a place of disgust into one of compassion. "How are you feeling about it?"

"With how things are going with my father, I'm sad to think what she'll be coming home to."

"Well, he's not making it easy," I said, letting a bit of my own anger slip through.

I observed her subtly, checking her reaction. She seemed to agree.

"I'm trying harder to keep things good between us. I… I even agreed to cooperate with the fertilization."

I couldn't hide my shock, and her face flushed with embarrassment. It was impossible not to feel an onslaught of emotions and opinions when it involved not only cruel practices, but also someone I loved so deeply. I was staring into the eyes of the girl who would be carrying Tye's child. It was hard to process.

"I understand," I managed to say, though my voice wavered slightly.

"Will you come with me tomorrow? My father's convinced that if I spend some time with the guy, I won't be so angry about the baby stuff. What do you think?"

My heart was caught in my throat. Of course, I would jump at any opportunity to be close to Tye, but the baby was the one topic I'd rather not hear them talking about. "Where are you going?"

"I need to get out of this glass ball of a prison. I said I'd go if he let us take a walk through the Grand Gardens. Kill two birds with one stone."

"Am I even allowed to go?"

She scoffed. "The fact that I agreed to go at all? My father wouldn't dare say a word to me about bringing a friend. Besides, we'll probably have twenty guards with us anyway. It won't exactly be a private moment."

There was no denying it—both getting to see Tye again and grabbing some fresh air sounded amazing.

"Sure. Anything for you."

The logistics of leaving the Basilica for the gardens were, as expected, extensive. I could tell Harlow was anxious when she requested that she and Tye take separate cars. Security protocols were complex before even getting in Harlow's transport, and then a small procession of security vehicles followed us across the city.

Even though it was only brief, each rare glimpse of Ylem beyond the heart of the city had me mentally mapping the layout. If this place were to become a battleground, knowing my way around might make the difference between life and death.

"This feels so weird," Harlow said, breaking my concentration. "Like I'm going on a first date or something. Wouldn't be the first time my father tried to force me to like a guy. He's embarrassingly traditional."

"I'm sure he knows this one won't be any different for you. Doesn't have to be romantic."

I hoped my sensitivity to their coupling didn't come through in my voice. It was clear Harlow wasn't attracted to men, but I couldn't help feeling a tinge of envy that she'd get to spend time with Tye.

"He seems nice enough. Anyway, it's clear my father's switched his efforts to making sure the Ichor lives on, rather than interfering in who I end up with. He's even putting resources into finding Tye's extended family out there. He hopes there's maybe another like him."

The way my hand tightened over the armrest almost broke it off. Had they not caused Tye enough pain?

Clearly she hadn't noticed, because she continued. "I'm praying when my mom's back, she sets him straight. Only one who ever could."

When we finally arrived, the reason behind the name Grand Gardens became immediately clear. It was no ordinary park—it was sprawling, filled with flowers I couldn't even begin to name, trees that must have been hundreds of years old, and statues that looked like they were from all corners of the earth. It was like someone had decided to rescue one of every kind of plant before the world crumbled and brought them here, to save what they could from the planned downfall of mankind.

Yet, even more arresting than the beauty of the garden was the view of the wall. I'd never been this close to it before. The sheer size of it was both terrifying and breathtaking.

Harlow and I stepped out of its shadow and into the sunlight. With the legion of guards in our wake, we made our way toward a massive fountain. Water cascaded from all sides like a veil, forming the centerpiece of the park. Everything seemed to orbit around it, like it was the core of this floral universe.

Sitting on the fountain's edge, flanked by a golden-clad soldier, was the core of *my* universe: Tye. It took all my effort not to smile when our eyes met. That urge quickly vanished, though, as the guard beside him removed his helmet, revealing white hair that gleamed in the sunlight. *Maverick.*

"Hey," Harlow greeted Tye, her tone upbeat. "Tye, this is Aria." She gestured toward me. "I wanted her to see the gardens."

He reached out, our hands meeting briefly. The second his skin brushed mine, it was like an electric pulse ran through me. I avoided his eyes, afraid that even a glance would give too much away. Pretending not to know him was hard enough, but with Maverick lurking nearby, it was unbearable.

Before the tension could stretch any further, one of Harlow's guards motioned toward me, pulling me away from the fountain.

"Stay put," he said gruffly, guiding me under a lone birch tree.

I watched him and the rest of Harlow's security detail fan out and position themselves at different points in the park, giving Tye and Harlow some space.

Harlow shot me an apologetic glance, but I waved it off, signaling that it was fine. It'd be interesting to know how she and Tye got along when she vented to me about all of this later.

My stomach lurched as Maverick unexpectedly made his way over to join me under the shade of the tree. We didn't look at each other, only stood side by side. Neither of us spoke for a while, the weight of unsaid words heavy in the space between us.

"Looks like you managed to get close to Harlow," he said, finally.

I fought to hold back the barrage of words sitting on the edge of my tongue. "Looks like you managed to get close to Midas ... "

We spoke softly, barely moving our lips, careful not to attract the attention of any distant guards.

"I'd ask what you're doing in Ylem, but I think it's obvious," he said.

"What *you're* doing here's the better question."

He shuffled his feet. "I feel like no matter what I say, you're not gonna buy it. You don't trust me."

"I wonder why that is."

"I saw you weeks ago, yet you're still walking around as Aria Sterling. I think you have reason to trust me, at least a little bit."

I put my hands in my pockets and clenched my fists. "It's going to take a lot more than that for me to trust you again, if at all."

Tye and Harlow were now strolling down a long path of magnolias, deep in conversation.

"When we went our separate ways, I stayed true to my word," Maverick said. "I stopped using. I told them I never found Tye. But they weren't gonna just let me walk away from all of this. I knew too much already."

"Tell me what they have over you that would make you do that to me. To Malik, for that matter. You promised him, and instead you betrayed us."

I could feel him turn to face me, but I kept my eyes straight ahead. I wanted to make sure nothing looked suspicious, but more than that, I couldn't bring myself to look at him.

"If you have to know, I'll tell you, but I know you're going to think even less of me."

I couldn't argue with that—I probably would.

"It was back when I was deep into drugs. One night, I was driving, high as a kite. I ended up causing a horrible car crash. The driver didn't survive ... I panicked and ran away from the scene. Somehow, I managed to avoid getting caught for years. You know, I actually turned my life around before the Outbreak Wars. I got clean, joined the military, and moved up the ranks.

"Just when I thought it was all behind me, that the world had bigger problems now, some government elites turned up. They knew everything about the crash. Turns out, the person in the other car was the attorney general's kid. And he hadn't forgotten. Of all the bad luck, right?"

Hearing the genuine pain behind his words had me fully engrossed in his story.

"They had all the evidence they needed to lock me up for life, but they offered me a way out. They roped me in. They knew my connection to you, and your connection to Tye. At the time, I didn't even know why they were interested in him, but the choice was clear. Either do this job for them or spend the rest of my life rotting in a cell. I couldn't imagine that, I'd come so far ... so I took the deal."

He must've seen my frown because he suddenly became defensive.

"Every day of it felt wrong. I never expected it'd get this out of hand. I was just gonna report back anything that would help them find him, like any other military mission, no questions asked. I didn't think about how much you cared about him, or how much it would hurt you. I didn't know about his blood. I went against everything I was trying to be ... I *really* do care about you, Willa."

His words hit me hard, stirring up the tangled mess of what I once felt for him and the bitterness that had taken its place.

I let the silence stretch, then changed the subject. "You're indebted to the government, but you're serving Ylem? So they're one and the same, then?"

"Not the same, but they're intertwined. That attorney general lives here. Most of the government officials do. I'm lucky I even ended up positioned where I am."

"Lucky to end up beside the man who caused it all? You told me you didn't want to help them anymore," I said bluntly. "Malik would still be here if Midas hadn't crashed that plane."

His hesitation to answer almost made me turn to him. I resisted.

"The best camouflage is standing with the enemy, where no one looks twice," he said eventually. "Isn't that what you're doing?"

I let out a dry laugh. "So prove to me you're really on our side."

"How?"

"Help me. Start by telling me where we are. Where is Ylem?"

He looked around cautiously to make sure the guards were still focused on Tye and Harlow, who were now sitting on a distant stone bench.

"The Patagonian Steppe. South America."

The fact that he actually told me caught me off guard. "What about the bombings Midas is planning? How much time do we have?"

"Early next month."

My throat felt like it was closing up, but I swallowed hard and managed to keep myself calm. The timing stunned me—before New Year's. That meant everything was closing in faster than we'd prepared for.

The chances of rallying for an attack afterward seemed completely out of reach, and I wasn't sure how much more mankind could endure. How could anyone survive another blow like this and still rise to fight? I desperately had to make sure someone in the network knew. Rowen and the others had to be warned.

Before I could push him further, Harlow and Tye got to their feet, and the conversation was over. Maverick had shown some promise of redemption, but there was still a long way to go before I could call him a friend.

As soon as Maverick turned to lead Tye back to their vehicle, I caught a glance from Tye. It was quick, but he knew. He could tell Maverick and me had exchanged words.

"Well, that was lovely," Harlow said, her voice strained but polite, still doing her best to maintain decorum despite everything that must have been going on beneath the surface.

"And quick," I said.

I couldn't see any visible signs of upset. They seemed to have gotten along, at least for now.

Before I could say anything more, the guards stepped in, efficiently sweeping us back to our vehicle.

The luxury car glided smoothly away from the gardens, and I found myself trying to read Harlow as she stared out of the window in silence. She was processing a lot, that much was clear, but it was hard to say what exactly she was feeling.

Finally, I broke the silence. "Was it bad?" I asked cautiously. "Felt like you cut it short."

"No, he's very sweet. And smart. I just didn't want my dad to think he was right and we hit it off like soulmates. But I think we got to a good place, considering the positions we're in."

Harlow was being vague, giving a noncommittal shrug that told me digging further right now wouldn't be a good idea. I'd find out later.

Suddenly, she started to smile. I blinked, confused. "What?"

"Maybe next time we should set *you* up with him," she teased, a playful glint in her eyes. "I know you're not into sleeping with anyone, but

I saw the way you looked at him. Admit it, you at least found him handsome."

I felt my heart jump, and for a moment, I was mortified. Despite all my efforts to act like I didn't know Tye, somehow our connection had still shown itself.

Harlow was sharp, of course, and I'd have to be more careful. I forced myself to stay calm and lean into it rather than deny it. "He was," I said with a casual shrug.

And, just like that, both of us dissolved into giggles.

The convoy of cars suddenly screeched to a stop, drawing our attention outside. A dense crowd had surged into the streets, completely blocking the vehicles from moving any further. Every person was staring at something up ahead.

"What's going on?" Harlow called to her driver.

She rolled down the windows and gasped. My stomach lurched violently.

Hanging by nooses in a city square were three bodies, swaying eerily in the breeze. Harlow's face paled as her eyes took in the gruesome sight.

I almost threw up when I recognized two of the figures. On either side of a hanged soldier was Mother June... and Chef Manny. My heart dropped.

The soldier in the middle must have been the gunman who'd tried to take Midas's life. My blood ran cold as the realization hit: Mother June and Chef Manny had been my only connections to the network. Ylem's forces likely uncovered them while investigating loose ends.

Harlow's expression shifted from shock to anger—likely directed at her father for ordering such a public display. She was still stunned, though, clearly shaken by the realization that traitors had been so close to her household.

For me, the unease ran deeper. This had been my only lifeline, the only way I could get messages back to Rowen and the others. Now, that connection was gone, and as far as I knew, I was completely on my own. Midas was always one step ahead of me.

The cars finally lurched forward, pulling us away from the harrowing scene.

When Harlow caught my eye, there was something deeply unsettling in her expression. "See how I try? I really do, and he always seems to make things worse..." Her voice was low, almost like she was talking to herself.

I hesitated before responding, trying to find some kind of reassurance that would mask any hint that I cared about their execution. "If they were traitors, he was only protecting you."

My words sounded hollow even to me, and Harlow's silence only deepened the tension in the car.

The rest of the drive passed in an uncomfortable quiet. When we finally arrived at the Basilica, Harlow wasted no time. She demanded to be taken straight to her father, and the guards escorted her away.

Separately, I was led down to the staff quarters, but on the way, I passed both Tye and Maverick. My heart raced as I made use of a brief second alone with Maverick when the other guards turned the corner with Tye.

I leaned in just close enough to whisper, "I need to talk to Tye. Tonight. Prove yourself."

The guards didn't notice a thing. Maverick didn't react, his expression unreadable, but I knew he'd heard me. My chest tightened. I hoped he would come through for me when it mattered most. I had to tell Tye everything I'd learned.

The rest of the day passed in a quiet haze. I hadn't seen Harlow, and I found myself at dinner alone with the staff, then helping out with the cleanup and the endless tasks of preparing the mansion for the night. At least the work was methodical, helping to keep my mind from the anxiety I'd built up through the day, though that could only last for so long.

Once the chores were done, I lay in bed staring at the ceiling, waiting to see if Maverick would come through. As the hours crawled by, my mind went to the good side of him—how he treated Archer like his little brother, how Malik trusted him, how he saved me more than once. He'd hidden so much from me, and I'd been mostly blind to his internal struggles that ultimately led to betrayal. My intuition had failed me there, but despite everything, deep down, I still didn't believe his spirit was evil. There was a part of him that was good. I felt it.

Just as I was about to give up hope of seeing Tye, a faint tap at the door broke the nighttime silence. I shot up out of bed, my heart in my throat. When the door creaked open, it was Maverick!

"This is the stupidest thing I've ever done. Hurry," he muttered under his breath.

Without another word, he gestured for me to follow.

Maverick led me through curved, candlelit hallways, his footsteps soft, careful. Every few seconds, he'd pause to check around a corner, his head snapping back as if expecting someone to appear out of thin air.

After what felt like an eternity, we reached Tye's door. Maverick gave me a stern look, eyes flicking to his watch. "Ten minutes," he said, his voice firm but quiet.

He opened the door. I slipped through, and as it clicked shut behind me, I threw myself into Tye's arms. He held me tightly.

"You two on good terms now?" he asked with a smile.

"He has a lot more to prove," I said. "A lot happened today that I need to tell you about."

"Tell me," he said, pulling me over to sit on the bed.

"The bombings are happening next month, way before the New Year's attack. There won't be any coalition if that happens."

"Next month?"

"Worse than that—Midas just executed the *only* two people I knew were in the network. How are we going to warn the others?"

He paled. "I hope they didn't get my friend Vale ..."

"I don't think so. The other one they got was a soldier. The one who attacked Midas, I think ... but it means they know there are others like me. They could be getting close to finding out who I really am."

"If I go back to the camps, I could try asking Vale if he can get a message out, but if they're cracking down, I don't want to be the reason they get him. He's being very careful."

"This is bad, Tye," I told him. "We're out of options."

"I did make a deal with Midas. If I got on Harlow's good side, he'd spare Safe Zone 32."

"Coming from him, that's as good as no promise at all."

"Then what can we do? We either trust Maverick for help, or hope Midas will keep his word."

A storm of conflicting thoughts was circling in my brain. Trusting Maverick enough to tell him about the attack and its details was still way too risky to chance. He was unpredictable.

"How did you get on with Harlow?" I asked, an idea forming.

He looked taken aback by the sudden shift in conversation. "Good. She opened up about her mom ... and we made a pact of our own. She seems to share a lot of the same opinions as us on her dad and what he's doing. We agreed to play the parts we've been given so it'll be easier on both of us. She's in a tough position too. No part of her wants to have this baby, but she'll do what she needs to do, and I'll do the same."

"Do you think we can trust her?"

He made a face, as if he was searching for hidden meaning in my words. "You'd know better than me. She seems trustworthy, but—"

"I trust her. Maybe she can help us."

His expression froze in disbelief. "Help us how? To do what?"

"Maybe ... Maybe she can get us out of here? We can get you on the right side, with the right people who can work on a cure, and we can warn the others about the bombs—help them prepare for it. Whether it hits them or not, that kind of destruction will affect the battle plans, no doubt about it."

I could see the wheels were spinning in his head. "You did the impossible getting into Ylem, so I don't doubt you can make getting out happen, but so much could go wrong. They'll lock me up, but they need me. With you ... I don't even want to think about what'll happen if we get caught."

Maverick tapped on the door, then peeked in. "Time to go."

I stood, still holding Tye's hand. "Let me figure it out."

17. TYE

With the traitors executed, the guards who had been repositioned outside for heightened security were back at their regular posts inside the Basilica, which meant seeing Willa again—even with Maverick's help—would be near-impossible.

The idea of Ylem investigating breaches in their midst was a constant worry gnawing at me that dug deeper by the hour—not just for Willa, but for Vale, too. If they connected anything back to the wider network, the entire plan for New Year's could be done for.

Worse, it could mean Willa's execution. That thought alone filled me with a fear so deep, it was hard to breathe just thinking about it. Losing her, especially in a place like this... that would be my final blow.

And then there was her suggestion of trusting Harlow. She seemed different from her father, true—almost his opposite in some ways—but the possible consequences of telling her anything about an escape were almost unthinkable. If even a word got out to the wrong person, it could unravel everything, and our one chance to bring Ylem to an end would slip away. Vale had stressed that fear to me more than once.

I wasn't sure what to think about Maverick in this case. He and Willa appeared to have reached some kind of understanding, but she still seemed more willing to trust Harlow. I couldn't blame her for that—Harlow's disapproval of her father was out in the open, while Maverick's trustworthiness was tangled up in their rocky personal history. She'd spent far more time with him than I had, so her judgment had to be sharper on this one.

Despite my doubts, I could see the sense in her plan. With the bombings approaching, we were running out of options. Getting Harlow on our side might be the only way to stay ahead of whatever Ylem had in store—and our best chance at saving not only our friends, but the entire resistance.

To add to my growing anxiety, Secretary Croft arrived at the Basilica the next morning to collect me.

"Whenever you're around, it never ends well for me," I said, stepping onto the metro.

"You're needed at the camp facilities for preparations," she announced. "The public resurrection is this weekend."

Although I'd been through endless rounds of testing and had already seen a body resurrected, I couldn't shake my nerves.

On the ride there, I tried grounding myself by thinking back to my recent walk with Harlow. The way she spoke about her mother lingered in my mind: *"Of all the terrible things my father's done, losing my mom is the only thing he truly feels guilty about."* She'd truly opened up, and the emotion she showed for her mother was genuine, even raw. From what Harlow described, I could see her mother had been a source of love for both of them—a big departure from everything I'd come to know about Midas.

I'd seen firsthand how the mere mention of her affected him. Maybe, if her mother were brought back, she'd be someone who could get through to Midas. And if Midas felt guilt, there could be a side of him that even he couldn't fully repress. The thought gave me a flicker of hope.

When I arrived at the camps, I immediately scanned the rec room, hoping Vale and Beckett were exactly how I'd left them. I was relieved when I spotted them, but I was expecting to see them together like usual. Instead, they were on opposite sides of the room. Vale was sitting at a table, locked into a game of checkers with one of the foreign Angels, while Beckett was curled up in a corner with a book, barely glancing up.

I wouldn't have thought anything was off until I tapped Vale on the shoulder, expecting a warm welcome, and all I got was a cold, dismissive "hey" before he went back to his game.

Having been so worried about him, the indifference was unexpected, and it stung. Maybe he was having a bad day or just needed some space, so I tried not to take it personally. Anyone locked up in here for this long was bound to have their patience tested.

I crossed the room to Beckett, who didn't even look up from his book until I stood right in front of him.

"Is everything okay with you two?" I asked, trying to keep my voice low. "What's going on?"

Beckett kept his eyes on his book, but gestured for me to sit beside him.

"We're good, but it's been weird," he whispered. "He's extra paranoid now that they've uncovered some of the network. He'll probably give me shit later for talking to you, but the silent treatment's driving me nuts."

"So what now? We can't be seen together anymore? You guys are my only friends here."

"I tried to tell him it looks weirder that we suddenly don't talk, but he said there's new guards weekly and they didn't used to pay attention like they do now. Best we interact as little as possible. I have to say, though, he's making me *wish* for a transfusion day just so I can get out of here and have some human interaction. This is the longest I've gone without being called for one. I guess all the security changes have held things back."

"Have you been following everything that's gone down?" I asked.

"Yeah, and so's Vale. Broken bits, but we know about Midas's new plan."

As if Vale could sense what we were talking about, he shot us a disapproving look over his shoulder.

"I'm gonna grab a different book," said Beckett, rising to break away from our chat.

This new charade we'd have to keep up was not making me feel good. The walls of Ylem were closing in even tighter.

I was barely settled when I heard my name called for my appointment. Without the usual pep talk from my friends, I felt the anxiety burrow even deeper. I tried to steel myself as the guards led me down the long, sterile hallways.

The familiarity of the chamber didn't make it any easier. The cold, metallic surfaces, the faint hum of machinery, the soft beeping of monitors—all of it felt depressing.

Dr. Chiron was already there waiting for me, his usual detached attitude in place. "Tye," he greeted. "Today will be very quick and easy."

I sat on the examination table. "Mm-hmm."

"You may recall we installed nanotechnology into your bloodstream not too long ago. It's been extremely vital in our newest developments."

"That's great."

Chiron likely noticed that his enthusiasm wasn't being shared. He began preparing a needle connected to a bag of neon-blue liquid, and when he caught my eye, he explained, "This IV contains a serum to ensure you're at your peak for this weekend's resurrection."

I couldn't wrap my head around how casually everyone discussed bringing someone back from the dead.

"That man you revived—what's he like now?" I asked, the image of his decayed body coming back to life still fresh in my mind.

Chiron busied himself at the monitor, which told me more than his words did about the experiment's results. "The longer someone's been dead, the harder it is for the mind to recover," he said, an edge of disappointment in his tone. "There's an adjustment period."

"Does Harlow know that?"

"Her mother's body was cryofrozen shortly after she passed," he replied, "which might mean a better outcome, since decomposition was halted. By anatomical standards, she wasn't dead for too long... but results vary."

We now knew my blood could bring someone back to life, but there were clearly a lot of unknowns hanging over it.

As he fed the liquid into my veins, he asked, "Your time with Harlow went well, I take it? She seems more open to the fertilization process now. I'll be seeing her not long after you for her follow-ups. It's best to get the difficult parts dealt with so she can focus on reconnecting with her mother."

The small talk was maddening. I had the urge to grab Chiron by the shoulders, to somehow jolt him into seeing the bigger picture. Willa had me imagining wild scenarios of turning more people from Ylem onto our side ... but Chiron had never struck me as the radical kind.

I could feel the euphoric sensation of the serum circulating through me now.

"I know the months of testing have been hard on you," Chiron said, "but you'll be glad to know it hasn't been in vain. We're on the precipice of making major breakthroughs with an actual cure, once and for all."

Despite how good the IV was making me feel, I wasn't smiling. "None of that brings me any comfort if Ylem's the only one gaining from it."

He threw a quick glance at one of the guards in the corner whose back was to us. "The first step is making it a reality. Then, *anything* is possible."

Chiron's words hung in the air, and when he glanced up, our eyes met. For a split second, I saw something different. It was like a flicker of understanding, maybe even of shared purpose. Subtle, but just enough to make me think he was suggesting more than he could outright say. Like he was acknowledging a possibility that went beyond Ylem's interests.

I didn't press him about it. Chiron had always been very guarded, and trying to dig deeper could make him pull back. I remembered the first time I met him at the border facilities. Even then, I'd sensed something decent in him, like he didn't quite fit. It was that small trace of humanity that made it so frustrating when he suppressed it and played his role so rigidly.

He quickly removed the needle and wrapped a bandage around my forearm, obviously eager to finish up the appointment.

When I returned to the Basilica, I thought the hardest part of the day was behind me. I'd managed to get through the lab appointment, but just as I was hoping for a moment of normalcy, Secretary Croft told me that Midas wanted to see me.

She didn't give me any details, just led me through the maze of curved hallways until we reached one of the grand parlor rooms. The doors opened, and there was Midas, lounging on an emerald-green couch with a glass of red wine in hand. The color of it had an unnerving resemblance to blood.

A man in a lab coat was leaving as I entered, and he slipped past me without a word, like he'd just been dismissed. Whatever they'd been discussing, it didn't seem like something I was supposed to hear.

Once he was gone, Croft left me there, and I was alone with Midas. Being one-on-one with him always felt strangely personal, but even in those close exchanges, he kept himself on another level—just out of my reach.

He looked up, eyes heavy with exhaustion, as he waved me toward a seat. "Come, sit," he said, his tone pleasant enough.

But if I'd learned anything at all, it was that a conversation with Midas only meant one thing—things were about to get worse.

I sat down, bracing myself.

"Your efforts to get through to my daughter seem to have proven useful. I can't say she's been any warmer with me today, but she has clearly come around to the idea of the child."

"Good to hear."

"I need you to give me your full cooperation at this upcoming demonstration, Tye. The people need some positive results to outweigh the mishaps this month has brought. The attempt on my life, the traitors among us … even the growing presence of Dark-Eyes roaming outside the wall. The resurrection will prove that we are still in a powerful position to maintain our stability."

"Don't worry, I plan on being the perfect little science experiment."

He didn't seem to like my sarcasm. He put his wineglass down and gave me that familiar look that always sent chills down my spine. "If all goes well this weekend," he continued slowly, "I think things will finally fall into place with Harlow again. Something broke between us when she lost her mother … "

His ice-blue eyes settled somewhere far away as he trailed off, and for a moment, he seemed almost human. Maybe he was just too tired to keep up his usual cold front. The sudden shift made me uneasy, unsure of what to expect next.

He exhaled, leaning back. "My wife was the one who kept our family grounded. She shared my ambition, but had Harlow's empathy. Even when Harlow was little, she was always asking why things were the way they were, always holding her own strong opinions."

A faint, almost reluctant smile tugged at his mouth. "My wife encouraged that side of her, while I worried that empathy would make Harlow vulnerable in a world like this. I still do. The world's a brutal place; there's no way around that. I've always wanted her to be tougher, to use her gifts to shape her own path without letting the ugliness around us bring her down. Naturally, she leaned toward her mother."

He glanced at me then, perhaps searching for some trace of understanding.

"I loved my wife," he said quietly, the words laced with an unexpected sincerity, "and I regret that my work led to her death. But having her back—this is our second chance."

He watched me closely, gauging my reaction, but he didn't know Harlow had already filled me in on why things were rocky between them. And from the look on his face, I could tell he knew it was mostly his fault.

He picked up the wineglass again and took a slow sip, savoring it like it was part of some private ritual. "My wife will finally see that all my efforts led us here, to this greatness, and that her sacrifice had a purpose. She was the first to fall to the virus at my hands, and now she'll be the first significant person I bring back. The way it's all aligned has only strengthened my conviction that what I'm building is our destiny."

I sat there watching him, unsure if his twisted conviction or the quiet ache buried in his voice reflected the real man beneath the surface.

As if catching himself for revealing too much, he set down the wineglass and picked up a gold-trimmed folder filled with papers, signaling a clear shift in the conversation. "I wondered why Safe Zone 32 was so important to you, but I think I figured it out."

My heart clenched, sending a new rush of worry through me. I knew naming that place would come back to haunt me. *He found my friends.*

"We've been looking for your extended family. Any relatives that may share your blood," he went on.

Relief replaced my worry, but realizing what the folder was, I suddenly became aware that he might have found relatives of mine that I wasn't even aware of. I'd had no relatives that I knew of living in the same state, but had never had the time to search beyond my parents—not a moment to breathe since arriving at the border camp and going on the run soon after.

Midas picked up his wine again, taking a self-satisfied sip as he watched my reaction, clearly reveling in what he thought was a win. "Tell me, where's your uncle Brooks now? Or your cousin Heath?"

I kept my face neutral. I recognized the names, of course—my dad's brother and my cousin on my mom's side—but I hadn't seen or heard from them in years. They lived nowhere near us, and aside from a few interactions at family functions when I was growing up, I wasn't close with either of them.

I realized I could use this turn of events to my advantage. If Midas was after more Ichor, and believed I was protecting them somewhere in Safe Zone 32, it'd be in his interest to keep his promise of sparing it.

"I don't know where they are now, but last time we spoke, they were in that area," I said, feigning cooperation.

"Well, hopefully I can arrange a family reunion of sorts when they're brought to Ylem for study," he said, with a tone that sounded hauntingly genuine. He seemed consumed by the idea that Ylem was the greatest place on earth, even for a prisoner.

"So there's others like me after all? *God's blood?*"

"As you know, we can't confirm without thorough testing, but if it existed anywhere else, it'd likely be in someone closely related to you."

"I see... Well, that's where I last knew them to be," I lied.

His fingers tapped contemplatively on the folder. "Since you and Harlow seemed to get on well, spend some time with her this evening. She's understandably anxious about the resurrection."

I managed a stiff, half-hearted smile. "Sure thing."

Word had traveled quickly through the Basilica that tonight, Harlow was meant to have her space. Her evening transfusion was set to take place soon, and everyone seemed to be on alert to ensure she'd have time to decompress. I was glad to hear that Beckett would be here tonight—but at the same time, I'd been hoping for some alone time, a chance to get closer to her, build her trust in me further. After my talk with Midas, that need felt more urgent than ever.

As I walked past one of the lounges on the way to my room, I noticed the staff setting up an elaborate arrangement of snacks—fruit, pastries, and an assortment of other small dishes. They were clearly trying to make her feel comfortable, to ease whatever worries she might have about the upcoming resurrection. I couldn't help but wonder if all these extra efforts were because they were doubting that everything would go smoothly...

Finally alone in my room, I had a rare chance to just breathe. The day had been one hit after another, and a hot shower seemed like the perfect way to unwind before meeting up with Harlow.

Showers were one thing I never took for granted. Every time the water hit my skin, it reminded me of those long stretches when we had no running water at all, when layers of grime and dried blood were just part of life. Getting clean felt incredible. It brought me back to when Otto rigged up that first makeshift shower in the warehouse. That day felt like a breakthrough, a moment when we were normal kids again, even if just for a while.

I caught my reflection in the mirror, almost surprised by the sight. Compared to my days back at the camps, I looked healthier, stronger. I still had bruises from all the needles, but it was nothing compared to the half-starved wreck I'd been at the beginning of the outbreak.

I unwrapped the bandage from today's IV, going through the usual motions—these bandages had become a near-constant part of me. As I pulled the last strip free, something slipped out and fluttered to the floor: a small, folded piece of paper.

I bent down and read the hastily scrawled message:

there are tunnels under Ylem

I read it over and over, processing the words. *Chiron must've slipped this to me!* He was taking a risk, finally pulling against his chains. He'd been careful at hinting that it was possible the cure wouldn't remain locked inside Ylem forever. But to leave me this message ... he wanted me to know, maybe even to use this information to get out of here.

Simply knowing there were routes beneath Ylem wasn't enough, but at least it was a starting point. I took a slow breath in. Why now, though? This was the most dangerous time to step in and help, with eyes everywhere on the lookout for traitors. Clearly, it was important to him that I knew. Had something shifted for Chiron—some new urgency? Was there a plan in motion involving me that had suddenly pushed him to help me escape? Or maybe Willa had somehow pulled strings to get him to help. She was more than capable of making the impossible happen.

The shower was already running, so I let the note dissolve under the stream, watching the ink and paper vanish down the drain, leaving no trace.

With a smile, I stepped into the hot water, letting the possibility of reuniting with my friends sink in.

Later that night, I found Harlow in one of the many lounge rooms, which was dimly lit, set up for relaxation with soft music playing. She was wrapped in a luxurious silver silk robe that matched the color of her hair. She was always well dressed, but I couldn't help feeling it was more than just a fancy outfit tonight—like she wore it to bring herself some sense of comfort.

She was already in the middle of her transfusion with Beckett, reclining on an oversized couch as the blood flowed through the IV between them. The male nurse sat quietly in the corner, watching the monitors and trying to be invisible.

I'd half-expected Willa to be here—they were practically glued at the hip these days. But since Willa was still technically staff, it made sense she'd be confined to her quarters at this hour.

"Hey," I greeted them, shaking Beckett's hand. The awkwardness from before remained; we still had to pretend we were strangers.

"You two will get along. Beckett's great," she assured me.

Beneath her smile, there was a trace of something heavier. Sadness, maybe, or nerves, which made sense. No matter how dressed up she was, it was hard to mask the kind of anxiety she must be feeling.

I took a seat across from them, sinking into the down-filled cushions. "You feeling okay?" I asked her. After our last encounter, it felt like we were on track to become something like allies. I wanted her to feel my support.

"I mean, I'm probably just as anxious as you are, and spending the day with my dad didn't help. No matter how much I try to bend to his wants, we still don't seem to click."

"Hopefully once your mom's back, she'll whip him into shape."

She gave me a rueful smile. "I'm sorry you have to be put through the ringer for it to happen. But I'm very happy I'll be seeing her again," she said, her voice breaking with emotion.

I couldn't tell how much Beckett knew about the resurrection, but he kept his focus on the IV as the nurse carefully removed it from both their arms.

"Beckett, you should stay for a while. We can have dinner soon," Harlow suggested, with a brief nod to dismiss the nurse.

"Sure, you know I'm never in a rush to get back to the camps," he said with a smirk.

"You want to hang out here with us, or get some reading done in the library?" she asked.

"Respectfully, if we were back at your place, I'd be all for getting some chapters in, but this place gives me the creeps."

She laughed. "Isn't my place so much better? Trust me, getting my personal space back can't come soon enough."

It was nice seeing them already comfortable with each other, and I instantly felt more relaxed that it was just us.

Harlow's gaze shifted to the doorway where the nurse had just left, her expression darkening. She lowered her voice and leaned toward me. "They did it today."

I blinked, my mind scrambling. "Did what?"

"They *started the process,*" she said, a hint of grim humor lacing her words. "Who knows if it'll take on the first try, but it looks like I'll be carrying our future kid soon. Congrats."

I barely registered Beckett's wide-eyed reaction as he turned toward me. The reality of it all was overwhelming.

When I didn't respond, Harlow went on. "After our talk, I feel better about it. As strange as it is, it almost feels poetic, like there's a higher meaning to it all. You're bringing my mom back just as there's a new life inside me. It's as if the past and future are merging in some way."

I felt calmer knowing that despite everything, her heart was still in the right place.

Beckett glanced from her to me, silent but attentive.

"I respect how you're handling everything," I said. "If the kid's anything like you, they'll do well in this world."

Harlow's eyes searched mine for a second, as if weighing up my words. "Will they? I just can't imagine the baby growing up in a world like this one, confined to this city forever. We said it best: we play our parts, but this isn't the way to live. I understand you have it worse than me in many ways, but we're two sides of the same coin."

Her raw honesty struck me harder than I'd expected. Willa's idea of trusting Harlow might not be so far-fetched after all.

"I want the same, but for there to be a better world out there, we both know a lot has to happen that your dad would never allow."

I took the chance to plant the idea, watching her carefully to see if it would take root. Even Beckett seemed to notice, casually reaching for a cookie to mask his interest.

"My father says he wants me to take over from him when he's gone, but he knows damn well I wouldn't run things the way he does," she told me. "He'll leave behind a well-oiled machine that runs without me. I'll just be the face of it. No real power."

"Machines can be reprogrammed," said Beckett, almost flinching at the sound of his own words slipping out.

Harlow, though surprised by his contribution, looked interested. "You're an intellectual, Beckett. Tell me what you'd do. Genuinely curious to hear your take."

I couldn't look away from him. Harlow didn't know how close to home she'd hit, and Beckett's mind was clearly turning over how to handle this sudden opportunity.

"Well..." he began. Harlow leaned forward in her seat. "From what I've experienced, you treat people great. I think you'll know what to do, when you can."

Even Harlow knew that was a cop-out. "So diplomatic, Beckett."

Clearly, Beckett's loyalty to Vale's agenda was unshakable. I respected it, but I was hoping he'd help me gauge how solid Harlow's loyalty to Ylem really was.

The head houseman stepped in, breaking the quiet moment. "Excuse me, ma'am, dinner is ready for you in the dining room. All courses have been laid out so you can continue your private evening with your... friends."

Harlow nodded, and the three of us followed him out into the hallway where several guards in gold were stationed. The 'space' Harlow was being given was merely an illusion.

In the dining room, an elaborate spread awaited us. The table overflowed with dishes, each one more ornate than the last. Beckett's eyes lit up, clearly pleased not to be heading back to the camps just yet.

We sat down and began assembling plates, Harlow serving us generously. As we grazed, the silence was only broken by the clinking of forks and knives.

A few minutes in, Harlow's voice cut through. "Tye... when you brought someone back, were they really... *human*?"

So, unanswered questions were weighing on her mind, too. I hesitated, not wanting to add to her worries by mentioning the emptiness I'd seen in his eyes—that eerie, unsettling void.

"They don't tell me much," I admitted. "I didn't really see how it all turned out." When her face fell a little, I quickly added, "But there's a lot riding on this for your dad. If he didn't feel sure it'd work perfectly, he wouldn't stage a big public event like this—especially given how much you say he cares about her."

That seemed to ease her mind, at least for now, but I couldn't shake my own doubts. She fell quiet, absently picking at her food, lost in thought. After a few moments, she spoke up again, her tone softer.

"What were your moms like?"

The question hit me hard. Coming from her, especially now with her mom about to come back, it felt so simple, almost innocent. But it stirred up something deep, a reminder of how little time I'd ever really spent grieving. Survival had always come first, with memories of them just running under the surface, like a program in the background I could never shut off.

I glanced at Beckett, catching a similar sentiment reflected on his face. His own loss seemed to weigh him down too.

As I let the memories of my mom come up, I started to smile. It was tough to get past the last, awful image of her—it was burned into my mind like a scar. But once I did, there was this warmth, this reminder of who she really was. She raised me well, all those years.

"She was really special," I began, eyes fixed on my fork. "Selfless, talented, kind to a fault. I could tell her anything."

Harlow leaned in, studying me. "Do you look more like her or your dad?"

I laughed lightly. "People used to say I was her spitting image."

"She must've been beautiful," she said warmly, then turned to Beckett. "What about your mom, Beckett? What was she like?"

His face softened, and his eyes were already glossy. "She was … cozy, you know? I used to joke she'd make a better grandma than a mom. We'd bake together, knit—she taught me. We'd even have reading contests to see who could finish more books in a month."

Harlow seemed captivated by these glimpses into our pasts. It was like she was looking at us with fresh eyes, realizing that our lives had started somewhere very different from Ylem.

Her expression grew sad. "I'm sorry for everything my dad's done. I'm sorry we're all without mothers because of him. He's so consumed by his own ambitions. He doesn't see the damage it leaves behind; he just keeps his eyes on the next goalpost, the next thing he can conquer."

"Maybe your mom will help him see everything he's done in a different light," I offered.

Harlow laughed bitterly. "I don't know. Sometimes I feel like he's taken things so far, there's no way he'd ever change course. To him, that would mean failure. That's why he keeps treating everyone—from me, his own daughter, to you Angels—like we're all just pieces in his grand design, moving parts he can control."

"All the world's a stage, and all the men and women merely players," Beckett muttered, almost to himself. "Shakespeare," he added with a sheepish laugh.

Harlow smiled wryly at him. "It's funny—no matter where I am in Ylem's ranks, or where you two are, we're all equally powerless."

The word hit hard. *Powerless.* Even with everything stacked against us, I couldn't let myself believe we were truly stuck.

"Sometimes, it only takes one person seeing things differently to start the change," I murmured.

Both Harlow and Beckett noticeably reacted to my words. Harlow looked at me with a kind of admiration, maybe even catching onto what I was hinting at. But Beckett... He was wide-eyed, clearly shocked I'd gone that far. I could almost feel his panic, like he was picturing Vale strangling me for getting even a little too close to the line.

But to my relief, Harlow didn't seem alarmed by my words. If anything, she looked deep in thought, as if she was actually mulling over what I'd said.

Beckett quickly steered the conversation back onto safer ground. "Well, I hope I get to meet your mom. She sounds amazing. What's her name?"

The question seemed to snap Harlow out of whatever thoughts she'd been turning over. "Olivia," she said, a small, reflective smile on her face.

18. WILLA

I found myself staring up at the sky more than once, picturing the terror in my friends' eyes as they watched a missile streak toward them. After everything they'd fought through to survive, it could all be gone in a flash. The thought sent a chill through me every time.

My personal mission had always been clear: find Tye and get him out of Ylem. But the urgency to escape—to get us both back to the safe zone—had skyrocketed. Midas had tried once to eliminate the rest of the world, and now, he was about to finish the job. The enormity of what needed to be done grew with each passing day, and with it, my hatred for him burned hotter.

But I wasn't the kind of person to sit back and accept the cards I'd been dealt. I never wanted to be ordinary, and if I was going to leave my mark on this world, there was no better way than by tearing down the empire built on our pain and suffering.

Harlow, of course, was a wild card in all of this. I still hadn't figured out how to pull her into my plan. She wasn't like her father, not by a long shot. She had heart, empathy—things Midas couldn't fake if he tried. And her position alone could give us access to things we'd never reach without her.

How I'd go about this was a constant question on my mind, but today wasn't the day to push her. Her mother was coming back from the dead. That was enough to throw anyone off. She was barely holding it together, and as much as I wanted to use her vulnerabilities to my advantage, I knew it wasn't the right time.

What would happen when her mom was back? Where would that leave me? Harlow confided in me, leaned on me, but if her mom became that person for her again, what then? After Rowen had managed to position me so perfectly, I could end up completely discarded.

The thought made my stomach ache, but I had to push it aside. I couldn't afford to overthink. My focus now was on figuring out how to get Harlow to help get Tye and me out of Ylem, or at least gain her trust long enough for us to make our move.

I couldn't ignore reality. If her mom's return pulled us apart, all of this could crumble before I even had the chance to try.

The preparations for the resurrection today were in full swing, but the mood in Harlow's quarters was dim. I stood by as she adjusted the corset of her opulent yellow dress in the mirror. Her hands trembled, though she tried to hide it.

"She hasn't seen me since I was a little girl," she muttered.

"You look beautiful," I said softly, my voice steady even as I felt her anxiety seep into me.

She turned to face me, her eyes glassy. "I've always fantasized about being able to go back in time, and stop it from happening... By the end of today, she'll be with me again."

I offered her a supportive smile. "I'm happy some good is coming out of all the madness. You deserve it."

She nervously tucked her silver hair behind her ear. "What if it doesn't work?"

"Well, you have me. I'm here for you no matter what happens," I said, with a sincerity I hoped she could feel.

She didn't say anything, just nodded, a loving warmth in her expression.

The procession of SUVs moved slowly through the city, flanked by golden guards on motorcycles. The streets were strangely empty—everyone must have already headed to the venue, buzzing to see the big demonstration.

We were in the car behind the one transporting Midas, who was riding with Secretary Croft. Surrounded by dark, tinted windows, Harlow sat beside me, her silence heavy. Maverick was in the passenger seat, his gaze shifting between the road and the buildings towering over us, alert to any potential threats.

When we came out of a tunnel, a massive satellite tower came into view, something I hadn't seen before.

"What's that?" I asked, pointing at the structure.

Normally, I would never let myself seem curious about anything Ylem-related, but the silence in the car was stifling.

Harlow's eyes were fixed on the view through the opposite window. Whatever she was thinking about had pulled her far away, so Maverick replied instead.

"Communications tower. Security, data, transmissions. It's all centralized there. It's also the source of Ylem's jamming signals. No aircraft outside of our fleet can fly within range of the walls."

Rowen had mentioned that obstacle. I filed that away as a major potential vulnerability.

The stadium came into view like a monument to Ylem's ego—intimidating and overtly grand. As we pulled up to the front entrance, everything ran like clockwork. Guards peeled off to their posts with military precision, the SUVs parked in tight rows, and everyone moved as if they'd rehearsed this a hundred times. The efficiency was hard not to admire.

Inside, the scale of the place hit me like a wave. It was packed with people, a sea of bodies, each one dressed like they were attending the event of the century. The noise was almost deafening, a consistent buzz of chatter.

Every step I took felt like being on display, the eyes of the crowd tracking us. My face heated up as we filed through the aisles toward a reserved section.

Ylem's people were always a spectacle. Everyone looked like they'd stepped off the pages of some high-fashion magazine. Sleek dresses, sharp suits, and sparkling jewelry were everywhere, each person trying to outdo the next. They weren't here to just watch—they were here to be seen.

The crowd was a mix of people from all races, their diverse backgrounds only confirming what I already knew—these were the wealthiest and most powerful individuals from all around the world. I thought I spotted a couple of faces I recognized from movies and political stories. It made my skin crawl.

The energy in the stadium was restrained excitement. People chatted to each other in hushed tones, eyes darting toward the stage at the center of the stadium pit. Everyone was waiting for the main event like it was the highlight of their lives. And maybe it was. For people living within Ylem's perfect walls, life probably didn't offer much excitement beyond its carefully controlled routine.

When we reached our section—blocked off, front and center of the raised platform—there was a shift. Conversations quieted, heads turned, and all eyes were on us. Midas and Secretary Croft led the way, their presence commanding in a way I hated to admit. Harlow followed close behind, and even in her anxious state, she moved with a grace that made people stare.

I stuck close to her. There was something about her—her silver hair catching the light, the subtle tension in her step—that drew people's attention. Whether that was due to admiration or pity, I couldn't tell.

As we settled into our seats, I scanned the crowd, hoping to spot Tye. Wherever he was, I could only imagine how he must be feeling, knowing they were about to exploit him for everyone to see.

"I'm going to use the restroom," Harlow whispered in my ear. As she stood, a few guards immediately fell in line to escort her.

It was clear she needed a moment to gather herself, so I stayed where I was. I had to hold it together, being right in the thick of everything—

Maverick next to me, Midas directly in front of me, and the looming threat of having to watch a dead body come back to life. It was overwhelming. Malik had told me to "stay bright," but every day, it felt like that light was getting harder to keep on.

Maverick eyed me shifting in my seat. "It's gonna be okay," he said, his voice low enough not to carry.

I didn't answer immediately, just stared out at the crowd. "…I was thinking of Malik," I admitted eventually.

His voice gentled. "I've dreamt about it a hundred times—what it'd be like to bring him back. I know Tye would do it for you in a heartbeat, but it only works on infected bodies…" His words faltered as his gaze shifted away. "Still, I'm glad he never became one of them. No matter how many Teeth I see, they still haunt my nightmares."

I couldn't deny that when I first learned about Tye's gift, a part of me had clung to the faint hope that Malik could somehow come back. That fragile glimmer of a possibility was dim to begin with, but feeling it extinguish entirely was crushing.

Even though I still had my guard up around Mav, Malik was the thread that connected us—I knew how much he cared about him. I took a deep breath, forcing back the tears threatening to well up. Our conversation couldn't look like anything more than casual small talk.

And luckily, I stopped just in time. Amid the stadium chatter, Secretary Croft turned her head, casting an irritated glance my way. She couldn't have heard what we were saying, but the fact that I was engaging with Maverick at all seemed to be enough to bother her.

As soon as Harlow retook her seat, the lights around the stadium dimmed and a hush fell over the crowd as Midas stepped onto the stage. This was likely his first public appearance since the attempt on his life.

"Even in the face of recent challenges, I want to thank each of you for being here today to witness what is truly a monumental moment—not just for my work, but for my family. I'll leave the details to our esteemed Chief Medical Architect, Dr. Chiron."

A polite wave of applause rippled through the audience as Midas stepped down from the podium and returned to his seat. In his place, a familiar-looking man in a pristine lab coat took the stage.

Dr. Chiron adjusted the microphone and looked out at the sea of faces, taking a moment before speaking.

"Good evening. Tonight, we stand at the cusp of something truly extraordinary—something that could redefine what we believe to be possible. For years, our team has worked tirelessly, testing, researching, and refining what has become one of the rarest and most astonishing discoveries of our time: a unique type of Angel's Blood, or as we've come to call it, Ichor."

He paused, letting the significance of his words settle over the audience.

"This remarkable substance is found only in one subject, who you will see here today, and has the unprecedented ability to reverse the effects of infection. Through countless trials, we've seen what Ichor can do—revive infected bodies, repair what was thought irreparable, and work compatibly with all blood types. But tonight, we go one step further. Tonight, we take all of that research, all of those breakthroughs, and we put them to the ultimate test."

Chiron's eyes scanned the stadium, stopping briefly on Midas, who sat stoically in his seat, holding Harlow's hand—something I'd never expected to see.

"Our leader, Midas, has not only made all of this possible through his vision and determination, but has also chosen to make this moment personal. His confidence in our work is unwavering, as is his hope for the future of Ylem. That is why, before all of you, we will bring back the person he cherished most, his late wife, Olivia. This is not just a test of science; it is a testament to what we can achieve together."

There was a tension in the doctor's demeanor, a mix of professional pride in his work and what looked like guilt over the demonstration he was about to perform.

"Should tonight's demonstration succeed, it will mark the beginning of possibilities so profound they stretch the boundaries of God's will. The loss of loved ones, the fear of infection, the grip of death itself—all of these could one day be things of the past. The seeds of immortality, longevity, and resilience—no matter how this virus evolves—can finally take root."

Dr. Chiron's tone softened as he delivered his final words. "Thank you for standing with us tonight, as we take this historic step together."

He gave a slight nod and stepped back from the podium. A platform rose slowly from the center of the stage, the sound of its machinery drowned out by the collective gasp of the audience. My stomach dropped as the sight came into view.

The pale, lifeless, warped body of a woman lay strapped to a gurney, her arms bound by an intricate web of tubes and wires connected to surrounding monitors. Beside her, Tye was strapped to his own gurney, directly linked to her through the network of equipment.

Her skin glistened unnaturally, wet and waxy, the telltale signs of having been recently thawed from cryofreeze. She wasn't quite a Mort, but the hollowness of her features and the lifeless way she lay there were enough to give me goosebumps.

And it wasn't just the sight of her—it was seeing Tye like this. Restrained. Used. Dehumanized. My fists clenched at my sides as my helplessness swallowed me whole.

In front of me, Harlow sat stiff as a statue, her hands gripping the edge of her seat. She was barely holding it together.

Dr. Chiron stepped forward, adjusting the IVs connecting Tye and the woman. Yet, when I looked closely, his movements were hesitant, as though the weight of what he was doing wasn't lost on him.

The transfusion started quickly, blood flowing steadily from Tye into the woman. The audience had fallen silent. For a moment, nothing happened, and I found myself holding my breath, probably turning blue in the face.

Then, gradually, her transformation began.

The gray hue of her skin started to fade, replaced by the faintest blush of color. It was subtle at first, but as the moments stretched on, life was creeping back into her body.

Tye's expression was unreadable, but I could see the strain he was under. Sweat beaded on his forehead, and his hands twitched slightly as if trying to resist his restraints. He looked so alone up there, and my heart twisted at the sight.

Then, it happened! The woman's eyes snapped open, black and soulless, and she let out a blood-curdling scream that echoed around the stadium. The sound sent a jolt through me, and I wasn't alone. The audience flinched collectively, a gasp rolling through the stands; Harlow buried her face in her father's shoulder, her whole body trembling.

The woman's body twitched violently, her limbs jerking as though she were being controlled by invisible strings. For a moment, I thought she'd leap off the gurney. But slowly—agonizingly slowly—the horror began to subside.

Her eyes started to clear, the blackness giving way to something recognizably human. Her face softened, and her movements became less erratic. Piece by piece, the haunting features melted away, leaving behind a visage that looked almost peaceful.

Chiron hovered nearby, his gaze flicking between the monitors and Tye. His professionalism hadn't faltered, but the tension in his jaw betrayed him.

He hated this.

By the time Harlow's mom began to look human again, the audience was on edge, caught between awe and disbelief. Harlow finally lifted her head, her face tear-streaked as she watched the scene unfold.

Her father, sitting beside her, looked emotional for once—so different from the stoic mask he usually wore.

Harlow's hands were shaking, but she didn't look away from her mother. And neither did I. It was impossible to. It was a miracle and a nightmare together in one.

The audience seemed to hold a collective breath as Harlow's mom became visibly more aware of her surroundings. Her gaze darted around the stadium, taking in the thousands of people staring down at her. Confusion crossed her face as she noticed the wet hospital gown clinging to her shivering body. Then her expression softened, her wide, bewildered eyes locking onto Harlow.

"Mom?" Harlow choked out, her voice breaking with disbelief.

But just as the word hung in the air, her mother swayed and crumpled back onto the gurney. Gasps rang out through the stadium, and chaos followed as the crowd buzzed with concerned murmurings.

Medical personnel rushed onto the stage, surrounding the woman. Harlow and Midas bolted from their seats, running onto the platform just as it began to descend out of sight.

My eyes locked onto Tye's as the stage sank lower. His expression said it all—this was the moment that confirmed he'd likely never be free from Ylem, not with what his blood could do. A heavy understanding passed between us before the stage vanished underground completely, taking Tye, Harlow, and her parents beneath the stadium.

Dr. Chiron's voice cut through the commotion, calm but firm as he took the microphone again. "It's important to understand that after years of unconsciousness, the body and mind need time to adjust. The stimulation can understandably be overwhelming. There's no cause for alarm—this is an incredible moment for science and humanity alike. The Ichor has once again proven its potential as a gift to us all."

The applause started slow, but grew into genuine excitement.

Secretary Croft then took the mic, her commanding tone silencing the crowd. "Please make your way calmly out of the stadium. Updates will follow once Madam Olivia has had time to rest. Thank you for your understanding."

The controlled efficiency of Ylem kicked in as the crowd began to funnel out. I stayed in place for a moment, the scene replaying in my head, until finally, Maverick pulled me towards the exit.

He and I walked down the empty aisle that led away from the civilian exits and directly to the row of sleek SUVs waiting to take us back to the Basilica. The crowd continued to buzz faintly behind us, but Harlow and Midas were still nowhere to be seen.

As the golden guards busied themselves readying the escort procession, I pulled away from Maverick, quickening my pace. He followed without hesitation, and spoke in a low voice.

"Don't take your anger out on me. I might be one of your only real friends here."

Keeping my own volume down, I shot back, "Tye's up there, being used like an animal, because of you—"

"I told you," Maverick interrupted sharply, "I didn't tell them he was on that plane—"

Before either of us could say more, Secretary Croft's pointed voice cut in. "Major, what color is your uniform?"

Maverick blinked, clearly thrown by the sudden question. "Gold," he replied slowly, looking like he was bracing himself for whatever was coming next.

"And what color is Aria's?" she asked coldly.

He glanced at me for half a second before replying, "Gray."

"Indeed," she said with a tight smile. "Harlow has the rank to bend rules and keep the help as company, but you do not. Stop fraternizing."

Maverick immediately stiffened, his usual air of confidence nowhere in sight. "I was just taking her back to the car we came in," he said evenly, though his jaw tightened.

"Then do it *silently,*" she said with a frown, then added, "As a matter of fact, wait with Midas's car. I'll take her back."

My stomach twisted. The last person I wanted to be stuck in close quarters with right now was Secretary Croft. Maverick's eyes flicked to mine briefly before he turned on his heel and headed for the car parked in the middle of the line.

Croft gestured for me to follow, and I reluctantly climbed into the vehicle after her. The doors shut with a heavy thud, and before long, the SUV started rolling. I sat across from Croft, trying to push down the unease that had been sitting in my chest all night, but the way she was looking at me, like she was silently picking me apart, made it near-impossible.

I'd have to deal with Croft for the time being. It would probably be a while before I saw Harlow again. It must be surreal to sit face-to-face with a mother you'd thought was lost forever. What do you even say to someone who's been gone for so long and missed so much?

Croft broke the silence. "So, you're not just a pretty face. You seem to keep finding your way in with Ylem's upper ranks."

I glanced at her, considering my response. "I was pretty shaken up from what I saw on stage," I said after a beat. "He was just making small talk."

"What you saw on stage should excite you," she said firmly. "That was the core of what will make Ylem the strongest nation, with the most valuable assets. It's about time we had something to remind our people of that. That rogue soldier, the infiltrators—that all falls directly on me."

I couldn't tell if she was sizing me up or looking for validation. "Well, you handled it quickly. I'm sure the people noticed."

"At least today's miracle will be at the forefront of their minds," Croft replied, her tone sharp but steady. "Not to mention, your best friend will have her parent back."

"That part I'm happy about," I said, wondering if she was testing me.

"Are you?" she asked, her eyes narrowing slightly. "I can see why Harlow gravitated to you. She needed someone strong, steady. I tried to be that for her for a long time, but anyone close to her father, she keeps at arm's length." She paused, her gaze boring into me. "I warned you to stay in your lane. Now you'll see—you were just a placeholder to her. You'll fall back to where you really belong."

The words hit hard, but I kept my composure. "I came here to work, not make friends. I'll be okay."

Her expression softened slightly, almost approving. "That's the strength I admire in you. I recognize it."

A compliment? I blinked, unsure how to respond.

"What? Surely you can understand a woman like me can recognize power in another?" Croft asked, her tone sharper again. "I'm proud of what we've built here in Ylem, and ranks matter, but I understand your position is just happenstance. You had a whole life before the outbreak. Immeasurable loss. I see it in your eyes. To apply for a low position like yours in Ylem means you were grasping for an ounce of hope and normalcy."

Was she baiting me to slip up? I quickly changed the subject. "Where were you before Ylem?"

She exhaled deeply, glancing out of the window as if pulling herself back in time. "I headed the U.S. military. I was in charge of clearing safe zones early on in the Outbreak Wars. I handled logistics and tactics at the height of the chaos. When the president allied with Ylem, I'll admit, I was confused by the whole thing. The redirection felt like I was abandoning the very people I'd sworn to protect." Her voice remained even, but there was a weight in her words I hadn't expected. She looked at me steadily, though not unkindly. "But then I realized there was no way to bring back what we'd lost, and with the virus spreading as it was, the U.S. became a permanent warzone. Ylem was a way to repurpose everything I'd worked for—to protect the people here."

I stayed quiet, lost for what to say, but she continued.

"I'd been so used to the men in power keeping me in my place, despite my rank. But when I met Midas, he saw me as a visionary in my own right. He never acknowledged my gender; he just let me take the reins and build Ylem's military backbone into the greatness it is today."

For a moment, I felt a twinge of respect for her. It was just unfortunate that all her talent had gone to the wrong side. Her legacy wasn't protecting people—it was helping Midas keep a chokehold on anyone outside its walls.

The SUV slowed to a stop, pulling up to the looming sphere of the Basilica. The guards were already there, waiting to escort me inside, and I welcomed it. I barely waited for the door to fully open before sliding out, eager to put some distance between myself and Croft.

As I walked through the entryway, the other staff shot me quick, judgmental glances, their eyes flicking over me like I was out of place. They were scrubbing floors, dusting railings, their hands busy with tasks that were becoming painfully familiar to me. They were rarely afforded the privilege to step outside this place. If Harlow didn't need me anymore—if this really was the end of the line—I'd just be another gray-uniformed ghost haunting these pristine halls.

The thought settled in me like a stone. I'd told myself this was all part of the plan, that getting close to Harlow was just a step toward blowing this place wide open. But now, with the possibility of her spending all her time with her mother, it hit me: I actually cared about her. It wasn't just an act. Somewhere between the laughs and the open conversations, she'd become someone real to me. And losing that—losing *her*—would hurt more than I wanted to admit.

19. TYE

Thousands of eyes watched as my blood drained away and finally brought Harlow's mom back to life. No matter how many times they'd tested my limits, I still wasn't prepared for the nightmare of being on display like this, used and made a martyr. Her scream echoed in my head, loud and sharp, like it had lodged itself permanently in my skull. And Willa's eyes, wide with shock, kept flashing in my mind on repeat as the platform lowered beneath the stadium, taking us out of the audience's sight.

When the platform finally reached the lower level, the atmosphere below was even more chaotic. Medical personnel swarmed Harlow's mom, checking her vitals, evaluating her state. Even though I wanted this for Harlow's sake, it was still jarring to see that my blood really was capable of such a dark miracle. The room buzzed with urgency, but no one came near me. There was no regard for the fact that my body was aching in protest, drained both physically and emotionally. Every pair of eyes was fixed on Olivia on the gurney.

I sat there, tethered by wires and probes, feeling like an afterthought, though my veins had been the reason for all of it. I moved to unhook myself, even reaching for the IV needle still in my arm, when Dr. Chiron appeared.

Without a word, he stopped me and carefully removed it himself. His face was tight, but his eyes gave him away. A silent apology for the role he'd played in this awful ritual.

For a second, his eyes lingered on mine, searching, as though asking if I'd received the note he'd risked leaving me. I held his gaze, just long enough to let him see that I had.

He wrapped a bandage around my arm and helped me to my feet.

The room seemed to suddenly fall silent as Harlow's mom stirred again. Slowly, she sat upright, her wide eyes darting around at the small crowd encircling her, taking everything in.

"Give her space!" Midas barked.

In seconds, the room cleared, leaving only him, Chiron, Harlow, and me to watch the scene unfold.

Her expression was of both confusion and quiet horror, her brows knitting together as though she were trying to reconcile with a fragmented memory.

Harlow stepped forward and knelt by her mother's side. I knew better than anyone that she had been anxious to know what her mom would be like when she woke.

"Mom ... ?" she said, her lips dry and trembling.

Her mom lifted a pale, shaky hand and took hold of her daughter's. "Harlow?" she rasped, her voice weak.

The tears came instantly, streaming down Harlow's face as she threw herself into her mother's arms.

It was the last thing I saw before two golden guards came to pull me away.

I was still shaking when the guards shoved me toward the row of sleek black vehicles out front, their polished surfaces gleaming under the stadium lights. Midas's car was parked in the middle, standing out as the only one with extra armor plating.

The car ride to the stadium had been tense and uncomfortably quiet, Midas lost in thought the entire way. Harlow had mentioned his lingering regret over his late wife, but seeing him like that still felt unsettling.

I'd used the time to prepare myself, but now, after the ordeal, I could use this moment alone to recoup.

When I opened the car door, I sadly realized I wasn't alone. Maverick was there, just as surprised to see me as I was him. Even Midas's personal guard had been cut out of the Rothfields' private reunion. It was just the two of us.

I slid into the seat across from him, the soft click of the door sealing us in. The partition was up, shutting out the driver and creating one of those rare moments where a private exchange with Maverick was possible. Normally, I'd have jumped at the chance to prod him, but my head was still foggy from the transfusion.

Maverick seemed to notice. He plucked a bottle from the cup holder in the center console, handing it to me. The liquid inside was the familiar neon blue—Ylem's miraculous answer to replenishing whatever life they drained from me. It worked well enough, but it felt like a bandage on a bullet wound. Physically, I was fine, but no medicine or IV drip could patch the trauma inflicted on my mind.

I sipped it slowly as the car began to move, instantly feeling my headache disappear.

The late afternoon sun reflected off the metros that zipped past on the highlines between buildings, ferrying the wealthy back to their estates. Down on the streets, others walked home from the stadium, probably gossiping about what they'd just witnessed.

Maverick seemed relaxed but watchful as we both stared out of opposite windows. There was a familiarity between us, but it came with caution.

"I know part of you still thinks I turned you in," he said after a while, "but for what it's worth, I'm sorry you're being put through that."

I leaned back in my seat, watching him carefully. "Somehow, I believe you when you say you didn't," I said. "But what happened today just guaranteed Ylem will do whatever it takes to keep me here forever."

"Look, once I accepted I was here for good, I felt less like a prisoner. I stopped thinking about what comes after this. You should try it." He hesitated before adding, "But I guess I don't have anyone waiting for me like you do."

"You're not a prisoner," I said. "Your rank alone gives you more freedom than I'll ever have."

He let out a quiet laugh. "Everyone here's on a leash, Tye. The trick is figuring out who's holding yours and how hard you can pull before they yank it back."

"Feels more like a cage than a leash," I muttered.

The car rocked gently as we turned a corner, the giant sphere in the distance coming into view.

With my head clearer, the urgency to make this alone time count hit me again. The resurrection trauma still hummed under my skin, pulling my thoughts back to escape.

"What's the deal with these tunnels underneath Ylem?" I asked, keeping my gaze fixed on the window to make the question sound casual.

I could feel his attention shift toward me. "What are you up to?" he asked, his tone mildly suspicious.

"Nothing," I replied quickly. "I overheard someone mention them. Just curious."

"... Right." His voice shifted into something more serious. "Look, if you've got people in the insurgency helping you, you should tell me. It's for your own good. They're cracking down hard, and I can at least try to keep an eye out. Besides ... " He hesitated again. "Maybe it'll give me hope in believing someone's finally slipping through Ylem's iron fist."

"You could be that someone," I said, turning to meet his eyes again. "It could bring hope to the whole world, even. You're quite literally next to Midas every day, with a weapon in hand at that."

"Then what? I'm dead on the spot," he shot back. "Most of my life, I was killing myself. And now, for the first time in years, I actually *want* to live. The irony's sick. It'd be much easier to survive all this if I didn't care."

I knew it had been a long shot, so I dropped it. Pushing too hard might shut him down, and I couldn't afford to lose this fleeting moment of openness. I switched tack, still hoping to salvage the conversation. "So, about those tunnels?"

Maverick laughed incredulously, then hesitated, like he was deciding if sharing anything would be indirectly helping me. Finally, he relented. "They hold all of Ylem's infrastructure. The water systems, power grid, storage. They're riddled with high-security systems, but somehow, there are still underground clubs and hotspots operating illegally down there. If it weren't for Midas's own daughter being a regular in that scene, the security units wouldn't turn a blind eye like they have been."

I blinked, surprised. "Harlow? What do you mean, clubs? Like parties? Didn't think Ylem citizens were the type."

"Half these billionaires partied nonstop before they came here," he said with a shrug. "They need somewhere to use their drugs and feel that high again. That's why I steer clear of that scene."

His words stuck with me. A new piece to the puzzle—one I wasn't expecting.

The SUV pulled up to the grand entrance of the Basilica, its tires squeaking softly against the polished stone drive. As soon as we stopped, the golden guards fell into formation, lining up to escort me inside as if ready to fend off some unseen attack. The theatrics always annoyed me, like they thought a drone might swoop down at any second and snatch me up, hauling me over the wall and out of their precious grasp.

Inside, the frenzied energy was noticeable. Staff scrambled everywhere, polishing, tidying, rearranging. It was like they'd been told Harlow's mother might return, but had never believed it would actually happen. Now, faced with the reality of her resurrection, they seemed determined to make sure everything was up to par.

Maverick caught up to me as I lingered near the grand foyer. "They've made some food for you," he said, his tone even but detached again. "You should eat and rest."

I gave him a brief nod, too tired to say much, and let a maid lead me to the dining room, where a hot meal was waiting. The scent hit me immediately, rich and savory, but it didn't stir my hunger the way it should've. I was starving, weak from the day, but my mind wouldn't stop spinning long enough to focus on food.

As I sat, my thoughts drifted back to the tunnels. If they were highly secured, that presented a massive problem. I was already a spotlighted person in Ylem—every movement of mine was watched. Even if I managed to sneak down there, I imagined navigating the labyrinth of infrastructure would be nearly impossible.

The idea of Harlow sneaking into underground clubs through these same tunnels was interesting. If she could move freely down there without raising alarms, maybe there was a way. Maybe the system wasn't as airtight as they wanted us to believe.

Even if I could figure a way out, what then? I didn't even know where Ylem was. For all I knew, it was surrounded by nothing but endless wasteland. The thought of being trapped outside was almost as terrifying as being stuck inside.

I'd seen what it was like when a prisoner escaped—the Angel who had broken out of the camps. Ylem's forces had descended on them like wolves. If they'd reacted like that for one escapee, I couldn't imagine the lengths they'd go to to drag me back. The risk wasn't just mine to bear; if anyone helped me, they'd be crushed in the aftermath.

Even if escape felt impossible right now, Willa deserved a way out of this place. I knew she'd come here hoping we'd leave together, but if the tunnels could be her chance, she had to know about them—whatever happened next.

After I forced down what little food I could stomach, I headed to my room and let the hot water from the shower wash the stress of the day away.

When I was ready for bed, a knock at the door startled me. I froze for a moment, half-expecting it to be Maverick. Maybe it was another chance to see Willa.

I crossed the room in a hurry and opened the door. But it wasn't Maverick. It was Harlow.

She stood in the doorway, her eyes red-rimmed like she'd been crying all day, but somehow there was a new sense of peace about her. The golden guard stationed in the hallway stepped back, clearly choosing to mind his business.

"Harlow," I said, masking my surprise as best as I could.

She offered a small nod and stepped inside without waiting for an invitation. After closing the door behind her, she moved to the armchair in the corner and smoothed her wrinkled yellow dress as she sat, as if savoring her first moment of quiet all day.

"How are you holding up?" she asked, her voice quiet but steady.

"Bit better now," I said, weakly offering a smile. "How is she?"

Harlow exhaled, leaning back slightly. "Finally home. They pumped her full of meds and sleep aids to get her back on track…I don't know what I was imagining, but I guess I should've expected it'd take time for her to be fully like I remember her."

"Of course," I replied. "It must feel so strange…but I'm sure she's happy to see you again."

A flicker of something crossed her face. "I wanted to thank you for what you did today," she said. "I know it was in part by force, but it really is an incredible gift."

I hesitated, glancing down at my hands. "I'm happy some good came of it, but sadly, this gift is why Ylem owns me."

Her expression tightened, and she quickly shook her head. "I know. I didn't mean it like that. You know I don't align with any of it, but I at least wanted you to know how much it means to me to have her back."

"I get it," I said, meeting her eyes. "I'm happy for you, really. How's your dad feeling about it?"

Her lips curved into a faint, bittersweet smile. "He hasn't left her side. I haven't seen him so concerned about anything since I was a kid. It's nice to know he still cares about her. Still has a heart buried under all that ruthless ambition."

"Hopefully your mom bounces back soon," I said. "Might be what it takes to shift things around here."

Harlow tilted her head slightly, her expression softening. "I've got to hand it to you. Staying positive after all you've been through takes a lot of strength. I admire you a lot for it."

The words caught me off guard, but I nodded. "Thanks."

She stood, brushing her fingers through her disheveled silver hair, smoothing away the signs of an emotional day. "Anyway, I'll let you get some sleep. It was just important to me that you knew how I felt about what you did. I'm going to head back up to stay with my mom."

As she reached the door, I called after her. "Harlow."

She turned, eyebrows lifting slightly.

"I admire you, too."

She smiled—a real one this time—before slipping out into the hallway.

The energy in the Basilica had shifted completely since Madam Olivia had returned. It was like the place had been holding its breath and now couldn't exhale fast enough. Experts of every kind came and went: medical professionals, therapists, and other specialists whose roles I couldn't even guess at.

I started catching glimpses of Olivia here and there. Sometimes she was walking with staff, or sitting with Harlow, deep in conversation. She seemed coherent, even commanding at times. It was clear she was getting back on her feet.

I never got a chance to interact with her myself, and I wasn't exactly looking for one. Left to my own devices, I found myself enjoying the relative freedom. No one was breathing down my neck or dragging me into another experiment. For once, I wasn't the center of attention.

A week after the resurrection, I was walking through the dim hallways toward the dining room, my thoughts fixed on the waning days before the bombing—until I stopped dead in my tracks at one of the large parlor rooms.

There, standing by one of the antique floor candelabras, was Willa! She was busy lighting the tall candles, the golden glow flickering across her face, and for a moment, I just watched her. Willa was staff here, but I was still surprised to see her working.

She glanced over her shoulder, her eyes meeting mine. A flash of surprise crossed her face, quickly replaced by a quiet smile. We both scanned the room, ensuring no one else was around. When I knew the coast was clear, I stepped inside.

She set the lighter down on a small table and turned to face me. The moment felt electric, like every second was borrowed time. I closed the distance between us quickly, and before I could even think, we were kissing.

It was quick, but it was real. It wasn't just a kiss—it was relief, a connection. When we pulled back, our eyes met again, and for a moment, things felt right.

She leaned in close, her voice low and urgent. "Are you okay? It took everything in me not to jump up on that stage."

"I'm fine," I assured her. "I've been more worried about you, with Ylem digging around for more operatives. Any updates?"

Her face fell. "They executed the only two I knew about. Harlow's our best shot now, but I haven't had the time with her I need—not with her mom being back."

"I've been working on it," I said. "I don't know if he's in the network, but the head doctor from the resurrection gave me game-changing information. I think he wants me to use it to get out of here before it's too late."

Her eyes locked onto mine, her eagerness palpable. "What information?"

“There are tunnels under Ylem. I asked Maverick about them—”

“Tye, I told you, he’s not—”

“I think he’s okay, Willa,” I cut in. “Really. I believe him.”

Her expression stayed doubtful, her eyes narrowing. “And what did he tell you?”

“The tunnels are filled with Ylem’s mechanical systems, but what’s more interesting are the underground clubs hidden among them. Clubs that Harlow apparently visits from time to time. I think the tunnels could be our way out.”

She paused, processing. Her eyes darted around the room, double-checking that we were still alone. “So, what? I ask Harlow to take us clubbing? That’s probably the last thing on her mind right now.”

“I haven’t figured it all out yet,” I admitted, “but I needed you to know. With or without me, you have to warn the others about the bombings.”

“What about your friend at the camps?” she asked. “You said he was in the network.”

“I’ll ask him if I get the chance, but he’s determined to stay out of anything that could compromise the New Year’s plan. I’ll try my—”

The whine of a vacuum broke through our conversation, growing louder as it approached us from down the hall.

Without a word, Willa turned back to the candelabras, resuming her work as if nothing had happened, while I set off in a brisk walk toward the opposite end of the corridor. I smiled to myself, grateful for the unexpected stroke of luck.

I remembered something my dad used to say: every good thing in life comes with a tax—it’s how the world stays balanced. The week I’d spent left to my own devices, free from blood draws, and even getting that rare glimpse of Willa, had finally revealed its price. Midas had summoned me for a transfusion, slipping right back into our hellish routine now that his wife was steady on her feet again.

The houseman didn't bother hiding his annoyance as he led me through the halls. It was the same every time—like just having me around threw off the equilibrium of his perfectly managed world. I didn't care enough to say anything, but I always noticed.

When we got to the lounge, it was exactly the same as every other time I'd been dragged there. Chiron was busy at the workstation, setting up the equipment with a little too much focus, like he was trying to pretend I didn't exist. It was obvious he was being extra careful, probably paranoid that Midas might pick up on the fact that he'd helped me.

Midas, on the other hand, looked almost thrilled to see me. He was seated in his usual spot, radiating smug satisfaction. The resurrection had clearly left him feeling untouchable, and now here I was, back on his schedule, ready to fuel whatever plans he had next.

"Tye," he said, like we were old friends. "I'm very pleased with you."

I made my way to the chair, keeping my expression neutral. "Thanks. Although, to be fair, I didn't really do anything except be born with freak genetics," I said dryly.

Midas grinned, clearly amused. "Your cooperation and resilience throughout all the trials have been commendable. The resurrection is all anyone can talk about—it's inspired everyone, just as I'd hoped it would." His smile softened. "And, of course, having my wife back after all this time ... It's a dream."

I flinched as Chiron slid the needle into my vein, the spot still tender and bruised from the resurrection transfusion. I couldn't help but get a dig in. "Even after all this blood of mine has mixed with yours, you'll never be able to resurrect people too?"

Midas's eyes hardened. "Doctor, why don't you explain it better?"

Chiron didn't look at me, his focus locked on the monitors. His voice was detached, professional. "The immunity transfers, but based on our testing so far, the ability to revive an infected body must come exclusively from the source."

"That's why finding others with Ichor is so crucial," Midas added.

I hesitated, then decided to press him. "Have you found them yet? My family?"

His expression shifted, his air of cool dissolving slightly. "It's becoming increasingly clear that they're no longer in Safe Zone 32 … if they ever were to begin with."

I refused to let his words rattle me. "Like I said, that's the last place I knew them to be. If you recall, I was at the border checkpoint for all of five minutes before I was made a prisoner. It's not like I could get in touch with them again."

My words came out bitter, and I didn't try to hide it.

Midas didn't react. "As much as you believe you're trapped here, this is the best thing that could've happened to you," he said smoothly. "The few safe zones that remain are in chaos—civil unrest, rebel groups tearing down the order we've worked so hard to maintain, infections spreading unchecked. Whatever you imagine them to be like, I promise you, the reality's far worse. Anyone would much prefer the luxuries of Ylem."

His certainty was infuriating, the way he always painted Ylem as a paradise—even for prisoners and those forced into servitude. But beneath my anger, his words left a cold knot in my stomach. If he was right, if things had truly deteriorated that badly, then Willa's last update about my friends might already be outdated.

Things were likely worse than I imagined, and the urgency to get back to them and help burned even hotter. I didn't need another reason to feel desperate, but Midas had handed me one anyway.

Sudden movement near the doorway broke through the noise in my head. It was quick, just a glimpse, but the long, golden hair was unmistakable: Madam Olivia.

She passed by without looking in, her steps a little too deliberate to be steady. Midas sat up straighter, his soft voice laced with control when he asked, "My dear, is everything alright?"

An aide trailing behind Olivia stopped in the doorway, her posture tense but composed. "She's having a spell of confusion right now, but she wants to see Harlow."

Midas's jaw tightened. He waved the aide off with a quick motion of his hand. She gave a brief nod and disappeared past the door, leaving an awkward quiet in her wake.

Midas leaned back in his chair, drumming his fingers on the armrest before turning to Chiron. "Cut it short," he said briskly.

Chiron moved to shut everything down. The low hum of the machine faded, and I felt the slight sting of the needle being pulled from my arm. It wasn't much, but I'd take any break I could get.

When I glanced up, Midas had already risen from his chair, adjusting the cuff of his sleeve with precise, deliberate movements. He didn't meet my eyes, his focus entirely on straightening himself out, like his image of control needed reinforcement. It was clear he didn't want to acknowledge what had just happened—or let me see that his perfect family façade had cracks.

Olivia's return might have been a showcase of Ylem's power, but even Midas wasn't exempt from the tax that came with it.

20. WILLA

Over the next week, I started to understand the looks and whispers from the other staff—the ones I'd been catching even here at the Basilica. They weren't outright mean, but the quiet judgment was there, and now it was becoming more obvious why.

Harlow had always kept me by her side, more as company than anything else, which meant I hadn't been assigned as many tasks as the others. I hadn't given it much thought at the time, but with Harlow spending most of her days with her mother, that protection was gone.

I was now fully available to be part of the daily rotation of chores—cleaning, errands, setting up for meals. It wasn't backbreaking, but the steady stream of tasks was enough to wear me down, especially with everything else that weighed on my mind.

It hadn't been long enough to warrant a conclusion that Harlow had replaced me with her mother, but the new distance between us was undeniable. And without the chance to spend time with her, I couldn't build the trust I needed to ask for her help.

The urgency was eating away at me. Tye had to get out of Ylem—the public resurrection had made that clearer than ever—and the others had to be warned before time ran out. With every day that passed, it felt like the window was closing.

I folded another towel, my hands moving on autopilot, then carried the neat stack across Harlow's spacious bedroom, the faint scent of lavender from the detergent calming me slightly.

The linen closet was tucked away on the far side of the room. I opened it and crouched down to the drawer where the towels were stored. As I placed them neatly inside, something caught my eye—an odd shape under the folds of linen.

Curious, I moved the towels aside, and a jolt of surprise shot through me. There, at the very back of the drawer, was a pistol. The mother-of-pearl finish on the handle told me it must belong to Harlow. She must've hidden it here—maybe the assassination attempt had shaken her more than she was letting on.

I stared at the sleek, cold metal and felt memories rushing back, unwanted but vivid. The first time I fired my father's pistol during the outbreak. My hands trembling as I gripped the weapon, the recoil making me jump, the sound of the shot ringing in my ears. That was the moment everything changed. Whatever innocence I had left was gone in the pull of the trigger.

I swallowed hard as the pistol sat there like a quiet invitation. If anything went down, I'd remember this was here.

My mind wandered for a second, imagining Midas walking the halls of his home, smug and untouchable, his guard down. My fingers twitched as if the gun were calling to me, daring me to pick it up. I reached for it, my hand hovering just above the handle—

"Where's Harlow?"

The voice snapped me back to reality. I spun around, heart hammering in my chest, to find Madam Olivia standing in the doorway. She looked worried and slightly dazed, but there was no denying her beauty, even with the tiredness in her eyes.

I quickly covered the weapon with the fresh laundry. "I-I'm not sure, ma'am," I managed, stumbling over the words as I straightened up.

Olivia frowned slightly, her expression distant, like she was still trying to process her surroundings.

Another woman appeared beside her in the doorway—one of the aides I often saw around the house. She stepped forward slowly, her tone careful, like she was dealing with a delicate thread she didn't want to snap.

"We'll bring her to you, madam. Why don't we wait in the solarium? Your favorite."

Olivia tilted her head slightly, her gaze softening, but she didn't respond right away. Instead, she stepped further into Harlow's room, her attention landing on me. For a moment, she just looked at me, and to my surprise, her expression was warm, almost loving.

"You're my daughter's friend, aren't you?" she asked, her voice calm and sure. "She's told me about you."

"Madam—"

The aide tried to interject, but Olivia lifted a hand. Her tone was still gentle, but also commanding. "Leave us."

The aide hesitated, clearly torn, but eventually bowed and slipped away, leaving me alone with Olivia.

I took a moment to really look at her. There were no signs that she'd ever been a creature of nightmares: her golden hair shining with life again, her green eyes far more serene than they'd been during the resurrection. Her alabaster skin was smooth and soft, suggesting a speedy recovery. The only thing that unsettled me was the thought that Tye's blood flowed through her now.

She looked like she belonged in this world of power and privilege. There was something grounding about her presence. I couldn't decide if that made her more or less intimidating.

"Yes, Harlow's wonderful. You've done an amazing job with her," I said, the words coming after a pause that felt longer than it should've been, but when they landed, they seemed to have an instant effect. Olivia was beaming.

The moment was interrupted again, this time by the soft creak of the door as someone else appeared in the doorway. My chest clenched so tight, the air was almost knocked out of me when I looked up to see Midas standing there, his presence taking over the room.

"Are you doing okay, my love?" he asked, his voice warm and filled with what sounded like genuine concern.

I felt it, but it didn't stop the intense hate from boiling in my chest. Before I even realized what I was doing, I'd taken a step back toward the linen closet—as though I had moved for the gun before my mind could catch up. But then, two golden guards appeared behind Midas, and the tension in my body snapped it back into place.

"I'm fine," Olivia said evenly. "I just wanted to see Harlow."

Midas's eyes were still soft, but calculating. "These men will take you to her. How does that sound?"

Olivia gave him one last, gentle smile and walked past him, moving out of the room and into the hall. Her expression hadn't shifted, but I could feel the subtle dismissal in her departure.

Midas stood there for a moment, a hint of embarrassment flashing across his face as he watched her leave. And now, with Olivia gone and the guards trailing after her, I was left alone with him for the first time ever. The room felt smaller, the air thicker. My heart was pounding so fiercely, I was sure he would see it pressing against my chest through my gray shirt.

I expected Midas to leave too. After all, I was just a housekeeper—nothing more than background noise, in the grand scheme of things. But instead, he remained, his eyes locking on me in a way that sent an uncomfortable chill through me. Unlike Olivia's warm gaze, his was cold, even though his smile stayed in place like some well-practiced mask.

"I've been meaning to talk to you," he said, like he was making casual conversation.

I froze, caught off guard. This was the last thing I'd expected. A wave of panic hit, and for a split second, I almost wished I'd grabbed the gun earlier.

"I've noticed how fond of you my daughter is," he continued, his voice tinged with something almost thoughtful. "You've been noticeably inseparable. I don't need to know the full details of your... relationship, but it's clear she values you."

I was struggling to process his words. My head spun as I tried to come up with a response. "She's been very kind," I finally said, keeping my voice steady.

"Of course, I don't approve of the way she does things, but I'm happy she has a friend."

Was this really the same man I'd always thought of as pure evil? He sounded so human for a moment. Just a father, trying to connect with his daughter.

But then, like a switch had been flipped, that coldness crept back into his expression. "I've tried to get her to mingle with others her age, on her level. But she seems to enjoy being contrarian. Normally, I would snuff this out for her own good, but if you're willing to help me with her, I'll let you two continue as you are."

The manipulation, the control—this was who he really was.

"Help how?" I asked cautiously, trying to keep my tone neutral.

"If she comes to you with anything that I should know about, share it with me. I don't mean your personal business, but if there's something that concerns you, or that might help me understand her better, I'd like to know about it."

I might've almost admired his attempt at being a better parent if I hadn't read between the lines. *He's asking me to spy on Harlow.*

With great effort, I forced the words out. "Of course, sir."

Midas gave me a sharp nod, his smile returning, though it still didn't reach his eyes. "Good. Continue your tasks."

Without another word, he turned and left, the sound of his footsteps fading down the hall. The moment the door clicked shut behind him, the air in the room suddenly felt breathable again.

The rest of the afternoon passed in a blur of tasks and quiet contemplation. My encounters with both of Harlow's parents had left a lasting impression on me, but in very different ways.

Midas's words stuck with me, though I had no intention of actually spying on Harlow for him. I would never help him with anything—not for as long as I lived. But the door he'd left open, the possibility of going to him in the future, was intriguing.

As I finished up the last of the chores, I caught sight of Harlow in the solarium, laughing with her mother, sounding light and carefree. I could tell how much this time meant to Harlow. She'd been waiting and hoping for this for so long.

The aide from earlier entered the solarium, and I overheard her telling Olivia that the physical therapist had arrived for her appointment. Olivia kissed Harlow sweetly on the cheek and followed the aide, leaving her daughter alone again.

Harlow's eyes met mine through the glass, and she gave me a warm smile and waved me inside. Finally, after the whirlwind of the past week, we had a moment to ourselves.

"She's doing so well," she said, gesturing for me to sit where her mother had just been.

I tried to come across as sincere. "That makes me so happy."

"It's crazy how much she's like how I remember her. Everything's coming back to her more and more with each passing day. You know, I try not to pay too much attention to all the strange experiments and stuff my dad works on, but I have to admit, this was truly incredible."

I kept the smile on my face, even though it pained me to hear her talk like that. She didn't know the toll it'd taken on me, seeing the horror Tye had been subjected to—and that was just a small glimpse of what they'd been putting him through since the border facilities.

"I'm really happy it all went well. So many people wish they could get time back with their loved ones," I said. "I'm happy it's you who gets to experience it."

"Are your parents still… alive?" she asked, her voice softening, a look of concern crossing her face. "I know you said you weren't so close with them."

I hesitated as a lump formed in my throat. It was hard to open up when I was pretending to be someone entirely different, but I didn't want to lie to her. "I lost touch with them, but yes," I said, offering some truth.

"Oh, Aria, that's horrible," she said, her face full of sympathy. "Well, your brother must've been amazing if he was anything like you."

I instantly perked up at the thought of Malik. "He was my best friend. I could tell him anything he'd never judge me."

She smiled kindly, her eyes scanning my face like she was trying to imagine what he might've looked like. I felt a sense of urgency—this might be one of the few moments I had with her in the midst of everything else going on.

"Speaking of..." I began, a little nervously. "Can I tell you something?"

Her brow furrowed slightly. "Of course, any time."

I took a breath, choosing my words carefully. "Your father came to me."

Her expression shifted, a flicker of anger darkening her eyes. "What did he want?"

"He wanted me to tell him if you came to me with anything he should know about," I said, trying to soften the truth. "To be fair, I think it was out of concern, but I wanted to tell you, as a friend."

She appeared to be processing a range of emotions before her smile returned, this time with a hint of gratitude. "You're a real girl's girl, Aria. Thanks for telling me that. He knows I've always been closer with my mom, so his hovering is probably on overdrive. Normally, I'd jump on him, but I'm going to focus on getting things back on track with my mom first."

"I think that's a good call," I said, relieved. "You've been so stressed with everything—the baby stuff, the resurrection. Maybe we should do something fun."

The suggestion had been on the tip of my tongue, but even I was surprised by how bold I was feeling. I supposed now was as good a time as any.

"Like what?" she asked, her interest piqued.

"At my last grocery run, I overheard one of the soldiers talking about an underground club. I don't know if you're into that sort of thing, but maybe—"

"Oh my god, Aria? I didn't think you had it in you!"

I froze for a moment, unsure of how to take her reaction. Had she caught on to my ploy?

She laughed, clearly amused. "I'm *very* into that sort of thing. I haven't been in a minute, with everything going on and security off the charts, but it'd be the perfect night to go."

I blinked, caught off guard. "Tonight? I mean, I was just throwing it out there, but—"

"My dad's taking my mom to his favorite dinner spot tonight," she said, her eyes lighting up. "Half the security team will be with them. It's the perfect storm."

A rush of excitement and fear hit me all at once. This could be my chance, the start of an escape, but the opportunity had come so suddenly that it brought a wave of anxiety. There was no time to make a solid plan, no time to get Tye involved.

"Maybe that handsome Angel, Tye, could come?" I blurted out. "Um, and whoever else you want?"

She flashed me a mischievous grin. "This side of you is sexy. Where the hell have you been hiding?" she asked playfully. Suddenly, she yanked me to my feet. "Of course he can! Let's get you an outfit!"

Harlow's room was a mess of clothes, the bed and floor covered in discarded outfits. After I'd tried on countless pieces, we finally settled on something. I looked at the tube top, leather skirt, and matching jacket in the mirror. It was much more revealing than anything I would usually wear, but it had the rock'n'roll edge I liked, even if it wasn't exactly me.

Harlow picked a navy silk minidress, elegant with long sleeves and a high neckline, but also with a plunging back that was definitely inappropriate for the Basilica. We both knew we couldn't be caught wearing these outfits around here.

I slipped back into my uniform, and while she went back to her closet to change into something more appropriate, I realized: if the opportunity was there tonight, and Tye and I ended up beyond the walls, we'd be empty-handed against any trouble.

I moved quickly, grabbing the gun from the linen closet and wrapping it carefully in the leather outfit I was to change into later. I was tucking it under my arm when I heard Harlow coming back.

Her full lips twisted into a smirk. "See you tonight, my lil' rebel."

I winked at her. "You bet."

The house had settled into a strange, quiet calm after the frenzy of both the crowns of Ylem leaving for dinner with their security detail.

I'd been in my room for hours, dressed and anxious, the loaded pistol securely tucked into the waistband at my back, covered by my jacket. I had no idea what tonight would bring, but I was ready for anything. It had all gone too smoothly, too perfectly, for it not to feel like the universe was guiding me.

Finally, in between the guards' shifts as planned, a soft knock came at the door. I took a deep breath, steadying myself before opening it. Harlow stood there, radiant in her minidress, her blue eyeliner and shimmering skin gloss making her look like she belonged in another world.

She grabbed my hand and led the way until I was following her down hallways I'd never seen before. With every step, my nerves grew. I half-expected a golden guard to jump out at any moment, but Harlow had promised me she knew this escape route like the back of her hand.

"I told Tye where to meet us," she whispered, her voice low but excited as we approached a service elevator in the pit of the Basilica.

She pressed the button, and the doors slid open. But I'd been expecting to feel relief at seeing Tye; instead, my stomach dropped. His face was tense with stress, and it didn't take long to see why. Maverick stepped out of the elevator next to him.

"He caught me," Tye said, his voice strained.

Harlow looked beyond annoyed. "Why aren't you with my dad?" she snapped.

"He's more concerned about your safety lately than his own," Maverick replied.

Harlow threw her hands up. "So now what? You're crashing our party?"

I exchanged a quick glance with Maverick, trying to silently communicate the need for his cooperation.

He sighed. "It's best I come with you. If you get into trouble, your dad will at least be happy I was there to look after you."

Harlow rolled her eyes, clearly irritated, and shoved him back into the elevator. The doors slid shut after we filed inside and we descended together. Adrenaline began to pulse through me.

We spoke in hushed whispers as we followed Harlow down the dimly lit tunnels. The walls had clearly been carved out for some emergency escape route, and for a moment, I couldn't help but think it was a major security lapse—this direct link to the Basilica was just sitting there unguarded. But then, at several points, Harlow would swipe some sort of keycard, and massive, thick metal doors would open, allowing us to pass through. The whole thing felt surreal, like we were trespassing in a hidden world beneath the surface.

We walked for what felt like thirty minutes, the tunnels stretching on endlessly, until we reached an unlit section. Harlow moved ahead and pulled a small lever on the wall. Tiny blue lights flickered to life, leading to a regular-sized door at the end.

We followed her through it, and the muffled sound of music instantly hit my ears.

We approached a small line of clubgoers forming in front of a doorman at the final door, the one that clearly led inside the club.

"Welcome to The Blacklight Scorpion," Harlow said with a grin, looking back at us excitedly.

My own excitement vanished when I saw two burly security guards near the doorman, patting people down before letting them through. I felt the pistol at my back grow red hot.

I thought about tossing it, ditching it somewhere before we got too close, but Harlow now had her arm around my shoulder and was leading me forward.

"Been a minute," the doorman called over the thumping music, pushing aside a few patrons to let Harlow through.

"Good to see you, Razz," she said with a warm smile, planting a kiss on both of his cheeks.

I tensed as the two security guards stepped toward us, but before they could search us—

"They're with me," Harlow interjected firmly.

Razz flashed a grin at us. "Enjoy," he said, waving the guards aside and swinging the door open without the required pat-down.

The second we stepped into the cavernous club, I had to pause for a moment to adjust. The black lights were casting everything in a neon glow that made everyone look almost ghostly, the appearance of their skin shifting between vibrant hues. It felt like stepping into a different dimension.

The otherworldly music hit me like a wave. The deep, pulsating bass wrapped around me, and I felt an instant euphoria. It was almost as if it were set to some mood-altering frequency.

A hostess, wearing nearly nothing, motioned for us to follow her through the crowd to the far side of the room, where VIP tables lined the walls.

En route, we passed the sleek chrome bar, where drinks that seemed to shimmer in the light were being served.

Even at the underground raves I'd used to hit with my friends in the inner cities near my hometown, I'd never seen anything like this.

Before we reached our table, a man in a broad-shouldered suit suddenly grabbed my arm and pulled me toward him. "Even in this light, I can tell you have beautiful eyes," he said, in some accent I couldn't make out over the music.

Maverick appeared by my side, but the man hardly seemed to notice. It wasn't until Harlow shot him a pointed look that he released me, allowing her to guide us toward the hostess now waiting at our corner table.

"Steer clear of him if you can," Harlow murmured in my ear. "He's some mafia capo my dad did business with."

The hostess leaned in with a smile. "Can I get you guys anything? Drinks? Sting?"

"Sting?" Tye asked, raising an eyebrow.

"To get high. Powdered scorpion venom," Harlow replied casually, as if it were no big deal.

Maverick shifted uncomfortably in his seat, while Tye gave a slight shake of the head to signal he'd pass. Harlow waved the hostess off just as a second girl approached, her arms open wide for Harlow.

"And this," Harlow said with a mischievous grin, "is the mafioso's daughter." She leapt into the girl's arms, and the way they embraced made it clear they were very familiar with each other.

Harlow was quickly pulled toward the dancefloor by the girl, disappearing among the fog and lasers.

"Maybe I should get a drink," I muttered, glancing at the boys.

Tye stood and nodded. "Yeah, I'll come with."

As we started pushing through the crowd, weaving our way toward the bar, I noticed Maverick trailing behind us. I hadn't anticipated the challenge of having him here. I knew he cared for me, but he was always looking out for himself first. If Tye and I disappeared, it would be on him. He'd never willingly let us escape on his watch.

We reached the bar line, and I turned to Tye. "Grab whatever looks good. I'll be there in a sec." I then turned to Maverick, shouting over the music. "For someone staying sober, this is a dumb place to follow us to."

Maverick anxiously surveyed the crowd. "What are you guys up to? No way was this all Harlow's idea."

"Are you asking because you want to help, or because you're going to stop us?"

He didn't flinch. "Tye asked me about the tunnels, and now you guys are here. If you're planning to make a run for it, don't. There's hundreds of tunnels beneath Ylem—you'll get lost and die. Or worse. There's Morts deeper in."

"Morts?" I asked, confusion tightening my chest. "I thought Ylem was Mort-free."

Maverick shook his head. "Do you know how many experiments they've done on Morts since the start? They've trapped some in underground annexes. There's even a bunch of openings that had to be closed up when some of them wandered into the tunnel systems. Besides, if you take Tye, they'll send their entire army after you. You stand no chance."

"Thanks for the vote of confidence," I scoffed, unable to hide my annoyance.

"If you stopped being so angry with me," Maverick said, his eyes intense, "you'd realize I'm trying to protect you. I love you, Willa."

Finally, after all this time, I felt a tiny spark of the care I used to have for him, a flash of the love we shared before everything turned to ash. It was enough to catch me off guard.

Maverick's voice softened, almost pleading. "I've apologized. I've tried to prove I'm on your side. I don't know what else to do."

I took a deep breath, shaking my head. "Look, I'm willing to start over. But for *your* safety, you should stick with Harlow and let me do what I need to do. Don't get mixed up in it."

Maverick looked disappointed, but he relented. "Alright. But think about what I said."

21. TYE

I was in awe of how quickly Willa had gotten us beneath Ylem, but I wasn't surprised. She'd always been the one to make things happen, able to handle situations with a calm tenacity that I could never match.

When Maverick caught me, I thought I'd ruined our best shot at escape, but now, watching how Willa was locked in conversation with him under the cover of the disorienting lights, it seemed she had a plan for that too.

I'd always dreamed of running off with Willa. I'd even tried to convince her to come with me when Canada seemed like a real option for safety. And now, this escape plan was as good as it was going to get—if we could somehow navigate the tunnels and not get caught. Even after everything we'd seen in Ylem, it was far more complex than we could ever imagine.

It was all happening so fast. I couldn't shake the feeling of guilt for leaving Vale and Beckett behind with no word. But I knew that if we made it back to the safe zone and regrouped, we'd all be able to join in on the New Year's attack plan... if that was still on the table at all. And maybe I could even set them all free.

With two glowing, bubbling drinks in hand, I made my way back to Willa, just as Maverick was returning to the VIP table.

"Everything good?" I asked, handing her one of the drinks.

"Let's hope," she replied, taking it from me before her gaze flicked toward the dancefloor.

I followed her eyes and caught Harlow looking at us over the shoulder of the girl she was dancing with. They were locked in an embrace. Willa raised her glass to Harlow, getting a smile in response, before leaning in close to me.

"Dance with me," Willa whispered in my ear. Without hesitation, I let her pull me deeper into the crowd, and we started moving to the beat.

I felt strange dancing with Willa so openly, with no hiding. But at the same time, I remembered where we were. This was a place where everyone was breaking the law. A place for sinning in peace.

When I placed my hand on her lower back, I felt something that made me pull back quickly. *A gun*. Tucked under her jacket, but unmistakable.

"Seems like you've thought this through. What's our next move, then?" I asked quietly, my voice barely cutting through the thumping music.

Willa, pretending to enjoy the dance, replied, "I'll be honest, I never thought we'd make it this far. The rest we'll have to improvise."

I felt a knot form in my stomach. "We've survived worse odds, I guess."

Her smile faded just slightly. "No food or water, and we'll be in the middle of nowhere, if we make it out. And Maverick just told me there's Morts underground."

"Jesus ... " The weight of her words sank in. "Well, just because we've made it this far, doesn't mean we have to be impulsive if it's not the right time. I'll follow your lead."

Before we could say anything else, Harlow was walking toward us, her energy infectious as she cut through the crowd, everyone staring at her like she was a star.

We stopped talking, slipping back into the rhythm of the music, our bodies moving together as she approached.

"Isn't this place amazing?" she asked, joining us and starting to dance.

"Insane!" Willa said, the excitement in her voice landing perfectly.

Harlow grinned. "You guys are the hottest couple. I love this."

My face grew warm at the compliment. "Thanks for bringing me."

"Of course."

Feeling a sudden need to do something in return, I said, "I'll grab you a drink. What do you want?"

She paused, then subtly placed a hand on her stomach. Both Willa and I froze, the implication apparently hitting us at the same time. "It worked? You're pregnant?" I asked in disbelief.

Harlow cracked a weary smile. "Weird, I know. Confirmed this afternoon." She nodded toward a group of guys a few feet away, all snorting powder from a table. "Motherhood's off to a good start, huh?"

I knew this was the planned outcome all along, but hearing it had worked made me feel conflicted. There was no emotional attachment to the baby, of course, but something about the reality of it left me with an odd feeling. I suddenly felt guilty about ditching Harlow here if I managed to escape, especially after the kindness she'd shown us.

Willa must've seen the doubt forming on my face because, without missing a beat, she said, "I'm gonna go to the restroom real quick."

I caught on immediately. "I'll walk you."

Harlow smirked at us, a playful squint in her eyes. "What a gentleman!" she said, slapping us both on the butt as we turned to make our way toward the back corner.

As we walked away, I couldn't shake the feeling that the choices we were making now would ripple far beyond this night.

We walked past all kinds of colorful characters, each one stranger than the last. There was a glossy veneer of fun to it all, but beneath that, it felt like everyone here was shady, even by the corrupt standards of Ylem.

Willa and I kept our heads down, staying out of the way until we reached a narrow back hallway. Further along, I could see the doors to the men's and women's bathrooms. I was ready to wait for her while she went in, but to my surprise, she walked straight past them, heading to the end of the hall without a word.

I glanced around quickly, making sure no one was watching us, then followed her, keeping close as she walked to a point where even the glow of the club lights didn't reach. This end of the hall was lined with a few unlabeled doors.

She tried the first one, but it was locked. Without hesitating, she moved to the second and twisted the knob. This door creaked open, and we both paused, glancing at each other before peeking inside. It was just a mechanical room, full of pipes and old equipment.

Willa closed the door and moved further down the hall, not saying a word, and I followed. The next one she opened revealed something entirely different: a long, barely lit tunnel. Only a few emergency lights flickered down its length.

Before stepping in, I grabbed her arm, stopping her. "I'd follow you anywhere, but are you sure you're ready for this? If anything happens to you because you're trying to save me, I'll never forgive myself."

Willa kissed me quickly on the cheek. "Shut up and hurry," she said, her voice low but firm. She pulled me inside and closed the door behind us.

The moment it clicked shut, an eerie silence took over. No music. No sounds from the club. Stifling darkness.

I could hear the soft click of Willa's gun being cocked as she led the way. The small emergency lights cast just enough of a glow for us to move forward.

Adrenaline pumped through me, my heart racing with each step. I couldn't believe we were actually doing it. Willa's steps were steady and focused, but behind her, I couldn't help but smile. We were escaping, finally free from the endless tests and transfusions.

The uncertainty of our plan was gnawing at me, though.

"You said if we make it out, we'd be in the middle of nowhere. You know where in the world Ylem is?" I asked as I stepped over a puddle of strange liquid.

Willa glanced back at me briefly. "Patagonia, apparently. Somewhere in South America."

I froze, taken aback. *"Patagonia?"* The word felt strange in my mouth. I had no idea how far from home that was, but I knew it was too far.

"I'm betting once Ylem realizes we're missing, it'll go haywire. Word will get back to my contact, Rowen. He'll send people to come help us... We'll just have to hope it's quick enough."

I tried to believe her, but the doubt kept creeping in. "I don't want to be negative, I'm just trying to think ahead so I can help... What if no one comes?"

Willa's pace didn't falter. "I don't know. Maybe we can find another cargo ship. Ylem imports tons of stuff, so there have to be ships or planes coming and going. Both of us were brought here from far away, so there's a route somewhere."

It sounded far-fetched, but I couldn't help clinging to hope. If we made it out, we'd find a way. Still, the memories of my time surviving alone in the desert kept creeping up on me. I remembered the loneliness, the constant battle to keep moving forward when taking another step felt impossible. The thought of going through that again made my chest constrict. But then I glanced at Willa, and her presence grounded me. She was with me this time, and somehow, that made everything feel a little more possible.

Willa seemed to pick up on my worry. "Look, the bombings are one thing. Maybe Rowen already caught wind of it from someone inside the network, and they're already preparing. I really hope so. But getting *you* out of Ylem is just as important. The world stands no chance without a cure, and Ylem will never let you go. We have to try. That's the first step—getting you out so there's a fighting chance against this virus. And hopefully, one day, we can make it back here and free the other Angels."

I felt the pressure of everything that lay ahead. Once I made it back to the safe zone, it wouldn't mean the end of the testing and experiments. With Ylem keeping everything under wraps, new doctors would have to start all over again, trying to figure out how to use my blood for a cure. But at least this time it would be on my terms—willingly, for people I loved and cared about, and for the right side.

Minutes passed in silence as we walked through the damp, musty tunnels. The air was thick with the smell of mildew. Just as I started to feel my nerves settle, Willa stopped short. I squinted, my eyes straining in the darkness to see what was ahead of us.

Then I heard it. Muffled music. It was faint, but unmistakable.

"Shit. It took us in a circle!" Willa exclaimed, frustrated.

I reached cautiously for the nearest door. I hoped to peek through and see some sign of an exit, but it didn't open. I figured it was the same locked door from earlier—the one we'd first tried. We were back where we'd started!

"Damnit," Willa whispered, sounding as worried as I felt.

We were about to turn back when a door suddenly swung open and Maverick appeared, pulling us both through it.

"What are you—" Willa started, but Maverick cut her off.

"There's a raid!" he said, eyes wide with panic. "They're shutting down the club."

I felt the blood drain from my face.

"Follow me!" Maverick ordered.

Willa quickly tucked the gun back into her jacket, and without a word, we followed him back toward the chaos. When we hit the dancefloor, the scene was pure madness. The lights had flickered on, flooding the space with blinding brightness. People were pushing and shoving, desperate to get out, while golden soldiers swarmed the room. I scanned the crowd, but there was no sign of Harlow.

We pushed toward the entrance, where the chaos seemed to escalate. That's when I saw Harlow, surrounded by golden soldiers, two of them shouting and pointing directly at us.

"Those two!"

Before we could react, Maverick stepped in front of us.

"They're in my custody," Maverick said, his tone firm and commanding. "Harlow ordered them to come. They'll cooperate."

Willa and I exchanged a look as dread washed over me. This was the worst possible outcome. We were caught between the soldiers and Maverick's cover story, not knowing whether to trust his help or fear it.

Willa and I spent the night in separate holding cells at some facility. It was uncomfortable, with bare walls that made everything feel cold. Harlow, of course, hadn't been brought here like us, though I was sure her father would be furious once he found out what she'd arranged.

If it hadn't been for Maverick's cover story, things could've gone much worse for us. He pinned it on Harlow, knowing she was the only one who'd get off with just a slap on the wrist. What came next was still up in the air, but I knew the punishment wouldn't be nearly as bad as if we'd been caught trying to escape through the tunnels.

Hours dragged on, each one heavier than the last. My mind drifted to Willa and the gun. Even with Maverick's help, how would she ever explain that? I was on the brink of a panic attack, stuck in the tiny box, and just when I thought I might actually crack, a guard came to my door and unlocked it to pull me out.

I was led through the hallways to a lobby where Secretary Croft stood, her face twisted in anger. Willa was there too, standing next to another golden guard, her eyes purposely avoiding mine. We were back to pretending we didn't know each other.

"I don't want to hear a word out of you," Croft snapped, her voice icy. "You're going back to the camps until we've investigated further."

My face got hot. I was relieved to know I'd see my friends again, but it also meant I'd be separated from Willa. It felt like I was trading one cell for another. Just a different kind of cage.

Without even getting the chance to say goodbye to Willa, I found myself back on the metro. The rhythmic clatter of the train was almost soothing, but the tension in the carriage made it hard to focus on anything else. Secretary Croft was seething, her eyes narrowed in quiet fury as she stared at me, but I didn't engage.

Finally, she couldn't hold back any longer. "Harlow and Maverick filled me in," she began, her tone tight and controlled. "I understand she gave you an order, but you answer to Midas, not her. So many things could've gone wrong by you going anywhere near that nightclub. Though you may have even gotten away with it if it weren't for her mother going to look for her in her room. You're very lucky, considering how this could've all gone down."

I just nodded, not bothering to say anything. I had no energy for a fight with Croft—and it wasn't just because I was physically drained, either. Croft had been making my life hell since the day she'd pulled me off that cargo plane, and now that my escape had failed, I had even more contempt for her.

As the train slowed, a guard approached and quickly blindfolded me. The familiar motions of being checked back into the camp were automatic now.

When the blindfold was finally lifted, I blinked against the bright fluorescent lights, trying to adjust. I found myself in the Commissary area of the camps, the sterile white walls and buzzing lights unchanged from the last time I'd been here. The same dull loop of mundane existence; the same faces, moving through the same routines.

I scanned the room eagerly for my friends, spotting Beckett first. He was sitting alone at one of the Commissary tables, a book open in front of him. A wave of disappointment hit me as I realized he was still separated from Vale, who I guessed was as determined as ever to keep their interactions to a minimum.

Beckett saw me almost immediately, his face lighting up. But he quickly masked it, perhaps making a conscious effort not to react too strongly. Guards were nearby, watching everything closely these days.

I grabbed a cup of water from the Commissary counter and sat down near him, but not directly opposite.

"How'd the resurrection go?" Beckett asked, his voice barely above a whisper.

"It worked, if that's what you mean," I replied. "But I'm not sure how her mom's doing now that it's done."

Beckett shot me a quick, knowing look. "I thought for sure you were gonna blow our cover, the way you were testing the waters with Harlow like that."

I leaned back slightly, glancing around before responding. "But you see what I see, right? She's different. And she wants to help. I know deep down—"

Before I could finish, Vale walked into the Commissary and made his way over to us, cutting the conversation short. Beckett rolled his eyes, not even bothering to face Vale as he closed his book. With a practiced motion, he stood and turned toward the rec room, like he was used to following their new playbook.

But then, to my surprise, Vale stopped him with a hand on his shoulder.

"Hey..." Vale's voice was soft, and for a moment, there was an odd vulnerability to it. "I love you, you know that, right?"

Beckett looked back with a smile, a quiet affirmation, before heading off.

Vale slid into a seat at the table behind me. He was sitting with his back to mine, but we were close enough to speak without raising our voices.

I heard him shift, likely glancing over his shoulder at the guards, who were absorbed in conversation on the opposite side of the room to me. "You back for more testing?" he asked, his tone dry. "I thought they'd chill for a second after that resurrection. It's all my assigned family can talk about."

I sighed. "I'm in timeout." I paused, not sure how much to explain. "Don't freak out...It's a long story, but I caught wind of some tunnels under Ylem, and I tried to get out. They didn't catch me escaping, but I wasn't where I was meant to be, so they're evaluating what to do with me next."

Vale's voice was full of disbelief. "You're a madman, Tye. That was a suicide mission."

"Well, I'm desperate. I can't take it here anymore, and with the bombing Midas is planning, my friends back home are as good as dead. There won't be a New Year's plan if they're not ready for what he's about to do... unless you can get a message out."

His voice dropped lower. "Trust me, I've been trying, but I've lost track of who's on our side. If there's anyone left in the coalition, they've gone silent. No one's reached out, no usual whispers through the grapevine, not since the executions. They're paranoid, and rightfully so."

I glanced over at Beckett, who was trying hard not to look at us, clearly uncomfortable with the situation. "You included?" I asked softly. "I hate seeing you and Beckett apart like this."

Vale's tone darkened. "I hate it too, but I'm protecting him. I shouldn't have gotten him involved in any of it. I can't do anything about Midas's plan, and neither can you. My job's to stay on course while we're only a few months away from New Year's. Any more rips in the sail and we're dead in the water."

I nodded, forcing myself to accept it, but the thought of having to stand by while my friends went through yet another catastrophic event didn't sit right with me.

Vale must have sensed the gears turning in my head and quickly added, "Just be really careful, Tye. You're not the only one trying to save people you love."

I finally turned to face him and found him looking over at Beckett.

22. WILLA

A couple of days had passed since my night in the holding cell, and a sense of unease hung over everything. The whispers had spread fast, and it wasn't long before I started to hear the comments behind my back. Not only had Harlow taken me to an underground club, but I'd been arrested on top of it, only to be released without real consequence. Even with the gun found on me, Maverick must've said something convincing, because it was never brought up again. Clearly, there was a double standard in play. None of the other staff would ever be afforded the same luxury of escaping Ylem's extreme punishments. Now, they were being especially cruel to me, as if dishing out their own version of retribution.

Even Harlow had been noticeably distant. Her absence had replaced the warmth I'd come to expect from her. It was true she was spending more and more time with her mom, but I couldn't help wondering if it was more than that. Was this what I'd feared all along? That she wouldn't need me anymore once things were back to 'normal?' Or was there something more to it? I couldn't tell. The uncertainty gnawed at me, especially when I felt like I'd been finally making progress with her.

And without Tye here, I felt more isolated than ever. Though we could rarely talk as it was, his presence still made the isolation easier to deal with. At least I knew someone else understood what it felt like to be stuck in this hellhole. Now that he was gone, I was alone, truly alone, and it felt like I was being swallowed up by the space itself.

On top of that, the stress of the impending bombs dropping had reached an all-time high. I could barely focus on anything else. The thought that my friends could very well die, and that Midas's destruction could be far more widespread than any of us had predicted, left me with a pit in my stomach. I had to accept the reality that we were stuck here until, at least, New Year's—if the plan could be pulled off at all.

I kept holding onto the hope that Tye's deal with Midas to spare Safe Zone 32 would hold. If nothing else, at least they might be safe. But even that seemed fragile.

The only thing keeping me grounded was the tiny grain of hope that things could have ended worse. Had we been caught trying to escape, we would've been in far deeper trouble. It didn't make everything better, but it was something to remind myself of. There was a chance, however small, that freedom could still be possible.

While I was vacuuming the long hallway, I passed one of the many sitting rooms, and something caught my eye. The familiar setup of transfusion equipment—the sterile bags, the tubing—was being arranged in the corner by a nurse. This was the lounge where Harlow usually had her sessions, and I figured she was probably in her room right now, changing into one of her elegant, comfortable robes as she always did beforehand.

I took the opportunity and steered the vacuum toward Harlow's room. My heart was beating a little faster than usual as I reached her door. I switched the vacuum off and knocked gently.

"Come in," came Harlow's voice.

I pushed the door open, and as soon as she saw me, my stomach dropped. Her face had fallen; she was clearly unhappy to see me. Something was definitely off.

"Hey, I just wanted to check in ... see if everything's okay," I said, trying to keep my voice steady. "I haven't seen you much since the other night, and I wanted to at least thank you for getting me out of there."

She pretended to be deciding between two silk robes, but there was an edge to her tone when she spoke. "Of course. It was my fault for thinking it was a good idea ... " She trailed off for a moment, then looked at me seriously. "Aria, I need to ask you something, and I need you to be honest with me."

I instantly felt my temperature spike. Harlow took a step back. "The guards told me they found a gun on you. My gun. I covered for you and said I'd asked you to hold it, but ... what were you doing with my pistol?"

The question hit me like a punch to the chest. The hurt in her eyes unsettled me. I wasn't prepared for this.

My heart was racing now. There was no way to dodge this one. What could I possibly say that would make sense? Harlow was sharp. She knew something wasn't right. I could feel myself grinding my teeth, hesitating, caught between wanting to come clean and fearing her reaction.

When I took too long to answer, Harlow's barely-audible voice trembled as she asked, "Are you part of the coalition?"

The question hung in the air like a pressure I could barely breathe under. I froze, every muscle in my body locking up. But then, as if a switch had flipped, a realization hit me. Maybe this was it. Maybe I had to just tell her the truth—be honest, no matter how brutal it would be—and hope that the bond we'd built would survive the shock of my confession.

I swallowed hard. *"Yes."*

Harlow's eyes went wide and she fell back onto the bed, her mouth hanging open in shock. But she didn't scream. She didn't run. The fact that she didn't freak out gave me a small glimmer of relief.

I took a deep breath. "Harlow, listen—"

"What's your real name?" she interrupted.

" ... Willa."

The silence between us felt like an eternity.

"You know that boy, Tye, don't you?" she asked eventually, her voice quiet but with an edge to it.

I'd already come this far, and I couldn't stop now. "I do. From before we knew anything about Ylem's existence."

Harlow's eyes flickered with confusion as I continued, each word pushing me further into uncharted territory. "And Maverick. He was friends with my brother—the one who passed."

Each new revelation visibly hit her like a blow, and I could see her mind scrambling to piece it all together.

I pressed on, knowing she was still with me, still listening. I had to stay bold while the moment was mine. “Harlow, I care about you. I care about everything we’ve shared. But if any of that was real, I need you to listen to me, carefully.” I paused, trying to find the right words to make her understand, to make her believe me. “I’m trying to get out of Ylem. Not just for myself. I need to make it back to my friends in the safe zone. You have no idea how bad it is out there. And if your dad carries out his plans—if those bombs drop—it’s over. Everything me and my friends have fought for will be gone. But there’s still a chance... There’s still a chance for us to warn them.”

I took a deep breath before continuing. “The bombs aren’t even the worst of it, Harlow. Tye is the only way anyone outside these walls has a chance for a future. He’s the key to finding a cure, to saving lives. There are people rallying behind him, fighting for him, because they believe in what he can do. And he wants to see his friends again, the people who are like family to us. *We need to get to them, Harlow.*”

I saw her hesitate, and I pushed a little further, not willing to let her slip away from me. “Remember what you said to me once, back when we were talking about the Angels? You told me that if it were up to you, you’d set them free. Well, at least one of them can be freed. This is your chance to make it happen. To be the one who changes everything.”

Her eyes softened for a moment.

“I know you’re different, Harlow,” I went on. “You’re nothing like your father. You’ve always had a good heart, a good soul, deep down. You’re capable of so much more than what’s been asked of you here. You’ve shown me that. And now you have the chance to prove it—to show the world, to show me, that you’re the person I’ve always believed you are.”

I took a step closer to her, my voice steady, but I couldn't hide how emotional I was. "*Prove* to me I'm right about that. I don't want to be wrong about another person I trust."

I waited, my heart still racing in my chest, praying that somehow, against all odds, Harlow would see the truth in my words. That she would understand.

But instead, her expression slowly turned blank, the warmth I'd seen moments before slipping away like it'd never been there at all. She stood up, her movements stiff, and softly said, "Aria, I need—" She stopped herself. "*Willa*. This is a lot. I need some space, okay? Please leave."

I could feel the blood drain from my face. I didn't know how to respond, so I just nodded automatically. I backed out of the room, my breath shallow, feeling like I'd just put the final nail in the coffin of everything I'd been working toward.

I went back to vacuuming, my hands shaking with the adrenaline of what I'd just done. The quiet hum of the machine barely registered as my mind spiraled. The fear of what I could've just ruined crashed down on me. Rowen's careful plans... Had I just destroyed them? Had I just condemned myself, Maverick, and Tye to a fate worse than death? The bombings, the betrayal, everything I'd feared, were closing in on me. And worst of all, if Harlow cracked, I could be hanged in the city square by this time tomorrow.

A sudden, desperate need for the comfort of someone who could make me feel better hit me—like Malik, who would listen without judgment and offer his calm perspective, his steady words making everything feel less overwhelming. Archer, with his innocent optimism, always able to make the worst situations seem brighter, even if just for a moment. Or Imani, who would understand me better than anyone, with that logical calmness that always helped me see things clearly when I was lost in my head.

But none of them were here. And all I had now was the overwhelming anxiety that had taken root in my stomach.

I tried to shake it off, focusing on the chores laid out before me. I found myself almost grateful for the endless tasks. At least they gave me something to occupy my mind. I didn't know how much longer I could keep waiting on edge, expecting any moment for the golden guards to come for me. If they did, I'd most likely face intense interrogation, maybe even torture. The possibility of that was all too real.

Just as I was becoming lost in the monotonous rhythm of polishing silver in one of the parlor rooms, trying to block out the dread eating away at me, a sound made me pause. The familiar, methodical steps of the golden guards echoed through the halls as they entered the Basilica. My pulse quickened. I thought for sure this was it—they were coming for me.

But then I saw Tye being escorted through the hall by Maverick, his posture stiff. He'd been brought back to the Basilica. This was a good sign. It meant that Harlow hadn't spilled yet.

I couldn't risk making any sort of eye contact with him, though. Not now. If anyone saw even the smallest sign that we were connected, it could end everything. I kept my focus on the silver, buffing it methodically, going through the motions.

It wasn't until a few minutes later, when the sound of the guards faded, that Maverick came and found me. He pulled me aside, urgently steering me toward the library. The heavy oak doors swung shut behind us.

"They already questioned Tye," he began, his voice low and firm. "I coached him on what to say about the club nightmare—"

"I fucked up, Mav." The words came out in a rush, and his jaw tightened. "I know you think I'm impulsive, reckless—crazy even—but this ... this tops it all."

Maverick froze, his expression hardening into a mask of barely contained frustration. *"What did you do now?"*

"I told Harlow. Everything. Who I am, how I know Tye ... that I know you—"

"Willa." The sharpness in his voice made me wince.

"Mav, I didn't have a choice. Everyone I know will die if we don't warn them about the bombs. I need to get back to them—and get Tye out of here. I asked for her help."

He stared at me, his expression a storm of disbelief and anger. "Willa, this is bad. You've just signed both of our death warrants."

"She hasn't told Midas yet," I shot back. "She could still come through for us."

"You're not thinking straight," he snapped, pacing now, his movements agitated. "Even if Harlow helps us, you won't make it out of here alive, let alone back to the U.S. The second they realize you and Tye are gone, they'll hunt you down. They won't stop 'til they have him back and you're *dead*."

"*You* could help us," I insisted. "Come with us. You know this place, the tunnels—you'd give us a fighting chance."

Maverick stopped mid-step, his back to me. "The safe zones are run by the military, Willa. They're directly tied to Ylem. You think they'll just let us walk back in as traitors?" He turned, his voice quieter but no less intense. "Even if we make it back, we'll be turned in before we can take a breath."

"Things are changing," I said, stepping closer to him. "More soldiers out there are abandoning their orders every day. They know Ylem abandoned them, that their leaders are using them. And they know what Tye represents. He's the key to ending this."

For a moment, doubt crept into his expression. But then he shook his head. "I know you've got people to fight for—friends, family—but I don't have anyone. At least here, I have a place, a purpose."

"You don't believe that." I spoke matter-of-factly, but my heart was pounding. "You're a pawn, just like those soldiers in the safe zones. The sooner you stop pretending you don't have anyone, the sooner you'll wake up and pick a side." I stepped closer still, holding his gaze. "I'm right here, Mav."

The words hit him hard, I saw it—the crack in his anger. His eyes glistened, the emotion unmistakable, but he blinked it away. Without a word, he turned and headed for the door. The risk of talking for so long had reached a breaking point.

"Maverick," I said seriously, "a final attack is coming on Ylem. You're either with us or against us. *No more playing both sides.*"

His hand hovered over the door handle, a moment of hesitation, but he didn't turn. Without a word, he opened the door and slipped out into the corridor, leaving a silent barrier between us.

23. TYE

Since his last transfusion had been cut short, I was brought back to the Basilica for a session with Midas. I wasn't sure if they were going to let me stay or if it was just for the moment, but the thought of seeing Midas again, especially after what had happened at the underground club, made me nervous. I couldn't shake the feeling that he'd be angry with me, or worse, that he'd press me harder than Croft's officers had.

Maverick left me with the houseman, who led me directly to the lounge. I could feel my pulse quicken as I walked in. Chiron was already hooking Midas up to the IV, not acknowledging my arrival. Midas waved a hand lazily in my direction, motioning for me to sit in the chaise next to him. My limbs felt tight as I lowered myself into the seat.

Chiron moved to connect me to the IV.

"I'm disappointed in you, Tye," Midas began. "You shouldn't have been anywhere near that place in the tunnels."

Chiron's hand jerked, and the catheter clattered to the floor. He quickly regained his composure, but I could see the tension in his shoulders.

Midas didn't even glance at him, his attention entirely on me as he continued. "But I will admit, I've put pressure on you to connect with Harlow. I understand you may have felt obligated to follow her... even if her actions were reckless."

I felt jittery. I didn't want to have this conversation, but I had no choice but to play along. "I wanted her to feel that we were friends and she could trust me," I said, forcing the words out.

Midas smiled, his eyes narrowing slightly. "Understandable." He paused, almost like he was enjoying the discomfort he was causing.

"That's why I will allow you to continue your stay here. But understand this: I will be making sure there's no more room to step out of line, for you or my daughter. With my wife back, our family unit is strong, and it must be seen that way by the people. My daughter, and you, represent us—the core of Ylem's power."

I tried to steer the conversation elsewhere, anything to avoid what he was saying. "How's she doing? Your wife?"

Midas didn't miss a beat, a smile curling his lips. "Incredibly. She's back to full health. Of course, there's the usual amount of adjusting to all the changes, but she's coping wonderfully." His eyes glinted with satisfaction. "It's all on course for the next phase of Ylem's growth. The airstrikes will begin at the end of this month. Preparations have already begun."

It wasn't just the blood draw making me lightheaded. The realization that the bombings were scheduled sooner than I'd thought made my head spin with worry.

"Additionally," Midas continued, almost casually, "as a result of the resurrection, there are other powerful families that want to meet you. It's good for political morale, so I'll be arranging a sort of tour. You'll have transfusions with them too."

His words drained the last bit of optimism I had left. It was like he knew exactly how to make me feel insignificant—like dust, with no feelings, no choice.

The sadness washed over me again. I couldn't shake the thought that I should've done more to escape that night.

Midas apparently noticed the drop in my energy. "Well, there's good news, Tye," he said, his tone almost too calm, like he was watching for my reaction. "Something I think you'll be happy to hear. We've finalized a cure, in vaccination form. Using the Angels and your blood. It's still in the early stages, of course, but it's a huge breakthrough. It'll be a while before it's ready to completely replace the transfusions, but you should feel hopeful. One day, you might be able to live here in Ylem as a normal citizen, one who's made a massive contribution to its history."

I let his words sink in, but instead of the rush of relief I expected, something heavier settled in my chest. Sure, it was incredible to think they'd actually created a cure, but the thought of it only serving those inside Ylem—those who had power and resources—was devastating. My friends, the people outside these walls, the ones who had lost everything to the virus... It would never reach them.

"I look forward to it," I said, the words coming out lifeless, lacking any trace of the excitement he might've expected.

After the transfusion, I was being escorted back to my quarters by the golden guards, my arm throbbing, when I heard someone calling my name.

"Is that Tye?"

I turned, startled, to see Madam Olivia standing a few feet away, looking more radiant than I could've imagined. She was in an elegant house dress that made me think of Harlow, that maybe she'd even picked out for her. She looked every bit the picture of health Midas had described, her skin glowing with vitality.

"Yes, hello," I said, a little timidly, unsure of how to act around her.

"I've been eager to meet the man who gave me my life back," she said, her voice warm and inviting. She smiled, and it looked genuine. "Come." She beckoned me forward.

I hesitated for a moment, then followed her. We rounded the corner, and I soon found myself entering an aviary I hadn't seen before. It was smaller than the solarium, but still beautiful. Lush plants filled the space, and a few exotic birds fluttered around in the open air—species that were probably rare even before the majority had been wiped out.

Olivia sat down on a small bench and patted the spot beside her. "Sit," she said, motioning for me to join her.

I hesitated again, but she had a calm air about her that made it hard to refuse. I took a seat next to her, and she immediately signaled for the guards to wait outside. They didn't question her, just nodded and planted themselves at the entrance, closing the glass door behind them.

The moment they left, the air felt different—more intimate, less guarded. Olivia's presence was commanding, but not threatening. There was something about her calm, collected energy that made me want to relax, even though I knew I shouldn't.

She looked at me for a moment, her expression thoughtful, as if she were trying to decide what to say.

"I heard something today," she began, her voice quiet but filled with a warmth I wasn't expecting. "I heard that Harlow is carrying your child."

I was quick to mask any reaction, trying not to let anything show.

"I know it was done unconventionally," Olivia continued matter-of-factly, "but she's told me so many wonderful things about you. She admires you, Tye." Her smile deepened, but there was something almost wistful behind it. "It makes me happy to be here for Harlow again. I missed so much of her life—so many years. I'll never get that time back, but now I have a second chance. And I have you to thank for that."

She spoke so freely, so genuinely. Her gratitude felt sincere, yet I couldn't help but notice the distance in her words. She hadn't been here long enough to understand the true weight of the 'gift' she was thanking me for. She had no idea what it cost me to be tied to this place, to this role they'd forced me into.

I swallowed down the bitterness, not wanting to ruin the moment. But I had to ask. It felt like the right time, even though I wasn't sure if I was prepared for the answer. "What was it like? When you were gone?" I asked carefully. "Is there ... *anything* after this?"

Olivia's smile faltered for a moment, and I could see the shift in her eyes. She seemed to hesitate, as if unsure of how much she wanted to reveal, but then she sighed softly and looked at me with the kind of gentleness I could only expect from someone Harlow took after.

"The moment you brought me back, I couldn't remember anything from when I was gone. My last memory is of the horrible sickness that overcame me, losing control of my body as the virus took hold. It was like I was fading away with no way to stop it." She paused, her gaze drifting as if she were still trying to piece together the fragments of something lost. "But deep in my soul, I believe there was *something*. I feel it, something I can't quite grasp, but it's there. I keep having these moments where it feels like I can almost hear something, or see something from when I was gone—like it's just out of reach."

I felt my frown give way to a small smile. The thought of there being something else after all this hell, something more than just survival in this endless cycle of suffering, gave me a brief, unexpected sense of hope.

I was still processing Olivia's words when the sound of soft footsteps interrupted my thoughts. Harlow appeared behind the glass, looking slightly taken aback at seeing us together. After a moment, she stepped inside.

"Everything okay?" she asked, her tone casual, though there was an edge of tension beneath it.

Olivia smiled. "Everything's fine, darling. We were just getting acquainted. I'll leave you two to have some time together."

Harlow gave her a quick nod, and Olivia stood, casting me one last glance before heading toward the door. The guards trailed behind her into the hall. I was actually a little disappointed to see her go. Her presence had been a small relief, but as the door clicked shut behind her, the air seemed to shift again.

Harlow didn't meet my eyes right away. She stood by the glass door for a moment, staring at it as if unsure of what to do next. But when she finally looked at me, I saw the stress written all over her face. Her usual confidence was nowhere to be found.

"Was your dad really angry about our night out?" I asked, trying to keep things light, but unable to hide the worry in my voice.

She hesitated before answering. " … Willa told me everything."

I nearly recoiled from the shock of her words. Even though I'd known Willa might ask for her help, I hadn't thought she was actually on track to making a move like that.

"About you. About Maverick. She asked me to help you escape."

I sucked in a breath. "And … ?"

She let out a long sigh, almost as if trying to steady herself. "And … I don't know, I'm a bit in shock. I feel lied to. Used."

I stared at her, trying to read her expression. She wasn't angry, but she wasn't exactly on board either.

"Well, if you're still thinking about it," I said slowly, "let me just say this." I paused, my heart pounding as I forced myself to speak the truth, to let her see how deep this ran. "Willa's the most special person in the world. If you think getting me out of here is too far-fetched, then at least help Willa. Let her go. She needs to warn our friends about the airstrikes. If she doesn't, they'll all be wiped out, just like everything else. They're the last family I have … and I *love* her, more than any words I say can make you understand."

The words came out more urgently than I'd intended. I held her gaze, hoping the sincerity in my plea had done enough.

Harlow took a long pause, and I still couldn't read her. Her eyes drifted away from me, like she was lost in a memory or trying to find the right words.

"When I was around fourteen, I was hanging out with a group of kids," she said eventually. "All from royal families living in Ylem. They kept me around because of who my father was, but they were determined to make me feel like the odd one out. One day, they brought me to a tunnel—one known to lead outside the wall. It's where they would dump Dark-Eyes after they experimented on them, sending them back out as an extra layer of security for trespassers. They dared me to go through it and bring something back from the other side … " Her voice trailed off, and she looked distant. "I was never going to do it—I knew better. But they wouldn't let it go. They wanted to see if I'd actually go through with it, like they got some kind of thrill from pushing me to prove I belonged.

"That tunnel's still there. It's dangerous, but it's the least complicated way out beyond the wall, and it's been neglected for years."

I was trying to process everything she was saying, to read her. Just when I thought she might leave me hanging, she spoke again, her voice firmer.

"I'll take you and Willa there. Give me a day to figure it out with Maverick, but be ready tomorrow night."

Tomorrow night?! For a moment, I almost jumped up to hug her, but I stopped myself. Instead, I just smiled, my throat tightening as tears threatened to form. She was serious. This was really happening.

"Thank you," I said quietly, feeling a weight lifting off my chest.

The next day dragged on, each hour stretching endlessly. I couldn't stop the nerves from crawling through my body, my mind thoroughly occupied by what was to come. One failed attempt was already crazy enough, but two? That would mean being caged like an animal for good, and I wasn't ready to accept that. This had to work—this would be my *final* chance. If we got caught, the consequences would be severe. Not just for me, but for Harlow too. She could lose her freedom completely. It was the highest of stakes yet.

Sitting on the bed after my evening shower, I could feel the anticipation building. I knew it could be weeks, maybe longer, before I'd have another chance to wash again. I pulled on a few layers of clothes, not knowing what kind of conditions we'd be facing. I wasn't unfamiliar with surviving on the bare minimum—I'd done it before. But what little I knew about Patagonia was that its wilderness was no joke.

A knock on the door broke through my thoughts—just as I'd predicted, it came between the guards' shift changes. Maverick walked in, tossing me a backpack. I caught it, feeling the weight of what was probably supplies.

We moved quickly through the halls until we reached a corridor behind the kitchen, then descended a long stairwell.

At the bottom, I spotted a small trolley surrounded by crates and boxes, their labels indicating they were filled with supplies. It looked like a transport cart, something used to bring goods in and out of the Basilica.

Waiting next to the trolley were Harlow and Willa, both of them looking eager to board. Willa looked different from the last time I'd seen her. No longer dressed in her gray uniform, she was in jeans and a heavy jacket that she'd clearly borrowed from Harlow, and had a backpack over her shoulders too.

Harlow swiped her access keycard keycard against a nearby panel, and a deep mechanical hum rumbled through the underground space as the cargo trolley came to life.

"This will take us close enough to the tunnel you guys need to take," Harlow said.

We boarded, and I glanced at Willa. Her eyes met mine. They were filled with uncertainty, but also something else—hope. We were ready to take on whatever was coming, side by side.

24. WILLA

I nearly collapsed when Harlow showed up at my room that night and told me she'd made up her mind—she was going to help us escape. All the doubts, all the fears I'd had about our trust, everything just melted away. My intuition hadn't let me down after all. Harlow was the ally we needed, and she was finally stepping up. But learning Maverick was helping her? That was the real surprise.

After a tense trolley ride and a long hike, the four of us stood at the mouth of a tunnel, not far from a maze of sewage channels. The rusted metal doors of the tunnel entrance were a clear sign that this place had been forgotten for years. The neglect of it all felt like a blessing—no guards, no interference. We were on the edge of Ylem's borders, and for once, it felt like luck was on our side.

Harlow turned to me, her eyes searching for something, maybe reassurance, but all I could offer was a tentative smile. She spoke first, her voice vulnerable in a way I hadn't heard before.

"I really hope I'm actually helping you two, and not sending you off to your deaths." Her voice cracked with emotion. "I get why you had to keep things from me, but I really do care about you."

I took a deep breath, stepping closer to her. "I care about you too. And what you're doing tonight could actually change history. I hope I see you again, but no matter what, I'll never forget you, Harlow."

She reached into her jacket and pulled something out from a pocket, her fingers now wrapped around the smooth, mother-of-pearl handle of her pistol. She handed it to me, and I took it without hesitation.

"You'll have this to remember me by," she said softly.

We hugged tightly, both of us knowing how much was riding on this plan. I didn't want to let go, but I knew I had to.

As Tye and Harlow exchanged their goodbyes, I found myself standing with Maverick. His body language was stiff. I could tell he'd made his decision, and I'd made mine.

"So you're staying?" I asked.

He nodded, not saying a word.

Disappointment flooded through me, but I kept my voice steady. I had no fight left in me to save him. "Take care then, Mav."

I turned back just in time to see Harlow scanning her keycard. The rusted port of the tunnel screeched open, revealing the dark path beyond.

"Take this with you," she said, and handed me the gold-plated card. "It's a master keycard to all access ports within Ylem. You might need it in there." Her eyes locked with mine, and the depth of her concern was clear. "Please be careful, Willa."

She handed us both a face covering. I gave her one last smile, then pulled mine on, Tye doing the same. Together, we stepped into the darkness. The door slammed behind us, and the shadows swallowed us whole.

The only sounds in the tunnel were our breathing and the occasional drip from the ceiling. Tye moved quickly, reaching into his bag and pulling out a flashlight and a gun. He let out a small sound of disbelief as he looked at the weapon.

"A *Desert Eagle*..." he muttered to himself, adjusting the gun in his hand. "Riley had one of these when we first left home."

I kept my focus straight ahead, remembering what Harlow had told me about this route once being used to release infected test subjects outside the walls. She'd described it as a straight shot, but the tunnel curved more than I expected. At least I could feel a gentle breeze, a small comfort, knowing that an exit was somewhere ahead.

"So, is the old plan the new plan? We wait to see if Rowen sends help?" Tye asked, his voice laced with that familiar doubt.

I offered a reassuring nod, though it felt like I was the one who needed it. "That, or we find our own way back." I said it as though I believed it, but inside, I was trying my hardest not to let the worry consume me. It wasn't the perfect plan. It was hardly a plan at all. But I'd find a way, like I always did. I couldn't afford to accept defeat before we even started.

We continued in silence, both of us hyper-aware of every sound. There were marks on the walls—scratches deep enough to make my skin crawl.

The tunnel stretched on, lined with metal pipes and mechanical structures that seemed to pulse with a life of their own.

But then we came across a strange puddle—a vibrant blue liquid. Tye saw it too. He moved toward it cautiously, his voice barely above a whisper. "What's that?"

I stepped closer, scanning the floor for more clues as to what it was. It looked thick. "Not sure. But stay sharp."

We maneuvered around the puddle, only to find the unnaturally blue liquid smeared across the floor, leading further down the tunnel. I felt the hairs on the back of my neck stand on end. Something wasn't right. We cocked our weapons without a word.

Tye's hand shook slightly, the flashlight's beam flickering as he pointed it ahead of us. Then, I heard it—a low growl, deep and menacing. Tye froze, and I pushed him back just a little.

Around the corner, something moved. *A Mort!* Its disfigured form was different—strange even by undead standards. Its skin was a vibrant blue, like that of some venomous, exotic animal. Where there should have been its usual black, orb-like eyes, there were only pale gray ones, a thick, cloudy film covering them. And from its neck, there was an enormous, grotesque growth—like a second head was beginning to sprout, its shape barely recognizable but horrifying all the same. The creature's needle-like teeth gleamed in the dim light as it lurched towards us.

It let out a shrill screech, sending a cold shiver down my spine.

I fired, hitting it in its rotted chest. It staggered, but kept coming, shrieking with rage. Tye opened fire too, a few quick shots that brought the Mort down with one last, horrible scream. Its body crumpled to the floor, blue liquid oozing out of it.

"I don't even want to know what they tried to do with this one," I said, my eyes straining to see along the dark tunnel ahead.

I stepped around the body. I'd never seen anything like it.

Tye's expression was grim. Both of us were now aware that more Morts—maybe even guards—could be drawn to the sound of the fight. We had to move quickly.

Our hurried footsteps echoed through the tunnel, our breath coming in short bursts as we pushed ahead, desperate to find the exit. Every now and then, a distant noise would startle us, but we kept moving, the cold metal of the tunnel walls seeming to constrict as we neared our goal.

We rounded a corner and froze. A lifeless Mort lay sprawled across the floor, its twisted body eerily still. There was something haunting about it, like it was waiting for the next bite so it could spring up again. I kept my pistol trained on it, but we didn't stop.

We walked a little farther, my lungs now tight.

Tye's voice broke the silence. "What'd you used to call them again?"

I smiled, recalling my grandmother. "Jumbees," I said softly. "It's something my grandma used to call evil spirits. A folklore thing from where she's from in the Caribbean."

Tye paused, then gave the word a try. "Well, let's hope no more Jumbees pop up."

I shook my head, a chuckle escaping me despite the situation.

The trek seemed to stretch on and on, and when we'd been walking for what felt like hours, the end was finally in sight. As we turned a bend, we spotted dim light ahead. The morning sun was just beginning to rise, a small glimmer of warmth in the endless darkness.

We quickened our pace, but an animalistic noise from the adjoining tunnel stopped us in our tracks. We exchanged a look, both knowing that sound well.

"Go!" Tye urged.

We ran. The growls grew louder, then—just as we neared the exit—a wave of grotesque Morts exploded into our path. They snarled and gurgled, a horrifying chorus of shrieks. We fired a few rounds but they kept coming, relentless. The tunnel was suddenly chaos. My only thought now was to get to the exit.

There was a mechanical screech of metal. The doors were beginning to close.

"What?! How?!" I screamed over the sounds of the approaching Morts.

Panic set in. *Has Ylem already discovered we're missing?* This could be the first reaction in a domino effect—closing all remaining exits.

We took off at a sprint, but to my horror, my foot snagged on something and I went down hard, crashing into Tye. It was another dead body. Both of us struggled to get up as the undead grew dangerously close.

"Come on, Willa!" Tye grunted, pulling me to my feet with one hand as he fired into the horde with the other.

We finally made it to the doors, just as the gap was almost closing. We jumped through to the outside, then—*crunch*—my backpack was trapped, caught between the doors. The Morts clawed at it, trying to drag me back inside by the straps.

"Shit!" I yelled.

With one hard yank, I tore my arms free, the backpack slipping off my shoulders and getting dragged back into the tunnel as the doors slammed shut with a final, deafening thud.

All my supplies were gone.

We stood, panting, our bodies trembling from the adrenaline, but after what felt like forever, I finally let out a sigh of relief. I looked up.

The behemoth wall of Ylem loomed behind us. In front of us, the vast, wild expanse of Patagonia stretched out. We'd made it.

But there was no time to stop, even though my legs still burned from the sprint. If the doors closing meant Ylem had realized we were gone, we couldn't afford to waste a single second.

I could see a distant patch of woods across the open plains. Beyond that, the snowy mountains stood in the background, a possible refuge but still so far away.

I reloaded my pistol. With my backpack gone, all I had was this gun and the single magazine that remained.

"We need to get to those mountains before they send search parties," I said decisively. "It's all open land otherwise. Nowhere to hide."

Tye nodded, his face set and serious. He zipped up his jacket, then stashed his flashlight back in his bag. He reloaded his weapon, the sound of the rounds locking into place cutting through the wind.

"Let's hurry," he said.

Without another word, we pushed forward, the cold air lashing against our skin as we ran.

The Patagonian Steppe seemed to stretch on forever, an endless expanse of dry, cracked earth with barely a hint of life. The wind was strong and biting as we walked, reminding me of how isolated we really were. The grass was sparse and yellow, barely clinging to the ground in places, while small, scraggly bushes dotted the landscape here and there.

The sun finally peaked over the horizon, casting a soft, pale light over everything. The flatness of the steppe and the sheer size of the mountains made everything feel vast and untouched, like we were walking through some untamed corner of the world. The quiet was almost overwhelming. There was nothing but the sound of the wind as we trudged forward, trying to make it to cover before people noticed we were gone.

They'd notice I was gone first. The staff always came to my room early, either to have me join in on the chores or help tend to Harlow, depending on the day. I hoped it would take them a while to realize Tye was missing too, giving us some time before they sent in the heavy-duty search teams. My biggest worry was Harlow and Maverick being exposed. We wouldn't be here without them.

We were almost to the woods when I saw another dead body, lying still on the ground. The lifeless Mort was unmistakable, its features distorted by the virus, but there was something else. A fresh bite wound marred its neck, and the arms were covered in bruises, the deep purple markings mirroring the IV scars I'd seen on the Angels. It was chilling to imagine it jolting awake again, but we couldn't risk drawing attention by firing off a shot. We had to move quietly.

We carefully stepped around the body, our footsteps light as we pushed through the tall grass, the woods finally coming within reach. The morning sun was fully awake now, flooding the land, casting long shadows under the trees, and illuminating the base of the snow-capped mountains beyond them. I felt a pang of faith. We might just make it.

But that was shattered quickly. The undeniable sound of a helicopter hit me like a slap. The search units had been deployed.

Panic surged through me. I grabbed Tye by the arm and we took off running again, heading straight for the cover of the trees.

We sprinted through the underbrush until I spotted it—a narrow crevice in the earth, a dried-up riverbed. I yanked Tye down into the gravel, quickly pulling together some dried leaves and branches that would work as cover.

"Get under, hurry!" I urged.

Tye didn't move. Instead, he stopped, and I could see the hesitation ripple through him.

"What are you doing?!" I asked desperately.

"Willa, they need me. If they find us, I'll be okay—but you..." His voice faltered, and his eyes were filled with pain. "They'll execute you... maybe worse. We should split up."

The sound of the helicopter was growing louder, and my heart was racing so fast I could hardly breathe.

I grabbed his arm tightly, pulling him down. "Tye, we are not going to be apart again. It's together or nothing. Whatever that means for me."

Tye's eyes mellowed, but there was a hardness there too, as though he knew the stakes. He finally relented and lowered himself into the riverbed with me, helping me cover us with the surrounding brush and debris.

We lay still, breaths shallow, hearts pounding in our chests, the sound of the chopper blades growing louder still. The trees rustled above us, and then—silence. For a moment, there was nothing.

I then heard the unmistakable voice of Secretary Croft shouting orders. "I want every inch of this place combed through!"

I stiffened, my breath catching in my throat. I heard soldiers' boots crunching on the gravel, their footsteps slow, deliberate. And then, a dog barked. The blood in my veins turned to ice. *They have a search hound.*

Tye and I exchanged a look beneath the leaves. We stayed still, so still that my muscles began to cramp. I could hear the dog's nose in the air, sniffing. I wasn't sure how much longer we could stay hidden.

Tye's eyes met mine again. His lips moved, and I only just caught his words. *"I love you."*

I swallowed hard, my throat tight. I was ready to accept that we'd done our best, but that this was where it ended. In moments like this, I could see how my impulsiveness often got the better of me. This plan was doomed from the start.

The dog's bark came again, closer this time, and then, before I could even process what was happening, the rough hands of soldiers were yanking us up from the ground.

Croft's voice rang out, cold and unforgiving. "Maybe what I sensed in you wasn't strength, but delusion," she sneered as our weapons were taken.

I couldn't look away from her, couldn't tear my eyes off the disgust in her face. But what hurt more was the sight of Maverick standing beside her, his weapon aimed at us, his face unreadable. He was playing both sides, as he always had.

Secretary Croft spoke coldly into her radio. "We found them. Deploy the second unit for backup to take the Angel to holding. I'll deal with the little girl myself."

Before I could even react, she grabbed me by the hair, yanking me down to the ground with a force that took my breath away. Her boot pressed against my back. I braced for the worst as I felt the barrel of her gun cold against my temple.

"Don't!" Tye yelled. "Please!"

"Think of this as an act of mercy. You'd die from the cold or starvation anyway if we didn't find you—"

BANG!

In the blink of an eye, chaos erupted as the guards holding Tye collapsed. I looked up in time to see their bodies crumpling to the ground.

Maverick had just shot his own men!

"Major?! What are you doing?!" Croft yelled, radiating shock and fury as she turned her weapon on him.

Adrenaline surged through me and I seized the moment, shoving her to the ground and grabbing my gun. In that same instant, Tye grabbed his and fired at Croft. She dove to the side, narrowly avoiding the shot.

Together with Maverick, we opened fire on the remaining soldiers as they scrambled to retreat and regroup. The gunfire was deafening, each shot making my ears ring.

Maverick was moving quickly to put distance between our groups, his shots precise as he took out the last of the search unit. The dog lunged at Tye's backpack, but he managed to slip it off, ditching it just in time to shoot and kill it.

We sprinted away, the distant whir of a second helicopter coming within earshot. My stomach clenched, but we didn't slow down. Croft was the only one left chasing us, firing as she did, the bullets whizzing past us and hitting tree trunks just inches from our heads.

I could see the mountains just ahead, promising some kind of cover. But before we could reach them, I heard a terrifying scream that made us turn in sync. In shock, I watched the Mort we'd passed earlier tackle Croft to the ground. The creature's inhuman growls filled the air as it dug its teeth into her, a horrible cry escaping her throat.

We didn't stop for long. We raced for the mountain pass, the sound of her struggle fading with every step as we entered the narrow gap.

We hurried through the frigid corridor, the sound of the helicopter's blades above reminding me we still weren't alone. It circled relentlessly overhead.

Maverick's voice cut through the noise. "We won't be able to lose them once we're out in the open again. And if we stay in here too long, they'll surround and trap us. Follow my lead and play along."

He'd made a clear break from Ylem that he couldn't take back, yet it still felt strange to rely on him with the stakes so high. But I didn't have time to question him. I kept my focus, my instincts telling me to go with him. There were no other options.

Mav moved quickly, leading us through the narrow path until we stepped out the other side and into the open. The chopper above swooped lower, and I knew it had spotted us.

"Mav—" I began, but he cut me off.

"Trust me," he said firmly.

Before I could say anything else, he waved his hand high, signaling for the chopper to land. He grabbed both Tye and me, pulling our arms behind our backs and pushing us toward where the helicopter was descending. It touched down and four soldiers emerged, weapons at the ready.

"Major!" one of them called out, looking relieved to see Maverick.

"I caught them, soldier," Maverick said, his voice smooth and commanding. "Give me a hand."

Just as the golden soldiers approached, everything happened in a flash. We fired, taking them down in a surprise attack before they could react. They collapsed like puppets with their strings cut.

Maverick didn't waste a second. He pulled us toward the chopper, urgency in his every movement. Once we were inside, he took control, settling into the pilot's seat and immediately starting the engines.

The chopper lifted into the air, soaring over the mountain peaks, and I finally had a moment to catch my breath. But once again, the relief didn't last long.

"This won't get us back to the U.S.," Maverick said, reaching for the satellite phone among the controls. "If you've got people helping you, now's your chance to get a hold of them."

I took the phone from him. My fingers were almost numb as I dialed Rowen's private number and pressed call.

There was a long pause ... then a soft click, and the line started to ring, the sound thin and broken like it was struggling across the sky.

Rowen's voice crackled through the phone. *"Who's speaking?"*

"It's Willa—"

"Willa?! How?! You shouldn't—"

"No time to explain, but I need you to send us help, as soon as possible!"

Maverick cut in, speaking clearly. "We have to get beyond the aircraft jamming signals. Send a plane to coordinates four-eight decimal five zero zero zero south, six-nine decimal five zero zero zero west."

"I have Tye. Ylem is after us!" I added desperately.

"Willa—I—I'll do my best."

"I'm sorry I didn't follow your plan, Rowen, but we had to get out of there," I said. "Midas is dropping bombs at the end of this month. Warn the others!"

There was a brief pause before Rowen spoke again, his voice shaky. *"Let's get you back as soon as possible. I'm already coordinating the pickup. Stay put."*

I took several deep breaths and stared out at the wilderness below, the sprawling city of Ylem far in the distance. We'd made it. But there was still a long way to go, and time was running out.

25. TYE

I watched Ylem merge with the horizon, the city growing smaller behind us. The last time I'd flown over it, I was blindfolded, with no idea of what lay ahead. I hadn't known I was about to face some of the worst things I would ever endure. But now, here I was—free, and with Willa.

From this height, I finally saw Ylem in all its sprawling, breathtaking size. It was bigger than I'd realized. Even now, as I felt the rush of relief to be leaving it all behind, there was a sinking feeling in my gut. Leaving was one thing. Taking it down for good? That felt like a whole other impossibility.

Maverick shifted the chopper's controls to bring it lower, then switched on the autopilot.

"Did we reach the coordinates?" I asked.

"Close," Maverick replied. "Get ready. We're jumping."

Willa's eyes went wide. *"What?!"*

"They'll be looking for the chopper," Maverick said firmly, though with a hint of fear.

The helicopter nearly skimmed the grasslands below us, the wind whipping around us as it dipped lower. We braced ourselves, and on Maverick's cue, we jumped.

I hit the ground harder than anticipated, but the grass softened it somewhat. I looked up just in time to see the unmanned chopper glide into the distance, vanishing from sight past the mountain range.

Maverick led the way and we set off at a brisk pace, trudging across the vast, windswept plains.

After what felt like an eternity, we reached a rocky outcrop that offered a bit of cover from the wind. We ducked into a gap between the stones, the three of us huddling close, trying to share whatever warmth we could between us.

I finally broke the silence, my breath fogging in the cold air. "No chance for a big fire, huh?" I asked, trying to sound lighthearted.

Willa rolled her eyes, but I could see the hint of a smile tugging at her lips.

"You missing Ylem already?" Maverick shot back, the smallest grin just peeking through.

Other than the wind howling through the rocks, we were in a rare moment of quiet.

"When you left with Croft's search party... did you plan on doing that?" Willa asked after a while, her voice soft but laced with something serious.

Maverick's expression became guarded. "I thought about what you said," he replied, quieter now. "I'm still nervous about going back to the safe zones... but I chose you."

Willa's hand found his arm. "You'll come live with us, and Rowen will help with the rest. I don't think Ylem has a hold on the military there anymore, not like it used to. We'll be okay."

"You did the right thing, Mav," I added. "I guess I should thank you for saving my life, again."

Maverick's lips curved into a full smile now. "I appreciate you guys being open to letting me back in. I don't want to be remembered for all the bad shit I've done. Whatever time I have left, I want to be on the right side, and remembered for that."

"Well, this is the start of a new path," Willa said warmly. "Stay on it, and you will."

Maverick's gaze was fond as he looked at her. "You know, Malik told me something I'll never forget. He said people die twice. Once when their physical body passes away—"

"—and again when the last person speaks their name... I told him that," Willa cut in, her voice thick with emotion.

Maverick glanced down, the words clearly meaningful to him. "I want to be remembered for something good," he said quietly.

The day dragged on, the cold settling deep into our bones as we huddled between the rocks. We heard helicopters a few times, but none flew too close. They were still searching for where our chopper had gone down. Maverick had assured us that the search parties would hesitate to cross beyond the jamming signal's range. Out here, they'd be vulnerable to air attacks themselves. For now, that kept us safe where we were.

As the day turned into evening, the anticipation grew. We sat in silence, listening for anything that might signal our salvation.

Just when we thought we'd made it through the day without being discovered, a distant drone appeared overhead. My heart jumped, and we immediately ducked into the tightest crevices we could find, trying to stay out of its sight. I held my breath, praying it wouldn't spot us. The minutes felt like hours as we remained still. After a painfully long wait, the drone flew off, and we could finally ease up.

We may have escaped being seen, but the worst part was the cold as night fell. We had nothing to start a fire with, no supplies to keep us going. I knew if we stayed out here much longer, we wouldn't make it through the night. The irony hit me hard—of all the dangers we had survived, we might die from something as simple as the cold.

Then, an unexpected sound rang through the sky, a loud engine that sounded nothing like the search helicopters that'd been circling all day.

Maverick was the first to peek over the rocks. "Those are U.S. military Concordes!" he said in awe.

Willa and I stood up, squinting into the sky. Three planes, sleek and moving at great speed, came into view. The U.S. military markings probably once meant they were loyal to Ylem. But Willa said things had changed—that their allegiance was with us now. And I believed her.

Willa grabbed mine and Maverick's hands. "They're here! Rowen pulled through!"

She let go and ran toward the open plain, waving her arms above her head. Maverick and I followed, caught up in the rush of disbelief and relief.

The planes lined up in the sky in a perfect formation. The middle one veered into position, leveling out for a landing, while the other two circled above, keeping watch like guardians.

We were jumping, shouting, laughing. It was a sight I hadn't thought we would ever see. Help. Real help.

With a deafening roar, the middle plane descended, its engines cutting through the air with a thunderous force. The Concorde's sharp nose tilted slightly upward as it slammed onto the ground, tires screeching against the dry earth, before it slid to a stop with a shudder that rattled my bones.

We sprinted toward it. The jet loomed in front of us, its hull painted in a deep matte gray with U.S. military insignia across the tail. Its body was thin and sleek, reinforced with armored plating.

A few soldiers disembarked, rifles held at the ready, scanning the area with sharp eyes.

As I caught my breath, another young man emerged from the plane, his glasses fogged from the cold. Willa's face lit up. She rushed to him, throwing her arms around him exuberantly. From her reaction, I could only assume this must be Rowen.

"Quickly, inside," he said, pulling away from her after pressing a quick kiss at the crown of her head. "They'll be aware of our landing. We need to move quickly."

We hustled inside the aircraft. The dim lights flickered to life as we entered. The interior was nothing like a civilian plane. The individual seats were gone, replaced by utilitarian benches. Overhead, compartments were stacked with equipment—medical supplies, combat gear, and ammunition. The walls were lined with tactical consoles, their screens glowing with faint blue light, displaying coordinates and security footage. Even the windows had been modified with dark reinforced glass.

Rowen led us to sit near the middle of the plane, and we strapped in as soldiers moved around us, preparing for takeoff. The engine roared to life, the powerful hum of the turbines shaking the entire airframe.

The planes that had circled above began to pull away, retreating into the skies as our Concorde's massive engines surged forward, lifting us from the barren steppe and into the air with a force that pushed us back.

The plane quickly picked up speed, and soon, the unmistakable whistle of flight filled the cabin. We were in the sky and headed home!

I exchanged a hopeful look with Willa, then Maverick. His usual grim expression had softened.

Rowen appeared shortly, bringing us water, warm sandwiches, and blankets. We chugged the water, devoured the food, and wrapped ourselves up. The warmth sank into my cold, aching bones. For a moment, we were allowed the luxury of respite.

I noticed Willa and Rowen exchange a glance. Willa looked nervous. "Rowen, I'm really sorry—"

"Don't be," he said immediately. "I'm not mad. Just shocked. This is a turn of events I never imagined. We had no word of the bombings you mentioned. It's been radio silence from our contacts in Ylem. It seems their security measures have tightened significantly."

"There was an assassination attempt on Midas," explained Willa. "Not by one of ours, from what I gathered. Ylem killed Manny and June anyway. Whoever else is in the network had to lock down or be caught. These bombs Midas is dropping, he wants to take out everyone who's left."

I felt a weight settle in my chest. "He really believes everyone that matters is there in Ylem," I told Rowen. "He has no reason to spare the outside. He tried it once with the virus, but now, he's bolder than ever."

Maverick spoke up. "He won't go through with it now that you're gone." I looked at him incredulously, and he shrugged. "Not on Safe Zone 32, at least. He'll know you're there, and others like you. He won't risk the loss."

"Others?" Rowen asked, his gaze shifting between us. "There are others with Ichor?"

My mind was moving faster than my mouth could. There was so much to relay. "They had a theory that maybe my family members would have it. I lied and said I had some relatives in Safe Zone 32 so they wouldn't destroy it."

Rowen's face darkened. "Well, if he thinks that's where you'll be, it's only a matter of time before Ylem sends troops to retrieve you. We may be pressed to launch our attack plan before New Year's, whether he carries out the bombings or not."

Willa's voice trembled slightly as she asked, "Is the U.S. military fully on our side now, or did you hijack this plane?"

Rowen's answer came with a weary sigh. "More soldiers gave up or gave in, and when more confirmation surfaced that the very leaders controlling them had abandoned them for Ylem, the majority joined us. There've been many shifts since you were away. The protests and rebel attacks grew to a boiling point, and the base camps finally caved in to the pressure to join us.

"Your friends were instrumental in spreading the word about Ylem's existence, and Tye's gift. The remaining states, even military forces in other countries, are as united as we could've ever hoped for in our cause against Ylem."

The three of us were silent for a moment, his words settling over us. Willa's hand reached for mine and I squeezed, trying to process it all.

"Are they safe? Our friends, their families?" I asked Rowen hoarsely.

"Yes, but I'll be honest. Although the military joining us has been an incredible feat, the safe zones are becoming increasingly prone to infection. There've been many infections popping up weekly."

"Well, I'm here now," I said, feeling a new surge of determination. "Put me in touch with the top scientists available, and I'll tell them everything I've learned so we can get started on a cure. Ylem says they've made one, so it is possible."

Rowen's face fell. "All the top scientists are in Ylem, and though we have our fair share of experts spearheading the pursuit of a cure, without Ylem's technology and access to more Angels, it'll take us years to catch up to where they're at."

"So our best hope is bringing Ylem to its knees and *taking* what it has," Willa said, her voice heavy with the realization.

Maverick nodded. "Even more reason to fast-track your attack plan. I was a high-ranking officer in their military. I'm happy to connect with anyone I need to to better your cause, share what I know."

Rowen met Maverick's gaze, then reached out and shook his hand firmly. "The three of you have changed our odds exponentially. Take the next few hours of our flight to rest, because there's a lot of work to do when we land. I'm going to start making some calls."

Feeling hopeful, I watched him head toward the cockpit. The three of us exchanged quiet, positive smiles, and the sense of a new purpose settled in my chest.

Outside, the clouds zipped by faster than I could track, the plane cutting through the night sky with an impressive smoothness. I tried to rest, knowing we'd need all the energy we could get, but my mind wouldn't shut off.

I was grateful for the two fighter jets escorting us. The way they flanked the Concorde gave me a sense of security. I couldn't shake the memory of thinking I was finally free on my way to Canada, only to be shot down and captured again. But now, I was holding onto the hope that this would end differently.

I glanced over at Willa. I could tell her mind was racing just like mine.

"What are you thinking?" I asked gently.

She turned to me with a pained smile and took my hand tenderly. "Thinking about Dustin. We're all going to be together again soon. When I left, he was still on the frontlines."

Before I could respond, Maverick shifted in his seat. I remembered how they didn't exactly get along, and the tension was clearly still there.

"I heard the frontlines have gotten worse, that soldiers are retreating," Willa continued. "You were out there, Maverick. Do you think he'll be okay?"

Maverick took a long pause, like he was picking his words carefully. "Dustin's got what it takes, but you know as well as I do—there's stuff out there that's no joke, no matter how experienced you are."

Willa didn't like that answer. She looked down, clearly unsettled, but before anyone could say anything else, Rowen reappeared in the cabin.

"Tye," he said, his voice low, "I need you for a moment. Come with me."

I stood up, giving Willa's hand one last squeeze before heading toward the front of the plane.

Rowen sat across from me just outside the cockpit doors, the dim light of the cabin casting a faint glow on his tired face. My attention was drawn to a small kit in his lap, the contents barely visible but enough to make me feel a little uneasy. He must've noticed because he was hesitant in opening it.

"I know you've been put through a lot," he said, meeting my eyes, "but with your permission, I'd like to take a blood sample so I can immediately get it to my people."

My stomach tightened, though I knew it was necessary. "Of course, whatever I can do to help."

He opened the kit to reveal a syringe and needle. "I don't want to gloss over the fact that you said Ylem claims to have finalized a cure," he went on. "While I hope we can retrieve it from them, I'd like to learn more about your blood and its capabilities."

Rowen's hands were steady as he prepared the needle. The small prick in my arm didn't hurt much, but it reminded me of everything I'd endured over the past months.

When he finished, he placed a Band-Aid over the spot, then reached for a tablet. "We have a long flight ahead," he said, his eyes focused on the device. "If you can take the time to write out everything you know about Ichor and any related information, I can get it into the right hands. I'll ask Willa and Maverick to do the same about what they learned during their time there. Time is of the essence."

I hesitated before taking the tablet from him. The thought of reliving it all, especially after I'd finally gained some distance from the trauma, was almost unbearable.

But the reality was clear. The whole world was counting on me. That was a weight I had to learn to carry.

Rowen moved to step away.

"Rowen," I called out, my voice more strained than I intended.

He turned back, pausing at the threshold of the cockpit.

"The head of Ylem's medical research was a man named Dr. Chiron," I said, watching him carefully. "He wasn't in your network?"

Rowen stood still for a moment, his expression thoughtful as he seemed to try to mentally trace the name. "No, we had no one on the inside in that department, sadly. It's been a bit of a blind spot for us."

I mulled that over for a second. Dr. Chiron had helped me of his own will, no coercion, no ulterior motives. There was honor in that.

"If we bring those walls down, remember his name," I said firmly. "He'll have everything we need to know."

Rowen nodded in understanding, mouthing the name to himself. Without another word, he turned and headed to the cockpit, leaving me alone with the tablet.

I couldn't help but think of Dr. Chiron and Harlow, Vale and Beckett—good people caught up in a corrupt system. Even the Angels in Ylem were just victims of circumstance. But as I thought about how the final attack was meant to level Ylem, I realized how many lives may be caught in the crossfire. The thought unsettled me.

I managed to rest for a bit, but as the last stretch of the flight wore on, the excitement of being so close to seeing my friends again made me antsy. My mind raced with thoughts of what was ahead, of the people I'd been separated from for so long. I shifted in my seat, unable to stay still.

The plane eventually landed at an airbase just outside the bordered city. As we approached the outer wall, I couldn't help but notice how much more decayed and heavily guarded it looked compared to my last visit. It was clear that the threats we once faced had moved much closer to the safe zones, and the walls now felt like the last line of defense against the creatures closing in.

Rowen led us through a quick reentry process. You could tell he was respected just by the way the border agents and soldiers talked to him.

As we walked through the facilities, a strange feeling crept over me. This was where I'd once been separated from everyone I cared about. At least, this time, it would be where I was reunited with them.

Once we'd followed through with the protocols and passed into the safe zone, a small military convoy waited to escort us. Rowen introduced us to the man at the front of the group: a tall, formidable-looking soldier with a handsome, weathered face.

"This is Commander Oren," Rowen said. "Ylem originally appointed him to lead the U.S. military after Secretary Croft stepped away. Fortunately, he's been part of my network for some time—and now, he's made the official decision to lead the cooperating military forces in the attack against Ylem."

Maverick saluted Oren respectfully, clearly recognizing the man. Oren turned to me.

"I've heard a lot about you, Tye," he said, his voice thick with a strong Texan twang. "I'm proud to stand with you on the right side of things."

I nodded shyly, still processing everything.

Oren gave us a reassuring smile. "Let's get you home quickly," he said. "We have security outside the place where you three have registered to stay. You can rest easy."

I felt a rush of excitement in my chest. It was finally happening. We were going to go home.

I watched out of the window on our drive through the safe zone, taking in everything for the first time. The streets were crowded, but the atmosphere felt lighter than I'd gotten used to. There was a balance between military and civilian life—soldiers held their posts while civilians moved calmly, waiting in organized lines at supply tents. Though a quiet fear still hung in the air, it wasn't as tense as I'd imagined. The energy felt different—there was a sense of order, but nothing like the suffocating control I'd felt in Ylem.

Certain parts of the city even resembled the old world: clean, well-kept, and almost normal. It wasn't luxury, but it felt like a patch of the state had held on. It made me think, maybe the people still had some fight left in them.

Eventually, we pulled into a neighborhood. The houses here were unassuming, nothing extraordinary, but I'd trade any grand palace to be in one of them with my friends. When the car came to a stop in front of a classic suburban-looking house, I felt a burst of adrenaline.

Willa placed a loving hand on my shoulder. "Welcome home," she said softly.

I couldn't hold it in. The excitement swelled inside of me and I practically jumped out of the car, rushing for the front door. With trembling hands, I pushed it open—and there she was. Ava.

Her eyes met mine and she instantly burst into tears where she stood. Her smile was so wide, so full of joy. I stayed in the doorway, frozen, until she screamed—

"TYE!"

She ran into my arms, and the world seemed to stop as I held her tight, feeling her warmth, her energy, everything I'd missed so deeply. I couldn't help it—I laughed, even though tears threatened to spill over. How had I survived without this kind of love for so long?

They must've heard the commotion because moments later, Otto and Riley appeared just beyond the doorway. The moment they saw me, they threw themselves around me and Ava, their sobs mixing with laughter.

Willa joined the pile-on, and as if time didn't exist, we stayed there, tangled in each other's arms, shaking with tears and smiles. We exchanged overjoyed greetings, words tumbling over each other in our excitement. None of it felt real. Even now, it was hard to put into words just how much I'd missed them, how much I needed them. The toll of everything I'd gone through suddenly seemed to lift. I hadn't realized how much I'd been holding onto, how much I'd buried in the name of survival, until this embrace, where I felt safe again.

And as I was absorbed by the group hug, surrounded by the people who'd been with me in spirit, even when we were worlds apart, I couldn't stop the tears. They came flooding out, not from sorrow, but from the overwhelming relief of finally being here. I'd made it back to them, after all this time.

For once, I felt like I was home. Whole.

I cried in their arms, letting the months of loneliness, of uncertainty, and of endless fighting wash away. This was where I belonged. This was my family.

26. WILLA

The first few hours back in the safe zone felt like a whirlwind—frantic protocols and meetings with military higher-ups, each one more urgent than the last. It was like we were three people coming back to Earth from a planet never visited by humans, and everyone wanted to know every last detail about what we'd seen.

Rowen was all business, coordinating everything with a focus that made it seem like he'd always been in charge like this. I couldn't help but think of Thirteen—how valiant he'd been in leading the fight against Ylem before its name was even a whisper on anyone's lips.

Thirteen had always been one step ahead, calculating the best way to strike, never wavering. Rowen had that same calculated edge, but this time, he wasn't working from the shadows. The network he once ran in secret was now operating out in the open, and he'd stepped seamlessly into the role of commander-in-chief, overseeing preparations for an attack already set to launch ahead of schedule.

The flurry of operations was a lot for any of us to adjust to, but especially for Tye. He'd spent months being isolated, and I could see the daze in his eyes as he tried to keep up with everything happening around him.

At times, he seemed distant, lost in thought. I could tell he was still finding his footing in his new reality. But amid all the commotion, I saw the relief in him, too—he was with us again, and that seemed to be enough for now.

The eager questioning didn't stop at home—our friends might as well have been with us in Ylem because we talked every detail into the ground. We spent hours catching up until the sun finally began to rise.

None of us wanted to go to sleep, but eventually exhaustion took over, and we all crashed together in the living room.

When I woke up a little later, the soft light of the morning sun poured in, and the smell of toast filled the house. The parents were in the kitchen, busy preparing what I assumed was a welcome-home breakfast.

Tye, Otto, Ava, and Maverick were already up, sitting around the table with Riley at the head. The space was a little tight with everyone here, but it was the kind of crowded that felt comforting.

Tye was happily holding baby Rio, completely in awe of her. It was clear on his face how much he'd longed for these moments. I couldn't help but smile.

Maverick, usually withdrawn, had been even quieter than usual since we'd arrived, but even he seemed lighter now. Like the weight of his past had lessened under our roof.

Still, there was no denying the awkwardness between the laughter. I knew my friends well enough to catch the glances they exchanged, the unspoken confusion when Maverick was around. They didn't say anything outright, but it was obvious they were still processing his presence.

Later, I would take the chance to speak to each of them privately—stealing quiet moments in the kitchen or slipping into one of the adjoining rooms—and the tension would start to ease. That was when I told them the truth: Maverick was the only reason we'd made it back home.

He noticed the whispered conversations, I knew he did, but he gave us space. He understood the weight of his past and how word of it might've reached them by now.

But for now, with breakfast ready, I joined the others at the table, where we took turns serving ourselves a humble plate each. The parents had done their best to spare no expense, but it was clear that rations were tighter than ever—meager helpings of bacon, toast probably repurposed from stale sandwich bread, and powdered eggs. Yet even with such a simple meal, the group was buzzing with the energy of a full house.

The mood shift wasn't just about being together again. It was the sense that even with the looming battle against Ylem, we had each other.

I thought about my own parents and my aunt, and how I'd need to see them soon. But even as I looked forward to that, I realized something: my true sense of safety wasn't with them. It was right here, in this room, surrounded by these people. Bonds forged in the fire of survival.

I glanced across the room at the parents here—the ones who treated us like their own. They'd been in Tye's life for years, long before I came into the picture. They were beaming at both Tye and me, their faces glowing with pride.

Riley's dad had his hand on Ava's mom's back, casual and familiar. No effort to hide that whatever was between them had grown into something more. I smiled back.

Riley's dad spoke first, his voice warm and sincere. "You're probably going to hear me say this a hundred times, but I've heard the stories. I'm just glad I finally get to thank you in person, Tye, for looking out for Riley and the others when we were all apart."

It was easy to see what those words meant to Tye, just from the way he glanced at Riley and the others.

"They all helped me just as much," he said with a smile, handing Riley her baby girl.

"I'm just astonished that you're both sitting here again," Ava's mom added. She raised her glass of water, a grin spreading across her face. "And to Willa," she said, lifting it toward me. "What you did was unbelievably brave."

We all clinked our glasses together before Riley chimed in.

"Of course they're back, it's them. Willa's a secret agent and Tye has magic blood. What can't they do?"

Her words were met with a burst of laughter.

"You guys going to work today?" I asked, dreading any minute we wouldn't be together.

Ava shook her head. "Sadly, yeah. There's a lot of changes happening around the city with everything going on."

"Lots of role shifts and protocol changes," said Riley's dad.

Otto shifted in his seat. "I'm off work, but later ... I'm seeing my birth mom. She got here a few weeks ago."

Tye's eyes widened with excitement. "Otto, what?! That's amazing! How's that going?"

Otto paused, a proud smile spreading across his face. "You guys know I hadn't seen her in years, right? Well, you won't believe what she's like now."

I raised an eyebrow. "Uh oh ..."

Riley laughed. "No, it's good. It's badass, actually."

"Oh, I need to hear this," said Tye, leaning forward eagerly.

With a grin, Otto began. "She totally turned herself around. It's crazy. Years back, she started a small business, led some volunteer programs ... until everything fell apart. Then, apparently, she ended up in one of the safe zones and from what she told me, she made herself useful, worked her way up the shitty system, then eventually she started helping groups of rebels under the radar—getting them intel, planning raids—whatever she could do to fight back against the forces making all their lives hell. At some point, they trusted her enough to the point where she had major pull. She became *head* of one of the *biggest* rebel factions in her state."

The room fell silent for a moment. Otto's mom sounded like a force to be reckoned with. It was incredible to see how his entire demeanor was different when he spoke about her now.

"She's trying to convince them all to join in on the fight against Ylem now," he concluded proudly.

"Her faction?" Tye asked, his voice filled with awe.

"Hers and tons of others," Otto replied. "While Rowen and Commander Oren have been assembling as much military as they can, my mom's been helping unite the rebel groups. It's coming together."

"We've finally made some headway," Ava added. "What your blood can do has brought hope to a lot of people, Tye."

I saw the words hit him like the pressure of a ten-ton weight, though he did his best to hold onto his smile.

"Tye, how about I show you the rest of the house? We can figure out a room for you," I said, offering him an escape.

His look told me he appreciated the excuse to step away.

"You can move my stuff into Otto's room," Ava offered, "even though he snores like a trumpet. I can sleep through anything, so I'll take one for the team. Tye should stay in your room."

"Thanks," Tye said, getting up and giving her a quick hug.

He followed me upstairs, and as we climbed, I could hear the others starting to fumble through some small talk with Maverick.

I showed Tye around, and despite the cramped shared spaces and our minimal personal belongings, he just seemed happy to be here.

When we reached my room, I was suddenly filled with emotion. I hadn't known if I'd ever see it again when I left. I stood still and just took in the space, memories flooding back.

"We can push these two beds together," I suggested after a moment.

I moved to my mattress, lifting it to find the folded-up band t-shirt I'd left behind. I placed it on the bed and unwrapped it.

There they were—Malik's gun, and my father's. Harlow's gun, somewhere downstairs, meant something to me too, but these two were different. These carried so much meaning.

Another wave of emotion hit me, and before I could stop it, tears started to well up. Tye gently put his hand on the nape of my neck.

"Hey, Willa, what's going on?"

I wiped my eyes, trying to calm myself. "Sorry. I was just thinking of Imani... Now that we're all back together, I just know she would've loved to make it this far."

Tye hugged me. "Look, I don't know the full story, but I know you. And I know you were an incredible friend to her."

That did it. I cried even harder, my hands shaking as I pulled away and wrapped the pistols again.

"Willa, what has you so—"

"I killed her, Tye," I whispered, my voice breaking. Saying it out loud felt both intense and a little relieving. "She was infected and turning, but I'll never forget what I did."

Tye didn't flinch, his face showing no judgment. He just pulled me in close. "Willa, we've all been pushed to do things we never thought we'd have to. That's what survival is."

The doorbell rang, interrupting the moment between us. Voices followed, and I didn't need to hear much to recognize who it was—my parents and my aunt. I could hear everyone downstairs exchanging pleasantries, then my parents asking where I was.

I wiped my face quickly, trying to pull myself together, and turned to Tye. "Guess you're meeting my family now," I said, realizing just how much was being thrown at him all at once.

Tye turned red. "I guess so."

We both laughed nervously, then headed back down.

As soon as we reached the bottom of the stairs, my family crowded me, enveloping me in a group hug.

"Willa! We were so worried!" my mom said, her voice thick with emotion.

"We came the second we heard you were back," added my dad, his arms tightening around me.

Aunt Solana squeezed me next. "Baby, we had no idea where you were until Rowen told us. We were all worried sick."

“I’m sorry. I had to be discreet... but I’m here now. I love you guys,” I muttered softly.

My mom pulled back slightly, looking at me with a mix of relief and pride. “It’s okay. I was just so scared. But we’re very proud of you. Both of you,” she said, finally spotting Tye. “I assume this is Tye?”

Tye smiled and shook her hand.

Aunt Solana raised an eyebrow, clearly putting together who he was from the stories she’d heard. “When things settle down, we’ll have to have you over for a good home-cooked meal,” she said to Tye with a knowing look.

He smiled warmly. “I’d love that.”

“Well, I don’t think things are settling down anytime soon,” I said. “Not until Ylem’s dealt with.”

My family looked worried at the mention of Ylem. My mom’s eyes started to glisten.

“Willa,” she began, her voice shaky, “I’m proud to have raised two brave children, but it worries me that you’re putting yourself in dangerous situations. Malik went back out, and... you’ve been so lucky to make it back more than once. I just can’t bear the thought of something happening to you, too.”

I took her hand in mine, squeezing it gently. “It’s okay, Mom. I’m not alone this time.”

I looked over at my friends, who were all giving me reassuring smiles. But my dad’s eyes fell on Maverick, and his expression changed.

“I know you,” he said softly.

Maverick looked like he was holding back tears. He’d met my family a few times during his closest years with Malik, but it had always been tense. My parents weren’t warm with him back then—especially my dad, who’d told Malik he should have friends who were more scholarly, not troubled types with tattoos. But now, I could feel the difference.

"You were friends with my son," he said, his voice tight. He stepped forward, shaking Maverick's hand like he could feel a piece of Malik through him.

Maverick was visibly fighting back tears. "I was. He meant a lot to me. Helped me a lot in my life."

Without another word, my dad pulled Maverick into a hug. My mom joined in right after, her embrace lingering.

"He lives on in us," she said softly.

A sudden ring came from the phone. From the other room, I heard Ava's voice as she picked up.

Riley's dad smiled at my family. "Do you guys want any breakfast? Some water?"

"Just water, thank you," Aunt Solana replied.

We all moved to sit in the living room. My parents were immediately enamored with baby Rio, cooing and fawning over her as Riley's dad brought out a tray with cups of water.

"Wish I could offer you more," he said with a small laugh as he handed them out.

Just then, Ava walked into the room, her face lit up with excitement. "I have some really good news before we all head out to work," she announced. "Or at least, it has potential to be."

We all leaned in, hanging on her words. Good news was a rare gift these days.

"Rowen called. He said they're recalling a ton of units from the contamination zones to return to their assigned safe zones in preparation for the Ylem attack. According to the paperwork, one of those units coming back is Dustin's!"

A ripple of excitement spread through the room.

"Do we know if he's okay?" Riley asked immediately.

Ava's face dropped slightly. "There's been no update from him in a while. Trust me, I've been tracking it nonstop," she said, her worry evident. "But Rowen said the units will start arriving tomorrow morning through the border facilities. We should be there when they come through."

Tye looked emotional. "He'll be there. I know it."

I met Tye's eyes and tried to look reassuring. We didn't have confirmation yet, but we had to believe—*I* had to believe—that Dustin would be among them. He was the last missing piece to make us whole again.

The next morning, our group was up bright and early, each of us alive with excitement. I'd slept so well, the comfort of Tye beside me reminding me that he made me feel complete, filling a space I hadn't even known was there. The connection between us felt stronger than ever, and I couldn't help but smile as I watched him move around the house.

Riley's dad was already off to work at the border facility, a part of the early operation to ensure everything was in order for the incoming units. Ava's mom had offered to watch the baby at home so the rest of us could head to the border together.

Maverick had been called to meet with Commander Oren for more debriefing. It was for the best. The last time he and Dustin had seen each other, the tension between them had been at an all-time high.

Otto drove us to the border, the engine humming steadily as we made our way there. It was a new addition since I'd left—an old van he had salvaged from scraps and refurbished.

After passing through what seemed like an endless number of checkpoints, we finally reached the border facility.

We were led into a large atrium at the military entrance, similar to the one I'd entered through during my past returns. The giant LED screen overhead flickered with the ever-changing names and statuses of survivors and otherwise, the information constantly updating. The atmosphere in the room was heavy, with families milling about, all waiting for the homecoming.

We made our way directly to the screen, our eyes scanning desperately for Dustin's name. And there it was—his name, with the symbol for *Deployed* beside it. My heart skipped a beat.

"That's still hopeful," Ava said. "If he was reported MIA, they'd have updated it by now." But there was still a hint of worry in her voice.

"He has to come back," Tye said, more to himself than anyone else.

"Look, Dustin's tough," said Otto, "and I know he got even better after training, but the frontlines are no joke. I hear soldiers talking about the stuff they've seen, and things are worse than we even went through. We have to be ready for whatever happens today."

Riley was nervously braiding the end of her hair, her eyes glued to the screen, checking it over and over.

I felt sick to my stomach, a gnawing unease growing with every passing second. The reason Dustin had volunteered for the frontlines in the first place was to help me find Tye. If he didn't return ... Losing Dustin would be the kind of loss that could finally break me for good.

Just when the weight of the anticipation was growing unbearable, soldiers began to funnel in. A few families rushed towards their loved ones. Most of the soldiers, however, had no one to greet them. They began to line up in an orderly formation.

We frantically scanned the faces of nearly one hundred soldiers. They looked worn, injured, hollow—like they'd seen unimaginable nightmares. There were more soldiers with bloodied bandages than not, and eerily, most of them looked to be under thirty. If my friends and I, and Rowen, weren't proof enough, it was clear right here that the younger generation had been left to carry this fight.

With every passing minute, my anxiety grew, and I still hadn't spotted Dustin's dirty-blonde buzzcut in the crowd. Until, finally—

"Dustin!" Otto yelled.

I nearly collapsed as I turned and spotted him in the back corner of the room. There he was—alive! We made a beeline for him, nearly slamming him against the wall as we piled on in a chaotic, joyous heap. Dustin fell to his knees, tears instantly streaming down his face.

"Tye?!" he exclaimed through a tearful laugh. "What the heck are you doing here?"

"We're back, buddy," Tye said, the emotion making his voice waver. "We're all back."

Dustin's buzzcut was overgrown, replaced by shaggy brown-blond hair, but his friendly eyes were still the same. When they met mine, I felt everything inside me fall back into place. He reached for me, pulling me into a long, tight hug, holding me like he never wanted to let go.

"I'm so fucking happy right now," he whispered into my ear, his voice shaky.

Though there would inevitably be more challenges to face, at that moment, all I cared about right then was that by some miracle, we'd all made it through.

27. TYE

Everything that had been broken inside of me felt like it was suddenly piecing itself back together, and Dustin was the last piece of the puzzle. The word 'friends' didn't even begin to cover what we all were. We'd bonded in a way that was beyond anything typical of the human experience. And despite the storm of war still brewing on the horizon, I felt like I was floating on air.

I tried to stay in that space, to soak up the feeling of peace, because if I stopped to think for too long, the harsh realities would come crashing back. Just beyond the border wall of our contained city lay a warzone—monsters, decay, chaos. With everyone I loved around me, it almost felt like we'd won already, but the world outside was still falling apart...

The disaster out there was a scene Dustin knew all too well. Though, no one was quick to ask him about the frontlines; we could see from his haunted eyes that he'd been through the wringer.

But even with that unspoken boundary between us, we couldn't stop talking about everything else. From the moment we left the base until we were home, we caught up on everything Dustin hadn't been filled in on—the good, the bad, and the ugly. It was like we were all trying to make up for lost time, speaking over each other and telling him every detail of what had happened since he'd left—since I'd left.

The last he knew, I'd boarded a plane to Canada, and we both thought we'd never see each other again. But now, Dustin couldn't stop smiling, stunned that we'd both made it back to the safe zone, despite the odds stacked against us.

Dustin clearly fought to stay awake with us as long as he could, but by the afternoon, the exhaustion finally caught up to him. He collapsed into the bed the parents had set up in the back corner of the living room. It wasn't much—a blow-up mattress on the floor with some extra blankets—but he didn't seem to mind. He said it beat the rocky ground he'd gotten used to sleeping on.

Dustin slept so deeply, it rivaled even Ava's legendary sleepathons. I could only imagine the level of burnout he must have been giving in to, knowing he was safe here, knowing he could finally let his guard down.

He slept through the rest of the day, the night, and into the next afternoon. It wasn't until just before lunch that he finally stirred, waking to the warm, spiced scent of stew, something Willa's aunt had dropped off for his homecoming, and the soft murmur of voices around the indoor picnic table. Everyone was here now, including Maverick, who sat quietly among us, doing his best to blend in.

Dustin sat at a spare chair at the end of the table, his eyes quickly locking on Maverick. His gaze faltered for a split second before meeting Willa's. She gave him just enough of an assuring look to let him know that, for now, it was best to set the matter aside. Dustin made the choice to ignore the surprise guest and settle into his seat.

The conversation picked up again, lighthearted at first—chatter about silly safe zone rules, gossip from everyone's jobs, and small talk that felt both normal and surreal.

Riley kept her eyes on Rio as she fed her, but it was clear something was weighing on her mind. When she spoke, her tone had shifted to something more serious. "When I saw how few of you guys returned, my heart sank."

Dustin gave her a weary smile. "We definitely lost a lot of guys on the battlefield," he replied, his voice neutral, like he was trying to cover the hurt. "But if you can believe it, some of the soldiers pledged to Ylem. Half of us marched this way, and half the other way ... *Losers*."

He made eye contact with Maverick across the table, and I could immediately feel the tension between them rise.

Dustin had always used humor to mask pain, but even now, it was clear that things had gotten far worse than we'd previously seen.

Ava scoffed. "Midas was willing to drop bombs on them, and they're running back to him. Talk about the wrong side of history."

Dustin let out a low sigh. "Look, based on everything you guys told me about that place, it's not surprising. I don't want to be a cynic, but there's an uncountable number of Morts out there. Until there's a real cure, I'm not sure things are even rebuildable at this point. Maybe living behind a walled city isn't such a bad idea."

There was an uncomfortable silence.

"So basically, Willa," Dustin grinned, "you fucked up. You and Tye should've stayed in Ylem."

We all laughed, but even that was strained.

Otto shifted in his seat, looking around at the group. "We'll be back there soon enough. Rowen wants us all at this big meeting they're having today to discuss battle plans. My mom will be there too."

"Excited to finally meet this legend," Dustin said with a smirk.

That afternoon, a convoy transported us back to the border facilities. Otto was driving, with Dustin in the passenger seat next to him. Riley, with Rio in her lap, and Willa were beside me. Ava was in the back. Maverick chose not to join our military escort, likely a deliberate move to avoid any unnecessary run-ins with Dustin.

As we drove, we passed by the medical tents and holding chambers, and a chill ran down my spine. The sight of them brought back memories I wasn't ready to face—those first seeds of realization that I was different, that I'd been flagged for Ylem. It felt like a lifetime before, but the memories hit like it'd happened just yesterday. I could almost feel the cold steel of the chamber walls again, the sense of being watched.

Riley definitely noticed the shift in my body language, because she placed a hand on my shoulder and gave me a kind smile. I returned it, grateful for her silent support. Rio gave a soft coo as if echoing her mother's sentiment.

Dustin turned to us from the passenger seat. "Seeing Rio's wild, dude. I swear, she's like a shrunken version of you. Looks identical."

Riley chuckled. "So she's perfect, is what you're saying?" She pressed a kiss to the baby's plump cheek, then turned back to me, her eyes still full of affection. "She seems to really like you, Tye," she said warmly. "Watching you hold her was kind of surreal."

I laughed softly. "She's adorable. And motherhood really suits you. I always knew it would."

Her gaze shifted to the window. "I actually feel like I'm doing a good job, all things considered. But... I'm really scared about the world she's gonna grow up in. I feel guilty."

"Guilty? How?" I asked.

She looked down at the baby. "Well, I made a bad decision in the moment, and she'll have to live the rest of her life in this mess because of it."

Dustin and Willa glanced over at her as her words settled over the car.

I propped my head on her shoulder. "It won't be like this forever. Not if we can help it."

She leaned her head against mine, like she was remembering I'd been there for the longest. The one who truly understood her.

The convoy continued its journey past some checkpoints and into a massive hangar. We were greeted by soldiers, but what caught me off guard was the unexpected respect in their attitude toward us. These weren't the same kind of soldiers I'd encountered before. There was no harshness, no suspicion, just a quiet acknowledgment of our group.

"Mom! Hey!" Otto called, waving across the hangar.

I looked over and saw a woman with wild hair and wearing a vintage-looking trench coat. She approached and opened her arms to Otto; they embraced, her smile wide and genuine.

Otto seemed completely at ease around her, even after all the pain I knew he carried from his childhood. It was clear he just wanted a family member in his life. He was glowing in a way I had never seen before, and it made me genuinely happy to see it.

"You ready?" she asked him, her voice rough and gravelly, like she'd been smoking for years. Her gaze then landed on the rest of us. "I feel like I know you all. Otto's told me so much," she said, shaking each of our hands. "Evelyn."

"Likewise," I said. "It's so good you two reconnected. Honestly, having you with us means more than we can say, especially with what's coming."

"Mama's here," she said good-naturedly.

We began to follow her behind the soldiers, down a hallway that felt like it was leading us into something bigger. The sense of purpose in the air was undeniable, like the entire journey had been building to this moment.

As we entered the second hangar, an extraordinary sight hit me. One of its massive walls was taken up by a huge screen displaying a detailed overview of Ylem, like a blueprint. Hundreds of fold-out chairs stretched in neat rows before a single podium at center stage.

I scanned the room, and recognized some familiar faces—Maverick, Ava's mom, Riley's dad, Commander Oren, and Rowen. But there were also a lot of unfamiliar faces, people dressed in different uniforms, giving me the impression they were heads of various military branches and rebel factions. I even spotted a few sporting patches of flags from other countries. It was clear we were dealing with a united front, people who had put aside their differences to focus on the greater cause.

The hum of conversation filled the room until Rowen spotted us. The room fell silent, all eyes turning toward us. The weight of their attention was different this time—there was no distrust, just a shared understanding of what was at stake.

"We have a long day ahead of us," Rowen said to us. "Find a seat when you're ready."

He wasted no time with pleasantries. We found some empty seats near the front, and the rest of the room followed suit, settling into their places as Rowen took his spot at the podium beneath the screen. His eyes swept over the crowd, assessing, as if taking stock of the people he trusted most to be here.

"Many of you have been working with my father on getting ahead of this indescribable misuse of power that Midas began implementing over a decade ago. I thank you for trusting me to take the torch from him in leading Ylem's demise. The rest of you, who've been called upon in this crucial time of need: now that there's a literal fork in the road determining what the rest of our history will look like, I thank you for being on the right side of things."

A few people exchanged grave looks, like the recognition of such an enormous responsibility was weighing on them.

"And to our young heroes, Tye and Willa, and their friends who have contributed in ways that have tipped the scales in our favor more than once, the parts you've played will always be remembered, no matter the outcome of this war." Rowen's eyes briefly flicked to us, a sharp but appreciative look that made me feel both proud and exposed at the same time. "It's an unpleasant irony that the heaviest of burdens has fallen on us who are still in our youth. Tye, you've already done your part and beyond. You'll stay here in the safe zone, while our force—"

"What d'you mean? No way," I cut in, my frustration instantly flaring. He had to know I wasn't going to just accept this.

Rowen seemed to have expected my resistance. "Tye, you are an asset that we cannot risk losing. You've paid your dues," he tried to reason, his tone calm but firm.

"I'm not an *asset,*" I snapped, the words coming out harsher than I intended. "I'm a person! And I'm done being treated like I'm not in charge of myself."

The room went silent. This clearly wasn't how anyone thought the meeting would start.

Willa's hand gently rested on my leg. I felt a lump form in my throat, but I wasn't backing down.

"I know a lot's riding on me, I get it. I know you're trying to keep me safe, but what those people did to me, the horrible things they've done to this world… There's not a chance in hell I'm staying behind. This is my fight too."

Rowen's face remained neutral as he considered my words, but it was clear he didn't think it was a good idea. His silence said it all.

Dustin spoke up, his voice steady. "I'll keep him safe, don't worry. Give me a few Special Ops, and I'll stick with him like white on rice."

I couldn't help but smile at that, and I saw my friends exchange hopeful looks with each other.

Rowen looked down at his tablet, typing something quickly, then glanced up at me. A small, reluctant smile tugged at the corner of his mouth, the kind you give when you're impressed but don't want to admit it. "Very well."

I felt a rush of relief wash over me—but then, as the weight of what I'd just agreed to registered, my stomach twisted. The truth hit me: I was committed now. I was going to war, and there was a very real chance that I wouldn't make it out alive, or that I'd lose more friends along the way.

Everyone in the room was hanging on Rowen's next words.

"Today, using the extensive information my father and I have been gathering, we'll go over a battle plan for a hard-hitting attack on Ylem to take it down, for good, and before it launches these new airstrikes across the country. We have our air forces surveilling to make sure no such attack is launched earlier than anticipated."

He clicked a few buttons on his tablet, and the map on the wall zoomed out, highlighting a marked point at the northern tip of Argentina. "This attack plan will have multiple phases," he said, his tone becoming businesslike. “I’ll walk you through each one, starting with the first. Phase one will be the insertion point. The entirety of our forces will be transported by military cargo planes to a remote sector of Patagonia, outside the reach of Ylem’s aircraft-jamming satellites and surveillance networks. Troops from other countries who have answered the call will meet us on the ground. Once there, our joined forces will offload equipment and begin staging a long march toward Ylem’s perimeter. Fuel reserves will be rationed for vehicles that will be used later in the assault. We’ll have to travel undetected across the steppe to get as close to Ylem as possible before the next phase.”

Rowen’s eyes flicked over each person around the room as he continued. “This trek will be challenging. We don’t expect to run into many infected, as the area’s remote, but we must be prepared for encounters all the same.”

Rio made a soft whimper, as if she felt the fear in the room.

Rowen clicked his tablet again, and a red line appeared on the map. “Phase two will take place just before reaching Ylem’s electronic jamming perimeter. Crossing it will likely be its first indication of our presence. The army will split into two flanks. A supporting flank, which will consist of a smaller unit, will move toward Ylem’s Eastern Wall. According to Major Maverick, this area is the least defended, due to the treacherous mountain pass beyond it that Ylem counts on. The challenge will be moving through the pass and maintaining stamina for the battle ahead.”

He continued to scan the room as he spoke, making sure everyone was following. “This flank will consist of the rebel factions led by Evelyn, various units of foreign soldiers led by their commanders, and Maverick, who will support in leading our forces towards the city’s center.” He met my gaze briefly, then turned to Willa. “Willa and Otto, I’ve placed you in this flank.”

Willa and I exchanged a quick look, the realization sinking in that we wouldn’t be together during the attack.

"And where will Tye be, now that he's going?" Willa asked, her voice edged with worry.

Rowen's expression remained calm. "Tye will be part of the larger leading flank, where Dustin will lead his Ops team. We'll continue marching forward and engage Ylem's main forces head-on at its Front Wall. Maverick is well-versed in its military operations. He's adamant that Ylem will likely send all its forces to face us directly to protect that wall, while unaware of the secondary flank at the other. And with its head of military, Croft, disposed of, it will likely be less prepared."

Rowen's strategic foresight was impressive. He went on.

"Commander Oren and supporting foreign commanders will lead the main flank. I'll be in a mobile base camp on the border of the battlefield, coordinating the plan. Ava, I could use your organizational skills to support and assist if you're willing."

Ava nodded without hesitation. "Of course," she said, sitting up a little straighter.

"And me?" came Riley's voice, loud enough that everyone turned toward her.

I blinked, surprised. Surely Riley wasn't planning on going to war.

She met Rowen's eyes steadily, with an air of determination that surprised me. "Just like Tye," she continued, "I want to fight for my own reasons."

Rowen regarded her for a moment, probably weighing the risks of allowing her to join the fight. He nodded slowly, since it was clear that there was no convincing her otherwise. "You'll be with Dustin and Tye in the lead flank."

Riley's dad looked over at his daughter, a wordless exchange passing between them. He was smiling, clearly supportive of her decision.

"Phase three will fall to our bombing squads," he continued, the map zooming in on the blueprint. "We have enough explosives to level ten skyscrapers. Each flank will have its own bombing squad, targeting strategic points at the Front Wall and Eastern Wall, giving our forces entry points into the city. This is where we'll each have our roles to play."

Everyone's attention sharpened.

"Willa," Rowen said, turning to her, "your reports noted that you have a master keycard capable of opening security points within Ylem, giving you full access. We tried to copy it, but with no luck. You'll be an integral part of this operation. You and Maverick will head towards the Basilica while your units cover you. You two know your way around Ylem and the Basilica better than anyone else. Maverick brought to our attention that Midas will surely retreat to his bunker underground, and that your keycard is one of the few capable of opening it. You must do whatever it takes to get there and, with your unit, eliminate Midas. From your past successes, I know you will not let us down."

Willa's fists tightened so hard in her lap that her hands paled from the pressure. I could feel the significance of what she was about to face.

I moved my hand over to her knee, offering the same support she'd given me earlier. She didn't look at me, but I could feel her racing pulse under my touch.

"Otto, Evelyn," Rowen called out as the map highlighted a structure within Ylem, "you and your units will be tasked with taking out the jamming satellite tower. If successful, we'll be able to call in air support for backup and for the retreat plan later. This was part of our original New Year's attack plan, but with no contact from my network inside, it'll now fall to you."

Otto's mom ruffled his hair reassuringly.

The projection on the wall shifted again, now highlighting a secondary structure.

"Tye, now that you'll be with Dustin, your knowledge will come in handy here. You two will take your units to the camps alongside a convoy. You'll infiltrate the facilities and release the Angels. The convoy and its commander will evacuate them to safety. Any surrounding units will offer support as you execute the operation."

I thought of Beckett and Vale, picturing their faces when I came to free them. I couldn't help but smile, though the anxiety of how heavily the place was guarded was bubbling beneath my excitement.

Then, I remembered. "What about Dr. Chiron? The labs are in the same facility. Whether he'll be there or not, I can't say, but that's where all the tech and data that we need are—for the treatments. For a cure."

Rowen smiled. He was already one step ahead of me. "I have a special task force specifically designated for that mission. As you all know, even with Tye's abilities and any Angels we'll come to have in our care, we don't have the means or equipment to utilize their blood. It will be of utmost importance to get hold of these invaluable assets. It's the only reason we're not bombing Ylem to the ground, as they would do to us." His jaw clenched; clearly, he wished he could. "Any Ylem scientists open to coming with us willingly should be collected and brought to safety, like the Angels. They'll be key factors in how we can apply the salvaged tech."

A quiet murmur rippled around the room. The potential of a cure was clearly a major reason many had committed to this cause. Though the others looked at me with a sense of hope, I knew the reality: my Ichor was useless without the tech that Ylem held.

"Lastly," Rowen continued, "the final phase will commence upon my orders. When the jamming satellite is decommissioned, I will call in helicopters and transport planes to arrive en masse to extract our forces back to our original landing point. We will then, hopefully, head home with the prospect of a new era on the horizon."

The applause started slow, hesitant at first, likely driven by fear. But it grew stronger as Rowen's words sank in.

"We will deploy in two days," Rowen declared gravely when the room quietened. "Please take the time to make your peace with your friends and loved ones. The road ahead is uncertain. Are there any questions or concerns that need to be addressed?"

The room buzzed with whispers again, but it was Willa who shifted uncomfortably in her seat and raised her hand.

28. WILLA

Rowen's plan was solid, well thought out, and masterfully coordinated. Still, one question remained unanswered.

"What about Midas's daughter, Harlow? And her mother?" I asked. "You didn't mention them at all. I don't expect them to resist, but—"

"She's next in line to take over from Midas," Commander Oren cut in before I could finish. He raised his voice to address the room, his tone blunt. "I don't mean to sound cold, but we can't let his bloodline continue if we're trying to destroy Ylem for good. She'll be their leader, but his agenda will still be in place."

A murmur of agreement spread through the room. To them, Harlow and Olivia were just as evil as Midas himself. They didn't know them like I did. I cared about them because Harlow was a good person, and it hurt to imagine something happening to her or her mother.

Rowen paused, considering. I could tell this wasn't something he'd fully taken into account. "Anyone who wants to willingly join us will be treated as an ally..." His voice trailed off, clearly reluctant. "But this is war, Willa. We won't be able to protect them if they stand in the way of our objective."

I stood up to make my point clearer. "Rowen, you put me with her to learn what I could, to stand by and observe, and I did that... but while I was in the heart of Ylem, I learned that there's still good there, and it's in Harlow. She's not like her father. She'll understand what needs to be done. She may even be the key to reaching some agreement with Ylem once Midas is gone."

I heard chatter in various languages, most of which I couldn't understand, but it was clear there were those who didn't agree.

I turned to face the room now. "All I'm asking is that we make an effort to get her and her mother to safety. To not harm them in any way."

Tye stood up beside me. "I've gotten to know Harlow and her mother, too. They're good people, and..." He hesitated, a flicker of uncertainty passing over his face. Then, almost reluctantly, he added, "And she's carrying my child."

The room filled with uncertain chatter. I wasn't expecting him to share this. He'd made it clear he didn't feel a connection to the baby in that way. I looked at each of my friends, seeing the pure shock on all of their faces.

Tye took a deep breath, gathering his confidence. "Midas forced her to conceive the child artificially, hoping to copy my blood. If we save her and the baby, there's a chance the child could have Ichor too. If I'm not the only one, there's hope for the future if anything happens to me."

Further discussion broke out throughout the room. Tye clearly hadn't put this in his reports because Rowen was wide-eyed with shock.

"Settle down, please," Rowen called out, trying to regain control. "Settle..." He scanned the room thoughtfully as everyone quieted, then turned to me. "We'll do our best to get them out safely."

I held his gaze and nodded, making sure he knew that his effort was important to me.

The next day, a strange quiet settled over the safe zone. The streets felt emptier than usual. The military forces that had once patrolled the area, keeping us in check, were now preparing for deployment. The citizens, knowing the gravity of the upcoming battle, spent their last moments with loved ones, unsure of what the future would bring.

With the reality of returning to the battlefield looming, our friend group gathered at a military shooting range. We'd been granted access because we were with Dustin and Maverick, both of whom had military credentials, but the tension in the air was unmistakable. Dustin and

Maverick had been avoiding each other awkwardly, and with only seven of us in the group, it was hard to miss.

I stood at the firing line, holding both of my pistols, aiming at the human-shaped target ahead of me. I fired two shots. One missed, the other hit the target's neck. I wasn't terrible, but I was definitely rusty.

Dustin, on the other hand, hit his target with precision. One shot, and the head was blown clean off. "Watch and learn, Willa," he said with a smirk.

"Shut up," I laughed, playfully shoving his arm.

He laughed along with me, though a quiet sadness lingered in his eyes.

"Dustin, selfishly, I'm glad you'll be with me on the battlefield, but how are you feeling about being deployed again so soon?" I asked over the gunshots ringing out around the range. "Not the best timing."

He scoffed. "You think soldiers scare me? I've faced Morts so deformed and creepy you couldn't even dream them up in your imagination. I can't tell you how many times I thought it was my last day on earth."

His words stirred something tight in my chest, but he didn't give me a chance to respond before continuing. "I have to say, though, I didn't picture *him* being around when I got back."

He shot a look over at Maverick at the end of the lineup, who, with a quick, confident shot, made a perfect bullseye through the head of his target.

"Trust me, I didn't think I'd ever talk to him again," I said, "but he's proven himself, at least to me. What he did to get us out of there, the information he's handed over... It's enough for me to at least consider him an ally."

I could tell Dustin wasn't fully convinced, but the look in his eyes softened, just a little.

"It's a dangerous thing, Willa," he said, his voice laced with concern. "Only seeing the good in people. I just worry about you."

I tried to offer him a heartfelt smile, but his words gnawed at me. There was an unease deep down inside me that I couldn't shake. Could my intuition really fail me twice? The battlefield would be the worst place to find out.

Maverick's ears must've been burning because, without a word, he put his gun down and walked over to our lane.

Dustin kept his weapon in hand.

"Can I talk to you for a minute?" Maverick asked him.

Dustin looked at me, but I turned back to my target, making an effort to seem overly interested in my next shot as I reloaded and aimed.

"You can talk to me right here," I heard Dustin say.

After a beat, Maverick said, "We both had very different paths to enlisting for duty, but you know the code all the same—when brothers go to war together, we set aside our differences. We fight as one."

There was a long pause, one that dragged on a little too long, and I finally dropped the act, turning back to them to gauge Dustin's reaction. He'd lowered his weapon and was kicking a small rock around in front of him, lost in thought.

"Code or not," he finally said, his voice thoughtful, "I heard how much you put into the battle plan. It's clear you had a huge hand in how we're going to take down Ylem. But more than that, you got these two home," he added, gesturing to me, then Tye a few lanes away. "We're okay."

To my surprise, Dustin offered his hand to Maverick, who shook it eagerly.

"I promise, I have your backs. All of you," Maverick said firmly.

Just as the significance of the moment settled in, Ava's voice rang out from the last lane.

"Thank god I'm not gonna be on the battlefield. Look at my target!"

Everyone burst out laughing at the sight of it. Shell casings were scattered all around, but not a single hole had been made in it.

"Sis!" Dustin called through his laughter. "Okay, let me show you how it's done."

As he stepped into Ava's lane, Tye joined Riley in hers. I watched him hand her the gun he'd been firing moments before. She set aside the standard pistol she'd borrowed from the gun range and took it from him in awe.

"No way, bro. Is this a *Desert Eagle*?" she asked, eyes wide with excitement.

"I want you to have it," Tye said with a smile. "I'm proud of you for stepping up like that. You'll need it for the fight."

Riley pulled him into a hug. "I'm scared to leave Rio behind, but I don't think I could live with myself knowing I didn't give my all in trying to make a better world for her. I know my dad will take the best care of her when I'm gone. He'll be happy to."

"No doubt," Tye replied softly.

"And there's no way I'm letting you out of my sight again," she added.

They both smiled.

"Take a shot," Otto called out. "You have to christen it."

Riley's smile turned into a smirk as she carefully took aim at the target in front of her.

BANG!

The bullet hit its mark, right through the target's chest.

"Holy shit, Ry!" Tye said with surprise. "Thought you'd forgotten how to use one of these."

"I'll never forget," she replied playfully, blowing the smoke from the barrel like a cowboy in an old western.

That evening, I visited my family's house, where they'd cooked chicken and spiced rice for Tye and me. Under normal circumstances, bringing someone home to meet my parents would have been a monumental, out-of-character event for me. But with everything going on, it barely felt like something to stress over.

They'd been insisting on spending time with me before I left again. I wanted to see them, of course, but my fear and anxiety about what was coming made it hard to even consider their worries on top of everything else already going through my head.

My aunt served Tye his small plate at the decorated table, which held a centerpiece of half-melted candles and a vase of flowers she'd cut from her plants outside.

"Thank you," he said warmly.

My family didn't pry or ask too many questions about us, which I appreciated. It was clear they were more concerned about what lay ahead than any romantic connections.

Halfway through the meal, my father put his fork down, his expression serious as he looked between me and Tye. "I know this may be a sensitive subject, but it's been on my mind. You've both seen Ylem—do we *really* stand a chance in bringing it down?"

The question was exactly what I'd been dreading, the very thing that had been on my mind too. I'd even rather have talked about my relationship with Tye.

Sensing my hesitation, Tye replied before I could speak. "I think Ylem really believes it has everyone who would be able to stand up to it already on its side. The leaders who live there, the billionaires with power—they'll never expect unity like this. I think that'll be its downfall."

My family smiled at the thought, and even I couldn't help but feel comforted by Tye's confidence. He'd always had this effortless sense of leadership about him.

I noticed my mom getting emotional. Without thinking, I reached over and gently put my hand on top of hers.

"Mom?" I asked quietly, unsure of how to handle what she might be feeling.

She looked up at me, her voice trembling just slightly as she spoke. "I just can't believe what's fallen on you, so young, being in the middle of this. I know Malik would've been better at giving advice and helping you figure it all out. I want to be there for you in the same way."

I squeezed her hand, feeling the familiar sting at the mention of Malik. "I feel your support, Mom. Don't worry," I reassured her.

"We're really impressed by the person you've become," she added. "All of us are."

I didn't know what to say, but I couldn't deny the warmth that spread through me, something I hadn't felt from her in a long time.

"I didn't get to know Malik," said Tye, "but I know how important he was to you guys. Just know, I'm here for Willa 'til the day I die. I'll protect her, always. Just like she does me."

I could see a quiet sense of reassurance settling over them.

My aunt, who had been quiet until now, lovingly placed a hand on Tye's back. "The only silver lining about dark times is that there are bright lights like you and your friends that shine through."

I watched as Tye's cheeks turned rosy. My aunt went on, her voice full of love.

"I'm serious. And you, Tye—your story, your abilities. They've really restored my faith in a higher power. When the outbreak happened, the way things turned out, my confidence in the divine was torn. What you're capable of has reminded me of miracles again."

I looked at Tye to see his reaction, but unlike the last time it'd been brought up, he didn't seem burdened or uncomfortable. Instead, he appeared to take my aunt's words as a compliment, not as pressure.

His gaze dropped down to his lap for a moment. "I only wish I had some control over it. It seems like there are more limitations than miracles."

His words caught my father's attention. He leaned forward slightly, his expression curious. "I'd love to hear more about it, if you're open to sharing."

My mom spoke up, concern evident in her voice. "I don't think he wants—"

"No, it's okay," Tye interrupted gently. "I wish I could explain it in more depth, but essentially, with a specific transfusion method, my blood can revive someone. They have to have been infected, though. My blood heals the virus, and even wounds. That's what separates it from the blood of the other Angels. They have immunity, and can pass it on, but mine's the only kind that can actually reverse the virus and bring someone back. Well, the only one they've found so far."

My aunt made her way over to the kitchen to start a timer for a cake she was baking for dessert. She called over to us at the table. "I was wondering if there were others like you." She came back and took a seat again, her eyes fixed on Tye. "There must be."

Tye looked thoughtful but didn't say anything, his fingers tracing the edge of his glass.

"They think others in his family could have it too," I replied for him.

"Are you connected with any of your family?" my mom asked. "We'd love to have them over if you are."

Tye's posture stiffened slightly.

"I'll help clean up for dessert," I said, eager to steer the conversation away. I started to pick up the plates, and my family caught on that it was time to drop the subject.

Back at our group house, the rooms were filled with the quiet hum of last-minute preparations. It was the last night before we'd be separated again, and even though we'd been lucky enough to find ourselves together under the same roof, it felt like the cruelest kind of irony. We'd barely had time to settle back into this fleeting sense of normalcy before being called to battle once again. It was something none of us wanted to think about, but it was the very reason we fought—so that one day, we could be back here again. So we could carve out a future where this togetherness didn't feel like a dream we'd be shaken awake from.

In the few hours we had left, we stayed near each other. The house was busy for a while with everyone moving through their routines, checking gear, organizing weapons, and sorting out the few things we'd take with us. Quiet conversations and the soft shuffle of movement were heard as we each privately grappled with the unknowns ahead. But none of us wanted to think about it alone—not tonight.

By some unspoken agreement, we all ended up in the living room. I stepped in and found Dustin, Otto, and Maverick on the floor, playing cards, probably in an attempt to distract themselves. The laughter and shuffling of cards was a nice background sound over the quiet anticipation that hung in the air.

Tye was sitting on the couch next to Riley, who was cradling Rio in her arms, while Ava was sitting on Dustin's makeshift bed in the corner, files and blueprints spread out before her. She was studying the battle plans, scribbling notes every so often.

I sat next to her, eyeing the small dreamcatcher by her side. I remembered it well—it was a gift from Otto. She'd told me it used to hang in the car she'd left home in, and it had always held a special meaning to her. I'd stared at it on countless sleepless nights, its frayed tassels swaying in the moonlight above her bed. It made me think about the old world and everything we'd lost.

She saw me admiring it and smiled. "I'm taking it with me. For luck."

"We could all use some of that," I said, watching Otto put down a card in the middle pile. My eyes immediately went to his trembling hands.

"Otto, you're shaking," I said gently. "You okay?"

He quickly tried to hide his hands, a slight flush creeping across his face. He let out a nervous laugh. "Yeah, just anxious. I've seen my fair share, but this feels different. At work, I've overheard what the real battlefields are like. I don't know how you did it, Dustin. How you joined so willingly…"

Dustin didn't look up from his cards. "Well, maybe I wouldn't have if I knew what I know now. But back then, I just didn't want to leave the border camps with no direction, lost in a broken system. It gave me direction, I guess. A purpose."

Maverick nodded to himself. Their stories weren't all that different, after all.

Otto picked up another card, his fingers lingering on it for a moment. "Seeing my mom in action, I guess I feel some kind of pressure. I spent so many years imagining she was a good-for-nothing, and now she comes back like this? I gotta step my game up."

His tone was light, a laugh escaping as he shook his head, almost as if he couldn't believe the absurdity of it himself.

"It's okay to have nerves," Maverick said, drawing a card from the deck. "But better soldiers in shiny gold uniforms than Morts."

"Rowen might stop in, by the way. He wants to see us before we head out tomorrow," Ava said.

"It'll be nice to see him before we head out," Tye remarked.

Riley, who'd been quietly bouncing Rio to sleep, stood up, gently shifting the baby onto her shoulder. "I'm gonna put her to bed," she said, her voice a touch quieter now.

As Riley made her way upstairs, Tye motioned for me to sit next to him. I moved without hesitation, settling in beside him. He wrapped his arm around me, and we shared a look—one that didn't need words. We both understood. Soon, we'd be back in Ylem, facing the hardest part of our journey. The part we both feared but knew we couldn't run from.

We held each other's gaze until the doorbell rang.

"I'll get it," Ava's mom called from the kitchen.

Moments later, faint voices came from near the door, and then Rowen walked in carrying bags. He looked drained, but the sight of all of us together brought a tired smile to his face.

"Evening," he said, putting the bags down at his feet. "How's everyone holding up?"

"We're ready," Dustin said.

From the truck lights shining through the living room window, I could tell he'd come with a military convoy.

"Good," Rowen replied, unzipping one of the bags. He pulled out a set of silver armbands. "I've brought some tactical gear in your sizes, but these bands will be worn by everyone to mark that you're with our forces. Rebels, allied troops, civilians alike. We don't want any friendly fire once our forces mix with the people of Ylem."

I appreciated the attention to detail. Taking a few, I passed them out to the others. Riley came down the stairs just then, hugging Rowen as he greeted her.

He then passed the bags around, and the others began pulling out their gear. As I watched, it hit me—this didn't feel like the real reason he'd come by. The heaviness behind his eyes told me there was more to it. He wanted company. He didn't have a support system like we did, not for the weight of the burden that rested on his shoulders.

When he caught me looking, his smile faltered slightly. I gave him a small nod to follow me into the dining room.

Once we were out of earshot of the others, I asked, "How are you holding up, Rowen?"

He hesitated for a moment, eyes drifting away before meeting mine again. His shoulders were tense, and I could tell he was holding something back. I stepped closer, softening my tone. "I told you I'm here for you, right? Not just for missions, but as a friend. Whenever you need someone."

He took off his glasses, wiping them slowly as if buying time, then let out a heavy sigh. When he finally spoke, his voice came out quieter than I'd ever heard it before. "It's just... Everything my father worked on, everything we've been building toward, it's all coming to a head. It's been so secretive for so long, I didn't even know the full scope of it until recently, and now it's all happening. It's been a bit overwhelming, that's all."

I waited, giving him space to process. Rowen stared at the floor, his words coming slowly. "I don't even know if this is what he envisioned," he continued, his voice trembling slightly. "But I do think he'd be proud of what we've accomplished. Proud of the way we've all come together. What we're about to do."

"Rowen," I said quietly, stepping closer, "I *know* he'd be proud of us. Of you. We've all had to grow up really fast. Make choices no one should have to make. And we're all still standing together, strong enough to fight back. If he's not proud of us, I sure as hell am."

We both laughed, fighting back the flood of emotions. He gave me a small, appreciative nod and a big smile before we turned back to the others.

29. TYE

None of us slept that night. It wasn't just because of the unnerving build-up to the long journey ahead, though that alone would've been enough to keep anyone awake. It was also the relentless sound of aircraft flying overhead, their engines roaring as they cut through the sky. The planes were landing on a secured, wide patch of land just beyond the city, their arrival signaling the start of what was about to unfold.

In the morning, we were heading straight for the same place. By the time the sun had barely peeked through the horizon, we were sitting quietly in the military transport, our faces waterlogged from the emotional departure just before we left.

Willa's parents, her aunt, Ava's mother, and Riley's dad had all woken up early to see us off. They stood on the porch, their faces wearing a mix of pride and sorrow. The goodbye had already been emotional, but when Riley had to part with Rio, the weight of what we were doing—what we were leaving behind—finally hit all of us. None of us could hold back the tears, and once again, we were reminded of how important it was to make it back.

The car was quiet as we drove through the safe zone, the stillness inside matching the silence outside. We watched families standing together, saying their goodbyes. Some of those being seen off were soldiers, others civilians who had chosen to join the cause, and a handful were rebels who'd now become united.

The enemy was Ylem, and in the face of that enemy, we were all one. We were no longer divided by our past or our differences. Everyone, no matter their role, had become a part of the same fight.

The car slowly rolled up to a checkpoint, the officer glancing at the driver's credentials before waving us through. We passed under a large gate that creaked open, revealing a wide stretch of land where nearly thirty cargo planes were lined up in neat rows. Their backs were wide open, allowing vehicles and soldiers to funnel in one after another. The scene was a chaotic kind of organized, with soldiers arriving in waves, supplies being passed around, and health checks being administered. More planes flew overhead, filling the air with the roar of engines, as if the entire field was alive with movement and purpose.

As soon as we stepped out of the vehicle, I noticed the flags flying along the perimeter of the airfield. The U.S. flag waved proudly, but beside it were others from countries I didn't expect to see. I felt a strange kind of reassurance at the sight. Despite the corruption that ran deep in the higher ranks of leadership, it was clear that there were still men and women in the military who fought for something pure—for their people, not their warlords. There was honor in that.

Commander Oren appeared, strolling toward us with a confident, knowing look in his eyes. "Good morning, young bloods," he greeted us with a smile, his voice carrying that sharp authority I was beginning to recognize.

As his assistant officer checked us in on a tablet, a medical troop approached, ready to administer a quick viral test. A few other soldiers unloaded our vehicle, all of them wearing the same silver armband, though the uniforms varied widely.

After we were cleared, Oren motioned for us to follow, and we walked toward a plane I instantly recognized. It was the same one we'd taken when we returned from Ylem. The paradox of it struck me—I was boarding the same plane to return to a place I'd spent months trying to escape. But instead of dread, I felt an unexpected swell of pride. The sheer size of the army around me, the shared purpose, made me realize I was heading back as a completely different version of the Tye who'd left.

Just then, Rowen appeared at the base of the Concorde, his usual businesslike manner in place. "Good morning. We're leaving soon, so let's get you guys settled in," he said briskly.

As my friends began climbing the steps, I hung back. "This is impressive. I can't believe you pulled all of this off," I said to Rowen, in genuine awe.

He gave me a light pat on the shoulder. "I wouldn't have been able to pull it off without the supporting countries. We've gathered every fighting resource still standing from around the world... anything Ylem didn't take first." A plane roared overhead, and Rowen raised his voice to be heard above it. "The rest of our forces will be meeting us at the landing point!"

I had a sudden thought that I couldn't ignore. "What's keeping Ylem from dropping those bombs on us once we land in Argentina? They've got drones monitoring the area, even beyond their jamming signals."

Rowen's eyes held mine with calm confidence. "We have jamming satellites of our own. They'll be activated by scouts ahead of us, ensuring we can land safely. Ylem won't be able to use their aerial forces in this fight."

I felt a new level of respect for him as I processed that. It gave me a little more faith that we might actually pull this off.

Rowen led me onto the plane, where my friends were already seated and strapped in. A few high-ranking commanders, marked clearly by their uniforms and medals, were seated in the back, talking among themselves. They gave me a respectful nod as I took my seat next to Willa. She was gazing out of the window, her eyes distant.

"Rowen?" Dustin called. He was sitting a few seats away, his arm around Riley. "Is our fleet stopping anywhere to refuel, or is it a straight shot there?"

Rowen sat down across from us, facing Willa and me. "No time to stop. We've got a handful of refueling tankers meeting us halfway for an aerial refuel."

Willa's brow furrowed slightly. "How long's the flight?"

"Keeping pace with the rest of the fleet, three days," Rowen replied.

A heavy silence settled over us. We all either stared out of the windows or straight ahead, lost in our own thoughts. The only sounds were the final thuds of the cabin doors shutting and the rising hum of our plane's engines powering up. But soon, the air was filled with the cacophony of dozens of other engines starting up around us. It was a sound that didn't just signify departure—it was the sound of the unknown, what we might not return from. The engines roared louder, and the plane began to move.

3 Days Later

The journey felt endless. The first part of the trip was filled with anxiety, but then, somewhere in the middle, it began to fade, replaced by monotony. We all resorted to any means necessary to keep our minds busy—catching up on the things we'd missed about each other's lives, playing mindless card games, and sleeping as much as we could. Sleep would be hard to come by once we reached the steppe, so we made the most of it.

The food on board was decent at first, but by the second day, the reheated TV dinners started to all taste the same—one indistinct flavor of post-frozen, microwaved disappointment. Still, we ate what we could, grateful for whatever we could find to fill the time.

Even with the nerves simmering, I couldn't help but feel a sense of thankfulness for this strange, rare gift of time. We were trapped in a small space, unable to go anywhere, and yet it was the most uninterrupted time I'd ever spent with my friends. In all the chaos and the madness that usually followed us, this moment felt almost surreal—like we were strengthening our bonds, stronger than any war could ever break.

Then came the announcement over the intercom. *"Take your seats as we prepare for landing."*

The anxiety hit me again, sharp and sudden. We'd arrived.

I strapped myself in, my heart rate picking up as I looked out of the window. In the distance, I saw cargo planes flying in formation. They were on either side of us, and probably above and below as well. The sight should've calmed me, but it didn't. Despite Rowen's assurances that our jamming signals would keep us safe, I couldn't shake the worry of a mid-air attack. What if they'd missed something? What if Ylem had some hidden plan?

So far, so good. But the closer we got, the tighter my chest felt, and the more I couldn't stop scanning the sky.

After a smooth landing, we sat in the plane waiting for orders as the rest of the fleet touched down around us. Through the window, I could see other cargo planes and jets already parked in the distance. It was clear this meeting point had been carefully chosen. The vast, open landscape stretched out in every direction, the perfect place for the sheer size of our forces.

Rowen stood up and made his way into the cockpit while the rest of us unstrapped ourselves. A soldier on board started opening the hatch and lowering the steps.

We all filed out, stepping onto the ground and taking in our surroundings. Camps were set up around the aircraft like each plane was its own apartment building—it looked like a new city that had appeared overnight.

In the distance, snow-capped mountains stood tall, the sun beginning to dip behind them. Ahead, the land stretched out endlessly, an open expanse that seemed to go on forever. And somewhere out there, Ylem was waiting.

One of the soldiers passed each of us our tactical bags, and we threw on jackets, the wind already reminding us of how cold it was going to be out here.

"Let's get you guys to the main camp before it gets dark," Rowen said, stepping out of the plane and leading us toward a hub of huge, sturdy-looking tents in the middle of the field.

Inside the first tent, the place was buzzing. Troops and commanders were milling about, monitors flickered with data, meetings took place around tables littered with maps, and phone calls were being made in a dozen different languages. It was clear this was the command center—the heart of the operation.

Rowen walked us past all of it into a neighboring tent. Inside, a series of cots were set up with blankets. Heating lamps hung in the corners, casting a soft light. It gave the tent a surprising sense of coziness, though I knew the comfort wouldn't last long.

"We start the march bright and early," Rowen said. "Get all the rest you can. I have to attend to other matters, so this may be the last time we see each other for a bit." He turned to Ava. "Ava, I'll need you to come with me for a few hours for briefings."

She paused and looked at Otto. Duty was calling. They shared a kiss and a tight hug, and then Ava followed Rowen out of the tent.

The rest of us silently dropped our bags next to our chosen beds.

"Quite the slumber party," Dustin muttered, flopping onto his cot with a tired grin.

The wake-up call came quickly, a squad leader pulling us out of sleep with a sharp command. "Pack up! You've got five minutes to report to your stations!"

I sat up groggily, rubbing my eyes, and the moment I stepped out of the tent, the sounds hit me. The first roar of engines filled the air—planes taking off, followed by the steady hum of military vehicles starting up. It was like the entire base was waking up at once, the rhythm of war already being set into motion.

The squad leader walked us across the field as the sky filled with more planes taking off. Most of the planes had left overnight, the military vehicles already offloaded. Soldiers were lining up all over, with others packing up the camps, preparing for the next phase.

We came upon an armored SUV with an intimidating turret mounted on top. I was about to comment on how familiar it looked when Otto turned around with a huge grin on his face.

"Surprise!" he said, and for a second, we were all confused. "I've been working on it between jobs," he continued, pride filling his voice. "It's a *real* super SUV, like the one we used to have, but military-grade."

Riley's eyes widened, and she hugged Otto tightly. "Bro, this is insane!"

"Are we going in this thing?!" I asked, laughing at how epic it looked.

"Of course," Otto said, as if it were the most obvious thing in the world.

Dustin grabbed him and gave him a playful noogie. Willa smiled from ear to ear, but I noticed Maverick looking left out.

"We had a car like this that got us to the border," I explained.

He nodded. "Looks like it can get us through hell and back."

"Precisely," Otto said, opening the driver's door.

Just as we were all getting settled, Ava arrived, eyes wide. "Oh my god, I missed their reaction!" she said, grinning. "Were you guys surprised?"

"You knew?" I asked incredulously.

"Course I knew," Ava said, her excitement evident. "Couldn't wait for you guys to see it."

We all piled in, the squad leader giving us a quick salute before walking away. As the engine roared to life, we were waved in the direction of a large procession of vehicles already beginning to move. Legions of soldiers marched between and around us, their footsteps synchronized.

Butterflies fluttered in my stomach as we started forward, but there was also a surge of joy—having my friends with me like this, feeling like we were a unit again.

The way we all settled into our seats felt oddly reassuring. So naturally, like this was how it was always supposed to be. Otto drove, Dustin sat beside him, and Riley and Ava were in the middle seats with me. Willa and Maverick took the backseat.

"Should we play the animal game, Ry?" Dustin called from the front.

A chorus of "no" came from everyone, but Riley was quick to counter. "We actually should," she said, grinning. "I won't pick a narwhal this time."

I glanced over at Ava, who was nervously biting on a fingernail, her eyes lost in the landscape through the window.

"Ava?" I asked, nudging her gently.

She didn't answer right away. After a beat, she sighed, her eyes never leaving the horizon. "I'm fine... My head's just swimming. I shadowed Rowen for all the briefings. By nightfall, we'll reach Ylem's jamming signal perimeter, and by morning, we'll have to split. I just don't like the thought of us not being together again."

Her voice caught, and I could see the tears threatening to spill. I reached across Riley's lap to hold her hand. "You think we made it through *all of that,*" I said, "just to let some city full of prissy rich people take us out?"

A small laugh escaped her, and she took a deep breath.

"It's gonna be okay," I added, but as I said it, I didn't fully believe it myself.

I could feel the static of uncertainty in the air. From the way I heard Willa and Maverick shift in their seats behind me, they weren't so sure either. Ylem was undoubtedly going to be ready for a fight, and nothing about the next few days was going to be easy.

We drove for hours, moving as one massive battalion. There were moments of banter among us, jokes that helped break the tension, but they were always followed by long stretches of silence, where the next steps of battle started to creep into our thoughts. Often, only the rushing of wind sweeping over the vast, grassy plains made it through the quiet.

As night fell, we grew more alert. Ava had warned us about this moment—the beginning of the next phase. The split.

The whole march came to a sudden halt. It was like a domino effect—row by row, vehicles stopped in place, as if an invisible wall had suddenly appeared in front of us. We had reached the perimeter of Ylem's jamming signals.

There was no noise for a moment, just the whir of the engines fading into stillness. Soldiers quickly began to set up tents, tanks strategically parked in formation to block the wind, and Otto shut off the engine with a soft click.

"So it begins," he said, putting the SUV in park.

A sharp tap on the window startled us. Otto rolled it down cautiously. A soldier stood there, his silver armband clearly marked, with a small Canadian flag just above it.

"Your food rations for the night," he said, handing Otto a big bag like we were at some remote drive-thru.

"Thank you," Otto replied, quickly rolling the window back up to stop the cold air from rushing in.

"It's freezing," Riley muttered, blowing into her hands for warmth.

"Better that way, if we run into Morts," Willa said matter-of-factly. "Tye and I had some run-ins. Wouldn't have made it if they were at full strength."

Dustin shook his head. "Can I enjoy this meal without picturing rotting corpses?" he laughed, pulling a sandwich and water bottle out of the bag before passing it around.

We all grabbed our share, the simple comfort of food grounding us.

As the hours dragged on, darkness fully fell over the camp. Little lights began to pop up all around the grounds—heat lamps glowing, campfires flickering. It created a cool effect, making the whole place look like the stars above were mirrored on the ground, little twinkling lights scattered in the middle of nowhere. Any other day, I'd think it was a comforting sight, but tonight, it only made me feel more restless for what was coming.

I tried to find a comfortable position in my reclined seat, but no matter how I adjusted, I couldn't rest. We'd been told there'd be no tent tonight. We'd be moving again before the sun even rose, so proper sleep was off the table. At best, we'd get a few naps in. Otto and Dustin were both seemingly asleep up front, Riley and Ava were sharing a blanket and looked to have managed it too, but Maverick was outside, standing with a few other soldiers and smoking a cigarette. I couldn't tell if Willa was asleep or not. She was lying across the backseat under a blanket, her eyes closed, but I couldn't escape the feeling that she wasn't fully at rest either.

I finally gave up on the hope for sleep. I quietly slipped out of the car, gently shutting the door behind me.

Maverick gave me a nod, probably seeing on my face that I was anxious and needed a moment to myself. I nodded back and silently made my way over to a small firepit dug into the ground. The flames were struggling to stay lit in the wind, but I didn't care. I zipped up my jacket and sat down next to it, pulling in whatever warmth I could get.

I didn't expect to feel so miserable about splitting up again. I knew it would be tough—I certainly didn't want it—but I understood why it had to happen. The plan was well thought out, and each of us had a crucial role in Ylem's demise. Now that it was here, though, with morning just hours away, I couldn't shake the uncomfortable pressure building in my chest.

I heard the trunk of the SUV shut and looked over to see Willa, wrapped in a jacket and blanket, walking toward me. She sat down beside me, the glow of the fire illuminating her face in a way that hit me right in the heart. She looked so beautiful, so strong. I knew I was going to miss her. Even if it was only temporary, the thought of being apart again felt unbearable. But I didn't need to say it out loud—Willa was always in tune with me, and the briefness of her smile meant she felt it too.

"You ready?" I asked quietly.

"It's strange," she said, her eyes looking somewhere far off. "When I think about what's to come, I don't even think about the battle. That part feels normal now, always fighting for survival. I'm more worried about what comes after."

I was struck by her words, unsure of how to respond. She went on, her voice softer. "Rowen's managed some stability for us—for now—but like Dustin said, the world as a whole is so far gone. Even with a cure, I just can't imagine anything coming close to what things were like before."

I scooted closer to her. "When we think of winning this war, or even curing this virus for good, it's impossible not to hope that things will look like they did before. That's what we know. We can't picture whatever comes after this, because it's not gonna be like anything we've known. It hasn't happened at any point in history before. It'll be a new normal ... kinda."

Willa smiled at my attempt to ease her mind. "A new *kinda*-normal, got it," she said lightly.

We shared a quiet laugh, but the moment passed quickly. Her smile faded again, and the seriousness returned. "And the baby? With Harlow?"

The question hit me hard. I'd been trying not to think about it too much—after all, the baby was only mine by genetics, and it was a strange kind of detachment I didn't feel comfortable with. But I couldn't avoid it anymore.

"If Harlow comes with us, I'll support whatever she wants," I said, keeping my voice steady. "But I can't lie, I'm worried about the kid. If they end up having Ichor, they'll be like me, an oddity. And I don't want a target on their back like I have. Everything changed for the worse when my blood was discovered, and it's not a good existence."

I could tell my words made Willa sad. She turned to face me more fully, her eyes locking onto mine. "That kid will have me and a whole group of friends protecting them 'til the end of time," she said, her voice full of certainty. "That's the one thing I know for sure—whatever the future ends up looking like, we are all gonna be there together, making the best of it."

That brought me a sense of relief, but only for a moment. I leaned over and kissed her, not caring who saw. Whatever the future held, I wanted to hold onto this moment with her for as long as I could.

30. WILLA

Before sunrise, the roar of engines and the sharp commands of officers broke the early-morning silence, signaling the start of the next phase. I didn't need the wake-up call; I hadn't slept for even a second. From the looks of it, neither had most of my friends. Some were already awake, while the others who stirred looked exhausted. I rubbed my eyes and began mentally preparing myself for what was ahead.

I started packing my few items into my tactical bag—a small canteen, my thermal blanket—and as I zipped it up, the comm speaker on the SUV's console crackled to life.

Otto pressed a button on the steering wheel, his voice groggy. "Otto here," he muttered.

"It's Rowen," came the voice over the comm. *"Phase two is commencing. I'll send transport to bring you to your assigned stations. Ava, you'll come my way."*

She started gathering the files from the seat pocket in front of her.

Rowen continued. *"Tye, Dustin, Riley, you'll be in the main flank. Dustin, your Special Ops team will connect with you there."*

"Copy," Dustin replied.

"Willa, Maverick, and Otto, you can remain in your vehicle, but proceed to right field to join Evelyn and her forces in the second flank. When your flank reaches its mark, we'll deploy the bombing squads."

There was a brief silence as everyone adjusted to being thrown into action so quickly.

"Speaking of bombings, Rowen," I couldn't help but ask, "has there been any sign of Midas's plan moving forward? We expected it to happen around this time."

Rowen was quiet for a moment before responding. *"We've been monitoring U.S. airspace closely. It seems he's held off, for now. As Maverick predicted, without knowing Tye's exact whereabouts, he won't want to destroy areas at random. Our scouts have only spotted search planes near here, still looking for you guys out in the steppe. With our jamming satellites, they've all been disabled since, which means they're already well aware something's off. Our presence will be confirmed as soon as our march continues forward. The secondary flank may still go unnoticed, but we should all be ready for anything."*

A chill ran through me as his words sank in. The radio call cut off abruptly.

In no time, the first escort vehicle pulled up beside us. The driver called out for Ava, and as she turned to us, I saw the tears in her eyes. The gravity of the moment hit all of us at once, and we quickly disembarked to say goodbye. We hugged her tightly, each of us taking a moment to hold on just a little longer.

"You got this," I said softly.

Otto scooped her into his arms, lifting her off the ground as he kissed her long and hard. "See you on the other side," he whispered, his words filled with both love and a kind of sad acceptance.

"We 'ave to move quickly," the driver of the Jeep said, his French accent thick as he looked at us impatiently.

Ava took in a deep breath, bracing herself. She pulled away from us, casting one last glance over her shoulder before she climbed into the Jeep. As it sped off, we stood in place, silently watching her leave.

Before her departure could even sink in, another Jeep arrived, kicking up dust as it came to a halt nearby. This one was different, loaded with soldiers and heavy artillery in the back basket. They called for Tye, Dustin, and Riley, and I felt my heart lurch.

Tye turned to me, his eyes meeting mine, and in that instant, we said a thousand words without speaking a single one. I didn't need him to say anything out loud; I already knew how hard this was for both of us. We shared a quick kiss—one that was more painful than comforting, but at the same time, exactly what I needed.

He broke away and gave me one last smile, a small, bittersweet gesture, before he boarded the Jeep.

Everyone traded hugs with Dustin and Riley.

"Give 'em hell," Dustin said to me, his grin fierce as he hopped into the Jeep.

"I'll be mustering up my Willa energy out there," Riley added playfully, throwing her tactical bag over her shoulder before climbing in.

Maverick, Otto, and I waved them off as the Jeep rolled to the front of the battalion. The moment felt suspended in time, the goodbyes echoing in my mind as I watched them disappear into the bustle.

Back in our SUV, we slowly drove through the camp, inching past troops moving in their formations and weaving through other vehicles until we finally reached a detached battalion. This had to be the secondary flank.

From my seat in the front passenger side, I couldn't help but notice the variety of people around us. Through the window, I saw faces from all walks of life. Some soldiers looked sure of themselves, their military uniforms sharp and their postures straight—soldiers from various states and countries. They were the ones who seemed most at ease in this environment. Others, though, looked a little more uncertain. I guessed they were civilians, people who'd come to fight but were now faced with the reality of war. And then there were the rebels, their rough-and-ready demeanor marking them clearly as those who'd been on the front lines of resistance long before this.

One troop flagged us down and directed us to the middle of the camp, where a dense convoy of military vehicles surrounded a hefty-looking Humvee. Standing outside the vehicle, confidently trading orders with different commanding officers, was Evelyn. She was wearing the same vintage trench coat as before, but now with a silver armband over the sleeve and a commander's uniform underneath.

Otto immediately parked the SUV and jumped out, going straight to her. They exchanged a quick hug, one that looked like it still held a hint of unfamiliarity, but Evelyn definitely looked proud to see Otto here.

Maverick and I joined them.

"Major." Evelyn greeted Maverick with a nod. "Glad to have your support."

Maverick gave her a respectful nod in return. "Likewise."

"I saw the reports," she said, her voice steady but sharp. "You expect we'll run into any Needle-Mouths on our way?"

The soldiers and rebels around us, who'd been chatting among themselves, fell quiet at the mention of the creatures.

"It's likely," he said. "Ylem ran tons of experiments on bodies and the infected during their research. They'd dispose of them out here as an added line of defense. And if traitors weren't killed, they'd end up dumped out here to feed them."

Evelyn's expression soured. "Lovely..."

Just then, the ground vibrated beneath us as the main flank started to move forward.

Evelyn straightened up, her eyes scanning the horizon. "That's our cue," she said determinedly. "Let's get moving!"

On her sharp command, the battalion began undulating into motion, soldiers taking their places like parts of a well-oiled machine.

Evelyn climbed up into the back of the Humvee. "Stay close to my convoy," she said to Otto, and with that, the formation sprang to life, rolling out with the hum of engines firing up.

The battalion moved steadily towards the distant mountain range, a solid line of vehicles stretching out ahead of us. I occasionally glanced out of the back window, watching as the lead flank grew smaller and smaller until it eventually disappeared from view. The sense of separation became real now.

Maverick had moved to the front seat with Otto, leaving me in the middle row. He was already on the radio, speaking with other commanders to organize the movement of troops and vehicles. His voice was calm and precise; he was clearly in his element. As I listened to him, I couldn't help but think this was the best version of Maverick—the version of him when he had a clear place and purpose. When he was needed, and he knew he was good at something.

He'd been quiet ever since we returned, probably because the weight of heading back to Ylem was just as intense for him as it was for Tye and me. But even so, his confidence had been steadily growing. I could see it in the way he was handling his duties.

Still, Dustin's words from before repeated in my mind—about not letting the good in Maverick cloud my judgment. I didn't want to ignore that warning, even though I had faith in my feeling that Maverick had chosen a side and there would be no turning back now. Ylem wouldn't let him. He was in too deep. But there was also something about the way he carried himself here, the way he'd stepped into this role, that made me think he'd find redemption in this fight.

I kept thinking back to Malik, and how he'd continued to believe in Maverick. Malik had known Maverick's struggles but also seen the goodness in him. He'd believed in Maverick's soul, always. It was a belief I held onto, even now. Because if Malik could see that in him, then that's what I trusted most.

We moved slowly through the vast grasslands, the vehicles maintaining a steady pace so that the soldiers on foot could keep up. Slow enough to ensure no one was left behind, but fast enough to keep the momentum going. Occasionally, the soldiers in the vehicles would swap out with the ground troops, giving them a much-needed break. The battle tanks and larger vehicles were strategically positioned on the outer edges of the formation, providing a barrier against the sharp, biting wind.

Though the cold was nipping at my skin, it wasn't the wind that had me on edge. It was the thought of Morts. The altered ones I'd seen in the tunnels were unlike any I'd seen before, even among the more developed phases.

Even without Ylem's experiments, I'd seen enough natural variations to know that the mutations weren't just limited to appearance—they were evolving in ways we didn't fully understand. The thought made my stomach turn.

I recalled hearing about colonies that had moved to the coldest parts of the world, hoping to avoid the undead altogether. The cold was supposed to slow them down, limit the Morts' movements, but now, I couldn't help but feel a deep, unsettling fear that one day, the Morts would adapt, even to low temperatures. The idea of them surviving in these freezing conditions—being able to thrive, no matter how cold it got—was nightmarish.

I hugged my jacket tighter around me, as if it could shield me from the dread creeping up my spine.

When we later approached the base of the mountain pass, the battalion began to restructure its formation, splitting into two rows side by side to fit the narrow path. The movement was smooth and calculated, the commanders coordinating effortlessly to ensure that every vehicle and troop was in position. There were moments when the path got so narrow, we'd be squeezed into a single line. The upside was that the wind was now much more manageable. The jagged, rocky mountains stood as a natural barrier, protecting us from the worst of the cold, and for that, I was silently grateful.

I couldn't help but feel some guilt about getting to stay in the SUV. The men and women who'd been on foot for hours had a weariness about them that made me wonder how they were still standing. I found myself silently hoping that, somehow, they would have enough stamina left to fight once we made it through the pass.

Every once in a while, the convoy would slow to a stop as the front of the line redirected to a better path to avoid an obstacle or get around a tricky section of the terrain. It was a pattern that had become familiar, but each time we stopped, I felt the strain building.

As we moved through the pass, I caught glimpses between the jagged peaks of the mountains: the unmistakable summit of Ylem's wall, just visible through the gaps. Each time I saw it, my stomach dropped. It was like seeing the mouth of a beast waiting to devour us.

It was hard to tell exactly when the sun had gone down at the end of the day; the mountains blocked most of the light, casting everything in shadow. But I could feel the change in the air—the march slowing to a stop, the bustle of soldiers setting up camp around us again. We'd reached our limit for the day and would stay in place for the night.

Otto parked the SUV behind his mother's Humvee as troops began to mill about, getting to work on setting up the camp. Maverick left to help lead the efforts, coordinating with other commanders. Large tents began to go up near Evelyn's main convoy, with her directing things with a confident ease.

It felt strangely quiet and empty in our section of the pass. The battalion was spread out over a thin line, so it wasn't as tightly packed as I'd grown used to. Only the immediate camp would be our company tonight.

Otto and I began helping with the setup, moving quickly to make sure everything was in place. The sky was darker now, the temperature dropping with the absence of sunlight. Once everything was finally settled, we headed into our assigned tent. There, a handful of cots had been set up. We chose two near the corner, tired but not ready to sleep.

As the camp began to settle down, Evelyn entered the tent, moving quietly to sit on a cot near us. The other commanders and Maverick hadn't returned yet, leaving the space feeling even more empty. I could feel the lack of sleep from the night before starting to catch up with me, and I rubbed my eyes as I sat back, trying to stay alert.

I watched Otto and Evelyn as they exchanged a few quiet words, a smile passing between them. But there was something else there too, a hesitancy in Evelyn's eyes, like she wanted to say more but wasn't sure how. I glanced from her to Otto and back again.

"Do you want me to leave you two for a minute?" I asked.

Evelyn chuckled softly, but it didn't quite reach her eyes. "No, no, let's not make it more awkward than it needs to be."

There was a long pause, and I saw Otto shift uncomfortably. He probably knew what was coming and wasn't quite ready for it.

Evelyn cleared her throat, and when she spoke again, there was a gentleness in her voice that I hadn't expected. "I can say it in front of your friends, because I mean it. Under all the war stuff going on, the one thing that's been on my mind, the one thing I'd regret not saying if anything happened to me tomorrow, is that I'm really sorry for not being there for you when you were growing up."

Otto's hand instantly went to his face, nervously scratching at his cheek as his eyes filled with emotion.

"I simply wasn't ready to be a mom," she continued, her voice breaking a little. "And worse, I had no clue who I was. I had no tools to raise a kid and face the failure I would've been…"

He was hanging on every word she said, as if they were the most important words ever spoken.

"And looking back, through the eyes of who I am now, I one hundred percent regret it. And maybe nothing will ever fix the damage that did to you, but I'm so astounded by the man you turned into. You got all your father's best qualities and beyond."

Otto moved closer to her, his emotions breaking through. She wrapped her arms around him as he cried into her shoulder. It was a moment so intimate, I felt like I shouldn't be there. But I couldn't look away.

"I'm very, very sorry," Evelyn whispered, holding him tighter.

I felt my own emotions bubbling up, knowing how much this meant to him.

I stood up quietly, excusing myself to give them some time alone.

The night air was uncomfortably cold, but it was a relief to have a moment to myself. I leaned against a nearby vehicle, watching people head into their tents and start small fires nearby.

My hand moved to the zipper of my tactical pants, reaching for the pocket where I kept the master keycard Harlow had given me. It'd stayed there since the moment we set out, a quiet presence against my leg, never letting me forget what I'd have to face tomorrow.

Just then, Maverick came around the corner, his neck tattoos barely visible above the collar of his jacket, which was zipped all the way to the top.

"Why aren't you staying warm?" he asked.

"Otto and his mom are having a talk," I explained. "Just giving them a sec." I noticed him lingering, his posture stiff, so I added, "You can hang here with me for a bit if you want."

He smiled, but there was no warmth in his eyes. "I'm feeling the pre-battle nerves. I'm ready, but it always happens when I know what's coming."

"*Do* you know what's coming?" I asked seriously. "Looking at the forces we have now... do we stand a chance?"

He was quiet for a moment. "I never thought I'd see a day when people from all over came together like this," he finally replied. "And knowing Midas, the way he thinks the rest of the world's so weak, he won't be expecting it either."

Tye had felt similarly, but doubt must've shown on my face because Maverick continued, his voice growing more somber. "We both know he's ruthless, and keeping Ylem at the top is his biggest priority. This isn't gonna be easy, no matter how we cut it."

I took a deep breath, processing his words.

"And what about you?" he asked, his eyes focused on me. "Are you ready for what you'll have to do? When you have to take that shot?"

The question struck me hard. "I've thought about killing that man every single day since Malik died," I said sharply. "He made the world like this. If it weren't for him, I'd still have my brother. I can't *wait* to take that shot."

But as the words left my mouth, I heard them, and the darkness in them scared me. As much as he was a tyrant, the thought of shooting Midas point-blank felt strange. He was evil, but he was Harlow's father, too.

Maverick's expression hardened. "I'll be right there with you. If you don't take the shot, I will. I'm done wearing the chains of Ylem. And I'm still gonna keep my promise to Malik, to protect you. I broke it once, but I won't break it again."

I could see the regret in his eyes, and I knew how much Malik's death still haunted him. The pain was raw and real, something he buried deep.

"Maverick," I said gently, "you don't have to hold everything in anymore. I know when it happened, you put your feelings aside to be there for me. I wouldn't have made it through that moment without you. If you want to talk about him, if you need me for anything, I'm open. I've forgiven you."

He looked at me with what seemed like deep admiration, but before he could speak, we both jumped at the sound of men yelling in the distance.

Then a shriek echoed off the rocky walls, a terrifying noise that made the hairs on the back of my neck stand up.

The unmistakable call of a Mort.

In the same breath, I drew both of my pistols, while Maverick swung his rifle off his back. The primal sound was like an order, and every soldier who'd been ready to rest moments before was now up and armed.

More growls and screams came from down the pass. I could picture it in my mind—someone must've disturbed a hibernating Mort and set off the rest of the horde. My heart pounded in my chest as my eyes searched across the camp, looking for any signs of what was approaching.

But what I saw was even more shocking than I was ready for—a body flying through the air, torn and bleeding. It landed on top of a nearby tank with a sickening thud, and I froze.

Whatever had the strength to catapult a man like that from that great a distance had to be massive. No Phase Two Mort could do that, especially in this cold. My stomach dropped.

Otto ran to the turret gun mounted on top of the SUV, quickly readying it as Evelyn began shouting orders while arming herself. The camp was chaos now, soldiers scrambling as the swarm spread through our flanks. And then, a collective gasp rippled through the pass.

A towering Mort emerged, its body deformed and covered in grotesque, fleshy knots. It looked like a juggernaut of muscle, taller than even our largest tank. It flipped a Jeep effortlessly, sending it tumbling, before throwing several soldiers into the rocky walls. I couldn't believe what I was seeing. Whether it was the result of another unknown mutation or some twisted experiment, I knew one thing—it was the largest Mort I'd ever seen.

I fired my pistols at the common Morts charging into our camp. One went down, its body collapsing into the icy dirt, but more kept coming as the soldiers around me worked to take out the rest.

The grotesque form of the behemoth lurched toward us. Otto and the others behind turrets opened fire, their shots landing with deafening cracks.

Its black eyes narrowed, and its anger exploded. It thrashed, killing several soldiers at its feet. The beast then charged in our direction, its heavy footsteps shaking the ground beneath us. Maverick and I both jumped out of the way, narrowly avoiding being trampled as it stomped on the tent behind us.

I fired at it from the ground, my shots hitting its thick, muscle-bound torso. It turned its attention to me, and before I could react, it grabbed me by the leg.

Upside down now, I fired into its arm, but the pustules covering its body acted like some kind of fleshy armor, and the creature was barely deterred. It growled at the onslaught of bullets from all directions, and swung me around like a ragdoll, enraged. My stomach lurched as I was hurled through the air, my body twisting helplessly.

I landed with a hard thud, a sickening jolt of pain shooting through me when I hit the ground. When my vision cleared from the impact, I realized I'd been thrown far from the camp. Dazed, I struggled to stand, my legs unsteady beneath me. I saw my pistols, scattered far away from me across the icy ground.

I stumbled toward them, but before I could reach one, another Mort tackled me from behind, shrieking wildly. I had no time to react as its needle-like teeth sank into my ribs! I screamed in agony, punching at its face in a desperate attempt to get it off me. For a moment, it backed off, pulling away just enough for me to collapse next to my pistol.

I grabbed it quickly and fired directly into the Mort's brain. It fell limp, its body crumpling before me.

Barely catching my breath, I saw soldiers rushing toward me. One of them yelled, "We have a bite!"

Even though it'd happened to me, hearing those words brought everything into sharp focus. It hit me like a cold wave—*I've been bitten.* Whatever traces of the vaccine still swam in my blood might not hold up against this direct an exposure. Was this really how I was going to go out? Before I even reached Ylem? As much as I trusted in the universe, it had a knack for cruel irony.

The soldiers started carrying me back toward the camp, my blood leaving a trail behind me. I could barely hold on to consciousness, but I did catch the bombing squad throwing a mine onto the giant's back. The explosion made my ears ring. I could feel the ground tremble as the behemoth finally collapsed, its body smoking, black blood bubbling from its wounds.

I was fading fast. I listened for any other signs of movement, for any more gunshots, but the camp settled again. We'd made it through the attack—but not unharmed.

The last thing I saw was Maverick and Otto running toward me, their faces filled with worry, before everything faded to black.

31. TYE

The trek through the grasslands felt endless. The sun beat down relentlessly, and the day seemed to go on forever. I was lucky to be inside my own armored personnel carrier—a large, tank-like vehicle situated in the middle of the battalion. The heavy armor around me provided a sense of security, but it couldn't help me shake off the unease growing in the pit of my stomach. Ylem's Front Wall was now visible, several miles ahead of the camp we had set up for the night, an eerie reminder of how close we were to enemy territory.

It was clear that the extra security had been arranged for me after I insisted on coming to the battlefield. But even with the armored walls and soldiers stationed on night watch outside my carrier, I couldn't help feeling vulnerable.

I kept waiting for Ylem to strike, for its forces to confront us in a surprise attack. Whether it knew we were here or not, it hadn't shown any signs of raising the alarm. And somehow, that made it worse. Did Ylem know we were coming? Was it so confident in its power that it was waiting and watching for its entertainment?

Riley was anxious, too. She'd taken up smoking again on marching breaks, a habit I hated but couldn't bring myself to call her out on now. After we'd had our small rationed meals, I found her sharing a cigarette with two British soldiers. When they saw me approaching, they quickly backed off, as if they thought Riley and I were an item or something.

"You seem to be making the most of all this," I said, trying to keep the mood light.

"Don't be jealous," she shot back, grinning. "A little flirting to keep my mind off missing Rio's a good trade-off."

I eyeballed her cigarette pointedly, and she snuffed it out in the dirt with a sigh. "Sorry. It just feels nice to be able to feel like pre-mom Riley for a bit."

"Understandable," I said, smiling a little.

She glanced at me, her expression shifting to something more serious. "We better get through this. I was so happy having you back, helping with her, being by my side again. Having to give birth while you were away… It was really tough on me."

"Riley—"

"Of course, it's not your fault. I'm just saying, you were my biggest support, and I didn't have you there. And it was weird because, you know, my relationship with my dad hasn't always been the best, and suddenly, he became my rock."

"It was so good seeing him again," I said, recalling how every interaction I'd had with him while I was dating Riley had always been positive.

She nodded. "I think he regrets not accepting my sister for who she was. I don't know how much of his support is for me, or for his regrets with my sister."

I put an arm around her, offering what comfort I could. "You know as well as I do, with all the changes in the world, perspectives shift. You guys were apart for a long time. He probably realized all that stuff wasn't important, and now he's making up for lost time. I think he's just trying to make things right."

"I could tell when we were saying goodbye that he was really scared about losing me—another daughter…" Riley smiled softly, her eyes glistening, but then visibly pulled herself together. "Okay, I need another cigarette," she said with a laugh.

Before I could respond, one of Dustin's men—a Special Ops soldier, dressed in all black—came rushing over to us. His face was serious, his posture rigid.

"They want you guys at the command center," he said quickly.

"Is everything okay?" I asked, immediately on alert.

"They'll brief you there," he replied, not offering much more, before he started leading us toward the large mobile center at the back of the battalion. Rowen and Ava were stationed there, and I had a sinking feeling this was going to be more than just a routine check-in.

When we arrived at the command center, I saw Dustin already inside, and the moment I caught sight of Ava, I knew something was very wrong.

"What is it?"

Rowen looked to Ava, who hesitated for a moment before finally speaking, her voice tight. "The second flank was attacked by Morts. They lost men, and it seems … Willa was bitten."

I hadn't expected to hear anything even close to that. The words hit me with such force that I stumbled back slightly, as if they had physical weight. My mind instantly flashed to giving her my blood, but the reality was that without Ylem's technology, without someone like Chiron to do the transfusion, there was no way to do that. That was the whole point of this battle. *How is this happening now?*

I was too stunned to speak, but Rowen quickly picked up where Ava left off. "There's no fear of her turning. They administered all the vaccines within minutes of her exposure, and they're treating her now."

A flicker of relief washed over me, but it barely dented my panic. "I need to go to her—"

"Tye," Dustin interrupted firmly, "we knew you'd say that, but be realistic. We're in position for the next phase tomorrow. You think a little nibble's gonna take Willa out? Hell no. She'll be up and running at the crack of dawn."

His reassurance helped, but I could tell by his pale face that he was worried, too.

Rowen's expression was solemn. "They're giving her the best medical care possible. Multiple field medics are tending to her."

I realized at that moment that I could handle strange experiments, I could withstand abuse, even imprisonment, but my one weakness, the thing that would hit me the hardest, would be to see the people I loved in pain—especially Willa. Hearing that she was hurt drained every ounce of energy I had left.

"Can we talk to her? On the radio or something?" Riley asked.

"Yeah, I want to talk to her," I said immediately.

Rowen gave me a sympathetic look. "When they stabilize her, we'll make it happen."

That hit me like a hammer. It implied Willa wasn't stable yet.

"Rest easy," Rowen continued. "We all care about her. And on top of that, she's a vital part of the operation. They'll work through the night to get her back on her feet."

After a tense silence, Dustin put his arm around me, offering a genuine smile. "Let's take a walk, buddy, keep our minds in the game," he said, leading me outside.

The cold air was a small relief, even if only for a moment. I tried telling myself that Willa had been through way worse than a bite, that she could handle this. As long as she wasn't going to turn, I'd try my best to push it out of my mind—for now.

Dustin and I walked through the camp, the quiet chatter in various languages providing a strange kind of comfort. The sounds brought me back to the moment, grounding me, even though my thoughts kept drifting to Willa.

It was extra dark tonight—no campfires or lights were allowed this close to the wall for risk of being spotted. In turn, the stars above seemed brighter than ever, as if the universe was trying to fill the void of the light we'd lost.

"My parents used to tell me wild cop stories," Dustin said lightly. "Things they'd see on duty. I always think about how they'd never believe the kind of shit we go through now. Makes their craziest stories sound like something out of a children's book."

I forced a laugh, though Willa's face was still fresh in my mind. I understood that Dustin was trying to keep me from panicking, but I could tell he had a lot on his mind too. I'd noticed the way he'd wake up in cold sweats during the night, and how he kept himself busy even during our short breaks on the march. He'd done a good job of hiding it, but I could see the pain he carried, just like I did. His time apart from the group had also left its mark on him.

"I never met your parents," I said, wanting to reach out in return. "Tell me about them."

He was caught off guard for a moment, but then his expression softened, like his mind was drifting to memories of them. After a minute, his face lit up, and I realized how much they meant to him.

"They were the best," he said warmly. "I just loved how they let me do my thing. They were serious, no doubt, but they never tried to make me into what they wanted. They supported my skating and surfing, let me join the wrestling team. They hoped I'd be more like them, but still, they let me do me. Loved that about them."

His smile faltered then, and the light in his eyes dimmed. "I still imagine myself finding them one day. I don't know if it's because I left home without seeing them, never knowing truly if they died or turned, but I keep having this vision. I'll be out and about one day, and I'll just run into them."

My heart broke on seeing the emotion in his face. Unlike Dustin, I'd seen my parents change into demonic versions of themselves, twisted by whatever the virus had done to them. But I could understand that hope, that fantasy of finding them again, as if it'd all been a terrible dream.

We reached the carrier and climbed aboard. I started going through the motions of getting ready for bed, unpacking my blanket and stripping off my gear.

Dustin was already halfway out of the door when he turned to me. "I'll see you in the morning," he said quietly.

"You're not in for the night?" I asked, surprised that he wasn't staying.

He shook his head. "I have to get my unit in order. There's no sleeping tonight."

With that, he shut the door behind him. I knew then that I wouldn't be sleeping either. But I also knew that staying awake, worrying about Willa, would make it that much harder to function tomorrow.

A few minutes later, Riley entered, closing the door behind her. "They heard Willa's doing good," she said, her voice filled with relief. "They gave her steroids and patched up her wound."

"Okay, good," I said, feeling the tension in my chest ease just a little. It wasn't enough to make me push the thoughts aside, but it was a great bit of news to hold onto as the long day finally came to an end.

I woke up surprised I'd actually fallen asleep at all. I rubbed my eyes and looked through the front window of the carrier, where the battalion was already forming up. The army was packed, ready for the next phase.

I quickly got up, pulling on my gear and heading outside. I looked around at the organized mayhem unfolding in front of me.

Dustin wasn't far off. A unit of about forty Special Ops surrounded him, all suited up in black and ready, listening intently as he spoke with them.

Riley stood a little farther away, having one last cigarette before entering the fray. Her loaded gun was resting by her side, and I could see her hand shaking as she took another drag.

A soldier approached, handing out earpieces. I put mine in and clicked it on. Rowen's voice came through immediately, sharp and clear. *"... Bombing squadrons are approaching the wall. Ready formations."*

I climbed up the side of the armored carrier, my eyes straining to see further into the distance. In the haze of the early morning light, I could just make out a brigade of vehicles speeding across the grasslands, headed straight toward Ylem's Front Wall: the bombing unit.

"Tye," Dustin called.

I jumped back down to the ground, noticing the way his unit surrounded the carrier. They were ordered to protect me at all costs, and while it should have made me feel safe, it only made me feel singled out.

"We'll be moving soon," Dustin said, his voice lighter than before. "I've got someone on the line for you."

He held out a radio phone and I grabbed it eagerly, my heart hammering in my chest. "Willa?" I asked, desperate to hear her voice.

"Hey," she replied, sounding calm and normal.

My heart lifted a little at the sound.

"Barely a day away from each other, and you go and get yourself bit?" I joked, trying to mask my worry.

She laughed, but I could hear the exhaustion in it. "The whole time I was in that medical tent, I wanted to let you know I was okay."

"I was going crazy," I admitted. "And now? How are you feeling?"

"Sore," she replied, "but they pumped me full of steroids and gave me the latest vaccine immediately, so they said I won't turn. I've got bigger things to focus on right now, though. Our bombing unit just moved into position below the wall. Waiting on orders."

I frowned, my mind racing. "Here I was, thinking that Morts would be the least of our worries out here."

"This one was different than any we've seen before," she replied worriedly. "Whatever chemicals Ylem messed with under Zenith, they sure knew how to abuse them."

The battalion started in a slow march forward. My grip tightened on the radio. "I have to go. I'll see you on the inside. I love you," I said quickly.

"I love you too," she replied, and then the line went quiet.

Dustin grabbed the radio from me, his expression serious. "Back in the carrier 'til we're inside."

I rolled my eyes. "Yeah, yeah," I muttered, but did as I was told.

I had my automatic and a pistol, ready for the fight ahead, though I couldn't help but wonder if they were going to keep me inside the carrier until absolutely necessary.

Suddenly, a piercing alarm blared across the plains.

Riley came stumbling inside the vehicle as it started to move. "What's that?" she yelped.

We both rushed to the narrow front window, straining to see through the armored glass. It didn't take long to realize the alarm was coming from Ylem.

"They know we're here," I said, the words leaving my mouth more shakily than I intended.

Without warning, cannons fired from the top of Ylem's wall, launching huge shells toward the bombing squad's vehicles. The first explosion rocked the convoy, sending a plume of smoke billowing up into the sky. Even from this distance, I could see the damage was major.

"Shit!" Riley shouted in disbelief.

Dustin and a few Special Ops soldiers climbed on board the carrier, locking the thick door behind them. I couldn't tear my eyes away from the bombing squad. Another vehicle exploded just before reaching the wall. Already, there were only six of the ten left.

I could hear Rowen's voice crackling through the driver's intercom. *"Take evasive action! Fan out and regroup at the demolition point!"*

The squad scattered on his command. The cannons overhead only managed to take out one last vehicle, while the remaining five regrouped and pushed close enough to the wall to deploy their explosives.

At least a hundred rockets fired off from the crown of their vehicles, streaking in unison toward the massive structure. Just as the bombing squad's convoy began retreating to rejoin the battalion, a deafening sonic boom swept over the grasslands. An explosion, nearly as bright as the sun itself, made me squint, my eyes stinging from the intensity of the blast.

The floor shook violently beneath me as huge chunks of the wall crumbled, smashing into the earth like falling asteroids. Then, something I never thought I'd see: in one massive, crushing motion, an entire section of the wall deteriorated under the explosion's force. Fire and smoke rose in a gigantic black cloud.

Before I could even process the magnitude of what I'd just witnessed, our whole battalion was charging at full speed toward the breach in Ylem's wall.

32. WILLA

Our armored SUV passed through the opening in the Eastern Wall, the massive pieces of broken stone still smoking from the blast. The rest of the battalion followed, carefully moving over the rubble as we made our way deeper beyond the breach. The sounds of boots on the ground and the occasional shouted orders reverberated off the part of the wall still standing.

I didn't feel any pain from the bite, for now. The steroids I'd been given were still masking it, but I knew that wouldn't last forever.

Being bitten had once been one of my deepest fears—especially after what happened to Imani. But that was before there was any version of a vaccine, before I'd witnessed things far worse than a bite. Now, I had no time to think about it. Not when we were stepping back into a place that could very well be the setting for my last day alive.

We funneled further into Ylem, the only sound the blaring alarms in the distance. This part of the city felt deserted—no golden soldiers, no signs of the usual life that once thrived here. The streets were empty, the buildings standing like hollow giants. It was clear the citizens had retreated at the first sign of danger. And as planned, this part of the wall hadn't been reinforced like the heavily defended front-facing side.

Gunshots and the distant cries of battle travelled from across the city, but for the moment, our battalion continued through unchallenged. We had to move quickly.

Evelyn's convoy pulled up alongside our SUV, just as Rowen's voice buzzed in through my earpiece. *"Evelyn, Otto, head straight to the satellite tower with your units. It'll be heavily guarded. We'll send more support as we make progress. Willa, Maverick, you know how to proceed."*

I barely had time to give Otto a quick hug. Maverick jumped from the vehicle, shouting for his unit to assemble. I watched as the soldiers moved into their positions.

Otto and Evelyn's platoon of rebels and troops were already heading toward the distant tower, its shape a dark silhouette against the smoky skyline.

I raised my two pistols, checking the familiar weight in my hands as I fell into step with Maverick's unit. The flow of soldiers marched towards the heart of the city.

Before long, our unit had broken away from the greater battalion, which was now fanning out to its assigned stations.

When we veered in the direction of the Basilica, our presence was finally challenged. Golden soldiers began showing up, some on foot, others emerging from the rooftops of the surrounding buildings.

"Stay sharp," Maverick muttered, signaling for his men to move quickly into a large city square.

We ducked behind a grand fountain, its ornate façade now cracked and chipped from the hail of gunfire coming from all directions. The sound of bullets whizzing past me made me flinch, but we fired back, taking out the first crew of guards with relative ease. But more kept showing up. Reinforcements in security vehicles flooded the area in no time.

The square erupted into chaos. Gunfire rang out from all corners. Windows shattered, sending glass raining down onto the pristine Ylem streets. Water splashed from the fountain as bullets pelted it.

I saw civilians running for cover between the luxury buildings, some of them caught in the crossfire and collapsing on the pavement. Blood began to pool on the cobblestones.

I fired again, taking down a few more Ylem soldiers as they advanced, but it was already starting to get overwhelming. Every time I looked up, more soldiers emerged, pushing us back. Maverick's men were trying to cover us from different points in the square, but more of them kept falling. The tide of battle was beginning to turn against us, and we hadn't even made it near the Basilica yet, which would be even more heavily guarded.

Just as things seemed like they might tip into a loss for us, a band of rebels roared in on Jeeps, guns blazing. They fired at the Ylem soldiers, shifting the balance in our favor. The golden soldiers began to fall hard and fast, their positions crumbling under the barrage of fire.

A girl ducked beside me. I recognized the fiery red hair and silver armband and my heart skipped a beat.

"Cleo!"

"Don't think they covered this in FORESIGHT training!" she yelled over the gunfire, her voice thick with adrenaline.

I snapped back into action, taking down a soldier charging toward us. Then, I turned to Cleo, smiling despite the madness raging around us.

"You're a crazy bitch, Willa," Cleo laughed. "And I love it!"

She opened fire, her automatic weapon spitting rounds towards the golden soldiers, giving Maverick and me an opening to run.

"Go!" she shouted.

Maverick and I dashed between the adjacent buildings, sprinting through the narrow alley that separated them. Maverick's men followed suit, running to join us as Cleo and her group stayed back, providing cover for our escape.

We reached a new section of the city, having covered a decent distance, but were still nowhere near the Basilica. It was a reminder of just how vast this city was. Even with the few streets I recognized, I still felt disoriented by its scale.

Maverick, heading up the unit, stopped in an alleyway, his men immediately doing the same.

He turned to me. "Do you have the keycard? Is it safe?"

I quickly reached into my zipper pocket and found it tucked safely inside. "Yeah, I do."

Maverick glanced around, eyes narrowing in focus. "I have an idea," he said, his voice low but sharp. "They'll have already shut off the metros, but we can walk the tunnels and railways to get closer to the Basilica."

There was a brief moment of acknowledgement from his men. We all braced ourselves and moved swiftly, following Maverick's lead.

We advanced in short bursts, covering each other as bullets stitched the walls around us, until we reached the metro stop and scrambled down into the dark, shadowy tunnels. The click of our boots echoed around the empty space as the group descended.

I couldn't shake the feeling of déjà vu. The dark tunnels reminded me of when we'd escaped the mall, the horror of that moment still fresh in my mind. I scanned the shadows, half-expecting Morts to appear from every corner, but nothing moved.

We came to a stationary metro train, its windows dark and lifeless. We moved quickly around it, Maverick leading the way. But some of his men were lagging behind—they were hurt.

"Medic!" he ordered, and the rest of the unit stopped.

A few of the soldiers were leaning against the tunnel walls, blood staining the concrete. Maverick and a field medic immediately moved in to tend to them.

I watched Maverick tear off a sleeve from his shirt and tie it around a soldier's bleeding arm. As he did, I noticed a new tattoo, the ink looking fresher and brighter than the rest on his arm. I'd spent a lot of time taking in every detail of the canvas of his skin, when Maverick had once been my only comfort. This new tattoo was of a bone and an arrow crossed over in an X, and my stomach tightened with the realization of its meaning.

"Maverick?" I whispered, the word catching in my throat.

He glanced up at me, then followed my gaze down to the tattoo. His expression softened for a moment. "It's for Archer and Hound."

The words hit me harder than I was prepared for. I couldn't help the tears that welled up in my eyes. We were alive because of their sacrifice at Ground Misery, and Maverick's new ink told me he knew that too.

I swallowed hard, trying to keep my composure. "He's probably so happy knowing you have that. That they meant that much to you."

Maverick gave me a pained smile but didn't break focus. He kept working, making sure his man was stabilized. We couldn't afford to stop for too long.

Minutes later, the medic finished and the injured soldiers were back on their feet. We all moved forward, following Maverick down the dark tunnel, the distant sounds of battle keeping us alert.

We meandered through Ylem's complex metro system, the dim beams of our flashlights flickering on the walls as we moved. I wasn't sure Maverick knew exactly where he was going. Every now and then, a fork would appear in the tunnel and he'd hesitate before choosing one direction over the other, as if gambling on which path would lead us to where we needed to be. But I knew he had a much better grasp of Ylem's layout than I did—or any early blueprints Rowen had gotten his hands on.

I suddenly noticed that I wasn't at the front with Maverick anymore and had fallen behind toward the middle of the unit. Fatigue was taking its toll, and it wasn't normal for me. I didn't want to show any sign of weakness. Too many people were counting on me. But I was a fool if I thought the bite wouldn't have any repercussions at all. I felt it begin to throb under the bandages, a dull ache that pulsed with every step I took.

I was startled by a wet sensation on my face. It wasn't water; it was warm. I instinctively reached up to touch it and saw a red stain smeared across my fingers. *My nose. Blood.* My stomach flipped and I wiped it quickly away, hoping no one had seen. The medics had warned me that I might experience mild symptoms of the virus, but actually feeling it happen...

I shoved the panic down. As long as my head stayed clear enough to finish what we came for—to end Midas—I could deal with the rest later.

We kept moving forward until finally, we reached a metal door in the tunnel, its dark surface almost blending into the wall. Maverick's face lit up with recognition. This was clearly the place he'd been aiming for.

"Willa?" he prompted.

I stepped forward, digging into my pocket, and pulled out the golden keycard. I slipped it into the port, the mechanism flashing green before it clicked open. The heavy door slowly slid open, revealing a ladder that led lower into the depths of Ylem.

"This is a shortcut to where we need to go," Maverick said, and climbed through first.

I followed the unit down, dropping into the narrow space beneath the ladder and landing in what was clearly a water duct. The shallow stream of water rushed under my boots, and though it smelled clean enough, the pressure of the current made it harder to keep up. The rest of the unit had already begun to march ahead, and I fought to keep pace, every step feeling more difficult than the last.

After nearly half an hour of trudging through the cold, rushing water, we climbed a very long ladder, my hands slipping on the rungs from the damp. When we reached the top and emerged into a secondary tunnel, I blinked against the sudden exposure to light. We were now out of the claustrophobic confines of the underground and higher above the city. This tunnel opened to the outside.

Ahead of us, an elevated railway snaked through the modern buildings. The ominous shape of the spherical black Basilica stood out against Ylem's skyline. We were closer now, and the battle sounds were deafening. It was clear we were in the heart of the fight.

Maverick stopped to address our unit just before we exited the safety of the tunnel, his tone commanding. "This railway will take us close to the Basilica," he said, glancing back over his shoulder. "But we'll be exposed, so we need to move fast and cover each other. No stopping. If we make it past those two skyscrapers up ahead, they'll know what we're after, and they'll throw everything they've got at us. If you fall, you fall with honor, and I'll remember what you've done to get us this far."

His words were sobering, and I felt my heart rate quicken.

We all reloaded and cocked our weapons, and my hand instinctively went to the third pistol strapped to my thigh—the one Harlow had given me. Its mother-of-pearl handle was just visible above its holster.

Maverick gave the signal, and we charged forward onto the outer railway that hung above the city. I moved quickly, but my eyes couldn't help but take in the chaos unfolding below us. War vehicles clashed, their turrets swiveling as they exchanged fire. Explosions ripped through the air, sending bodies soaring across the streets; harrowing cries rang out, mixing with the deafening gunfire.

A few of Ylem's war vehicles turned their turrets toward the railway, and I felt the structure of the tracks sway as massive bullets blasted through it. My heart hammered in my chest as I stooped, but I kept moving.

Golden soldiers began appearing on the rooftops of nearby buildings, firing down at us. I had just enough time to roll out of the way as a spray of bullets sliced through the air, narrowly missing me. I heard the thuds of men falling around me. My ribs ached, but I couldn't slow down. I fired back at any Ylem soldier I saw, not bothering to aim for anything other than the threat.

We eventually made it around a bend in the railway, and for the briefest moment, we had cover from the assault. Our unit quickly reloaded, but I could see that we were already down to half the men we'd started with.

Far away, the satellite tower still stood strong, smoke billowing from beneath it, but its lights were still glowing bright. There was no sign that it'd been taken out. The anxiety in my gut flared—Otto could be in trouble.

I heard Rowen's voice in my earpiece. *"Maverick, Willa, report your status."*

Maverick responded first, his voice strained as he caught his breath. "We're nearly there, but taking heavy fire. I'll need more men near the Basilica when we reach it."

Rowen's stress was clear in his tone. *"We're spread thin, but I'll do my best."*

Clearly, Maverick wasn't exaggerating. When we reached the perimeter of the Basilica, the streets were swarming with so many golden guards that it almost seemed as though the area around it had been gold-plated. The sheer number of soldiers was staggering, and for a moment, it felt like we were walking into a trap. But to my relief, Maverick didn't lead us directly toward the sphere. Instead, he ducked into a utility stairwell off the railway, guiding us down to street level.

We exchanged fire with nearby guards, taking them out one by one, but not without loss. My heart nearly stopped when one of Maverick's men was shot in the head. The bullet's force slammed his skull against the wall behind him, and blood sprayed across my face. I wiped it away quickly, but the image of his body slumping to the ground stayed with me long after we got out of there.

We were down to about ten men now, and I couldn't help but wonder how the hell we were going to stand up to the Basilica's defenses.

"We're going through a back way," Maverick said, as if reading my thoughts. "But we need to get some distance and move through the city."

"How do you know all these secret channels?" I asked him, scanning our surroundings for more threats.

"I followed Harlow through every path imaginable when she was sneaking out. Memorized most of them. Believe me, I thought about running from Ylem more than once. Some of these paths have been forgotten over the years—too many staff and worker turnarounds—and the higher-ups don't care about this low-level infrastructure shit."

We traversed quickly along a few more streets, ducking into alleyways as we moved through the battle zone. I saw silver armbands among the fighting crowds, still holding strong. I looked out for Tye, or any of my friends. Not seeing them brought clashing waves of both relief and worry over me.

But then, the unmistakable shriek of what could only be a Mort pierced the air. My blood ran cold.

Our unit froze. The sound went through me like a dagger. I watched in horror as a sudden horde of them surged forward, having likely entered the city through the breaches in the wall. They were feasting on anything that moved. It didn't matter what side you were on.

"C'mon!" Maverick shouted, urging our unit away down another series of alleyways. My legs felt like lead. The pain in my side was becoming unbearable, and I knew the steroids were wearing off.

I was falling behind, and Maverick noticed. His eyes flashed with concern.

"What's wrong?" he asked, his voice low.

I didn't reply right away, but my hand naturally went to my ribs. That was all he needed. Without missing a beat, he ordered the unit to take cover.

"Move into that underpass!" he commanded, and then, much to my surprise, he gently scooped me up into his arms. The gesture felt familiar, comforting even.

We made it under a bridge, and Maverick carefully sat me against the wall, the rest of the unit forming a perimeter around us, guns at the ready in case anything came our way.

"Medic, let me get that steroid shot," Maverick called out.

The last standing field medic approached, producing an auto-injector pen. I lifted my shirt, and Maverick clicked the needle into my side. I flinched, the sharp pain making me grit my teeth. I quickly pulled my shirt back down and stood again.

"Willa, take it easy," Maverick said, gently but firmly.

I felt the chills sweep through me, leaving me feverish and unsteady. I knew I needed a moment to recover, as much as I hated to admit it. The timing couldn't have been worse. We were so close ... I relented, and sank back down onto the ground.

"If you're not in good shape, you'll end up getting killed," Maverick said seriously. "We're walking right into the viper pit. The steroids will only take a few minutes to kick in."

"We don't have a few minutes," I bit back.

Maverick regarded me with concern, and something else I couldn't quite place. "I wanna know where you get this fire from," he said, half-laughing. "Why d'you have to be so unstoppable all the time?"

At first, I thought he was just trying to distract me from the pain, but the way he was looking at me made me pause. He was genuinely waiting for an answer.

I hesitated, looking around us before meeting his eyes. "Maybe it's a side effect of having the parents that I do," I said, speaking more quietly now. "You saw it whenever you were at the house. How they always pushed this idea of success on us—the degrees, the job, the house, the family. It was all they talked about. Their ideas of what matters most. But it never felt right to me. I didn't want to be successful like that. I wanted to actually mean something. I wanted to be remembered for more than just checking boxes."

The steroids were starting to wash away the pain, and the sense of relief made my words flow. I pressed on.

"Malik was amazing, but where do you find enough support to be something that extraordinary? I had to generate it for myself, I guess. I'm sure it's not entirely healthy, but I just have this drive to fit as much as I can into this life, before I move on to whatever comes next."

Maverick let my words settle between us, and for a moment, it seemed like they'd given him something to think about. He let out a self-pitying laugh, but it didn't reach his eyes. "If only my parents being tough on me had made me turn out like you, instead of a junkie," he muttered. "Maybe I wouldn't be in this mess."

I realized how little Maverick had ever shared with me, especially about his parents. "They were hard on you?"

His expression became distant, like he was revisiting a memory he didn't want to.

"My dad was tough, not in a disciplinary way, but he was always guarded, never really got emotional. It was hard to connect with him."

I paused, letting his words sink in. "Did you ever find out what happened to them?" I eventually asked.

Maverick's face darkened, and I could see the sadness creep into his eyes. "No," he said quietly. "I lost touch with them way before the world tanked. They were so disappointed in me when I was using and wouldn't stop. They both had terrible upbringings, but they made something of themselves. And then there was me—raised right, given everything they thought I needed—and I still let the world get the better of me ... "

He swallowed hard. "I think they're still out there. I feel like they'd find a way to survive this. They've always been strong. That's how they were able to deal with me for as long as they did."

I didn't know what to say. I'd seen Maverick emotional before, but this was different. There was something in the way he talked that made me feel closer to him, more connected. I wanted to reach out, but before I could, we both heard it—the shrill screeches of approaching Morts.

Maverick helped me stand, and I felt almost as good as new. While my ribs still ached, it was manageable now. I nodded to him, giving the signal to the rest of our unit that I was ready to move on.

We didn't have time to linger on feelings. Midas was almost within reach.

33. TYE

Our battalion poured past the broken Front Wall of Ylem, and all around our armored carrier, I watched as gold and silver clashed. My jaw dropped at the sight of the instant slaughter that ensued. It was both brutal and strangely inspiring to watch—the burning passion in the eyes of our forces, fighting fiercely because they had all lost something to Ylem. We were on their land now, the land of the elite who had shut us out, who had hoarded all the resources while the rest of us were left to suffer.

The carrier shook violently as turret guns fired from the top of the wall, and gunmen rained bullets from high points on the surrounding buildings. The sound of lead against the armored car was deafening. It felt like we were being targeted specifically, but I reminded myself that Ylem still didn't know I was back—not yet.

Through the viewport, I could see Commander Oren on foot, fighting valiantly among his troops and shouting orders. Riley's hand gripped my shoulder tightly as we both watched the destruction unfold. The scene was harrowing. Golden soldiers turned red with blood, and in turn, our allied troops were falling en masse before we'd even made it a few yards into the city.

From inside our carrier, Dustin was strategizing with his men over his earpiece, coordinating his Special Ops team to protect our vehicle. I could see the angst in his eyes. He was itching to get out and fight, but he knew his mission was at the camps.

It felt like it took forever to crawl through the battle, slowly making our way to a break in the fighting. Once we reached that opening, the carrier picked up speed, racing ahead in the direction of the facilities.

Dustin's men followed in Humvees, swerving behind us through the streets. I recognized a few streets, but most of Ylem still felt unfamiliar to me. I'd hardly seen the city, never having had the freedom to explore it. All those months I spent here, blindfolded, kept in the dark about where I was ... Ylem made sure that no one who wasn't one of its own could truly feel at ease here.

I heard Ava's voice in my earpiece. *"Tye, I'm tracking your carrier. Just sent the driver coordinates to the camp structures. Expect heavy security around that area. Do not leave the carrier until it's mandatory. We'll send transport for the Angels once you're there."*

"Copy," I said, impressed by how Ava had slipped into her role so easily. She'd always had a steadiness to her that I could count on.

Our convoy swerved sharply as Ylem military vehicles sped around a corner, their heavy turret guns aimed directly at us. The contrast between their fleet's sleek designs and our mismatched vehicles—salvaged from whatever was left to fight with from around the world—was striking. We took evasive action, firing back with our own turrets in turn. The carrier sped up, plowing into a platoon of golden soldiers firing from the street. The force of the impact threw us back.

Riley, Dustin, and I were all pressed hard against the armored wall of the carrier as our convoy suddenly screeched to a halt. We'd hit a blockade of Ylem war vehicles. Their bullets hammered the carrier with such force that the front glass actually started to crack. The Special Ops Humvees provided cover fire from the rear so our carrier could break free in the other direction.

"My unit needs support!" Dustin yelled into his earpiece. "I need my guys to stay with me!"

Almost as if the words had triggered it instantly, help arrived. We watched out of the back porthole as a platoon of French and Canadian soldiers flooded the area, cutting a path for the Special Ops Humvees to rejoin us.

Our convoy surged forward again, moving at speed through the city. Ylem citizens scattered, desperately trying to find cover as we sped past them.

I kept my hand wrapped tightly around the grip of my weapon, ready to move at a moment's notice. Adrenaline kept me sharp, and braced for the inevitable fight ahead. The camps were always heavily guarded, but after my escape, I knew security would be tighter than ever. And once Ylem realized we were there to take the Angels, it would only get worse.

Even at the speed our convoy was moving, it was clear the battle was closing in on us. The city was becoming more chaotic as soldiers from both sides flooded the streets. The once pristine marble façades, gleaming with the luxury of Ylem's wealth, were now bloodstained.

Our driver hadn't said a word the whole time, and I wasn't sure he even spoke English. But he was sweating, his focus locked on the road ahead, hands gripped tight on the wheel. He slammed on the brakes again, and we lurched forward in our seats.

Riley nearly ended up on top of me as the front window shook with the impact of the Mort we'd just hit. Its claws scraped violently at the plexiglass like it was trying to tear into a can of food.

"We have Teeth!" Dustin yelled to his men through the earpiece.

Two of them outside moved quickly, taking out the Mort in a flurry of well-placed shots. But before they could even catch their breath, a clan of Phase Twos rounded the corner, clearly hungry for human meat.

Dustin didn't hesitate. He loaded his weapon and bolted outside without a second thought.

"Dustin!" I shouted after him, but he was already gone.

Riley and I exchanged a wordless look, then rushed outside to join him.

The sounds of battle were deafening now, much louder than they'd been inside the carrier. I felt disoriented, the chaos closing in around me as I fired at the charging Morts. Riley took one down beside me. More Special Ops jumped out of the Humvees, joining the fray. I heard the carrier creak, and when I turned to look, my stomach dropped.

A deformed, lanky Mort was slashing at the vehicle's armor, smashing the driver's side plexiglass with insane force. It reached inside, grabbed the driver, and yanked him out onto the street.

"Shit!" Dustin yelled over the man's screams. He fired at the monster, but it didn't relent; it lunged at him instead, sending him crashing to the ground. His gun skidded out of his reach as the Mort's needled mouth opened wide, aiming straight for Dustin's face.

Together with several of his men, I fired into its rotting flesh, but it refused to pull back. Dustin's face turned red with effort as he struggled to push the beast off, its teeth now just inches from his neck.

"No!" I shouted, charging at the monster.

It snapped at Dustin, but just as it was about to take a bite from his neck, it decided to turn on me. The pain hit like a shockwave as the Mort's teeth sank deep into my tricep. I yelled in pain, struggling against the force of it, until a shot rang out. The Mort's skull exploded, and its body collapsed. Riley had pressed the barrel of her Desert Eagle directly to its head.

I staggered back, still in shock from the pain, as a few of Dustin's men helped me up, quickly wrapping my arm. Riley looked like she was about to lose her breakfast, but I forced a weak smile.

"Better me than any of you," I said, trying to sound lighthearted despite the searing pain.

"Get him in a Humvee," Dustin ordered, his eyes hard.

Riley and I were pulled into the nearest Humvee and the convoy began to move again, leaving the carrier behind.

"You shouldn't have done that," Dustin chided, though a smile broke out across his face. "But I'm glad you did."

Our Humvee made a sharp turn. "The camps are up ahead," said the driver.

I realized I'd never seen the exterior of the camps, but I knew we'd arrived when I saw the platoon of golden guards, poised and ready outside a large compound. Certain parts of it looked familiar, like the rec area's domed ceiling sticking out of the brutalist-style structure. Other aspects were a surprise, like the secondary building adjacent to it.

"That must be the women's wing," I muttered. "They kept us separated."

Riley stared at it. "I'll take care of them," she said firmly. "You get the others."

Dustin called into his earpiece. "Half of you, go with Riley to the second building. The rest, stay with me and hold position."

"Copy," a chorus of voices responded.

As our convoy pulled up, reinforcements arrived to assist us. We hopped out of the Humvees, ducking behind them like they were shields while we worked our way through the guards. A group of Special Ops surrounded Riley and began moving toward the women's building while Dustin led us to the men's.

I could see why Dustin's team was elite—its members were agile and deadly. They moved as one, each knowing exactly what to do without a word spoken.

We blasted through the legion of golden soldiers blocking our path and reached the front entrance of the facility. Dustin ordered some of his men to use a battering ram while the rest covered them. After several heavy strikes, the door crashed open, and we flooded inside.

Alarms blared as more golden soldiers rushed in, opening fire from every direction. We fought our way through the hallways of the prison, each of us giving it everything we had.

About twenty minutes later, we found ourselves facing a massive metal door with a keypad beside it. I recognized it as the entrance to the Angels' holding facilities.

"It's here," I said.

"Get a charge on it!" Dustin ordered.

Three of his men approached the door and carefully placed explosives. The rest of us ducked into a nearby hallway and waited until the charge went off, sending a tremor through the building. When we returned, the door was still intact, though charred from the explosion.

"Damnit," I muttered. "If we don't have the code, it needs to be opened from the inside—"

I was stopped mid-sentence when the door hissed open on its own. Everyone raised their weapons, ready for an ambush, but it wasn't a guard standing there with a weapon. It was someone in a familiar jumpsuit, holding a taser as a group of paralyzed guards lay sprawled on the floor behind him.

"Vale!" I shouted, relief washing over me as I ran toward him.

"Tye?! What the hell is this?" he asked, looking over the Special Ops team.

"New Year's came early," I joked. "We're getting you out of here."

More Angels began to emerge from their hiding spots, realizing that help had finally arrived. My eyes locked on another friendly face: Beckett. His eyes were red, tears pooling as soon as he saw me. We hugged, but the moment was cut short by the unmistakable sound of gunfire down the hallway.

Ava's voice came through our comms. *"Backup with transport is outside!"*

"Let's get them going," Dustin commanded.

Some of his men moved to direct the Angels toward the exit. Beckett and Vale lingered, however, both of them filching weapons from the fallen guards.

"Go, get yourself out of here!" I urged them. "We'll cover you."

But both stood firm. Vale's jaw was set. "The New Year's plan might've come early, but a plan's a plan. I'm fighting."

I nodded, understanding his decision.

As we heard footsteps thundering down the hall, I recognized another special unit of soldiers arriving: Rowen's designated team. They were here for the tech and data from the labs upstairs.

"We should help them," I suggested, looking toward the elevator shaft. "More Ylem soldiers will be here any second."

Dustin agreed. "Let's go."

Beckett, Vale, and I, with a few remaining Special Ops, headed down the hall, taking out any lagging guards along the way. My arm was still throbbing, but the wound was healing considerably.

We reached the elevators just as Rowen's team finished getting them open with some quick cross-wiring. The lead soldier of the group saluted Dustin, apparently recognizing his rank by his uniform. "Lieutenant Bradford," he announced.

"You can call me Dustin," he replied, shaking Bradford's hand firmly.

Without wasting any time, we all crowded into the elevator. It rose quickly, taking us up to the main floor of the labs.

The teams readied their weapons as the elevator doors parted moments later. The sight that greeted us was jarring. A handful of scientists were already kneeling, their hands raised in terrified surrender, while others scrambled in the back—some trying to pack up files, others feverishly erasing data from their computers.

Rowen's team moved in, tackling the resisting scientists to the ground, while the others were ushered out of the room.

My eyes darted across the scene, searching for one face in particular: Chiron's. Was he already gone? Did he use the cover of battle to run and finally break free from Ylem's hold?

As our units took control of the situation, Dustin and I moved toward the back of the lab, where a door led to the hallway of exam rooms and offices—including the one where I'd undergone so many tests. My skin prickled as I approached the door. I hadn't realized how much dread this place still held for me.

The door was locked, requiring a hand scan to open. Beside it, a tall pane of glass looked into the hallway beyond. Dustin and Vale didn't hesitate. Within seconds, they opened fire, shattering it to bits. We climbed through the broken frame, opening the door at the end of the hall.

Then, I saw him. Chiron. He was huddled behind the examination table, eyes wide with shock. "Tye?!" he called out shakily. "Why did you come back?"

I kept my weapon raised, my focus razor-sharp. "There's no time for a catch-up," I said, my words coming out colder than I'd expected. "You helped me once. Will you help now, or do you choose Ylem?"

Chiron stood slowly, trembling, but there was a flicker of determination in his eyes. "I need to know my family will be safe."

Dustin and I traded a look. "Chiron, I promise we'll do whatever we can to get them out alive, but right now I need you to focus on the bigger picture," I insisted.

The gears were visibly turning in his head. Finally, he asked, "What can I do?"

"How do we get the data we need for the cure? Everything you've worked on, everything you know—we need it."

Chiron moved quickly, scrambling into the adjoining office. He pulled a hard drive from his desk drawer, his hands shaking as he plugged it into the nearest workstation. "I'll get as much as I can on here, but it'll take time."

Just as he spoke, a violent explosion rocked the building. I could see through the windows that Ylem's backup had arrived. Soldiers were flooding the area outside. The clock was ticking.

"Get on it!" Dustin yelled, and turned back to prepare for the incoming onslaught.

"How much time do you need?" Vale asked Chiron, eyeing the door.

"No less than fifteen minutes," Chiron replied, already getting to work.

Another crash, followed by gunshots; the unmistakable sound of Ylem's golden soldiers storming the building. The elevator and stairwell doors on either side of the room burst open. They were closing in on us.

"Stay with him!" I shouted to Beckett, and Vale and I rushed toward the door to join the fight in the greater part of the labs.

We threw ourselves into the frenzy. Our men were trading fire with the soldiers pouring into the room. We ducked behind research stations, taking cover as bullets tore through the air, chipping away at the equipment around us.

I couldn't stop myself from feeling a rush of anxiety. Every shot fired seemed like a dent in the vital information that could've been retrieved from this room. I knew Chiron was working as fast as he could, but I wasn't sure how much longer he had before the lab was overrun.

I couldn't believe we'd made it this far, but half of these Ylem men probably hadn't seen battle in years, hiding behind their walls, while the other half had arrogantly thought an attack like this would never breach their city. Now they were forced to spring into action. Still, the sheer numbers they had against us were impossible to ignore, and knowing Midas, he'd have strategic plans for a scenario like this. I wasn't letting my guard down for a second.

I stood next to Vale as we cut down at least a dozen golden soldiers. His focus was unmatched. I could tell he was finally getting the chance to take his power back after everything they'd put him through. But even as we made those kills, it wasn't enough. Dustin's Special Ops team was nearly spent, and Rowen's unit was down to a few men, all while more golden soldiers flooded the area like they were pouring out of some revolving door.

"Fall back!" Dustin shouted as he reloaded behind a desk.

Vale and I jumped back through the window frame, moving swiftly toward Chiron's office.

We burst through the door. "How much longer?!" I yelled.

Sweat was beading on Chiron's forehead as he stared at the download bar on the monitor. "About five minutes!"

Five minutes sounded like a lifetime. Beckett was visibly shaken, his hands still trembling from the chaos outside. Vale noticed and pulled

Beckett close, wrapping his arms around him before gently cupping his face in his hands.

"We're gonna get out of this. We're gonna have a life together," Vale said, his voice low but resolute.

I overheard the quiet exchange, and for a moment, I wished I had the luxury of such optimism. But that brief, tender moment was shattered when Dustin barged in. Just as Lieutenant Bradford tried to make it inside behind him, he was shot in the doorway. His body hit the floor with a sickening thud, blood pooling on the carpet.

With Bradford's lifeless body blocking the threshold, Dustin had no choice but to quickly drag it inside the room. He managed to shut and lock the door, his back pressed against it as we heard more golden soldiers gathering outside.

"You're surrounded. Come out now!" came a shout from the other side.

I took a deep breath and spoke into my earpiece. "Ava, Rowen, do you hear me?"

"*Ava here!*" she replied quickly.

"Ava, we're cornered in Chiron's office! We've got the data, but we need backup. There are Ylem soldiers everywhere!"

"All forces near you are slammed with protecting the Angels," Ava responded, panicked. *"They're being overrun too."*

I looked out of the small window across the room, scanning the battle raging below. I saw the armored carriers for the Angels, fighting tooth and nail to move through the crowds of soldiers.

"If you can make it to one of the carriers, we can get you out of there!" Ava urged.

I thought about jumping, but we'd never survive the drop.

The banging on the door grew more intense, and Dustin's body jerked against the pressure of holding it closed.

"One more minute," Chiron muttered as his hand hovered over the hard drive, shaking from nerves.

I braced for the door to give in, but then Beckett, standing by a research station, spoke up.

"What's this?"

Chiron's voice cracked as he yelled, "Don't touch that! Not all of us are immune."

But Beckett was already reaching for a box of syringes labeled with a bright red biohazard sticker. I saw the Zenith label on each syringe and my heart sank.

"The virus?" I asked, my skin crawling.

"For test subjects," Chiron confirmed nervously, his attention returning to the screen.

Without missing a beat, Beckett pulled one of the syringes from the box.

"Woah!" Dustin shouted in disbelief.

Beckett didn't hesitate—he was immune, after all. He walked over to Bradford's body, lying still on the floor.

"Keep your weapons on him," Beckett said firmly. "I don't know how this'll turn out, but we don't have a lot of options."

We all kept our guns trained on Bradford as Beckett stuck the needle into his skin and pressed the plunger. The body convulsed as the liquid took effect.

"Help me," Beckett said, and Dustin immediately moved to assist, lifting Bradford's body with him.

"Chiron," Beckett said, "tell them you surrender."

Chiron hesitated for a moment, then shouted at the door, "It's Dr. Chiron! I'm coming out, do not shoot!"

We could hear the guards shuffling outside, evidently confused by the sudden turn of events.

"Ready?" Dustin asked as Bradford's body started to twitch.

"Now!" Beckett said, and they yanked open the door, tossing Bradford's body into the hallway like a human grenade. The guards fired immediately. Dustin managed to slam the door shut and lock it again, barely avoiding a hail of bullets.

"What the fuck?" one of the guards yelled from the other side.

"It's a Dark-Eye!" another shouted, and I heard the guttural screech of the newly-formed Mort.

Gunshots and chaos erupted as it tore through the enemy, creating the perfect distraction.

"Done!" Chiron said, unplugging the hard drive from the machine.

We didn't waste a second. Weapons raised, we charged out of the office, firing at anything that moved, but the golden soldiers were fully entangled with the Mort as it tore through their ranks.

Taking advantage of the commotion, we fought our way down the hall toward the nearest stairwell, and somehow, we made it. But it was too early to celebrate. We still had a long way to go.

Out on the street level, we ran through dust and smoke. Dustin and Vale picked off any Ylem soldiers who got too close. Beckett and I stuck close to Chiron, guarding him and the hard drive with everything we had.

I spotted an armored carrier up ahead, moving slowly through the flood of uniforms. We fought our way through the densely-packed warzone, weapons blazing as bullets tore past us, some so close I swore one grazed my hair. Even Chiron's lab coat had a hole near the hem.

I kept my focus on the carrier. We *had* to make it. We couldn't afford to fail now.

As we neared the vehicle, a foreign commander spotted us. I wasn't sure if he knew about the hard drive, but something in his eyes told me he understood how high the stakes were. He barked orders in what sounded like German, and his soldiers formed a protective ring around us, providing just enough cover to get us to the carrier.

We climbed inside, nearly collapsing from exhaustion. I could hear the loud clang of bullets hitting the outside of the hull as we huddled together.

Vale and Beckett shared a hug, both of them trying to catch their breath. Dustin and Chiron leaned against the armored walls, looking as worn out as I felt.

I glanced around, and my heart nearly stopped when I saw the young Angels. Girls from the women's wing were crowded in the back of the carrier. And then, I saw her: Riley, standing near them, blood dripping from her arm. Tears were in her eyes, but they weren't from pain—they were tears of relief.

"Told you I'd take care of it," she said, her voice shaky but proud.

I could hardly believe it. Relief washed over me, and for a moment, I let myself relax. As I exhaled, I realized my pain was gone. My arm had completely healed.

The deafening clatter of bullets striking the carrier pulled my thoughts to Willa. My mission might have been over, but my vendetta wasn't.

"Riley, stay with Vale and Beckett here," I urged. "Get this carrier to safety."

I turned to Chiron, who was catching his breath, his face still pale. "We'll call for help to find your family once we break through to a safer area. I'm heading to the Basilica."

"And I'm coming with you," Dustin said immediately.

34. WILLA

Maverick led us as close to the Basilica as we could get without drawing attention from the legions of golden soldiers at its base. We skirted the periphery, staying hidden in the shadows of a nondescript alleyway between buildings. The anticipation was building like we were in a pressure cooker, but Maverick's steady pace kept us moving, guiding us through the alley and into a series of maintenance tunnels.

To my surprise, we arrived to see a familiar sight: a trolley, sitting motionless on a slanted track. It was the same kind of trolley Tye and I had used to escape the Basilica the first time.

I stepped forward, reaching for the keycard port, but Maverick stopped me. "Same as the metros," he said. "The systems are shut down. We'll have to walk. But this'll take us right to the service entrance of the kitchens."

The remainder of his unit started up the incline, their flashlights cutting ahead of us through the darkness.

As we climbed, I became very aware of what awaited us at the top of this slope. We were about to step right inside Midas's lair. My palms started to sweat. The idea of facing him head-on filled me with unease. Harlow would be there too. I couldn't help feeling the sting of regret as I pictured how she might react. She knew where my loyalty stood—on the side of the resistance—but could she have ever imagined I'd be the one sent to kill her father? The thought made my stomach churn.

I'd known Harlow well enough to understand that despite her disagreements with Midas's ways, to her, he was still her father. It made me sad to think she'd most likely regret any friendship we once had.

But this was not the time for second-guessing. If I failed to take Midas down now, there might never be another opportunity. The truth was, I didn't want to think about what would happen to Tye if I didn't succeed. I couldn't bear the idea of leaving him behind in this mess if something happened to me.

As my steps became more hesitant, Maverick's brow furrowed. "What's on your mind?"

I bit my lip, suddenly feeling self-conscious. "Tye ... It scares me how much I love him."

Maverick's expression softened, and for a moment, I could see the turmoil of his own unspoken thoughts in his eyes. Something about it made me realize that maybe this wasn't exactly what he wanted to hear.

"Sorry," I mumbled.

"Don't be," he said quickly, his voice gentle. "I'll never be able to put into words how happy I am that you have him. I don't care about my weird, complicated feelings that I barely understand myself. What you have with him is so clear. And you deserve it."

His words struck deeper than I was ready for. A lump rose in my throat, and I reached out, placing my hand on his shoulder. I wanted him to know that his support meant more to me than he could possibly imagine.

"I know Malik would be over the moon knowing you had someone like him," he added.

For a moment, there was a quiet understanding between us. And in that silence, I felt a sense of peace, as if, for a brief moment, the world outside the tunnels had stopped spinning.

But we both knew the mission wasn't over yet.

I took a deep breath and followed Maverick through the darkness until we came upon the familiar stairwell leading to the kitchens. This was once a quiet service entrance, used to restock the kitchens, and where the upper echelons of the Basilica would never see the workers who kept things in order for them. Today, though, it was a forgotten entrance that would deliver them a deadly surprise.

Maverick waved his men ahead. At the top of the stairs, they flickered their flashlights to signal it was clear. Then, as one, we moved up, entering the butler's galley.

We crammed ourselves inside, shutting off our lights, the silence overwhelming. The only sound was the distant gunfire from the battle raging outside the Basilica walls.

Maverick's whisper broke through the quiet. "You ready?"

I nodded, though my heart hammered in my chest. Once we left the kitchen, there would be no turning back. They would know we were here. Guards would be in every room by now, and there were only about fifteen of us left to get to the bunker. My stomach twisted. Getting in was one thing. If I succeeded, how the hell would I get out?

I clicked my earpiece. "Rowen?" I whispered. "You there?"

"Copy," he replied quickly. *"Things are getting heated out here. And you?"*

"We're inside the Basilica. Any units you can send this way, now's the time," I said, keeping my voice steady despite the tightness in my chest.

"I'm already ahead of you. The British Army, along with any men we can spare at the moment, are fighting their way over."

"Rowen," I said, my heart heavy, "let's finally end this."

There was a pause before he responded. *"I'd like that, Willa. I'm right here with you."*

I clicked off my earpiece as Maverick signaled his men to move out into the halls.

Gunfire rang out almost instantly. Maverick and I didn't hesitate—we darted down the hall in the opposite direction of the attack.

We wound through curved corridors, passing parlor rooms, and firing shots as golden guards popped out of every corner, yelling warnings about intruders. It felt like the entire Basilica was closing in on us.

Maverick reached a metal door. "Keycard!" he yelled as he turned and fired over my shoulder at the advancing guards.

I scrambled for the keycard and swiped it into the port. The metal doors opened with a loud clank, and I instantly had to dodge as a shot rang out from behind it. The bullet zipped past me, grazing Maverick's thigh.

"Shit!" he shouted, jumping out of the way as the assailant charged forward.

To my horror, it was Secretary Croft—rifle raised, and alive. Her face and neck were marked by deep scars, but there she stood, gun in hand, and somehow still human. Ylem's transfusions had saved her.

I fired at her, but she ducked behind a statue, the bullet missing by centimeters.

Maverick grabbed me, pulling me out into a larger sitting room where there was more cover. He shot two guards before ducking behind a tufted couch.

Croft exploded into the room, bullets shredding through the furniture, sending fluff into the air. I barely had time to reload, the sound of gunfire making my ears ring. I rolled out from behind the couch, taking another shot at Croft, but she was quick, darting behind a sculpture. I heard her firing back, and I knew I'd missed.

Golden guards started rushing in to reinforce Croft, but Maverick's men joined the fight too. Ceramics shattered in the crossfire; artworks toppled from the walls. The room was chaos as Croft and Maverick circled each other, exchanging deadly shots.

I killed a couple of Croft's men, and as she turned her fire on me, I had to duck into an adjoining room. Croft followed, her steps quick and determined.

I aimed above her at a set of golden curtain rods. *BANG!* The heavy drapes crashed down on top of her. She struggled beneath the fabric, and I fired again. I heard her scream in pain. I'd nailed her this time, but my gun clicked empty.

Frantically, I reached for another clip, but before I could reload, Croft threw the drapes off herself, her face twisted in fury. Blood stained her shoulder, but she wasn't finished coming for me.

She raised her rifle again with her good arm, eyes wild with rage, and nearly unloaded the full clip at me. I dove behind a marble console, just narrowly avoiding the hail of bullets.

"Stand down!" came Maverick's voice as he stormed into the room, limping. Croft didn't hesitate for a second.

I dared to peek over the edge of the console, just in time to see Maverick take a bullet to the chest! He was thrown back into a china cabinet, the impact sending it toppling over with a crash.

"Maverick!" I screamed, my heart shattering as he hit the ground.

But then, I saw the vest. His bulletproof gear had saved him. He didn't miss a beat, quickly firing several rounds at Croft. She jumped and rolled behind a hefty oak door, just narrowly escaping his fire.

Then both guns clicked at the same time—Maverick's and Croft's. Empty.

I readied my aim, but Croft threw a vase at me, disorienting me for a moment, and I missed the shot. She was fast. Before I could try again, she was on me—grabbing me behind the console with an iron grip and drawing a combat knife.

My breath hitched, but Maverick tackled Croft and they both crashed to the floor, struggling violently. Maverick's leg wound was bleeding heavily, visibly slowing him down and making it harder to pin her.

Without warning, Croft expertly switched the blade to her other hand and thrust it into Maverick's neck.

I was paralyzed with shock as Maverick's eyes widened, and he collapsed, his body going completely limp. A guttural scream tore from my throat, and in a blind fury, I emptied my entire magazine into Croft, her blood splattering over a Persian rug.

I didn't even have a moment to process what had happened. A group of soldiers stormed into the room, their heavy boots thundering across the floor. But I wouldn't let them near Maverick's body. Not yet. My hands were shaking, my heart pounding with rage. I raised my gun, ready to fire at anyone who dared come near him, but then I recognized the group: Dustin, leading his Special Ops team, and right beside him, Tye.

They stopped short when they saw Maverick's lifeless form. I froze, my gun still raised, then dropped to my knees, unable to stop the tears. The dam finally broke. I couldn't even think straight as Tye pulled me into an embrace, his arms strong around me, his presence instantly comforting. But when he spoke, his words were urgent.

"We came with reinforcements, but we have to keep moving. Where's Midas?"

His words felt like a slap, shocking me back to reality. I couldn't let myself fall apart now. I swallowed hard and grabbed Tye's arm, pulling myself to my feet. We had to go. We had to finish this.

"I'll hold them off!" Dustin called out to us as he and his men opened fire on more golden guards arriving.

I didn't look back as Tye and I rushed down the corridor. The Basilica's maze-like layout was throwing me off balance. I was still reeling from the loss, my head spinning, but I couldn't afford to lose my senses.

I found the metal door, closed again. My heart pounded as I fumbled for the keycard, my shaking hand betraying me. I managed to slide it in, and the door clicked open. I reloaded my pistols and Tye mirrored me, his expression grim. We stepped into the hallway, heading deeper into the bowels of the Basilica.

"This way," Tye said quietly as he took my arm. "I recognize some of this."

We moved quickly, rounding a bend, but the sound of footsteps echoed down the hall. Three golden soldiers came into view and aimed at us. We retreated behind the wall.

"I came ready," he whispered determinedly. He reached into his pocket and pulled out a grenade.

He pulled the pin and tossed it. The soldiers tried to run, but were trapped between our guns and the dead end. The explosion erupted, sending a cloud of dust billowing through the chamber.

We rushed to the metal door at the other end of the room. There was a palm scanner and a keycard slot. My hand was still trembling as I slid the keycard inside. It flashed green. I was almost surprised it worked.

A low rumble started behind the door, followed by the grind of machinery waking up from underground. Tye and I stepped back, weapons at the ready for our last stand. Midas would have security with him, maybe even be armed himself.

The door shuddered open with a hiss, but what we saw beyond it made my stomach drop.

The bunker—Midas's last defense—was *empty.*

Tye and I exchanged looks of shock, and then we heard it: the distinct roar of a helicopter overhead.

"Midas!" I shouted, the realization hitting me—if a chopper was still operational through the jamming signals, it could only be his, and he was making his escape.

"The rooftop!" Tye exclaimed.

He grabbed my arm and pulled me into a nearby elevator. He bashed the button for the rooftop, and the doors slid shut slowly. We were running out of time.

The elevator creaked upward, the sounds of war reverberating around us with each passing floor. It felt like we were moving at a snail's pace.

Finally, the doors opened onto the roof garden. Tye and I moved in sync, weapons raised, scanning the area. And there it was—Midas's opulent helicopter, circling overhead as it dodged heavy fire from below, struggling to make its landing.

Then I saw Harlow and her mother, standing in front of *him.*

Midas, the man I'd dreamed of killing every single day since Malik died, stood right there, within my reach.

My vision tunneled.

My pulse thumped in my ears as we advanced, guns raised, my eyes locked on Midas. But Harlow was standing in my way, her eyes wide with shock.

"Willa?" she asked, her voice cracking at the sight of me. *"What are you doing?"*

I couldn't bring myself to respond. The pain of seeing her here, caught between us, was unbearable. My emotions were already spiraling, but I couldn't let them take over.

I kept my gun trained between her and Olivia, desperate for a clear shot at Midas. He wasn't walking away from here without paying for everything he'd done.

Tye spoke first, his voice steady. "You know what has to be done, Harlow. You and your mom can come with us. We can still change history."

The chopper persisted in its attempts to land.

"Please don't do this!" Harlow begged. "Just let us go! I'll make him stop everything!"

I couldn't stay silent anymore. "Harlow, listen to me." My voice sounded wrecked. "I care about you. I love you, even. You know deep down—everything that's happened, and everything that will happen, is because of him, and he won't ever stop. He never has. Think of your kid. Think of the world they'll grow up in. Think about how the world your father created will treat your child if his blood's like Tye's. *This has to be done!"*

Tears streamed down Harlow's face as she looked between her parents, Tye, and me. We were standing on the edge of something monumental.

And then, before anything else could be said, Midas made his move.

It happened so fast; he drew his golden pistol in a flash of motion, and suddenly, I felt a searing pain in my chest. The sound of the gunshot hung in the air, and no amount of steroids or vaccine could stop the agony that erupted within me.

My lungs exploded in my chest, and I gasped for air, but there was nothing...

This was it.

I knew it because the pain started to fade, replaced by a euphoric peace. A deep comfort, as if I could feel them—Malik, Imani, Archer, Maverick—standing with me again.

For a split second, I saw Tye's beautiful face turn white as snow, before my pistols clattered to the floor and the world slipped away.

35. TYE

Midas might as well have shot me too, because when the bullet tore through Willa, it felt like it pierced my own heart, shattering it into a million pieces. Her body, lifeless and covered in blood, was a sight so unbearable, it felt like my soul had left my body. I wasn't Tye anymore; I was just an empty shell, an observer to a nightmare I couldn't escape. But that numbness only lasted for a heartbeat. Because then I remembered—she was the love of my life.

And in that instant, a wave of rage surged through me, an anger so raw and all-consuming, it threatened to burn me alive. All I could think about was tearing Midas apart, making him feel every ounce of pain he'd caused me, and then some. The world around me blurred—nothing mattered except the need to make him suffer.

I rushed forward, raising my gun toward Midas. My hands shook, the weapon unsteady in my grip. I didn't care who stood between us, but before I could fire, Midas did something truly chilling. He turned his pistol away from me and pointed it at his own daughter.

Harlow's face was frozen in horror.

"Drop your gun!" Midas yelled, crazed.

Harlow's mother screamed at him, "This has gone too far, Midas!"

The chopper was drawing closer, weaving between the turret fire from below. Midas's gun pressed into Harlow's back, and all I could think about was how evil this man was—how pulling the trigger was a very real possibility for him if it meant furthering his twisted agenda.

Every muscle in my body was screaming for me to lunge, to stop him. But Harlow stood still, terrified, looking from Midas to me like the next move could mean the end of her. Everything felt like it was spiraling out of control. I couldn't let him take her, the baby. I couldn't let him do any more damage. I wasn't able to help Willa, but I wouldn't let Harlow die too.

I have to stand down…

I tossed my automatic to the side.

"And the other!" Midas barked.

I removed the spare handgun from my holster and threw it across the stone floor.

"Please, Midas!" Olivia pleaded, her voice quivering with desperation, but she didn't move, scared to set Midas off.

His gaze shifted to her. "You still don't understand, do you?" His voice dropped, laced with icy venom. "These people are here to destroy my work, to tear down everything I've built! They're the vermin of this earth, incapable of seeing greatness without wanting to destroy it!"

"Greatness?!" Harlow shot back. "Is this what you call greatness?"

His eyes were blazing with a manic intensity, something I'd never seen from him before. He'd always been so effortlessly calculated.

"I should've bombed them all when I had the chance! You question everything I do, but you still don't see the bigger picture! I've done what no one else could—I bent evolution to my will! My name, my legacy will be remembered for thousands of years to come. *I* will be remembered, long after their useless lives have faded into dust!"

Olivia flinched, a soft sob escaping her lips. She shot a glance at Harlow, who was visibly struggling in the face of her father's madness, unable to find the right words to say.

"And you, Tye…" His pale eyes narrowed, each word a poison dart. "I offered you the chance to stand beside me, to become part of something greater. But instead, you chose the vermin. You chose to betray me. And you'll be forgotten like the rest of them!"

I took a deep breath, my eyes not wavering from his. "You're right, Midas. You might be remembered, but it'll be for all the worst reasons.

You'll be remembered for destroying everything good in this world, for being so power-hungry that you burned down everything in your way—your family, the ones who stood by you, the very vision you once stood for. But me? I don't care if I'm remembered. I'm fighting for a world that'll outlast me *and* you!"

Midas appeared to register my words like no one had ever spoken to him in that way. For a moment, his eyes flickered with doubt. Madam Olivia seized the opening, her voice breaking the silence.

"Take the gun off of her… Please, my love," she pleaded, her voice still trembling.

It seemed like her plea reached him. His posture shifted, the madness in his eyes dimmed, and he finally lowered the gun.

Harlow backed away slowly, disbelief clouding her features as she put distance between herself and her father. Her eyes darted back and forth, from Midas to Willa's body, as if trying to make sense of what was happening.

The chopper finally set down on the rooftop, its ramp lowering just enough for Midas and his family to board.

He turned toward the chopper, stepping closer to the edge of the rooftop. But neither Olivia nor Harlow moved. They both stood frozen, looking at him with fear.

"What are you doing? Now's our chance!" he yelled.

Harlow was shaking, but her voice was firm. "I'm not going with you."

Midas scoffed. "Even now, when everything's on the line, you turn your back on your own family?!"

"You're not my family," she spat. "I tried! I have my mom again, but to me, you died a long time ago, and you just proved I was right."

Her words seemed to cut deep. His shoulders slumped as he realized his daughter was a lost cause.

Midas turned to his wife, his voice softer now, as if the last thread of his humanity was begging for connection. "Olivia?" He reached a hand out toward her.

Olivia looked between Harlow, Midas, and me, her face showing how torn she was, caught among the wreckage of her family.

Then, she actually took a step towards him. My heart sank, and Harlow's face fell. She looked utterly crushed by her mother's decision.

I couldn't believe it. After everything, Midas was about to get away. Even if we won this battle, if he escaped now, his dark ambitions would simply carry on somewhere else. I had to stop him.

I looked down at the spot where my pistol had fallen, only to realize it was gone. Panic hit me immediately, but before I could even react—*BANG!*

I looked up to see Olivia holding the smoking gun. The bullet had hit Midas square in the chest, his face contorted in pure shock. He stumbled back, hands clutching at the wound as blood began to seep through the fine silk of his shirt.

In the next heartbeat, he lurched back another step and tumbled over the edge of the rooftop.

There was a tense silence, then a loud *crack* as his body hit the ground below us.

For a breath, the world was still.

Olivia and Harlow stood in place like they were made of stone, unable to believe what'd just happened.

I couldn't help it—I ran to the edge to make sure my eyes hadn't deceived me. Sure enough, I saw him, just another lifeless body among the fallen soldiers from both sides.

Midas was dead...

I'd imagined his downfall countless times, but none of those fantasies had ever looked like this.

A strange, mechanical hum vibrated through Ylem. For a terrifying moment, I was certain Ylem was unleashing some final, devastating act of destruction. A secret weapon, launched once Midas had fallen.

But then Rowen's voice urgently came through my earpiece. *"Ylem's satellite jammer has been dismantled! Sending in air support!"*

Within moments, the familiar drone of distant choppers and roaring fighter jets swept across the sky above us. Midas's helicopter, now retreating hastily, was quickly shot down by our incoming air units. I watched it spiral into a fiery explosion.

Every part of me wanted to celebrate, to console Harlow, to shout from the rooftops that Midas was finally gone—but only one priority consumed me. Willa.

I sprinted back to her, collapsing to my knees beside her body, and all the emotions I'd been desperately holding back erupted. Sobs shook my body uncontrollably as I cradled her to my chest, her blood soaking my clothes.

My hand brushed the bandages covering her bite wound, and suddenly, everything became clear to me. Willa had been bitten, which meant—Ichor could revive her!

I could bring her to Midas's transfusion lounge, find the equipment, and make it happen myself. Surely it would work. She'd only been gone moments. But my eyes landed on the bullet hole in her chest, and doubt crept in. Would the Ichor really heal that, too?

I need Chiron.

Adrenaline gave me fresh clarity. Pressing the earpiece, I called desperately for Ava. "Ava! Where's the carrier with Dr. Chiron?"

"He's with his family—they're evacuating to the—"

"I need him airlifted here, to the Basilica rooftop, as fast as possible!"

"What's happening, Tye?" She sounded confused. *"We can get you out of there now—"*

"Just do it!" I shouted back. "Quickly!"

Harlow finally broke away from her mother's side and joined me next to Willa. She could barely bring herself to look down at her broken body.

"Tye, I'm so sorry—"

“I’m gonna bring her back,” I insisted, rejecting the painful finality of her words.

Harlow took a moment to process what I’d said, then slowly nodded, her eyes reflecting genuine hope.

In silence, we looked out at the battlefield below. Even with Midas dead, chaos continued to rage, but now, thanks to our air support, the tide had shifted significantly. Ylem’s soldiers were beginning to stand down, acknowledging their defeat.

A U.S. military chopper appeared, circling the rooftop carefully before finding space to land. I felt a surge of relief as Chiron climbed off, flanked by a few soldiers. He saw me crouched beside Willa and slowed as he approached, his eyes darting uncertainly between me, Harlow, and Madam Olivia. It was clear he was torn, realizing that helping me now would likely contradict Ylem’s goals.

He looked to Olivia, searching for direction, but to my surprise, it was Harlow who stepped forward.

“Dr. Chiron,” she said, her voice firm despite everything that had just happened, “do whatever Tye needs. That’s an order.”

Now that Midas was gone, Harlow had become the leader of Ylem. In a strange twist of fate, the person now in charge by default was someone I trusted.

Chiron hesitated for only a second before relief visibly softened his expression. He turned to me with renewed purpose. “Tell me what you need.”

“I need to revive her,” I begged desperately. “Please!”

Chiron looked distraught, but maintained his composure. “Let’s get her inside.”

I scooped Willa into my arms, her body heartbreakingly limp, and we all rushed for the elevator.

When the doors opened into the Basilica, the halls were littered with bodies, the eerie silence proof that, at least here, the battle had ended.

Following Chiron, we entered the familiar lounge, the machinery from my past transfusions still standing.

Carefully, I laid Willa down on one of the lounge chairs, flinching at how pale she looked. Just then, Dustin and his remaining men rounded the corner. His eyes landed on Willa, and his knees nearly buckled beneath him.

But when he noticed Chiron setting up the equipment, his expression shifted. "Are you gonna—"

I nodded, determined. Dustin crouched beside Willa, looking as though nothing outside these walls mattered more to him than this.

I quickly sat across from her while Chiron attached the IVs and wires, connecting us both.

"Will this work?" Harlow asked anxiously, her voice trembling.

Chiron spoke cautiously yet gently. "The results will depend entirely on the internal damage. Ichor accelerates the body's natural healing, but it doesn't always regenerate limbs and such. A bullet to the chest…" He paused, clearly worried. "We will try."

I'd never experienced anxiety like this before. My heart was pounding so hard it hurt. Every win we'd had today would mean nothing if this didn't work.

My blood began flowing into Willa, and I silently pleaded for the Ichor to move faster, watching her closely for the smallest sign of life.

Each passing second felt heavier than the last. Outside, the distant noise of fighting gradually died down. Even Ylem seemed to know it was over—but for me, the quiet only made things worse, forcing me to focus entirely on what was unfolding right in front of us.

Five minutes turned into ten, then fifteen. Soon, half an hour had passed, dragging painfully without any change.

I clenched my teeth as my veins started to ache from the draining. But my eyes stayed locked on her pale, still face. Every subtle flicker of movement in the room—Chiron shifting uneasily on his feet, Dustin clenching and unclenching his fists, Harlow anxiously brushing tears from her cheeks—only made the wait more agonizing. My mind spun, inventing signs of hope where there were none. The tension stretched painfully until I felt I might break under its strain.

I finally forced myself to properly look at Chiron, searching his face for reassurance, but when his eyes met mine, they were full of defeat.

"It appears the Ichor won't help in this case," he said softly, the words tearing through me like knives.

"What?! No, keep going!" I begged.

"Tye," Chiron said with finality, "it won't do any good."

Everything inside me shattered. My vision blurred, and the weight of unbearable grief consumed me. Dustin's arms tightened around me and I broke down, my body shaking uncontrollably as a wave of despair swept through the room. Harlow collapsed into tears beside Willa, her cries raw and agonizing.

I tore the IV from my arm and fell onto Willa, crying into her shoulder.

Olivia finally stepped forward, her voice quietly broken. "Let's give them a moment. I'll go to the battlefield and declare Ylem's surrender."

She guided Chiron and the soldiers from the room. The door clicked shut behind them, leaving only the suffocating sounds of our heartbreak.

The reality crashed into me all at once—Willa was actually gone. Gone for good. Somehow, despite everything we'd been through, I never truly believed this could happen. She'd always been the strongest person I knew, so unstoppable that it seemed impossible she'd ever be lost. Yet here she was, motionless, her body so still it felt unnatural.

The pain was so deep, so overwhelming, it froze me. My mind desperately scrambled to reject the truth, but seeing Dustin from the corner of my eye jolted me back to it. He was on the floor next to her, not even trying to hide that he was crying, the kind of tears that only come when you lose something you can't imagine life without. I'd never seen

Dustin break like this, and it brought home just how much she meant to all of us.

Our eyes met; his were bloodshot and haunted. It felt like he was looking straight into me, seeing exactly what I was feeling. Without a word, we shared something deep, an unbearable grief over the most important person either of us had ever known.

Finally, he wiped his face, gathered himself, and stood up. "We're gonna get through this, buddy. I don't know how, but I know I'll be here to make sure of it."

"I can't believe this is happening," I said, barely recognizing my own voice through my sobs. "I just ... I can't believe she's gone."

Harlow finally spoke up from behind us, her voice sounding shaky but sincere. "I'm sorry for everything my dad caused—for all the pain. But I promise you I'm going to fix things. You once told me it only takes one person, Tye, remember?" She swallowed hard. "I can't bring her back, I can't undo what he did. But I swear I'll do everything I can to steer Ylem in the right direction. Consider me an ally, and a friend."

Her words pierced through the darkness, offering a sliver of hope I hadn't expected. I didn't know how to respond, tears still streaming, but I managed a nod.

Dustin gently placed a hand on my shoulder. "We'll wait for you outside," he said softly. "Take as long as you need."

He took a deep breath, visibly pulling himself back into soldier mode, then quietly led Harlow from the room.

The second the door shut, loneliness swallowed me whole. My soulmate was gone, and all the reasons I'd found to keep going had vanished with her. Willa always said we'd known each other before, that we'd find each other again in the next life, but imagining even one more minute in a world without her was impossible. After everything I'd been through, my blood, my supposed miracle, had failed when it counted most.

Somehow, I managed to pull myself to my feet—not because I felt strong enough, but because there were still people worth living for. Friends who still needed me. They were the only reason I didn't end it right here; I had to keep going, for them.

As if she sensed exactly what I was feeling—and maybe she did, because our connection was always like that—Ava's voice suddenly buzzed through my comm. I'd almost forgotten I was still wearing it.

"Tye? Where are you? Ylem's standing down, the evacuation's starting soon."

My throat locked up, refusing to let any words through. Silence filled the gap until Ava tried again. *"Tye? What's going on?"*

I forced myself to speak, my voice sounding foreign. "I'm at the Basilica... Willa's gone."

"What do you mean—"

"Midas got her," I interrupted. "We tried to bring her back, but... she's *really* gone, Ava."

The silence on the other end shattered my heart all over again. When Ava finally spoke, her voice was broken. *"I'm on my way. Just stay put."*

I turned slowly, forcing myself to look down at Willa one more time. Her body looked hollow, completely empty of the fiery spirit that made her who she was, like her soul had truly moved beyond my reach. Forcing myself to step away felt beyond me. How was I going to face the days ahead without her by my side? And even worse, the thought of laying her to rest tore me up. That was a finality I couldn't imagine surviving.

I dragged my gaze away from her body and stumbled blindly for the door. But just as my fingers touched the handle, a sudden, sharp gasp came from behind me.

Willa!

36. WILLA

I woke with a sudden gasp, like I'd just broken the surface after being underwater for too long. My head spun and my vision blurred, shapes swimming into view around me. Then it hit me—Midas! In a panic, my hand flew for my pistol and I aimed it at the figure standing across the room.

My vision cleared slowly to reveal his wide-eyed, tear-streaked face, and it finally clicked into place. My grip relaxed, the gun falling to my side. Looking down, I noticed all the IV tubes and wires connected to me, and I realized: Midas had killed me. And somehow, Tye had brought me back.

Before I could check my chest wound, Tye was already pulling me into a passionate embrace. He sobbed quietly into my shoulder, and suddenly I was crying too, overwhelmed by the miracle of still being here, with him, alive. He pulled back, cupping my face gently, his eyes shining with disbelief. Nothing mattered except that we were here together. I wouldn't have to face whatever came after this life without him.

"Is he dead?" I managed to whisper.

Fresh tears spilled down his cheeks. "Yes. Olivia did it. We won the fight."

He held me again, tightly, and I melted into the warmth of his arms. This time, the embrace was different—it felt lighter, like we were finally free. From the quiet beyond the room's doors, I knew it was true. The battle was over. Ylem had fallen, and the future we'd fought so hard for was finally within reach.

We sat quietly for a few minutes, soaking up the hard-earned moment of peace after fighting so hard, and for so long.

I was trying to desperately grab onto any memory from whatever had happened in the blackness of my time away, but all I had were fragments—a feeling, mostly. I knew Malik was there, my friends too, but the details were lost, fuzzy, like a half-forgotten dream. It frustrated me that I couldn't remember it more clearly, but the feeling itself was comforting.

Slowly, reality trickled back in. "Did everyone make it?" I asked. "Where are the others?"

"I think so. But Maverick—"

"I know." I cut him off, my throat tight. I remembered that image too vividly. I wished I didn't.

"Let's go find them," Tye gently suggested, carefully disconnecting me from the IVs. "They're not gonna believe it when they see you."

He helped me stand, and I could feel my strength gradually coming back, though I wasn't sure if it was from sheer determination or Tye's blood flowing through me. My fingers brushed over my chest, finding a rough scar under the bloodstained shirt. It didn't hurt, just felt like an old wound.

I took Tye's hand, grateful for him—for everything he'd done—and together we stepped out into the hallway.

My heart leapt when I saw Dustin and Harlow standing there, completely frozen, like they genuinely thought they were seeing a ghost. Dustin let out a broken sob, rushing forward and pulling me into a tight hug, with Harlow quickly joining in. We clung to each other, crying and laughing at the same time.

"I knew it the whole time!" Dustin said, wiping tears away with a shaky laugh. "No way Willa goes out like that!"

We laughed again, but as my eyes met Harlow's, I knew her tears weren't just for me. If what Tye had said about what her mother did was true, I knew her pain ran deeper.

"Harlow . . ." I said softly, taking her hands.

Before I could say anything else, she squeezed mine back. "It's okay. It's finally over. We're gonna make things right, and I'm so glad you're here to see it."

Her words filled me with hope. Despite everything, our friendship was still there. She smiled, looking down to see her pistol strapped at my thigh.

Voices from downstairs caught my attention, and my heart skipped at the familiar sound of Rowen's accent.

We headed down a spiral staircase, my legs still shaky beneath me. Seeing the Basilica torn apart was unsettling. The spotless halls I remembered were now covered in rubble and bodies. I forced myself to look straight ahead, afraid I'd see Maverick if I looked too closely.

Just as we rounded the bend into the foyer, Rowen's voice rang out. "Which room is she—"

He froze mid-sentence when he saw me. Despite how many people were in the room, the way his eyes locked onto mine made it feel like we were the only ones there. His expression quickly moved from confusion to shock, before finally settling into quiet understanding as his gaze shifted to Tye, realizing exactly what must've happened between the moment he'd heard I'd died and now.

"Welcome back," he said faintly, a pained smile spreading across his face.

I hugged him, relieved to see another friend who'd made it.

Behind him stood Madam Olivia, watching me with an expression of quiet understanding. She alone knew exactly what was swirling inside me at this moment.

"I've ordered the black flag to be raised," she told Rowen. "It will signal to the city that Midas has fallen."

Rowen nodded gravely. "The battle might be won, but we've got plenty left to do before we can even think about leaving." He turned to Harlow, who straightened anxiously. "From what I understand, you're in charge now. We'll need you and your mother for the next steps."

"Whatever you need," Olivia agreed immediately.

Harlow took a deep breath as if to steady herself. "We should call a council meeting with the other family heads. Not all of them are going to be on board with changes."

"I agree. You two organize that," Rowen instructed. "In the meantime, we'll focus on stabilizing the city and recovering the dead."

The heaviness of such a task lingered in his voice, but he masked it behind a leader's tone.

"I'll start putting things in order here at the Basilica," Olivia replied. "We'll reconvene with the council this evening."

"Where's Chiron?" Tye interjected suddenly.

"With his family," replied one of the British commanders standing nearby. "He's beyond the wall with the evacuees."

"He should be at the meeting," Tye said firmly.

The commander acknowledged this with a quick salute.

"Ava said she'd meet us here, but I'm gonna try to get in touch with everyone else first," Tye added, turning to me. "I'll meet you back here soon."

He kissed me gently on the cheek before heading out, a small group of soldiers quickly falling into step behind him.

Over the next hour, an uneasy order settled over the Basilica. Staff emerged slowly from their hiding places, and soldiers from both sides silently worked together, carrying bodies out of the halls. It felt as if the rage that had fueled everyone only hours prior had finally burned itself out.

With Midas gone, even the golden soldiers seemed to realize our cause might end up benefiting them, too. Whatever anyone believed before, everyone was putting those feelings aside now, united by a shared need to restore some sense of normalcy.

I put it off for as long as I could, then finally approached Dustin in one of the hallways. He was taking charge, directing people with a calm confidence.

I pulled him aside and felt my throat tightening. "Did you see Maverick?"

His expression showed immediate understanding. "Yeah. We covered him with a flag, for now. I wanted to wait until you told me how you'd like to handle it."

A lump formed in my throat as I realized Maverick had fulfilled the promise he'd made to Malik—he'd kept me alive long enough to see this day.

"I just don't want him ending up in some pile of bodies," I said, my voice breaking. "He deserves to be honored. Can you make sure he is?"

Dustin didn't hesitate. "Absolutely. I'll handle it myself."

I hugged him tightly, knowing how complicated their history had been, and feeling grateful he was choosing kindness now. He squeezed my shoulder before stepping away to continue his work.

As he left, another body crossed my mind—Midas's. I needed to see it for myself, to truly believe it was over.

Slowly, I made my way up to the rooftop, realizing that, in the end, I didn't care that I hadn't been the one to pull the trigger. Just knowing he was gone made it feel like a weight I'd carried forever was finally lifted.

When I reached the roof garden, I saw Harlow standing at the edge, alone, silently looking out over the city. I approached quietly, following her gaze. Below, a group of golden soldiers solemnly carried away an ornate ceremonial casket. There was no doubt in my mind who was inside.

I stood quietly beside her, unsure of how to start a conversation neither of us was ready for. Instead, I watched the city below. Smoke drifted from buildings, military vehicles rushed through ruined streets, and crowds of people moved about in a daze, clearly still stunned by what had unfolded.

"I heard what your mom did," I said after a while. "Regardless of how I feel… are you okay?"

Harlow's gaze didn't leave the golden soldiers on the ground. "I don't know yet," she admitted. "But that person wasn't really my dad anymore. He was completely lost." She shook her head, drawing in a deep breath. "What's actually eating at me is that suddenly I'm supposed to take over Ylem. Of course I want to help—I really do—but I'm not sure I'm ready."

I let out a shaky laugh, but there was no humor in the situation. "I know a thing or two about having to grow up too fast and take on things you're not ready for. But trust me, no one's ever ready. It's just your turn now. You'll step into it, and you'll do your best—and we'll all be here to help you."

A faint smile flickered across her lips. "Thank you, Willa." She turned to me. "You know, I'd love it if you and your friends stayed here in Ylem. I realize it's probably not your favorite place, but we'll make it better. Together."

I hesitated. "Our families are back in the safe zones—"

"Bring them here," she interrupted gently. "I'll make sure you're all taken care of. You know we're not short on resources. Any friend of yours is a friend of mine."

I couldn't help but smile at her earnestness. "You're amazing, Harlow. Let's just see how this council meeting goes tonight first, okay? Something tells me not everyone's going to be thrilled to have us."

Harlow smirked playfully. "I'm the queen now! They'll do as I say!"

We both laughed, and it felt like a small release after the heaviness of the day.

Before either of us could say more, Olivia strolled over. "Harlow, Rowen needs you downstairs."

Harlow sighed. "Duty calls."

She gave my hand a quick squeeze before leaving me alone with her mother.

The two of us stood in silence, watching as soldiers below cleared the debris of battle. Finally, she spoke, her voice gentle but weighted.

"I can't know exactly how you're feeling right now," she began tentatively. "I was gone much longer than you were, but when I came back, something inside me had shifted. This world didn't feel real anymore—it felt like a meaningless simulation, some rigged game where nothing I did truly mattered."

She paused, and when she continued, her voice was stronger. "But today, seeing what my husband had driven himself to, the damage he caused while I was away, I realized something important. He was just one man, yet his choices changed the course of history. And for the first time since I returned, I finally felt like maybe our choices really do matter. Maybe we really can shape the future." She turned and looked at me, her eyes filled with resolve. "I did what I did to protect my daughter. But I also did it for myself. I made a choice. I did love him, once, but if there was ever a chance for the world to return to the beauty I once knew, he couldn't be part of it."

Olivia's words resonated deeply with me, bringing unexpected comfort. Despite everything, I felt like she might become someone I could rely on, someone steady to have in the aftermath. I held her gentle stare.

"No matter what we have to do for survival," I said, "it's never easy making choices like that. You really did change our futures. I won't ever forget it. Thank you."

She glanced down at the casket procession and then back to me, offering a warm, reassuring smile. We shared a quiet moment of understanding that only broke when familiar voices spilled out onto the rooftop.

I turned, my heart swelling at the sight of Riley, Otto, Ava, Dustin, and Tye—all battered and weary, but unmistakably alive. They rushed toward me, pulling me into a group hug that instantly let me know everyone had already been filled in.

"Nothing can take you out, huh?" Otto joked, flashing his big, bright smile despite the blood and burns across his face.

Riley hugged me fiercely, then turned to hug Tye just as tight. "Dude, your magic blood seriously came through. There's no way I'd recover from losing this girl."

I smiled, noticing Riley's bandaged arm, and feeling grateful we'd all somehow made it.

Ava latched onto me and wouldn't let go, crying softly into my shoulder. "I'm so glad you're alive," she finally managed.

"Me too," I replied. "That all of us are."

Dustin stepped in, lightly messing my hair like we were kids again. "And they say our generation's good for nothing. A bunch of teens saving the world? Come on."

We all laughed, and somehow it felt louder against the weight of the day.

Rowen and Harlow rejoined us, shifting the mood back to seriousness as Rowen got straight to business.

"We've discussed next steps," he said firmly. "Harlow will address Ylem tomorrow morning. It's important we're here for that. I adjusted our extraction plan so we can stick around to help with negotiations. But there's one detail that doesn't leave this circle." He met each of our eyes carefully. "Harlow and I agree that *no one* outside this circle should know Olivia was the one who killed Midas. It would cause too much political chaos. The credit has to go to Tye, if he agrees. With the baby Harlow's carrying and Tye's Ichor, it gives him leverage and protection that no one else has."

"I wish it *had* been me," Tye said.

"Then it's settled. We never speak of Olivia's role in this again, but I can say on behalf of all of us, we're forever grateful for it."

Olivia nodded humbly, and a silent understanding passed through us.

"Before the council arrives," Rowen continued, "Chiron's here to talk about getting the cure out beyond Ylem's walls before the topic is presented in tonight's meeting. If you'd like to join, your insight would be valuable."

By nighttime, the Basilica had transformed. Soldiers from both sides were guarding the halls, and staff had managed to restore most of the rooms into livable conditions. Still, the bullet holes and shattered windows were a reminder that any peace we'd found was fragile. The next few hours would be crucial—the council's reaction would decide everything.

Before that, though, we gathered with Chiron in one of the spacious parlors. We each took a seat around the room, quietly waiting. Chiron was there with a young boy and a gentle-looking woman. When the child hugged him tight and the woman kissed him softly before they left, I realized they were his family. The love between them was clear, making me see Chiron in a new, more generous light.

When the door shut behind them, Chiron let out a long breath, seeming to gather his thoughts.

"My work has always been about making the world safer—first for my family, then for everyone else. Until today, my hands were tied by those above me. Thanks to you all, that's changed." He paused, emotion evident in his voice. "Thankfully, most of what we've developed survived on that hard drive. Along with the Angels, Tye's Ichor, and the nanotechnology in his bloodstream, we now have enough data to distribute the cure on a wide scale. We've successfully taken the Angels' natural abilities and developed a vaccine. Unlike the current one that merely suppresses symptoms, this fully eradicates the virus—no trace left, no transfusions required."

We exchanged hopeful glances, but Chiron quickly tempered our enthusiasm.

"Though it can cure, it doesn't give permanent immunity; only Angels possess that gift naturally. But it's groundbreaking nonetheless. The real challenge is producing enough doses, and quickly enough, to stabilize the world before the virus spreads further. Even with Ylem's resources at our disposal, manually vaccinating everyone is impossible—especially considering how many bodies and infected are still out there..."

His voice trailed off, filling the room with heavy silence.

"So, you're saying it's not possible? Even with a cure?" Tye asked, frustration creeping into his voice.

Chiron shook his head. "I believe we need to push further. We need to revisit the original idea—the one Zenith was exploring before Midas took control."

The realization clicked. "Planes?" I asked. "Distributing the cure through the air?"

"Exactly. We still have Zenith's data and research. With some adjustments, we could deliver an airborne solution of Ichor."

Dustin leaned forward in his seat, wide-eyed. "Wait, you mean completely reversing the virus? Not just curing survivors, but actually bringing infected people back to life?"

"Yes," Chiron confirmed, his voice steady. "It would require massive resources and full cooperation from the council. These families hold tremendous power and wealth. If they agree, along with the scientists who share our vision, we could realistically achieve this within a few months."

We all stared at each other, realizing that not only could we end this nightmare, we could truly reverse it altogether.

Rowen's response was cautious but practical. "That raises an important question—can the world even handle millions returning at once? Our safe zones are already strained. Is the infrastructure out there strong enough?"

His words hung heavy in the room.

"That's a valid concern," said Chiron. "Our research shows the recovery of the infected largely depends on how long they've been lost. Those infected recently could regain consciousness quickly, like waking from a coma. Others who've been gone for longer might need more care, but recovery's still possible."

He pressed on, sounding more hopeful. "In fact, this could be a solution rather than a burden. People coming back means rebuilding communities, restoring abandoned cities, and restarting agriculture, transportation, and communications. Ultimately, we wouldn't need the safe zones anymore. We'd have a world actively repairing itself, regaining stability—maybe an even better world than before."

Everyone looked to be filled with hope at his words. I imagined a world not just restored, but renewed.

"I don't think it's our decision to say whether they should or shouldn't be brought back," Harlow said firmly. "My father destroyed their lives, and if we have a chance to reverse even some of that damage, we should do the right thing. We'll figure out the rest as it comes."

I admired how she was already stepping into her new role. Even if some of her confidence was just for show, it was still impressive to witness.

"I agree with Harlow," I said. "The Morts are changing, and before long, even Ichor might not be enough. If this is our chance to get the cure out there all at once, we have to take it."

Across the room, Tye's eyes met mine, and he nodded in quiet agreement.

Otto shifted uneasily, gripping Ava's hand tighter. "Well, let's just hope the rest of Ylem sees it that way."

No one else spoke. The silence lingered until Ava finally asked, "Shall we?"

Together, we stood, bracing ourselves for the meeting ahead.

37. TYE

It was late into the night, and the adrenaline from the battle had finally worn off, leaving us all struggling to keep our eyes open. We sat around the longest oak table I'd ever seen, deep into a tense discussion with the heads of Ylem's most powerful families. It was clear from their varied accents that they came from all different parts of the world, yet each was cut from the same cloth—as was apparent from their lavish clothing and jewelry. In stark contrast stood the translators behind many of them, dressed plainly in the dull gray uniforms of Ylem.

A few seats remained empty; some figureheads had flatly refused to cooperate, while others had already fled Ylem altogether. Those who'd stayed had listened as Chiron outlined his proposal for a worldwide cure, and while he'd presented it uninterrupted, the room had since erupted into heated debate.

Harlow stood at the head of the table, looking around at each council member as she spoke. "We need your support to carry out a distribution plan of this scale."

An elegant-looking woman spoke up, her posture stiff. "And once we help bring back these millions of people, what then? They'll need homes, food, and medical care. Will you expect us to prop up the unstable economies around the world too?"

A wave of murmurs followed, some heads nodding in agreement. Other faces were unreadable.

Madam Olivia, sitting to Harlow's right, responded. "We're not demanding your contributions. We're asking. You're free to do as you see fit. But my hope is that those of you who have stayed—those who showed up to this conversation—have at least some part of you open to working together."

Harlow's voice cut through the low chatter. "My dad promised you safety, and I'm promising you the same. If the infected are eliminated completely, Ylem's protection won't be exclusive anymore—there's no reason to challenge a safer world."

An intense-looking German man quickly piped up. "Ylem vill never truly be safe again. The countries behind the leaders who fled today vill regain their strength once the virus is gone, they vill seek revenge. These people have shattered the illusion that this city is untouchable, and that vill come at a cost."

My friends squirmed slightly at his tone.

Another council member leaned back and spoke quietly to his translator. From his accent, I guessed he was Swedish. After a short pause, his translator delivered the message clearly.

"That illusion was shattered long before today, when Midas chose isolation and dominance over unity. If we continue down his path, we'll remain targets forever. But if we offer a cure—if we build bridges instead of walls—then Ylem has a chance to become more than a fortress. We can gain allies rather than enemies."

Madam Olivia leaned forward in her seat. "We understand that resources are valuable, especially in uncertain times. But you must see the bigger picture: the longevity of Ylem itself. My husband's fist no longer grips your throats. Try to be open to the new direction our allies are offering."

Across from her, a man whose accent I couldn't place addressed the room sharply. "You expect we welcome them, ah? After they bring war to our doorstep. Let in the infected? Invade our city? After this boy kills our leader? No, madame. If one of us pulls out of Ylem, many resources leave with us. You must remember, it is you who needs us, *not* the other way around."

His words settled ominously over the table, followed by a tense silence, then more murmured conversations between several council members.

Harlow didn't flinch. She looked every council member in the eye before speaking, her voice clear.

"War came to our doorstep because my dad wasn't satisfied with just building this city. He was actively trying to wipe out everything beyond these walls. The ones you're seeing as enemies? They have families, too. Loved ones. And from where they stood, Midas had become a threat. That threat is gone now. So the real matter here isn't about helping any one person's cause. What I'm telling you is this: if you help undo the damage my dad caused, it's going to benefit *you* in the end. Your countries. Your legacies. Even Ylem." She let that land for a moment. "If you won't help us for the sake of the world, then help yourselves."

No one rushed to speak.

Willa cleared her throat. Everyone turned to her. She hadn't spoken since the meeting had begun, and the sound of her voice alone felt like a match striking in a cold room.

"When transfusions stop working, when a new strain evolves and it doesn't respond to what you've developed—what are you going to do then?"

The room stayed silent, but it wasn't the cold kind anymore. It was the kind that meant listening.

"Now's the time to get rid of it for good," she insisted.

Even the stiffest ones at the table looked less sure of themselves now.

Chiron stepped forward from where he'd been standing at the edge of the room to offer his support. "It's true," he said. "We've developed a cure derived from Tye's Ichor and everything we've tested on the Angels. It's highly effective against the current, known strains. But viruses change. And if we continue to let this one mutate in the wild, uncontained, we may never be able to reel it back in."

He paused, glancing around the room. "This isn't theory. This is fact. And we're running out of time."

There was no outburst. No argument. Just the pressing weight of his words settling into the minds of some of the most powerful people left in the world.

"Forgive our hesitation," one of the councilmen said carefully, "but we barely know you, Harlow. You were absent from nearly every decision made in Ylem before today, and Madam Olivia has only just returned. Now you're here with strangers and these young idealists, asking for our cooperation. Our reluctance isn't just selfishness—it's the result of difficult times and sudden change."

"I understand," Harlow replied, "and you're right. I kept my distance because I didn't agree with the way my dad ran things. I'm not proud of the decisions he made—but I'm here now. And I intend to use everything I've inherited to move us toward a different kind of power." She glanced around the table. "I want to hear your concerns and ideas. I want to work *with* you. But I also hope we can all agree that what's at stake here goes beyond personal politics." Her hand moved gently to her abdomen. "I want my child to grow up in a world that's not boxed in by walls."

She turned to me and smiled. It felt like my chance to speak.

"My blood, what it can do, it's been the biggest burden I've ever had to carry," I said. "But if it can give the world a second chance, I'd carry it a hundred times over." I looked around the table at each of them. "We're not going to agree on everything. Maybe we won't even agree on most things. But right now, let's at least agree on this next step."

The room was quiet after I spoke—tense, but not hostile. It felt like the idea of moving forward together was starting to take hold.

That was when one of the Indian councilmen leaned forward, a man I recognized from months earlier, sitting on the rooftop with Midas. His tone was calm, but every word he said hit like a brick.

"If you're thinking ahead strategically, I will do the same," he said, his eyes on Harlow. "You know I'm one of the wealthiest assets in Ylem. Your father knew it. And you come from possibly the wealthiest family. Let you and I merge our families and our assets, and I will agree to fund as much of this operation as needed. I imagine others at this table will be more inclined to cooperate if I front the majority."

A beat of stunned silence followed. Then Madam Olivia spoke. "Are you asking for my daughter's hand?"

He shrugged, like it was the most obvious idea. "A marriage alliance, yes."

The energy in the room changed in an instant. Discomfort flashed in Harlow's eyes before her expression hardened. Around the table, I caught the reactions of my friends, including Willa, whose fingers curled into a fist against the polished wood.

I felt sick. Because I knew—Harlow had already been used as a pawn once. Her father had decided her baby would be part of his power play. And now here she was again, cornered into another sacrifice in the name of strategy.

Some of the others at the table clearly didn't like where this was going. Urgent whispers rippled through the group, and then another councilman finally spoke up. "Midas hasn't even been laid to rest, and you're already after his seat? Shame on you."

The other man's jaw tightened. "I'm offering a solution in exchange. Isn't that what negotiations are for?"

More murmurs broke out—some agreeing, others clearly just as unsettled as the rest of us. That was when Madam Olivia cut in again, calm but firm. "What if I were to marry you instead?"

For a second, it was dead quiet.

Then, one of the Ylem commanders at the far end of the table spoke carefully. "I wouldn't advise that, madam. The optics won't be good. Your husband just died. If you remarry this soon, especially to someone at this table, it'll look like collusion, not strategy."

Olivia considered that in silence, while more side conversations bubbled up from all directions. Just when it felt like the room was spiraling out of control, an older woman with silver hair and a velvet suit stood up.

"This side of the table will commit to the cause. No marriage required," she said, her eyes flicking pointedly toward the man who'd proposed it.

Harlow offered her a grateful smile. But the man wasn't having it.

"So we're expected to make all the sacrifices, while the Rothfields make none? Understood," he snapped, pushing back from the table. A few council members stood and followed him out without a word.

The atmosphere shifted again—less noise now, but with a whole new kind of tension.

Harlow's face was flushed red, and I could see it wasn't from embarrassment—it was frustration. The kind that hits when you've done everything right and still get dismissed like a child. Her shoulders stiffened as she sat down, and I noticed Rowen glancing her way, eyes narrowing slightly. The moment wasn't lost on him.

He stood slowly, resting both hands on the table as the murmuring died down. When he spoke, his voice wasn't loud, but had enough influence to quiet the room.

"We don't need all of you," he said, looking each council member dead in the eye, "but we do need more of you."

He let that sink in for a second before continuing.

"You came to Ylem for protection. You stayed because it offered you control. And now, you're sitting here with a chance to be part of something that goes far beyond these walls. I'm not asking for a moral awakening or a leap of faith. I'm asking for a practical choice. The world's changing, fast. You can either help shape what's coming or get left behind when it does."

A few of the council members shifted uncomfortably, avoiding his gaze. But others—those still sitting, still listening—seemed to lean in.

"I get it, you're cautious," Rowen went on. "You've got resources, influence, assets to protect. So use them. You're here at this table where the future is being decided. Don't just hope the chaos doesn't reach your doorstep. Because it will. Maybe not tomorrow. Maybe not next year. But it will."

He straightened up, his tone sharpening. "This cure, this plan, doesn't just help the infected. It could bring stability. Trade. Global infrastructure. Your family's future. You want to preserve what you've built? This is how you do it."

One by one, heads began to nod. No dramatic applause, no speeches in return—just agreement in the way the room shifted, like the last of the resistance had finally given way to reality.

I looked over at Harlow, and though she didn't say a word, I saw it in her eyes: the tide had turned.

She stood with more control than I probably would've had in her shoes. "My dad valued your insights and contributions," she said. "You won't be punished by me for not taking part in this, so I'm asking you to make the choice on your own. If you'll help us, stay seated at the table. If you won't, I ask that you leave the room so we can carry on."

What followed was the tensest moment of the night. No one moved at first. The silence dragged, and I felt the air still like everyone was holding the same breath.

Then, little by little, a few chairs scraped back. A handful of council members stood, some with their translators right behind them, and quietly walked out. The door shut behind them, and things went still again.

The ones who stayed weren't saints—far from it. They were still the same polished faces who'd thrived inside Ylem's walls while the rest of the world burned. But at least they were still here. At least they were willing to try.

Harlow gave a small, tired smile. "From my heart, thank you," she said. "I'll remember who stayed."

Rowen and Chiron started flipping through thick folders in front of them, already shifting gears. "Thank you," Rowen said. "We have a lot to go over to see if we can actually pull this off. I'm going to need a generous amount of your time."

He turned to Willa and me. "You and the others should get some rest. I'll need your support tomorrow—there's more to do before we can head home."

Harlow led us all out of the boardroom and into an adjacent sitting room. No one said anything at first, just all kind of dropped onto whatever furniture we could find, exhausted and barely functioning.

The muffled conversation from the boardroom kept going behind the closed door, but no one had the energy left to follow it. One by one, my friends started dozing off.

Harlow looked around at us blearily. "I'm sorry I haven't been able to properly meet all of you. This has been the longest day of my life."

Otto didn't even bother opening his eyes. "You're telling me."

"There's gonna be plenty of time for that," said Ava. "I don't think we're going home as soon as we thought."

Harlow brushed her hair out of her face. "I should probably stay here tonight in case they need me, but why don't I have my drivers take you guys to my house? It's not far. There's space for all of you to sleep properly."

"Harlow, don't worry," Willa said through a yawn. "We've slept on dirt floors more times than we can count. This is fine."

Harlow rolled her eyes. "Well, get used to actual beds while you're my guests. My home is yours." She glanced toward the boardroom door. "And if things go the way I hope they do in there, maybe none of you will have to go back to living like that again."

Dustin let out a dramatic groan and stretched like he was an old man. "I'll take a bed over dirt any day. It's been rough."

Harlow smiled gently. "I told Willa earlier—this place might not feel like home yet, but I want you here. You and your families. You'll be taken care of, as long as I'm around."

"Thank you," I said. "As much as I want to get out of here, maybe it's better if we stay a while. At least until things settle."

"Not to mention," Riley added, sitting up a little on the couch, "the safe zones are falling apart. I'd rather raise Rio here, honestly."

I saw it before she said anything—Harlow's hand moving to her stomach. I reached for her other hand gently, and she didn't hesitate to take mine.

"I'm scared of what it'll mean if he has Ichor," she said quietly.

For a second, I froze. So did Willa.

"He?" I asked.

Harlow blushed, a sheepish smile creeping in. "Yeah. I only found out last week."

Riley's face lit up. "Oh my god, congrats! You're gonna be an amazing mom, I can already tell. Hopefully he won't look like Tye, though."

We all laughed, and for a second, the room felt lighter.

"Hey, with a cure in play now, Ichor might not matter the way it used to," Harlow pointed out. "Me and him, we might actually get to just live normal lives. Blend in, and be normal."

Harlow didn't look convinced, but I couldn't blame her. She probably wished she could disappear too, but her father's legacy wasn't something that could be shaken off. That burden would follow her and this child long after this war ended.

Still, she looked at me, Willa, and the others with something that felt like gratitude.

"I'm just glad it was you. Seeing you all together, the way you care for each other... I know you're good people. My dad spent so long trying to marry me off like it was some business deal. I always thought I'd end up trapped. Stuck in a marriage with a kid who reminded me of someone I didn't even love. But this? This is more than I ever hoped for."

Everyone in the room was sitting up by now.

Dustin pointed at her belly with mock seriousness. "We got you, kid."

The warmth in Harlow's eyes looked like it was about to become tears, but just then, the houseman passed by. He looked like he hadn't slept in days, and for once, he didn't shoot me a glare.

"Madam," he asked hoarsely, "do you need anything?"

"Yes," Harlow said, regaining her composure. "Please arrange transport to my house for my friends, and make sure they're settled in for the night."

He nodded respectfully. "Of course, madam."

"I'll meet you guys there in the morning," she told us.

The armored SUV rolled through Ylem's streets. I leaned my head against the window, looking out at the aftermath of the fight. The city looked rough—some buildings still smoldering, broken glass everywhere, bullet holes in architecture that used to look flawless. Soldiers were out in full force, cleaning up, helping people, and finishing off the last of the stray Morts that hadn't gotten the memo that it was over.

Here and there, I caught glimpses of people arguing—mostly residents yelling at some of the new arrivals. Still, the arguments didn't turn violent, and the soldiers stepping in weren't aggressive, just tired and focused. It felt like everyone was trying—awkwardly, but still trying.

Our occupying forces were already setting up camp wherever they could find space: in alleys, on rooftops, between buildings, even outside the wall where the gap had been blasted through it. Seeing the patchwork of different uniforms and flags all working together was making me feel hopeful that things would eventually even out.

Before long, the SUV pulled up in front of a sleek, ridiculously fancy building. It practically shimmered under the streetlights. I didn't need anyone to tell me this was Harlow's place.

The second we stopped, Riley leaned forward, wide-eyed. "Bro, I could get used to this."

38. WILLA

I woke tangled in silk sheets, the fabric soft and warm against my skin. It took me a minute to register where I was, but the heavy glow of sunlight pressing through the drapes told me it was well into the daytime. For the first time in what felt like forever, I'd slept in, and not just because the worst of the fighting was over, but because beside me, still breathing deep and even, was Tye.

We hadn't let go of each other all night, only shifting when one of us got too warm or a limb went numb. Even in sleep, we found each other again.

I turned to him, watching as he slept. His stubble had grown in, rough across skin that still had some youth under all the small scars that told his story. There was evidence of trauma in the lines around his eyes, but somehow his presence still felt calm. Grounding. Even after everything he'd been through, Tye was still a person I could anchor to.

For so long, I'd made peace with the idea of being alone. Not in a lonely way. Just ... realistically. I never saw the way I loved or experienced intimacy matched in anyone else. I never felt the desire the way I thought I was supposed to. I'd had relationships that felt important—but this was different. With Tye, it never felt like anything was missing. He never made me feel like my boundaries were a burden. He made me feel whole, exactly as I was.

He stirred beside me, then opened his eyes slowly, his hand already reaching for mine and pulling me closer.

"What are you awake thinking about?" he asked, his voice still heavy with sleep but warm.

He always knew when something was on my mind.

I studied him, letting myself sit in that moment—his hand in mine, his breath brushing my cheek. "I know how much I love you, because... when Malik was gone, I didn't think I could ever feel love that strong again. But *I love you*. Very much."

His eyes lit up with the kind of spark that showed he knew just how deeply those words mattered to me. "I love you very much, too," he said. "I'm excited to have real time together. Do actual life things. When the dust settles."

That's when a familiar worry crept in. What if, when everything actually settled, he'd start to realize all the things that I wasn't? That I couldn't give him?

"You're supposed to smile when I say that," he said gently, clearly catching the way my mood dropped.

I sat up slightly. "I'm just thinking about what we look like, after. When the world isn't burning. We've only ever known this version of us. What if when things get normal again, you realize *this* isn't enough?"

He sat up with me. "Is this about us, or about your boundaries?"

I hesitated before answering. "... I've just been in situations before, with people who thought it wouldn't bother them, until it did. And that's not on them. It's human nature, it's normal. But I don't want you to ever feel like you're giving something up."

He leaned closer, his hand still holding mine. "Willa, there isn't a single doubt in my mind that I want to spend the rest of my life with you. That has nothing to do with sex. I want you. Like this. Just with me, always. That's enough."

And just like that, the tension unraveled in my chest. That was the thing about Tye—his sincerity always found a way to bring me peace. He didn't just accept who I was. He loved me because of it.

He gave me a loving kiss, then rolled out of bed, already stretching and reaching for his clothes. "You know you can always tell me anything that's worrying you."

I smiled, a little wearily.

"Is there anything else?" he asked kindly, pulling his shirt over his head.

I pulled the covers off me and noticed clean clothes folded neatly on the dresser. The staff must've come in quietly at some point while we were asleep.

"I'm not worried," I said as I started to dress. "But I am thinking about the baby. We have to help Harlow raise him. And... he's going to be tied to Ylem forever."

Tye looked at me and nodded with a quiet understanding. This wasn't something either of us had really asked for, but we both knew it was a responsibility we were going to carry, whether we wanted to or not.

"Well," he said, buttoning his pants, "nothing about our lives has been traditional, so this won't be either. Kid's gonna have a whole army of parents."

We laughed. He reached for my hand again and tugged me toward the door. "Let's go get breakfast before Dustin eats it all."

We stepped into the hallway and made our way downstairs.

The big, open living room below was flooded with sunlight pouring through the huge windows lining the far wall. The long dining table under them was already busy, full of banter and activity. Outside, the city looked calmer than yesterday. No smoke, no chaos. Just cleanup crews and a stillness that made it feel like we'd finally turned a corner.

Everyone was already gathered around the table, but there were two faces I didn't recognize at first, until I saw the way Tye lit up at the sight of them.

"Vale! Beckett!" he said, rushing over to hug them. "You guys good? Thank you for everything yesterday."

"I've got a couple bruises that might never go away," Vale said with a grin, "but here we are. We're good."

"These are my friends from the camp," Tye told me proudly. "Vale was in on the network too."

I stepped in and hugged them both. "Good meeting you, finally."

Harlow smiled at me, offering the chair beside her. "I was just getting to know all your friends better. They're great."

A member of staff poured me a glass of orange juice right away.

I was happy to see everyone, but one presence was noticeably missing.

Maverick.

I stared at the fruit and pastries in front of me, trying to focus on anything that would push the bloody image of him on the Basilica floor out of my mind.

Through a mouthful of food, Dustin mumbled, "You two sleep good? I feel brand new."

"We did," I said. "Bit too long, though, it seems."

"No such thing," Ava chimed in as she served herself eggs from a silver dish. "I would've slept another four hours if *this one* hadn't been smelling bacon and begging us to get moving." She nodded at Otto with a smirk.

"Oh, c'mon," Otto tossed back. "You were drooling for it too, don't lie."

Ava grabbed a piece of bacon from the tray. "I was not," she laughed, then took another three.

Riley turned to Harlow. "You've got your speech today, yeah?"

Harlow immediately looked nervous. "Yeah. My mom and the council decided I should be inaugurated as soon as possible. They don't think it's smart to leave Ylem with open leadership while everyone's trying to make sense of things. But before that, I've invited Vale and Beckett here to talk about what we should do with the Angels. A lot of them don't have anywhere to go back to. I want to offer them a safe haven here, outside of the camps."

Tye sat forward in his chair, looking hopeful. "That's great. I know some of them don't even remember their lives before all of this. They're gonna need support. You spoke with them, Vale?"

"I did," he said. "I was taking the temperature. A handful want to try to find their families or go back to their countries, but most of them need housing and help. I told them Midas is gone, and I'll do what I can to make sure they're in good hands. They seem open to it."

"I'd love to meet all of them face to face before the speech today," Harlow said.

Beckett smiled. "I think that would go a long way."

As we continued eating, a group of medics entered the room. Harlow stood and addressed us. "They're here to check up on you guys. I called in the best. I know you've got injuries from the fight, so let's just make sure we're all in good shape."

I reached out and gave her shoulder a squeeze. "Already getting into mom mode?"

She smiled, then led us over to the sitting room where the medics started setting up equipment.

Tye walked over to Otto and Beckett, who'd ended up sitting next to each other on the couch. "Otto, I'm sure you already met, but this is Beckett. Beckett Taylor. He was close with Xander."

Otto's eyes widened the second he heard the full name, and tears welled up in his eyes. I'd heard him talk about Xander plenty of times, but it still caught me off guard to see it hit him like that.

Tye looked apologetic. "I didn't mean to spring it on you like that. But I think you two should connect."

Otto wiped at his eyes and smiled. "Nice to meet you, Beckett. I've heard a lot about you."

Beckett's face lit up with a sweet, pensive smile that told me he was happy Xander had shared their history.

While Otto and Beckett talked among themselves, I slipped across the room and took a seat beside Dustin on the chaise. One of the medics was already checking his vitals, a small device clamped around his finger and beeping steadily.

Another medic turned to me. "Is it okay if we check your bite and chest wound?"

I lifted my shirt just enough to show them the bite mark. It had scarred over, faded and jagged now, like something that had happened a lifetime before.

As the medic crouched to examine it, I leaned toward Dustin. "Where did Maverick end up?" I asked quietly.

He took a deep breath. "I personally brought him back to our camps outside the wall," he said. "I've got guys from my unit looking after him until you make the next call. We'll have to honor him when everything blows over."

I smiled at him, as much as it hurt. "Thank you. He deserves that."

The medic sprayed something cold across my bite, then dressed it in thin gauze. "We'll keep monitoring," they said, "but both your wounds are in good shape."

They moved on to Otto next. He'd pulled back his sleeve, revealing some pretty brutal burn marks snaking up his arm toward his neck.

I watched him wince as ointment touched the burns. Ava lovingly rubbed slow circles into his back without a word.

The medics moved between us, checking wounds, rewrapping gauze, handing out a few painkillers where they could, until the fragile calm was interrupted by the soft sound of dress shoes on tile.

Harlow's houseman appeared at one end of the room. "Madam, the Chancellor's in the foyer. He's here to discuss matters requiring your approval and signature."

Harlow didn't flinch. "Bring him up."

We all traded looks. Tye shifted in his seat. Riley sat up straighter. We might be Harlow's friends, but here in Ylem, we were still outsiders.

The medics quietly packed up their kits before heading out the way they came. Just as the last one left, the Chancellor entered.

He wasn't alone. Two other councilmen flanked him, and behind them, three guards, rigid and gleaming in gold. Their eyes swept the room like searchlights. One of them locked onto Tye almost instantly. I saw it in his stare, like Tye was a walking threat. To their knowledge, Tye was the one who'd killed Midas.

The Chancellor's voice was smooth, but carried weight. "I expected you to be at the Basilica with your mother during this time," he said to Harlow, "but we've come to you for your convenience."

The way he said it made it clear: it wasn't meant to be kind.

Harlow stood tall. "If you're here to dictate every word I'm going to say in my speech today—"

"We have other matters that need addressing," he interrupted.

"Go on, then," Harlow said coolly.

His eyes flicked over us all, one by one. I felt them linger on me, then Dustin, then land back on Tye.

"In all fairness, madam, I understand these are your friends. But the matters we must address are best not discussed in front of anyone who, only twenty-four hours ago, bombed our walls and occupied our city." He let that hang in the air for a moment. "Things need to be in order before we integrate these new arrivals," he added, "if that is your hope once you're anointed."

There was silence. Harlow's brow furrowed. I could tell she hated that these responsibilities fell on her, but she understood. She gave a small nod, then looked at us with an apology in her eyes.

"Excuse me," she said softly, and followed them into the next room.

The golden guards stayed, posted at the entryway like statues. Watching us.

The moment the door shut, it was obvious that the warmth had drained from the room. Harlow might've welcomed us in, but not everyone here felt the same. And it was starting to show.

None of us said anything right away. With the guards still standing there, watching the group like we might flip the table or pull out a weapon mid-scone, we slowly drifted back toward the breakfast spread. One by one, we retook our seats, putting some space between us and them.

After a minute, I turned to Otto. "Is everything okay with your mom?"

He brushed some crumbs from his lap. "Mostly. She took some damage, but I spoke to her this morning. She's up and running. She, Commander Oren, and Rowen are all bouncing around trying to keep things in order. Most of our forces have pulled back into one big camp outside the wall until the politics calm down. We can't head home just yet."

"There's no chance we would've won without you taking out the satellites," Ava said, leaning forward. "It was looking bad there for a second."

"It was a miracle we were able to," Otto admitted. "They had the whole thing heavily guarded. Even after we got past their blockade, the system was buried underground with backup generators and everything. I gotta say, the way my mom led the rebels, the way they listened to her, I was so impressed. Rowen's plan was solid, but she really brought it home out there. We were able to hit all the points at once, and it just... crumbled."

"You're a legend, Otto," Dustin said, grinning. "It's in your blood, clearly."

Otto shook his head, but he was smiling. There was a light in his eyes I hadn't seen since before everything fell apart. It wasn't cocky, just proud. And he had every right to be.

Once the staff had cleared the plates and wiped down the table, the quiet returned.

Harlow walked back in shortly after, and one look at her face told me everything I needed to know. She looked like someone trying to hold twenty things at once with no hands left.

The councilmen trailed behind her, but none of them looked at us. Not even in passing, like we were merely furniture. They walked through and slipped out of the door.

Harlow sat down slowly, like something was weighing heavily on her. Her hands stayed folded in her lap, her eyes on the table.

"They're arranging my father's funeral for tomorrow," she said, voice low. She didn't look up. "To be clear, I don't expect any of you to be there. I know he was the reason for a lot of your suffering. You should honor the ones who've fallen on your side, while we take care of ours."

No one said anything at first. It wasn't cold, the way she said it. Just honest. Like she already knew how much we'd given up to be here.

Then, she turned to Vale. "I want to see the Angels before any decisions are made about them."

"They're safe," Vale said. "Heavily guarded in the silver camps just outside the wall. We should get going if changes are happening fast."

I clocked the term 'silver camps,' clearly referring to the silver armbands our side had worn in opposition to Ylem's gold uniforms. Just another reminder that even if we were cooperating now, there was still division. The war might've paused, but the colors still hadn't blended together.

We arrived at the campgrounds just past noon. Everything had been moved closer to the breach in the main wall. From a distance, it looked like its own miniature city stretched across the plains. Tents, vehicles, supply crates, makeshift med bays. An organized system.

As we walked through, it got quieter. Soldiers rested along the edges of tents, some still being treated, some too injured to move. I saw a few flatbeds loaded with bodies—covered respectfully, but that didn't make it any easier to look at. Burned-out vehicles sat in rows like discarded toys, proof of how close this had come to failing.

In the distance, the air fleet meant to take us home stood waiting. For a second, I let myself picture it, that feeling of flying away from all this. But we weren't there yet.

Eventually, we reached a giant tent, more heavily guarded than the others. Soldiers in silver armbands stood outside, holding rifles across their chests. Vale stepped forward and exchanged a quiet word, and they let us in.

Inside, the energy was different.

There were at least a hundred rescued Angels. Most were our age or younger. And for the most part, they looked okay. In good spirits, even. Some were sitting on cots, others standing in loose clusters, chatting, smiling, breathing in fresh air like it was a luxury. After the two divisions had been separated for so long, the room now buzzed with reunion.

That buzz quieted the second they noticed us. Tye, especially.

A few of the guys broke from the crowd and hugged him, Vale, and Beckett.

Vale raised a hand to get everyone's attention. "I brought Harlow—the new leader of Ylem—and she wants to help us. I know I've talked with a lot of you already, but she wanted to hear it for herself. This is the start of you all having your life back in your own hands."

All eyes turned to Harlow. The Angels were smiling now, looking at her like she was some kind of lighthouse after a long storm. She didn't try to command the room. She just walked in, gestured for them to sit, and found a spot on the edge of a cot like she wasn't above any of them.

There was nothing of her father in her presence. No posturing. No fearmongering.

She took a deep breath and began. "First, I wanted to start with a deeply sincere apology for the pain and loss my father caused. He's gone now, and I hope this is the start of some kind of healing. I want to help make sure you have what you need to do that."

The room stayed quiet. Everyone was listening.

"If you choose to stay in Ylem," she went on, "you'll stay as free people. You'll be able to contribute in whatever way you feel comfortable. You'll have a safe place here. You've done your part. If you want to leave, we'll arrange that too. You can decide for yourselves."

There was some whispering, but no one spoke up. It was like they weren't used to being allowed to.

Finally, a girl with wild, sun-faded brown hair raised her hand shyly. "Hi, Harlow, I'm Ivy."

At my side, Tye leaned in close to me. "She was at the border with me. When they first took me."

I blinked. That had been ages before. It hit me then just how long some of them had been stuck in this system.

Ivy continued. "We heard there's a cure now. A real one. If we stay, will we still have to do transfusions?"

Harlow shook her head. "No. I'm going to make sure we're done with that. Our medical division might need support in keeping a cure available, but I want us to achieve that as a team, not as prisoners."

Another Angel, this one a boy with an Irish accent, asked, "Some of us are okay with helpin', but ... we're scared. That even with you in charge, there'll be people who won't treat us like we're equal."

"There will be," Harlow said honestly, "but this is a big city. And like any big city, you can find your place. You can stick together. And you'll have a friend in me. I know you haven't seen it yet, but there are good people here in Ylem. Families who've already agreed to help us circulate the cure so we can bring the world back—"

"So it's true?" a burly guy shouted from the back. He stood up, his large size in contrast with the anxious edge in his voice. "We were hearing rumors that Tye can bring people back from the dead. They're gonna bring *everyone* back?"

Tye looked like someone had thrown him into freezing water. But he stepped forward anyway.

"They're working on it, Brock," he replied, obviously recognizing the guy. "That's the plan. We don't know exactly how it'll turn out, but we're strategizing with Dr. Chiron to make it happen."

Harlow picked it up from there. "Some of you might have loved ones who could possibly be out there—alive, or ... somewhere in between alive and not. Once the cure's released, it'll take time, but we'll do what we can to help you find them. Until then, we'll have a place for you here."

The whispering started again. But it sounded lighter this time. More hopeful.

Harlow gave them a moment, then added, "You have time to think and decide. I just wanted to invite you all to my inauguration today. I'll be talking to the people of Ylem, all together, for the first time. And I want you to see what kind of leader I plan to be. Give me a chance. Give Ylem a chance to be a safe haven for you, too."

The mood in the room had shifted. I could feel it.

Beckett turned to Harlow. "Vale and I will stay here to get more thoughts, but we'll see you there later."

As we turned to go, Harlow smiled at the group. She looked tired, but her demeanor remained warm.

"You're a natural," I said to her as we linked arms and stepped back into the sunlight.

The scene looked familiar. Oceans of people were gathered at the foot of the Basilica, packed shoulder to shoulder, their faces turned upward, waiting for Harlow's address. It reminded me of when it was Midas at the mic, right before someone tried to take him out. This time, though, every major leader, from both Ylem and our side, stood on the balcony behind Harlow in a show of unity. Whether everyone really wanted to be there was another story, but the message was clear. This was the new way forward. And at least Harlow knew she had her friends by her side.

Golden soldiers lined the steps, and were stationed on rooftops and fanned out in waves below like a net. They weren't the only ones armed. All of us had our weapons with us. I'd even given Harlow her pistol back earlier that afternoon, just in case.

None of us were taking any chances.

The crowd was mostly cheering, a dull roar of applause rolling through the city. But beneath it, I could hear low booing from scattered corners. Security had already removed a few people before Harlow even stepped out. It looked promising from far away, but up close, it felt like walking a tightrope over broken glass.

Then Harlow stepped up to the mic.

And somehow, despite everything she'd told me about not feeling ready, she looked like she belonged there. Calm. Steady in a way that made people stop and actually listen.

Her mother stood just behind her. Both of them wore structured emerald dresses, not shying away from their wealth or power. And maybe that was the point.

Harlow began to speak. And the moment she said "Hi, everyone," it grew quiet in a way I hadn't expected. Like the whole city leaned in.

"First, thank you for being here. I know the past few days have been a lot. I know a lot of you are tired, scared, angry—maybe even unsure about what comes next. Honestly, I feel all those things too. But we made it through. And now, it's time to decide what kind of place we want this to be."

I could feel the energy change below, even if it was subtle.

"Tomorrow, we'll bury my father. I know for many of you, he was more than just a leader. He was brilliant. Strategic. And he protected a lot of people. But he also hurt a lot of people."

The words dropped hard. A few of the councilmen behind Harlow shuffled uncomfortably.

"He started making decisions based on fear and power instead of compassion and reason. And somewhere along the way, the version of him that I loved got lost in what Ylem became.

"I'm not numb to his death. It hurts deeply. But if we want to move forward, we have to be honest about what he stood for. We can honor his genius and the good he did, but we also have to let go of the harm he caused. When we bury him, I hope we can bury the fear and control with him. Because I want to build something different. Something better."

The crowd stirred again. Not agitated, but interested.

"This city doesn't have to be an isolated fortress anymore. The infection we were so afraid of will be cured. The outside world will start to heal. We can start living, really living. And that means opening up. I know it's not easy to trust. I know some of you are uncomfortable with seeing new faces in Ylem, especially people you once called enemies. But here's the truth: we've all gone through the same history. We've all suffered. We're all trying to figure out how to exist after everything that's happened. We're in the same boat now, whether we like it or not. And if there's finally peace within reach, then we have to try."

A small, hopeful ripple moved through the front lines of the crowd.

"I'm not here to be my father. I'm not going to lead the way he did. I'll take the best parts of who he was, and I'll use them to keep Ylem steady. But I'll also fix what he got wrong. And I won't do it alone."

She looked behind her at her mother, Olivia. Then at us.

"I have my mom. I have people I trust. And hopefully, I'll have you too. I know I'm young, and I know I have a lot to prove. But I want to earn your trust; I don't just expect it. I want to be a leader you choose to follow, not one you're stuck with. And maybe, one day, when you talk about me, you won't just say I was the great Midas's daughter. Maybe you'll say I was great too."

As thunderous applause rang out around us, it felt like a new chapter for Ylem was starting, with Harlow leading the way.

39. TYE

Yesterday ended with the city alive and buzzing after Harlow's speech. Today, everything felt somber. The streets were quiet. The black flag waved at half mast. The people of Ylem were preparing to bury their former leader, and we'd returned to the silver camps outside the wall to honor our own dead.

It wasn't just about giving Ylem its space; it was also what Harlow wanted. She made it clear, as gently as she could, that we shouldn't be there. She didn't want us standing there while they honored a man who'd caused us all so much pain. A man who'd destroyed life as we knew it.

And then there was Ylem's council. Word was spreading, loud and fast, that I was the one who'd killed Midas. I'd happily take the credit, but it also meant a bullseye was forming on my back. That liability alone made me a target at a funeral this important to Ylem's people.

Harlow told me she'd call for us when it was over, but we'd know when that moment came, when the smoke rose over the wall. They'd be burning Midas in the middle of the Great Gardens—a city-wide ceremony of grief and closure. I could picture it all: the slow procession, the tears, the speeches that would praise his brilliance while carefully dodging his cruelty. He'd be remembered by most as a visionary. As the man who built the great city of Ylem.

Meanwhile, all I could think about was that he deserved to rot in a gutter. But I kept that to myself. I was trying not to let the hate eat me alive. I knew this wasn't about me. This wasn't even really about Midas anymore. This was about what the people of Ylem needed to move forward with Harlow as their new leader. To bury the past in a way they could live with.

Today, my thoughts had to be with the people we'd lost from our side, the ones who fought and died to make this win possible. They didn't get a ceremony. No gardens. No speeches from their families. Just dirt and ash, buried in a land they should've never had to die in.

We kept ourselves busy around the camp, helping with the devastating task of gathering bodies, hauling them in flatbed trucks to a series of pyres out in the plains. The bodies had to be burned. We couldn't risk them turning.

Every so often, gunshots sounded in the distance. Morts kept charging toward the camps, drawn to the scent of flesh.

Even after all the death I'd seen, it was jarring to look at so many ghostly faces. Soldiers and civilians, all jumbled together. These were people who'd all chosen to fight and who believed in a cause that would change the course of history for the better, whether they lived long enough to see it or not.

I wheeled a cot over to one of the flatbeds, the metal legs squeaking across the dirt. Two soldiers came over, lifted the body off, and added it to the growing pile in the truck.

Ava appeared beside me. She held a clipboard in one hand and her dreamcatcher from back home in the other. She'd been keeping track of names all day, helping to catalog the fallen so they weren't just nameless bodies lost to history.

I glanced at the page and noticed the ink bleeding across the paper. I looked up.

She was crying.

I wrapped an arm around her and pulled her in. "I know I roast you for crying all the time," I said quietly, "but part of me's relieved to see that you're not numb from everything we've seen."

She wiped at her cheek, then looked tenderly down at the dreamcatcher. "I could use a little numbness. Being an empath during the apocalypse really sucks."

"I don't know... The numbness scares me sometimes."

Just then, Willa and Otto walked past us, heading to a truck farther down with two more stretchers. Ava's eyes followed Otto until he disappeared behind the flatbed.

"You know what really scares *me*?" she asked suddenly. "The thought of losing Otto. I've been a mess all day over how young some of these bodies are. I love him so much that if anything ever happens to him, I just know I won't survive it."

I pulled her into another hug. "I know the feeling, trust me. I don't think any of us expected to find our soulmates before we were old enough to drink, but the end of the world will do that to you, I guess."

She let out a teary laugh, then busied herself with her clipboard again.

I looked across the camp and saw Willa consoling someone in the distance. The sight reminded me. "What about Maverick?"

Ava didn't need to look at her papers. "Willa wants to have her own moment for that. We'll do it after the service."

Even though I hadn't known Maverick for long, his absence lingered with me. In the end, he'd been a crucial ally. And he deserved to be remembered as one.

Just then, Rowen and Chiron walked up, both of them looking exhausted, and not the kind that came from lack of sleep. They were the two pillars holding everything up right now, and it showed.

"Sorry we haven't been able to help with this," Rowen said. "It's been nonstop in the situation room."

Ava looked down at her clipboard. "I think almost everyone's been accounted for," she said, her voice low and eyes still red.

Chiron and I locked eyes. There was something thoughtful in the way he looked at me, a kind of unspoken understanding. I gave him a nod, and he returned it.

"I've been wanting to thank you," I said, stepping toward him. "For everything you did. For me. For Willa. And for what's still coming."

He lowered his head slightly, humbled. "There's still a lot of work to be done. But I'm motivated to get it done quickly so the world can find peace. So my family can."

I blinked, realizing. "Wait... you're not at Midas's funeral?"

Chiron shook his head. "Given everything, I felt it was better to sit this one out."

Something about that landed deeper than I'd expected. He wasn't just skipping the ceremony—he was choosing not to stand beside a legacy he no longer believed in. It felt like he'd freed himself of Midas, and was no longer just walking the line between his work and his morals.

"On another note," he said, "I wanted to let you know that, based on recent lab testing, the child Harlow carries is positive for Ichor."

I felt my breath catch for a second. "I guess I'm not surprised... but I don't know what good Ichor is now that there's a cure," I said slowly. "Does Harlow know?"

Chiron shook his head. "Not yet. I haven't told her. With everything going on, it didn't feel like the right time. I know it's comforting to think he won't be singled out, and I truly hope that's the case, but Ichor is still incredibly rare. We don't fully understand everything it's capable of yet. As things evolve, it may reveal more than we know now. Ultimately, this is good news."

So he said, but I didn't like the sound of it. The child would be born into the world already branded with something people would want. I'd spent so long wishing I could be free of it, and now someone else was inheriting my curse.

Rowen interjected, his tone gentle. "We still have several months before the baby arrives, so there's time to figure out what it all means. But right now, the more immediate focus is on our plan to deploy the cure. Together with cooperating nations and the Ylem families who've contributed, we've assembled a mega fleet to begin global distribution."

Ava and I caught each other's eye.

"When's that happening?" she asked Rowen. "Are we going back to the safe zones for it?"

"We're hoping as early as next month," he said. "But I'm sure you can imagine the logistical complexities of coordinating a global drop. We'll have to play it by ear. In the meantime, our presence here's helping keep the peace. That matters."

Chiron nodded. "Many scientists from around the world, and some I've worked closely with here in Ylem, are working tirelessly to make sure this version of the cure is ready for the operation."

I took a deep breath. "So what I'm understanding is, the same way the virus spread is how we're getting the cure out. But this time, it'll work in reverse?"

"In the simplest possible terms," Chiron said, "yes. The pathogens have been altered to reflect your abilities."

I only then noticed the small comms device in his hand, buzzing quietly. He glanced at it, then back at us. "I need to take this," he said, already walking away.

Rowen stayed behind. His expression shifted, more tentative. "Tye," he began, "I don't know your relationship to them, but I thought you might want to hear some good news in the midst of everything going on. When combing through the files on Chiron's hard drive, we found something interesting." He paused, like he wanted to make sure I was paying attention. "You have two family members alive. One in Safe Zone 23, the other in 17. Your uncle Brooks, and your cousin Heath. Were you aware?"

I just stared at him. For a second, I thought I hadn't heard him right. Heath and Brooks. It wasn't the first time I'd heard their names recently, but I hadn't expected any news about them to feel like this. Like something in me had clicked into place.

"Midas was looking for them," I said, my voice coming out barely audible. "For Ichor."

"There's no indication Ichor's been discovered in either of them," he said, "but they were located, alive. We're happy to get you in contact when you're ready."

Ava rubbed a hand across my back. I hadn't even noticed I was starting to tear up.

"I'd love that," I managed to say, swallowing hard.

The truth was, I hadn't been close with either of them. I barely remembered the last time I'd seen my uncle. And Heath had been out of touch, even before everything fell apart. But the idea of any family still out there... It hit me harder than I'd thought it would.

For so long, my friends had been my family. But knowing that someone out there still carried my last name, still remembered me, maybe even wondered if I was alive, made something in my chest ache in the best way. On a day filled with so much loss, the prospect of reconnecting with family brought a kind of warmth I didn't know I needed. I couldn't help but smile.

Before I could say anything else, Riley and Dustin appeared, their expressions solemn.

"They're ready to start the service," Riley said quietly.

I wiped the edge of my sleeve across my face, and together, we approached the pyres.

As we neared the edge of the camp, I spotted a crowd of dozens forming near a stack of crates, Willa and Otto among them.

"What's going on?" I asked, walking up beside her.

Willa's expression was soft. "Harlow just sent these," she said, nodding toward the crates. "Boxes of candles and tealights."

Dustin picked one up. "Are we *sure* she's related to Midas?" he asked with a small smile.

Rowen stepped closer. "This is a very kind gesture."

Everyone around us had started taking candles, so we did the same, joining the growing crowd that was now gathering in a ring around the pyres.

The bodies had been stacked respectfully in rows of cloth-wrapped forms, some with names pinned to them, others still unknown. But no matter how carefully it was done, it was still hard to look at.

A heavy hush fell over the group. No one spoke as the first candle was lit. Then another. Then another. Quietly, people turned to one another and shared their flames.

I lit mine from Ava's. She had tears in her eyes again, but she held the candle steady. And as I looked around, I couldn't help but notice how accidentally symbolic it all seemed. A few small flames, passed from hand to hand, and suddenly... an entire army of wicks, glowing bright.

Some people bowed their heads in prayer. Some knelt in silence. Others whispered soft words.

Eventually, someone stepped forward and dropped their candle onto the closest pyre. One by one, others followed.

The fires caught quickly. The flames climbed over the wood, then over the bodies laid to rest. No one looked away. We stood quietly watching the columns of dark smoke stretch into the sky, then blow across the plains in long trails.

Willa reached for my hand, and I took it. I turned toward her, feeling a soft squeeze. We were both still standing.

I looked around at the others—Ava, Otto, Dustin, Riley. Beckett and Vale a few feet away in their own embrace. Even in daylight, the fire cast a warm glow over all of them. Quiet but alive. If it weren't for them, I had no doubt I'd be burning on one of those pyres right now, too.

The fires burned for hours. People stayed as long as they needed, stepping away only when they felt ready, some alone, others in pairs. No one rushed it.

Eventually, the camps started to shift back into their usual rhythm. Soldiers resumed their rotations. Medics returned to their tents. Somewhere nearby, a radio crackled back to life.

We shared a rationed lunch inside one of the communal tents. No one really had an appetite, but we ate anyway. Chat was scarce.

Willa had mentioned earlier that she'd found a scenic point on a map where she wanted to take Maverick. A bluff by the coast, several miles out. She was set on laying him to rest somewhere peaceful.

Before we'd sat down to eat, I'd gone with her to arrange the transport. I could tell it meant a lot to her. She didn't want this to feel like some clinical send-off in a morgue tent. She wanted space. Something that didn't feel like a warzone.

No one hesitated to join her. Even though it was for a sad reason, the idea of putting distance between us and the pyres was a welcome one.

As we loaded into Otto's super SUV, we did our best to keep the mood light. None of us mentioned the second vehicle behind us, carrying Maverick's body in the back.

Willa sat between Dustin and me, her hand tucked into mine. I could feel her thumb tracing absent circles against my palm, like it grounded her somehow.

After a few quiet minutes, Dustin reached over and took her other hand. She smiled softly at him.

"I'm sorry I was so tough on him," he said, turning to look out of the window, "but he proved me wrong in the end."

Willa leaned her head on his shoulder. "I know you were just looking out for me. But thank you. I know he'd love hearing that."

"Of course," Dustin said. "I'm always gonna look out for you. You've got a brother in me."

"And a sister in me," Riley called from the backseat.

Ava spun around from the passenger seat and grinned. "And me."

Willa started laughing, a light and real sound.

"You've got another brother right here," Otto chimed in from the driver's seat.

I gave her hand a squeeze. "Well, I can't be your brother because then I can't do this."

And I leaned in and kissed her.

Laughter broke out around the car.

"Okay, okay, relax, guys," Willa said, laughing as she nudged me with her elbow.

Otto slowed the SUV and eased it into park. "We're here."

We all fell quiet again and climbed out.

The view was unreal. Golden light spilled across the ocean, the sun hanging low. Waves broke gently in a steady rhythm against the dark, pebbled shoreline. A salty wind rolled in from the water. It might've been the freshest air I'd ever breathed.

We followed Willa down to the beach, our boots crunching against the pebbles. The escort team moved behind us, carrying the wooden container with Maverick's body inside.

When we reached the edge of the water, Willa turned and nodded. The escorts carefully set the container down near the waterline and stepped back, giving us space.

The sound of the waves and the distant cries of seabirds filled the silence. We stood in a circle around him, none of us quite ready to speak.

Then Ava broke the stillness.

"I brought these," she said quietly, crouching to open her tote bag. Inside were tealights, the ones Harlow had sent earlier.

Willa hugged her tightly.

Riley pulled a lighter from her back pocket. "Pass 'em around," she said gently, flicking the flame to life.

One by one, we each took a candle, shielding them from the wind as Riley lit them.

Willa took a breath, her eyes on the horizon, then turned back to us.

"I've lost some of the most important people in my life, and somehow, it never gets easier... Losing Maverick is hard for a lot of reasons. But the hardest is knowing he was my last real tie to Malik. He knew the same parts of my brother that I did.

"Maverick didn't have an easy life. He took a lot of wrong turns. But he found his way back and literally helped change history. And despite those bad choices, he played a huge part in changing me, too. I hope wherever he is now, he finally gets to rest easy."

She stepped forward, crouching beside the crate, her voice softer now.

"Say hi to Malik, Archer, and Imani when you get there. And give Hound a treat from me."

With steady hands, she pushed the crate into the sea foam. The waves pulled at it instantly, like they'd been waiting for him.

None of us hesitated. We stepped into the shallows, shoes soaked, pants clinging to our legs. The sun painted everything in gold and rose, its rays stretching across the water like they were lighting Maverick's way.

We knelt together and, one by one, let our tealights float, like little glowing boats, drifting out to join him.

I was in awe of how beautiful the sunset was. It felt perfect for this moment, maybe even more striking because we'd finally made it to the other side of chaos.

Willa's eyes filled with tears, but she didn't look away from the horizon. I slipped my arm around her shoulders, and she leaned into me, quiet.

"He got us out of Ylem ... and we came back," she whispered.

It was true. Neither of us would've made it out without Maverick's willingness to risk everything when we hit a dead end. But the Ylem we escaped wasn't the one we came back to.

"Are we really staying?" I asked.

Ava piped up first. "There's no denying this place is worlds better than the slummy safe zones ... but won't we be just like the families who ran here while everyone else dealt with the mess? There's still so many people who'll never get the chance to live like this."

"We're not running from anything," Otto said firmly. "If anything, we're staying in the thick of it. We have to. We've seen what happens when people in power go unchecked. If we leave now, it could all backtrack."

"I just worry about Tye," Riley added quietly. "If they think he killed Midas, it's only a matter of time before someone comes after him for it."

I couldn't deny it. The thought that everyone would just forgive and forget because Harlow was in charge and protecting me felt far-fetched.

"I think we've earned the right to better living conditions," Dustin said, keeping his tone light, but clearly not joking.

Willa let out a small laugh. "The world's going to be a better place for everyone soon," she said. "But at least, if our families can come here, I think we should stay. Keep an eye on things. Help Harlow with the transition. With the baby."

That was Willa, always thinking of everyone but herself. I turned and kissed the top of her head.

"I think that sounds like a good plan."

We watched the crate drift farther out, small waves lapping against its sides. The tealights floated around it like magic until the ocean breeze blew them out.

Then the crate finally sank beneath the surface, and somehow, the sounds of nature around us felt more vivid. Like a heaviness had lifted. Like peace had finally arrived.

No one said anything right away. We just stood in the shallows, letting the moment settle. Then, out of nowhere—*SPLASH.*

"Hey!" Willa laughed, spinning to face Riley, who grinned and kicked another wave of water our way.

Willa splashed back, and just like that, the silence had broken and laughter took its place. Everyone joined in, and this time, I did too.

I tackled Dustin under the waves. Ava pushed me off him. Otto kicked his feet and soaked whatever dry spots I had left. It turned into a saltwater dogpile of all the most important people I had left.

My friends. My family.

Whatever came next, we'd face it the same way we got here.

Together.

www.ingramcontent.com/pod-product-compliance
Lightning Source LLC
Chambersburg PA
CBHW060817310726
48980CB00002B/328

* 9 7 9 8 9 9 3 3 3 1 5 0 8 *